THE WHITE QUEEN

The
White Queen

FREDERIC FALLON

DOUBLEDAY & COMPANY, INC., GARDEN CITY, NEW YORK
1972

EDITOR'S NOTE:

THE WHITE QUEEN is a novel, not a biography, and the author has
taken liberties with certain historical facts.

For my Mother,
Helen Margaret Walker Fallon

THE WHITE QUEEN

PROLOGUE

This is Edinburgh, traveler. Stay awhile.

You shiver. February's the coldest month. Edinburgh's winds may cut you to the bone, but they are the softest summer zephyrs when you have seen the tempests in the north. If you find the skies too chaste and white here, they are granite over the Highlands. The snow gives Edinburgh's hills a lost, monotonous aspect, but in the Highlands snow comes four and five feet deep and more—mile upon mile of endless hoar that looks for all the world like a huge platter of Queen Mary's iced cream, melting and formless. White is the Holy Virgin's color, true, and the badge of purity, nobility, and right, but so vast an expanse as you may see up there is a terrifying thing. Too much white is as much the color of nightmare as is too much black. It can make a man afraid, make him think about God, and the other one. White and black are sisters here in Scotland when autumn dies.

The northern streams are impassable; the Clyde, the Nairn, the Spey have gone to hibernating. Loch Ness and Loch Leven are frosted over now. Many men, finding their boats useless, will seek to cross those lochs and streams by foot. But the ice will not bear

them. Death is a siren, and easy, in the north. They say there are
men who eat men up there, near the outer islands, and that the
cold and lack of passing travelers drives them farther down this
isle each time winter comes and goes. They say there are men—
women and children, too—up north, that pray naked to the Devil
and that he comes to dance and love and lie with them.

There is no better faring south. England's border is a barren
and unfriendly place every month of the year. The robber
barons school their hoards down there and mercy is the one
commodity in which they do not deal.

No ships enter Edinburgh's harbor town until March, and sometimes not even until Maypole-time. The days of sowing, reaping,
and threshing are past. It is too chill and angry for the wooing
of gentle dames and burgher's daughters, or for foaling, shearing,
and calving.

But this is not the worst place on the earth. We have taverns
warm and cheap; meat, bread, and ale are cheap, as well.
Since Queen Mary's coming back from France, we've had fine
Flanders wines and wines from the Loire and Paris. Our storage
houses are filled with peas, barley, corn, beans, seafowl, and
mutton. If it's an easy woman you'd be wanting, we've women
willing and in plenty—big-breasted, thick-thighed, with all their
teeth.

The Presbyterian religion is a heavy voice in this country,
but even the Presbyterian religion couldn't kill the Black Man
—Old Cloven Hoof—in a day, if ever. If the psalm singing
and all the incessant sour faces get you low, why, then, wait
you by your window lattice and watch for Queen Mary to pass
by in the streets. She'll lift you high enough, friend, as high as
high can go. The Congregation of the Lord's Saints Assembled,
as our Presbyterian brethren like to call themselves, does not
like Queen Mary because she's a papist and because she's more
French than Scots, but most of all the Saints Assembled dislike
her because she is beautiful and she laughs sometimes. But I
swear I've seen some Presbyterian gentlemen drop their hands
over their laps when the Queen's gone by.

Ah, and she's a braw Queen, Queen Mary is—an Amazon,

too, near six foot tall she is. No wonder royal folk have taken to believing in divine rights, with such a representative as she amongst them. She's a warm-type, smiling kind of beauty that likes fun and gaming. She's bound to pass by soon.

Doubtless Harry Stewart, our King consort, will be with her. She left the capital to bring him back from his father's house. Whenever King Harry has a fit, he goes mewling to his father and thinks the old fox will patch things together again. Queen Mary's going to tend her husband (I'll not call him King; he is no King to me, nor to anyone else in this country), she's going to tend him at Kirk o'Field, that old monastery down there just outside the town wall. It's deserted now, but once a merry band of monks sang and danced there. Those old men were corrupt, even bad, but they loved their pleasure; having given up on God, they made the most of earth. When the Presbyterians seized Edinburgh, they hung the abbot's body over the city walls. They burned the other monks and threw what was left into the sea.

Queen Mary's bringing her husband to Kirk o'Field because, they say, he has the smallpox. A likely story. It's pox of a different sort, I'd guess. Under that damask mask he wears, his pretty face is probably all scarred and running. Like his soul.

That's the Great Castle up there above the sea. It's more than five hundred feet high. King Arthur and his sister sinned their sin there. It's a hundred thousand years old, maybe more.

Look you! Down there. They're coming now! Stand up here and you'll see them better. I'll tell you them as they pass by.

First, Harry Stewart in his sick litter. He looks like a hero, doesn't he? That giant's body, that bright yellow hair. But we know him better than that. He's pulling the litter curtain shut. Good.

And there's Lord James, Queen Mary's famous bastard brother. Their father loved the ladies, but Lord James is a different sort; Bastard Saint is what some call Lord James, though it is not likely the Pope of Rome will go canonizing him. He's the true cause of the Presbyterians here in Scotland. Were it not for him, the Presbyterians never could have taken power. But, also, if it were not for Lord James, they'd have more. He looks like his dad, King James V, except he looks as his father might have looked after twenty years in purgatory.

And, coming up now, that's James Hepburn, the Earl of Bothwell—there's a brave man for you. Look at the hacks on his helmet! He's a rash, proud, hazardous young man, that Jimmy Bothwell is! It does the heart good to know there's such as he about. The Queen trusts him more than anybody, even more than her brother Lord James. And what a pair they'd make. She should have married Bothwell, not that nancy boy Harry Stewart. Better for everybody in Harry Stewart were dead in hell.

And there, back there in the rear, all alone and by herself, Queen Mary! Wait till she gets close and maybe she'll look up. She's all in white today.

The little caravan seemed frozen against the white plain. The snow fell slowly and took a long time to cover the black tracks left by the horses.

A long, bejeweled hand pulled aside the sick litter's damask curtain and motioned for a rider to approach. The rider bent his head, listened, then rode back to the Queen.

"We approach the capital gates, madam."

"Yes."

"His Majesty the King wishes you to ride near him."

"Is His Majesty ill?"

"To be blunt, madam, he has a fear that—"

"There is no remedy against fear," said the Queen.

"Madam," said the rider, "I know my master desires nothing more than that the secrets of every person's heart were written on their faces."

"That would be nice," she said, above the broken flute sound of the wind. "Is there anything else?"

"No, madam." The rider returned to the sick litter.

The Earl of Bothwell, who was riding several yards ahead of the Queen, turned back and looked at her. She either did not see or pretended not to see him. The flurrying snow struck her face, but she did not lower her head or draw the ermine hood closer. Bothwell watched the colorless flakes melt down her cheeks. He quickly turned his head.

The caravan passed under the crumbling stone entry gate and entered Edinburgh. It proceeded down the snow-encrusted, deserted Cowgate Road. The soldiers and servants bent their heads against the cascading wind and snow. Nobody spoke.

The Queen moved her mount alongside Bothwell. "He needs another week of cleansing baths," she said, "before he can return to the palace. He chose Kirk o'Field himself, and told me, over and over, every day, that he loved me. You would have laughed, Bothwell, to hear him tell me that."

The caravan left the Cowgate and made its way up a steep incline of warehouses to a high stone wall, then passed through an orchard of barren trees. The Queen followed Bothwell onto a broad flagstone courtyard surrounded by a series of ruined stone buildings.

A bright red taffeta mask covering the upper part of his face, the King swung his long white legs onto the ground, pulled down his nightgown, and allowed a servant to adjust a robe over his shoulders.

"Mary," said the King. He lifted her hand to his lips and reverently kissed it. "It's snug, peaceful," he said, turning to Bothwell and resting his arm carelessly about the shorter man's broad shoulders. "It's a place where man can think. A monastery once, consecrated ground. There's even ghosts—not one ghost, mind you, but an entire monastic order. Though most of the buildings are dilapidated, this one's good." He squeezed the Queen's hand and smiled beatifically.

A week later the citizens of Edinburgh were awakened by a tremendous explosion. A few ran to their windows quickly enough to see the King's residence rise into the sky above the city. The sky turned bright yellow, then it was black again.

When Queen Mary was told the King was dead, she sent for the Earl of Bothwell, but he would not come. Three months later they were married, according to the Presbyterian rite.

CHAPTER ONE

Year of our Lord 1542. November 24. Scotland. The plain of
Solway Moss near the English border. The English army, num-
bering seventy thousand, stood on the southern portion of the
plain. Opposite, at the foot of a low sloping brown hill, stood
the army of the Scots—fifteen thousand foot soldiers, two thousand
archers, two hundred fifty horsemen. News of the English invasion
had spread through the country and Scotsmen were pouring into
the encampment from Galloway, Sutherland, the Highlands, from
as far north as the Orkney Islands, Caithness, and the Hebrides.
Some carried culverins and hagbutts, but most had only clubs,
pikes, and farm implements. There were women, too. The King
of Scotland's advisers counseled retreat, but he would not hear
of it. The armies waited.

King James rode back and forth in front of his troops, then
ordered the blowing of the horn. He raised the rubied sword
Pope Alexander had given his grandfather, and shouted, "Bruce!
And Wallace! And God and St. Andrew!"

A woman cried out shrilly, "An' dinna ye firgit Quene Mai-
garet, saint, who spak wi' the Lord."

The King laughed and called back, in the Highland dialect,

"Oh, guidwoman, we'll nae firgit St. Meg." There was laughter and scattered clapping. It began to rain.

King James was thirty years old and had been King of Scotland for twenty-nine years. To the Scots nobles, who hated him, he was known as "The Red Fool," but the people called him the "Guid Poor Man's King." His French Queen Marie, his mistress Lady Margaret, his half brother by marriage Lennox, and an interest in architecture, poetry, and the courts were his only comforts. The prospect of his forthcoming child was also comforting; he was certain this one would live. He believed in fairies. He was tired of all the blood.

The English began advancing across the plain.

Thousands of swords lifted against the sky. Nobles, soldiers, farmers, merchants and burghers, boys, women were lost in the sound of the screeching pipes and cracking steel, the drumming of mace on ax over shield into bones and flesh, the shrill clan cries. King James's banner moved above the confusion.

Suddenly an entire section of the field, directly behind the banner, seemed to wash away. A company of English archers, just as suddenly, filled the empty space again. The Scots were cut in half, the King surrounded. Above the roar, King James screamed, "Lennox! Brother! Traitor!" The banner fell.

There was a good deal of close skirmishing, and the King's men were shouting, "God save the King! God damn his enemies! God save the King! God damn his enemies!" The plain gradually turned to mud. Men ran from the field, throwing swords and weapons down in their haste to escape.

December 14. Falkland. King James lay in a corner of a small room, lighted by one candle. His red hair was matted, face pale, lips cracked. His mistress, Lady Margaret, sat on the floor beside him, holding his hand. Her bastard, cheeks raw from weeping, lay with his head in her lap, sleeping. A short stocky priest knelt at at the foot of the bed mumbling Latin.

"Little boy's sleeping," said the King.

"Yes," said Lady Margaret. "Rest, love."

"I know what you're thinking, Meg. Mustn't."

"Rest, love."

He sank back on the pillow, his face in shadow. The candle flickered as the door opened and closed and a soldier approached the bed. The man caught his breath and said, "Majesty, the Queen has been delivered."

Lady Margaret stiffened and withdrew her hand from the King's.

He sat up. "Delivered? What? Now? But . . . so soon, to be delivered. It's dead?"

"No, Your Majesty, alive and well and like to live."

"A Prince of Cumberland," sighed the King. "A live one." He smiled softly to himself.

"It is a fair daughter, sir."

"*Daughter!* Yes, he said it was a daughter, a fair one. Of course it would be. . . ." He stared at the priest, then reached down and knocked the missal from his hands. The priest lowered his head and whispered the words from memory.

"A daughter. Yes . . . that! The Devil take her! It will end as it began; it cam wi' a lass, now it gang gae wi' one. And the English; they're there now, of course . . ."

"Queen Marie and the child left the capital immediately," said the soldier. He raised his hand and brushed an imaginary hair from his forehead. "They'll wait you in the high country," he said quietly.

Lady Margaret nudged the bastard and he sat up, rubbing his eyes. She motioned for him to go to the King. The boy was about twelve, with dark red hair, tall for his age, but thin and unhealthy-looking. The King clasped his hand.

"Achhh, Jamie, you'd be King soon, had I done what I should by your mother, but Kings seldom can, Jamie; I know it, Meg —you would have him King." He started to laugh. "King of what?"

"Of Scotland," said Lady Margaret. "What is your name?" she asked the boy. "Answer."

"James Stewart," he said, slightly bewildered.

"It is the same name as your name," said Lady Margaret,

turning to the King. "Scotland needs a man to succeed you, not your traitor brother Lennox, and not a baby girl pissing her blankets. My son is your son."

"Cannot do it," he said. "Illegitimate. God'd be angry. No."

The boy started to cry. Lady Margaret ordered him to stop, to remember who he was. When she turned back to the King, he was dead. The priest closed the eyes.

The boy was looking out the small window. The countryside was fire. "Can I cry for him now?" he asked his mother. When there wasn't any answer, he looked back over his shoulder and saw her sitting on a straight-backed chair, holding her stomach. The priest was kneeling beside her.

"Another bastard," she laughed. "Another shame." She pointed to the dead man. "He said when the brat came to name it John. He was the disciple everybody loved, loved everyone, which was a thing that King there could never get enough of. John!" Lady Margaret was quiet a minute, then said in a tiny voice, "It'll be a bit, yet. But stay till then. It hurts, and I'm afraid. Please, Father." She motioned for the boy to stand beside her and hold her hand. "Mama's sorry she yelled, Jamie. Now God's punishing her."

"Am I the King?" said the boy.

"They say the first one's always the hardest," Lady Margaret murmured to the priest, "but it should be the last one, when you know it's the last one—"

The boy stared at his mother. "Am I the King now?"

CHAPTER TWO

Pierre Ronsard left the dirt path and made his way through the bushes to a secluded section on the little island's bank. Somewhere, in the distance behind him, past the honeysuckle, a child's laughter disturbed a family of jays. The birds squawked loudly, flapped their wings, and moved along the tree limbs. The lion roared. The child screamed delightedly. Pierre looked at the water and watched the birds fly across the sky's reflection and then return again.

He sat down and continued the letter he'd meant to write fifty times before. "Forgive, *grandpère,* this tardiness in writing, but the Earl of Lennox and the King of England's troops pursue us everywhere. Bad when it was only them, but now they've the Scots Presbyterian heretics, whose numbers grow by the day. Once, we could tell the enemy by his accent, but now—it's strange to think: King James has been dead five years now. Civil war—five years of it—no end in sight. They're always a step behind. But Queen Marie is more a man than any man I ever knew; she's brilliant, brave. Now we're on an island in a loch. There is a small whitewashed monastery here. The monks are gone, but one remains—Father Archibald, a good old man.

"We've been here two months; it's quiet, lovely. I can hear Queen Mary's laughter in the garden. She's grown; she's almost six. She's as tall as twelve and speaks—I swear—as intelligently as a woman of five and twenty. The Highlands are a strange . . ."

He chewed at the quill.

"Ronsard."

He stood and shook the sand from his breeches. "Your Majesty, you were not to return until the end of the month."

"Early this morning," said the Queen Mother. She was a tall, thin, aristocratic woman in her thirties, handsome rather than beautiful.

A young girl flew past the hedges, her long brown hair tangling about her shoulders. A lion pranced a few paces behind her. The Queen Mother smiled. "I have concluded a treaty with France," she said. "They have ended their war with the Spaniards, and troops are available now. My daughter will be brought up in Paris, betrothed to the Dauphin, and one day she will be Queen of France. That has been my dream, and now it will be accomplished."

Ronsard clapped his hands. "Excellent. I'd love to see the King of England's face when he hears of this." He started laughing.

"What does he look like?" asked the Queen Mother. "I know you can see him; your eyes always glaze up so when you have visions."

"Madam, you should see him," laughed Ronsard. "It's something marvelous funny."

"Make him do a jig," she said. Ronsard laughed till his eyes filled. She waited, then added, "I have letters I want you to give my brothers when you arrive in Paris."

Ronsard stared at her. "Madam, you will not stay here?"

"I must."

"Then I will not go!"

"You will do as you are told. *Mon Dieu,* Ronsard, you are capable of the most extraordinary faces."

Farther down the bank, the little girl was wading in the water. The lion lay on the sand, opened its huge toothless mouth, and yawned. The child giggled, ran from the water, and began to dance lightly about him. He beat his tail contentedly in the sand.

The Queen Mother rested her chin on her hand and gazed at the child and the lion. She was quiet a minute, then said, "Pierre, I cannot keep my Mary with me in this country. Scotland had one other Queen Regnant: she was seven years old when, they say, she was murdered."

The child started singing. It was a sad, pretty song.

"*Mignonne,*" cried the Queen Mother. "*Mignonne,* come here." The little girl ran to her mother.

"What a pretty song. Where did you hear it, Mary?"

"In Persia," replied the child.

"And when were you in Persia last?"

"This morning. The fairies took me." She crawled into her mother's lap. "I breakfasted with Robin Goodfellow and Saladin and King Arthur."

"What was King Arthur doing in Persia?" asked Ronsard.

The child stared at him. She took a yellow daisy from her hair and put it in her mother's cap.

"Well, what was King Arthur doing in Persia?" Ronsard demanded in mock impatience.

"What are you doing in Scotland?" she said imperiously. "Besides, it's splendid in Persia. We had lots of confitures and pears—and very good green melon. Then Arthur asked me to be his wife."

The Queen Mother held the girl at arm's length. "Now, Mary, love," she said crossly, "you don't really expect Mama to believe such tales, do you? I warned you not to make up stories any more."

"Of course I don't believe it, but I thought it would make you smile. Anyway, if Arthur had asked me to marry him, I'd have said no. You're the only one I love."

Ronsard's hand darted to his heart. "Ahhhhhghhh," he moaned piteously. "I swear I shall die of grief immediately. I swear it!" He closed his eyes and fell to the sand.

"I love you, too, Pierre," said the girl as she bent over him, "but I love my mama best." He didn't move. She pressed her lips against his eyes. He still didn't move.

"Get up," she commanded angrily. "Stop playing. I won't have it! You're not dead—I can tell. Please, oh, please, please, *get up!*" She jumped to her feet and kicked him in the ribs.

"There was no need for that," he groaned, sitting up.

"There wasn't any for pretending, either," she screamed. She buried her face in her mother's shoulder. The Queen Mother patted her on the head and gave Ronsard a small frown.

"It wasn't very nice," Mary sobbed. "It is awful to pretend." Her mother dug her fingers into the little girl's ribs. She laughed, ran off a few feet, then said gravely, "All right, Pierre Ronsard, I forgive. But you will promise never, never to pretend again." She extended her hand.

Ronsard pressed the hand against his forehead and said, "I promise."

"Now you may give me a horsy ride," said Mary. "Next to Sister Regina, you give the best rides." The sound of voices came from beyond the foliage and she raised her head. "I've got to go," she said nervously. "I've got to go."

"It's only Father Archibald and Sister Regina," said Ronsard.

"Have to go," said Mary. She kissed her mother quickly on the cheek and ran off down the shore. The Queen Mother got to her feet and sighed.

"Good day, Lady," rasped Father Archibald. "We have some dispatches left for you."

The Queen Mother took him by the arm. "Father, you look six months younger than the last time I saw you."

"That was two weeks ago," said Sister Regina. "Like Merlin, Father Archibald grows backward." She was perhaps seventeen or eighteen. Her hands were large and callused, but she had an open, pretty country face. She helped Father Archibald ease himself down on top of a smooth stone, then handed the Queen Mother the dispatches. Smiling, she sat beside Ronsard and draped her hand on his shoulder. Father Archibald gave her a disapproving look, and she folded her hands primly in her lap.

"Lennox has looted five villages," said the Queen Mother. "Thirteen mills. Three hospitals. The English have withdrawn a number of regiments—they are arming the Presbyterians, putting them under the command of Sinclair, Guthrie . . ." Finally she said, "And James Stewart."

"Him?" said Ronsard, his mouth dropping open. "He's a boy. He's Queen Mary's brother."

"He's a Presbyterian," she said. "And he's seventeen. It was clever of the English to put him in command. As my husband's son—legitimate or not—he's won many over to their side." She opened another dispatch. "The English have sacked Dryburgh, Melrose, and Kelso abbeys."

"I saw Melrose once," muttered Father Archibald, "when I was young. They were loose livers. But Dryburgh—I visited there, I remember—it was a holy place." He coughed and cleared his throat. "Presbyterians, hah! Traitors. God will get them." He stopped to watch a red deer lead her fawn to the waterside on the opposite bank. Halfway across the island, the lion roared. "As pretty and plump as a child could be," he continued, addressing nobody in particular. "She's big-boned and grown so sturdy that her dresses will not fit her. I think she will be taller even than Your Majesty. The English are so much more wealthy than us, and smarter than us, bigger. I can't think why we keep winning, or, at least, not losing. I've had to take her across my knee a time or two when you've been gone; she needs discipline most of all, and she makes up stories. She stole marmalade this morning. And, sometimes, I've seen her talking with the jays, I think, or the deer, or something. Her face is so round and bonny you cannot get enough of looking at her, but I think to myself: she's so young now, and you're here, Your Majesty, but someday you won't be here. And there'll be only the English and heretics and we Scots. God, too. But a woman—being Queen—here in Scotland—it's not a simple thing. It could bring a tear or two, even here. But it's all wolves here in Scotland, and her being a woman . . ."

Late that night Mary woke up. I made a pig out of myself, she thought, too many sweetmeats, and God's punishing me. Or maybe it's the devil. She drew a little blanket around her shoulders, unlocked the door, and made her way across the garden to the building where her mother slept.

There was a hint of rain, but it was a pretty night. The moonlight cast shadows over the broad flagged terrace. Mary leaned against the silent fountain, eyes half closed and fixed on the slowly shifting images. There was a lion changing into a dolphin. By the kitchen house, the elongated body of a monk trembled in communication with God. A slight shift in the direction of the slowly rising wind gave the saint a set of angel's wings and then he was Oberon, King of the Fairies. The shadows blurred and spread like a vast pool of black blood. Off somewhere beyond the honeysuckle, she heard a cry which she knew was not a part of the wind.

She made her way through the flowering bushes. Then she stopped. Some thirty feet away, by a cluster of young trees, she saw Oberon's wife, the Fairy Queen. The apparition flowed back and forth in front of the saplings, its long white robes lifting above the high grass. Mary prayed the vision would see her, beckon to her, take her in its arms. She extended her hand and left it suspended in the crisp air for a few minutes. When she opened her eyes, the Queen of the Fairies had vanished. The odor of some dying flower filled the air around her.

A little farther off, Mary heard someone laughing. She followed the sound to the secluded spot near the bank where Pierre had given her a horsy ride before supper. The white robes rose in the dark air and dropped to the grass. Mary knelt behind a rock. It wasn't the Fairy Queen; it was only Sister Regina, who had just taken off her dress and was naked. Mary had seen her before; they'd gone swimming together.

"What would Jesus think?" said a man's voice. Mary raised her hand to her mouth and stifled a cry. She looked slightly to the left and saw the back of a slim-muscled man's body. She could tell it was Pierre. Nobody else, except her mother, had that kind of accent. He was naked, too. Ladies have big round bottoms, she thought to herself, but boys have little skinny ones.

"Jesus would not mind," Sister Regina said pleasantly. "Father Archibald might, but Jesus wouldn't. He's glad."

"The first time," Pierre was whispering, "it wasn't love. But it

wasn't lust. It wasn't love or lust the first time, but . . ." His
voice was too low for Mary to make out all the words. The only
ones she could understand were "merry as a cricket." She liked
that. Merry as a cricket. That was nice. The shadows all around
them were purple, but their bodies were pale, like alum, or like
the color of eggshells. Mary closed her eyes and breathed in the
smell of the honeysuckle. Then Sister Regina cried out.

They were lying down in the grass and sand and Sister Regina's
legs were raised and parted and Pierre was lying on top of her,
between the legs.

At first Mary thought he was smothering her to death. Should
I run out and stop him, say I know he's an assassin? Should I
get Mama and Father Archibald? Should I pray?

"Ah, blithe," murmured Sister Regina. Her hands were on
Pierre's back, which was moving up and down from his bottom,
and her legs were going back and forth.

"I love you," said Pierre. He raised himself up on his hands
and bent back his head. He had a little smile like pictures in her
prayer book of St. Francis when he was talking with the birds.
Then he lay down on top of Sister Regina again and Sister
Regina laughed.

Mary pulled her blanket closer, wiped her eyes, and walked
back to the monastery. Her stomach still felt mean and aching
and she rubbed it with her fist.

The next morning the Queen Mother and Mary and Ronsard
began a journey to Dumbarton, home of Patrick Hepburn, Earl
of Bothwell. "He was your father's friend," Mary's mother told
her, "and he always stood for him." From Bothwell's castle, she
explained, they would be guided to a place called Cromarty Cove,
where a galleon would be waiting.

The clock at the end of the darkened corridor struck midnight.

"I'd no idea," said the Queen Mother. Her hands were shaking.
"There was nothing said. Not in the reports. Nowhere."

"I can't open the door," said the Bishop of Orkney, setting his taper in an iron holder jutting from the wall. "It is a necessary precaution. Remember, speak only through the partition."

"I'd no idea."

"It is the will of God," said the bishop. He left.

The Queen Mother hesitated, then whispered through the barred opening. "Patrick Hepburn. Patrick Bothwell." There wasn't any answer. She stared at the heavy bolts, then leaned against the wood and whispered again, "Patrick Hepburn. Patrick Hepburn."

"Who's there?" The voice was thick, dreamy.

"It's me. . . ."

"Who's me? I'm me. Are you me, too?"

She felt a heavy pressure against the door. She shuddered and drew back.

"Did you see the sea?" said the voice. "It's out tonight. I can see it from the window."

"It's me," said the Queen Mother, starting, despite herself, to cry. "Don't you know who it is?"

"At first I thought it was my son Jimmy. His mother was nothing but his mother. She was tight and dry and died, but not before she gave me him. But you're neither me, her, nor him. Yes," said the voice in a disgusted tone, "I know who you are. The moon is full tonight, but the Black Man, he can't get me here. It's too high and up. And if I can't get down, still, he can't get up. You know something, me, I think he's God—both the same through and through—that's a bad thought."

"It's me. Marie de Guise-Lorraine. King James's widow, his late wife, Queen Mary's mother. Me."

Silence.

"Patrick!"

"It's you then. Why? Will you marry me, love with me now? Is that it?"

The Queen Mother moved away.

"You were me," said the madman in a soft voice. "Partways, at least. I asked you if you'd make it all the way, but you said no." He waited a few seconds, then went on, "You loved the King. I did too. But the King is dead. A little girl can't be a king; you can't be the king either. Her father cursed her on his deathbed. That's bad. The air can eat you up here in Scotland —best leave, forget political stuff, forget dead kings. Leave while possible. Yes. And take my Jimmy boy with you; he's seen too much of me already. Save him. Be his mother for me. Do that for me; you never did anything else. It's coming on me again. Best leave. Don't stay and watch and make me shame myself again. But take my boy and leave. Leave! It cam wi' a lass, an' it gang gae wi' ane."

"Yes," she said. "Yes." She walked hurriedly away. She raised her hands over her ears to close out the sound of the shrieking. There was a lattice window at the stairs and she stopped and pressed her face against the cold glass. Down below, a shadow threw a stick at the moon. It whirled upward through the night air, stuck to the blue a second, then dropped into the rocks. A dog scampered down the jagged incline and caught the wood between its teeth.

A young boy ran onto the moonlit beach, caught up with the dog, wrenched the stick out of its mouth, and stumbled into the waves. He yelled something at the dog, who immediately sat down and howled.

The Queen Mother pulled her shawl over her head and walked down the staircase. When she reached the beach she saw the boy lying on his back in the sand, looking up at the moon as it drifted among the clouds and stars. She cleared her throat and he leaped to his feet. "What you want?" he snarled.

"You were such a nice boy once," said the Queen Mother. "Regardless, I've had a conversation with your papa—"

"I hate you," said the boy. "I hope you die." The moon passed behind another cloud, coloring the sky a blue-black.

"Why?"

"He always said you were beautiful. But you're not—you're like a stick, you got wrinkles under your eyes, you look like an old woman." He struck her on the shoulder. "He said he loved you but you didn't love him. He never loved anybody but you, but you wouldn't love him." He hit her again.

The Queen Mother reached out and boxed his ears, then slapped him across the face. "You're wrong, Jimmy Bothwell," she said calmly. "I did love your father. But I was not *in love* with him. I was in love with my husband, King James. It is late, and the others are waiting. You will be our guide." She wiped the long black hair back off his face. "I was watching you out the window. I never saw anyone throw a stick as high as you. Except my husband, King James. And he was a grown man."

By the time they reached Cromarty Cove the next morning, the sun was a third of the way above the water. The child Queen rubbed her eyes. The white galleon anchored below looked like a gigantic seashell. Mary felt she could reach down and rub her finger against it. She moved to her mother's side and caught hold of her checkerwork skirts and mumbled, "I don't want to go."

"*Mignonne,* you must."

"Mama, please, don't . . ."

Marie patted her on the head. "Darling, you must go. A whole new country! Just think! And you'll be Queen there, too, someday, when you marry the little Dauphin and he becomes King. France isn't cold and heartless like Scotland. And lovely clothes—levantine, brocades, silk—and teachers, and children to play with. *M'amie,* it's time to go now, and we mustn't keep them waiting."

Jimmy Bothwell led them down the rocky incline. Down below, burned boys and men were heaving heavy crates into rope nettings, as easily as if they contained nothing more than fairy dust. Mary liked Jimmy Bothwell; she liked the way he pretended not to look at anybody or anything, and the skill with which he'd maneuvered his way among the rocks that morning. Most of all, she liked the way he pretended not to be watching her mother. Every now and then he would look over his shoulder at the fading outline of the moon, and his face would lose its harshness and become soft. Mary knew he was looking out the corner of his eye and checking to see if her mother was all right. It was manly and gracious, the way he did that. The only other boys she knew were Pierre Ronsard and brother

James. But Pierre, if he wasn't really a man yet, was no longer a boy either. And brother James was so long ago. She wondered what he looked like now, now that he was an enemy. I have another brother, too, only as old as me, but all I can remember about him is that he had bright red hair and freckles and cried a lot.

After they boarded the ship, the captain showed them down below to her quarters.

Marie opened the port window, then sat down on the bed and pulled Mary into her arms. "We have to grow up now. Yes, sweetheart, we do. Lord God made you to be a Queen. Later, you must believe in no one, trust no one, but Him. And say your rosary every morning and every night." She pressed her lips against Mary's cheek. "Ah, *m'amie*, you know your mama loves you, and that she must send you away for your safety. You'll get to meet your grandmother, and your uncles, too. France is where Mama—"

"I'll never see you again," Mary said. "You'll die like everyone else and they'll kill you."

"Foolish," said Marie. Half laughing, half weeping, she lifted Mary into the air, then set her down on the floor. "Mama has no intention of being killed. Even if I were, it wouldn't make me sad, because then I'll be in heaven. And everything's happy there."

"Father Archibald said brother James was wicked and wanted to kill us all," sobbed Mary. "He did. I heard him."

"Father Archibald is wrong," said Marie. "But that does not mean he is wicked. James is wrong, too, but he is still a good boy. And he doesn't want to kill anyone."

There was a soft knock on the door. The captain stuck in his head and said, "It's time."

When they reached the deck, Marie bent down and kissed her daughter lightly on the cheek, then walked down the gangplank.

"Mama!" cried Mary. "Don't go!"

Her mother turned around, smiled, and said, "I must."

The plank was hauled aboard, the anchor cranked up and tied fast. "Two men above to the fore," cried the captain. "Cut

the bands and let the foresail fall! Haul the foresail sheet!"
The white ship lurched away from the pier.

Mary leaned against the deck railing. Down below, on the
wharf, her mother raised her hand and waved. Her checkered
dress fluttered in the cool breeze. Jimmy Bothwell did not wave.

The captain cried, "Let the topsail and the mains'l fall!" All
the mariners began to haul and to call out to each other. One
sailor started singing a sea ditty and soon most of the others
had joined in.

Mary covered her face with her hands. She heard Pierre say,
in a very gentle voice, "You know she would not like that."
Mary waved good-by, trying to smile. France was the most
rich and powerful country in the whole world. When she was
Queen of France, she would come back home and give her
mama everything, and show her how much she loved her.

The thick water alternately churned, splashed, and sighed as
the ship passed over. The vessel sped from the cove and the
people on the wharf disappeared in sea spume. Pierre was looking
at the hills. His face was sad, as if he'd just learned something
unhappy.

Up above, the nest boy waved at the shrinking landscape. The
music of the sailors changed abruptly, turned deep, autumnal:

> "Pull weill a', pull weill a',
> God send, God send,
> Fair wither, fair wither,
> Stow, stow, stow, stow,
> Maik fast and belay—"

CHAPTER THREE

August, year of our Lord 1561. On the sea, ten hours off Calais, six sea days on to Scotland. The captain stood on the poop and surveyed the receding landscape that was France. He felt a cold hand on his shoulder and turned around. "Your Majesty."

She was very tall. Her deep-set eyes were greenish blue; the water made them green. Light chestnut hair was swept back from the high forehead and pinned beneath a white coif which accentuated the heart shape of the face. Her lips were red and finely etched. She was dressed from head to foot in white cambric linen, traditional mourning for widowed Queens of France. Mary smiled. "If I asked you, Captain, would you take me south to Gibraltar?"

"Are there secret plans, Majesty?" said the captain. "We've no wind south. I was instructed Scotland—"

"Then we'll catch a western wind," laughed Mary, "and set course for America." She reached out and pressed his hand. "Forgive me; I'm not being serious. Oh, Captain, you're a lovely man."

"Let your ladies get you a wrap," he muttered. "It's chill, and you'll catch death here, and all."

Mary observed the topsails. "Why aren't we flying the royal French standards? You have the Scottish merchant ensign, but nothing else."

"Because, Your Majesty, you signed no agreement with Queen Elizabeth of England to pass through these waters, which the English like to call their own. Because English men-of-war patrol these waters, and because, Your Majesty, the Queen of England would like to have you in her country as a prisoner."

"We left Calais a week ahead of schedule," said Mary. "Nobody knows."

"The Queen of England knows everything."

"Everything?"

"Yes," said the captain.

Mary bent her head, started to say something, then reconsidered and walked farther down the stern. She stopped by the rudder and gazed at the retreating coastline. "Good-by, France," she said lightly. "It's ended. And adieu, adieu."

Her years in the royal nursery at the Louvre in Paris, marriage with the Dauphin François, coronation as Queen of France at Notre Dame, her mother's death, and sudden widowhood last year at age eighteen—it all seemed like something she'd had to memorize from history for recitation before a tutor. The one thing she clearly remembered—could, in fact, visualize now—was the cloister of St. Pierre les Dames, where, following the death of her young husband, she'd spent some weeks. The hushed sweep of white gowns moving through elaborate gardens, gnats and bees droning, mingled fragrance of flowers and the sound of vespers hymning . . .

The green water bubbled and spat against the side of the rolling white ship. White because, in the northern mists, white was a color that could not be seen by enemies.

"Madam, come below," said Mary Beaton, one of Mary's ladies.

"No," she snapped. Then, "Forgive me. It was a kindness, your coming with me. You might have stayed at Chenonçaux." She took the other girl's hand and raised it to her lips. "You understand, Beaton . . ."

Beaton smiled, shivered, and made her way down to the cabins.

Mary stared into the water. Once she'd heard a sailor say that drowning was all sweet coral sleep and sea music. The thin line that was France swallowed the sun and was in turn swallowed by the sea.

On the third morning the sea lost its green and the galleon slipped over reflections of pink clouds. Mary sat with the first mate on the taffrail, looking at the water cresting in the wake. "Look," she said excitedly. "Over there!"

"Why, Lady," said the first mate, "that's Leviathan."

Several hundred yards away, a gray hulk rolled in the waves. The monster elevated its enormous head for a second, then splashed beneath the crests and began following the ship.

"'Can you draw Leviathan with a fishhook?'" Mary said from memory. "'He makes the deep boil like a pot.' He—I can't remember the rest."

"'No one is so fierce that he dares to stir him up,'" continued the first mate. "'Who is he can stand before Me? Then Job said to God: Now my eyes have seen You and I know You can do all things and no purpose of Yours can be thwarted.'"

"Bravisimo!" she said, clapping her hands. "Scripture always sounds nicer in one's own language." She laughed again and squeezed his hand. "Leviathan liked your recitation; he's still behind us."

"No, no, ma'am, they always follow the wakes, for to have the garbage we throw out. But leeward—there's some dolphins. Friendly type, dolphins. Not like old Leviathan."

"Ship starboard," shouted a sailor from the mizzenmast. "Starboard. Setting fast here."

"What flag, boy?" cried the first mate.

"Unclear," returned the sailor, and a minute later, "Three ships straight back, setting fast."

"What weight?" called the first mate.

"Three back—six hundred tons. Another starboard—eight to ten hundred. No flags! Men-o'-war!"

"Pirates!" someone yelled from the nest.

"Haul aft," shouted the first mate.

The captain ran from the forecastle, scanned the sails, and bellowed, "Spring, and break the mains'l! Forty degrees north. Full speed!" The yards creaked and the ship heeled over. *"Spring,* God damn you, boys, or we'll all be pissing seaweed." He strode backward across the taffrail, bumped into Mary, and spun angrily about. "God damn it, watch you—Majesty—I—"

"No need," she said. Her forehead was sweaty and her cheeks were flushed. "Proceed."

The captain handed her his telescope. "Their cannon—muzzle-loading, twenty-four-caliber loading, at the least. Three-mile range."

"And ours?"

"Twenty-caliber—two miles," said the captain. "They've perriers and mortars, too. The Queen of England *does* know everything, damn her."

The pirate ships had joined ranks. Catching up slowly, they simultaneously fired a blast of shot across the water.

"They mean for us to surrender," said the captain.

Mary laughed. "Then they don't know it's *us!*" Her heart was drumming. If I were a man! she thought wildly to herself. A man and with a cutlass, blood, and swinging myself down the—

"It's to be a chase, then," said the captain, grinning. "Full speed," he roared. "Lively, boys! Ah, stow and row!"

The pirates fired another volley and a sheet of cold spray shot across the taffrail.

"Majesty, best get below."

"No."

The whale that had been following her ship was stunned by the last volley. It raised its gigantic head, reared, and disappeared beneath the water. Soon, one of the enemy vessels passed over the spot where he had gone down. The water filled with blood. Mary cried out. Suddenly the whale leapt halfway out of the water immediately in front of its assailant and hurled its huge bloody body against the ship's starboard side. The *smack!* sounded over the waves. The pirate ship buckled and jerked.

One of the other vessels changed course and went to the aid of its fellow.

"Fog rising five miles, twenty degrees north," shouted a voice from the crow's nest. The two remaining pirate ships were drawing close.

"Make fast!" cried the captain. "Split water there!"

The pirates opened fire. In the glare, Mary watched the mainmast totter, sway, and crack. "Load cannon," yelled the first mate. "Return—" Mainsail blazing, the ship moved into mist.

"Mortars here!"

"Make fast! Return fire!"

"Cannon here!"

The taffrail burst into flames, and Mary lost her balance, stumbled, and fell backward over the railing onto the quarterdeck. Dazed, she got to her knees, stared drunkenly at the men rushing madly around her, and muttered, "Don't let me die, *Jesu,* don't let me die." She slowly closed her eyes and started crawling on her hands and knees in the direction of the cabins. Somebody shouted something. She felt herself being lifted. Is it my soul, going up, she thought, going off? There was a loud crash and she dropped to the deck again. A heavy weight collapsed on her back and she screamed out in pain. She wriggled herself free and stared into the first mate's bewildered eyes. The ship rolled; blood gushed from the open mouth. She screamed again, ran to the railing, and vomited.

"God damn you," she howled. "Oh, God damn, damn, damn you, God damn you, Elizabeth! God kill you. Elizabeth!" She slumped over the railing again, then stood straight. A small black vessel loomed some forty feet away.

"Scotland!" a voice sang from the black ship. "Scotland! *Clan Bothwell gu braith!*" It moved away in the mist, toward the pirates.

By afternoon of the following day the fog still had not lifted, and the captain gave orders to heave to, take soundings, and bury the dead. It was dangerous to proceed, and so the ship sat in mid-sea for two days. Eventually the fog lifted somewhat, and the vessel picked its way through rocks and shallow water.

That night the alarum bell clanged, and Mary rose and went up on deck. She asked the captain what was wrong.

He pointed to a black mound dimly flecked with lights, rising high in the mist. "Scotland," he said.

CHAPTER FOUR

"The Earl of Bothwell to see Your Majesty," announced the captain.

A black-haired, plain-faced young man of medium height entered the cabin and dropped brusquely to one knee. Mary extended her hand. He looked at it, stood up, and stared at her. He would be at least twenty-five by now, she thought, but she could still see in his face, his eyes, the harsh intensity of the young boy who had led her and her mother down the rocks at Cromarty Cove all those years and years ago, when she was nothing more than a child, whimpering at the thought of leaving her mama.

Bothwell fumbled through the pockets of his canvas greatcoat and produced a small silver casket.

Mary examined the inlaid lions, stags, and partridges on the top. "I gave this to my mother," she whispered.

"Right. And before she died she gave it me to give back."

Mary undid the clasp and lifted the cover. The inside of the box was networked with gold-leaf work. Folded on its bottom was a letter sealed with red wax. The paper crackled in her fingers. *M'amie,* it read, *Great responsibilities are easy to assume, but difficult to carry well before God.* Here the ink faded into the paper and several sentences were lost. . . . *Wm. Maitland is a politician—use, but do not trust. The Catholic power is Earl of Huntly—he's a fool. What a pity. The Presbyterians won— accept—perhaps they deserved to win. John Knox is a figure leader. The real Presbyterian power is your brother James. He knows, were it not for his illegitimacy and you, he would be a King. Watch him. Morton, Ruthven* . . . Most of the lines that followed were unintelligible. . . . *be a faithful Catholic always* . . . *Trust Bothwell.* . . . *James is a saint* . . . *murderer.* . . . *The past in Scotland is never past* . . . *as much history as is the future* . . . *long to hold you one last time in my arms. Your father was* . . . *they say you have his blue eyes. Trust Bothwell. Mama loves you.* Here the letter came to an abrupt halt. Mary read it again, then a third time. She had wanted to come back and give her mother everything. But she had known, even then, that her desire was only a child's flimsy wish, and that death would intervene.

"Do you want to know what it says?" she asked.

"No," he said flatly.

Mary folded the letter and put it in the pocket of her dressing gown. She thought Bothwell had been looking at her all this time, but he hadn't. His eyes were fixed on the silver casket. "Take it," she said.

He reached over and slipped it into his greatcoat.

She waited for him to say thank you.

He let his eyes rest on her breasts, smirked, then said slackly, "She said to—your mother, the Queen Regent—she said I was to take you to a place."

"Where?"

"You will know when we are there. But you must promise me a thing: you won't puke if you get scared. Queens lose dignity when they puke in front of ordinary folk. It gives an impression of mortality."

"Forgive me," she laughed, walking toward him and taking his hand. "It was you out there. 'Clan Bothwell Good Bruth.' You saved us all."

"You must come," he said. "Before it gets later. Or they know you have arrived."

"I can't go with you now, Bothwell. It's almost two. I can't simply—"

"Your mother said I was to take you," said Bothwell. "I'll bring you back when we're through. Get some dark things on. I'll wait above." He gave her an ironic look, then left.

Insufferable, she thought, no respect, courtesy. And his eyes— as if I was—and his entire manner. Her mother had written: *Trust Bothwell.* It was late; he'd probably been roused from sleep. Three days before, he'd saved her life. Yes, that was it— it was late, and he was tired.

When she'd dressed and climbed on deck, she found Bothwell talking with the captain.

"Whales, fog, and the Lord High Admiral of Scotland," the captain was saying, "that's salvation from above."

"We sank one. Let the other go. To tell Queen Bess in London." Bothwell turned and observed Mary as she walked toward them. "Excuse me, Lady," he drawled, "but that outfit. You are—it's obvious—dressed in male gear to avoid detection. Nice. But what Edinburgh gentleman wears levantine clockwork hose, a French-cut velvet doublet, boots of Spanish leather, or a cap with a pink ostrich plume? Madam, you've been away a bit. This is a Presbyterian country. Take off the ostrich, at the least."

"Right," she said, imitating his flat voice. Her cap flew over the side of the ship railing and floated off on the black, lapping water. Bothwell suddenly broke into a completely good-natured smile that cut his face from ear to ear. He was almost handsome. Mary allowed him to take her hand and lead her down the gangplank.

The sky above was thick and black gray, but as they cantered over the cobblestones Mary saw the hazy outlines of house fronts and treetops. Here and there, long wooden flights of stairs vanished into the rolling white air. In the distance she heard a watchman intoning:

"Two o' th' clock, look well to your lock,
Your fire and light, and so good night."

After a while the horses left the cobbles and their hoofs began to crunch over a soft grassy slope. Mary wiped the thick drizzle from her face. The horses were breathing heavily. She felt dizzy, excited. Bothwell got off his horse.

"We walk from here," he said, helping her down.

Below, the mist churned angrily about steeples and gabled roofs. The moon passed from behind a cloud and covered the scene in a gauzy, yellow light. A huge mass of black stone walls and turrets towered above them. "The Castle of the Maidens," explained Bothwell. "Edinburgh Castle." Mary watched the moon alight briefly on the highest turret. There was a sudden, violent alteration in the direction of the wind and the moon was sucked behind the black clouds. Bothwell tightened his grip on her hand.

"Where are the guards?" she said.

"Scotland isn't France," he said.

He fumbled with some keys, then pushed hard against an iron gateway. They walked across a seemingly endless courtyard. A series of high stone buildings welled out of the murk. "In here," he said, pulling open a door. She stooped, entered, and followed him up a long, dark winding staircase. The odor was oppressive. He brought her into a small room and lit a taper. "She did not say to bring you here. I was to take you to the other place—the one down below. But up here in this tower, that's where it should begin."

Muddy tapestries lined the walls. A torn mattress had been thrown over two cracked mahogany chests in one of the corners. Mary rested her hand on a dusty table top. The broken head of a porcelain Virgin smiled uncertainly from a heap of rubble near the door.

"Is this . . . where my mother . . ."

"Yes."

"At least, you were with her, Bothwell. It said so in the reports. You were like a son to her. She wrote me of you. Often. At least, she wasn't alone."

"No," he said brutally. "She wasn't alone. Everybody was here. The English commanders, Maitland, Huntly, Ruthven, Morton, your bastard brother James. Everybody but Master Knox. And they had him outside." He struck his fist against the top of the desk. "A priest is so much refuse to me. But if that was what she wanted, they might have let her have one."

"But you were there," she whispered. She touched his hand. "When a person's dying, it's good to have a friendly face by. When I die . . . I'd want—that."

"Ay," he said softly, letting his eyes rest on hers.

"Dropsy," he finally said. "But you know that. I'd help her do exercises at first, but the pain was too much. She was the only *good* woman I ever knew." He turned away.

"When she died, she was forty-four," said Mary. "They told me she looked like sixty." It hurt her to say that, but she said it because she wanted him to tell her it wasn't true.

"Then 'they' never looked close," he said in a rage. "She was blithe!"

"She loved you very much. She'd always write that—"

"She never loved me! She never loved anyone—but you. She did everything—for you. She killed herself because of you. Your mother never cared about Scotland. But forget that. She was dying and she knew it. No one else did, but she did. It was Protestants and Catholics. Catholics and Protestants. You would look out that window there and the hills were burning. You would look out this other window and the French and English were butchering each other on the water. You couldn't make out anything sometimes, for all the smoke. The Queen of England sent four armies. The King of France sent four fleets. The Scots were incidental. It was happening in our country, and, still, sometimes—no, all the time—it seemed like we had nothing to do with it at all. It spread. First the south, then up to the Highlands, then past that and up to the outer islands. The

English and the French. The Protestants and the Catholics. Death and madness. Then she knew she was dying. Your mother called in the English and the French and the Scots, and she called them to her deathbed. She said she'd had enough of it. That if the English would go the French would go too. She begged them to swear fealty to you if you ever came back. I believe she expected your husband would die. She said she forgave everything, and asked for their forgiveness. She asked for a priest. James said no. She shrugged her shoulders, patted him— your bastard brother—on the head, and asked him to pour her some wine. After a few sips, she put it on the bed table—that one over there. 'One more thing,' she said. She shut her eyes as if to think. Everybody waited. You could hear the clock clicking; you could hear all the breathing. I don't know how long it lasted, but finally the bastard leaned over and asked her what it was she wanted to say. She was dead. Sitting there dead and she looked—*still*—so straight, so *patient!*"

"And my brother James—what did he do then?"

"Left the room. Nice of him. Your brother is a Pharisee." He observed her coolly. "You have her height. Taller, in fact. And your voice is low and soft like hers, as well. Even the accent."

"Thank you," she said weakly.

"Now I'll take you where she told me to take you," he said. At the doorway, he paused. "But that's not her face on you. It's your father's. And your brother's. That took me back first time I saw you tonight. The way you look like your brother James. I hate him very much." He lifted the taper, took her hand again, and led her down the staircase. Their shadows twisted and blurred against the rusty javelins, maces, and spotted shields which hung from the crumbling plasterwork wall. They walked along a short corridor on the ground level, then moved down another series of stairs. The taper spit high, momentarily shriveling their shadows. Mary stifled a cry.

"Saints," said Bothwell, holding the fire to the wall. Five young Romans, eyes transfixed, arms uplifted, ascended from the Emperor's fire pit to heaven. Further down, St. Barbara knelt and bent her head. The executioner raised his ax. "The sea is too close. These were painted some time back but will not last much longer, I'd guess."

After what seemed like a long time, the stairs ended and Bothwell shoved open a heavy iron screen. They passed into the low-vaulted interior of an ancient chapel. At the far end of the room ragged cobwebs moved slowly back and forth from the arms of the crucifix above the altar. It was cold. Mary hunched up her shoulders. Bothwell led her past some over-turned pews to a small crypt at the back of the chapel.

"St. Margaret," he said, indicating one of the slabs, "and there's Malcolm. Duncan. Bruce." He pointed to a steel urn. "Wallace's heart. Here's James I. James II. James III. Pity." The marble on James III's grave had been broken into chunks. Bits of bone lay scattered at the bottom of the bronze coffin. "James IV. And here." He fitted the torch into a brazier and stood aside.

Mary read the words: James V, Scotia, Orare. A red granite cross, filled with runic inscriptions, was embedded in the center of the long marble slab. A bouquet of fresh daisies, pine, and stalks of heather lay beneath the red cross. Mary looked at Bothwell. He shook his head. She sank to her knees and lifted one of the daisies to her cheek. "I never knew him," she mumbled. She bent and ran her hand along the cold marble. "I don't even know what he looked like. Why did she want you to bring me here; later, there'd have been time, but—why immediately? I don't understand."

The wind filled the cracks of the nave; its low, tender moaning was almost comforting. The taper hissed. "Somebody's here," she said, standing up.

"No one," said Bothwell.

The wind groaned heavily. Mary stared at the dusty reflection of the fire on a wrought candleholder. "There's somebody here, watching us."

"Nobody," said Bothwell. "Or the wind. Or ghosts, or the vampire ladies."

"Vampire ladies!"

He smiled. "A story. Whoever was here before the Celts were here carved this castle out of the sea rocks. The sea used to come up to the precipice, but the shore has receded since that time. The Celts housed virgins here for their chiefs. Highland women mostly, prizes from wars. Once, the virgins arranged a banquet for all the Lowland chiefs. Then, after they had been drugged, the girls cut their throats. Supposedly, they still flit about, sucking blood and such things."

"Well," said Mary. "Perhaps I did hear something. We'd better go, my lord."

"No need for worry," laughed Bothwell. "They only suck the menfolk."

"But, dear my lord, those ladies must have teeth like knives! Could that be why Scotland's gone so pure of late? Is it possible, Master John Knox himself might have once visited this very crypt and—and—" She threw back her head and laughed. It was the laughter of a gay, perfectly delighted child at a Mayday or midsummer festival, a fairy laugh.

"Braw!" Bothwell chuckled. He lifted his arms over his head and slapped his hands together. "That's cheer. Your dad there would say as much. After all the years under that cold stone, his girl comes to visit—and she lays a good, clean, dirty laugh at his feet. Prayers and tears are prayers and tears, but that's *best!*" He crossed his arms over his chest and smiled broadly. When he smiled, he looked like a fourteen-year-old boy, wonderful, good.

Mary performed an elaborate curtsy. Ah, here's a *man,* she thought, a true, honest one, one to fight me victories, one to confide in, laugh with, admire. In France—well, France, you have your men—but not straightforward manly men whose faces you can read. She stared at Bothwell, fascinated. La, God, let me have three such as he, and I shall have a marvelous time here in Scotland. He was my mother's champion.

She accidentally upset the taper. The chapel glowed and disappeared around them. Bothwell suddenly stopped laughing. She felt him standing very close to her, then he said brusquely, "Time we went, at any rate."

She reached out, took his hand, and raised it to her lips.

"What are you doing?" he said, pulling away his hand. "Come."

When Mary arrived back at the ship, she found the captain on the quarterdeck. She was touched that he'd waited for her and wanted to thank him, but when he saw she was safe he grumbled at the hour and went below. He's been kind to me, Mary thought, but I'll make it up to him.

Halfway through her rosary, she lay back in bed and stared at the ceiling. There was something comfortable, comforting about white wooden ceilings. Bothwell was an entirely likable man. A person to trust. If he were only half a foot higher. If I were a full foot less. If . . . if . . . and only if . . . but I've grown accustomed to it. If one can't change a thing, then one accepts it. Accepts it. But only an inch, two inches—no more, only two— from the legs.

Mary rolled over onto her stomach and pressed her cheek against the cold sheet. It is altogether fitting that kings stand higher than ordinary men and women. It is dignity, sets us apart, above. Did not God himself call us "little gods"? Mary lay on her left side and stared vacantly at the watery reflection of moonlight on the wood floor. It is altogether fitting. They hate me.

Edinburgh has twenty thousand men, women, children. Glasgow's next in size with six. After that—villages, hamlets, scattered shacks and hovels, hills, ruined monasteries, lakes, and Presbyterian churches. But Bothwell is a likable man. The French were fighting and the English were fighting, and the Scots, all fighting here. Last year—a little year ago—the Presbyterians overthrew—all. The Mass, abolished. The Pope's authority, abolished. Transubstantiation, monks, nuns, purgatory, and indulgences—abolished. Master John Knox did it. My brother James did it. Now I'm here. I know they won't like that. They have mainly—in open fields—barley, wheat, rye, some flax, wheat, boar and herring, sheep, wolves, gulls, apes, leopards. . . . I'm a Catholic, and they hate Catholics.

She remembered, as a child, having read in a book: *There has been in this realme of Scotland one hundred and five kings, of whilk there was slaine fyftie-six.* That was the first line of the book.

Edinburgh had twenty thousand people, approximately nineteen thousand nine hundred and ninety-nine Protestants and then there would be, of course, the Queen.

But we'll be sleep and sea music . . . we'll live. She was on the sea again and as she drifted down and down, the skiff jerked and leaped from the reedy shore. Mary leaned against her mama and the yowling of the sleuth-hounds grew louder and more frenzied and closer, closer. The lapping water and the moon and the reeds swaying in the breeze. Men splashed in the shallow water with hagbutt pistols exploding in their hands. The boat rower's face was dirty, intent. He noticed her staring at him and smiled nervously and managed to wink before his face spattered red.

Mary woke up screaming. Her hands shot to her throat and struggled to undo whatever it was that was strangling her to death.

Mary Beaton held the rosary beads up to the candlelight. "They caught around your neck. There. Only that. Sleep now. It's almost three-thirty. Sleep, dear. Lie back and sleep."

"What . . . a dream . . . and I dreamed I saw . . . I don't know."

"All is well." Beaton lifted the covers and slipped in beside Mary. Mary burst into tears.

"Madam, are you afraid of tomorrow? There's nothing to fear."

Mary buried her face in Beaton's shoulder. "Oh, my poor mother," she wept. "She never had any *happiness.*"

Beaton took Mary in her arms and started crying too. "But your mother is in heaven," she said, "and if any woman ever belonged in heaven, she belonged there. She's happy now. And if she is not there, *chérie,* then no one is."

"Do you believe that there's a heaven?" said Mary, sitting up. "Madam!"

"But if there wasn't one. If there wasn't any heaven at all—if we were born, and had to live and die—and simply die and not have anything after, nothing . . . if there was only God, but no heaven, then what would God be? I never knew what it was like for her. Until I saw what they'd done to her room. If they could do that to her, what could they do to me? Oh, Beaton, she never had any happiness at all. I wanted to see her with everything, but I never thought she'd *die!*"

"And isn't that the way it always seems to be," sighed Beaton, dry-eyed, as much to herself as to the girl who lay shivering in her arms.

Mary examined herself in the mirror. She unfastened her high white ruff and threw it on the dressing table. She undid the two top buttons of her white cambric widow's weeds, thought a second, then undid two more. "The multicolor scarf, Beaton, and, yes, the eye kohl—silver-blue, I think." She unlocked her jewelry chest, took out a diamond necklace with a gem-encrusted crucifix, and clipped it around her neck. "Did you see him when you were up on deck? Beaton!"

"Madam, they've been waiting at least an hour."

"Did you see him?"

"Who?"

"Him! My brother. James."

"Yes, yes. Everybody. Madam, they're waiting." Beaton stared at her in disbelief. "Surely you're not going up like that. At least do the last button—you look like the Whore of Babylon."

"I would imagine, Beaton, that even Presbyterian women have breasts," said Mary, irritably fastening two of the buttons. "Well, what does he look like?"

"What does who look like?"

"My brother! Is he dour? Does he have a Presbyterian face? A small rain cloud above his head?" Mary laughed, picked up a cup of cinnebar water, and gargled.

"I saw him only a minute, from the back. But he's a very tall man."

He wouldn't allow her a priest, Mary thought. My mother was dying, but he could not do that one thing. No, no, these heretics are very pure when it comes to matters of religion. As representative of the Presbyterian traitors who defeated my mother in the field, defeated her at negotiation tables, seized upon the lands of the Church, and drove the Church out of Scotland, my brother James has deigned now to welcome my return. Splendid, marvelous, good of him to grace my arrival with his Presbyterian presence! To even take notice! Brother

James, who all these years has acted as if he—a bastard—would, could be a king. On my throne. In *my* country. Well, we shall see who is king and who is not.

"Get me my high-heeled shoes," she told Beaton.

"You never wear—"

"Get them, damn you. They're with the others. White ones. The only ones I have." She accidentally upset the cinnebar cup and watched it crash to the floor.

"Madam, you can't mean to wear these," purred Beaton, handing her the shoes. "They're four inches. They might mistake you for one of the masts. Or are you Atalanta this morning?"

Ignoring her, Mary re-examined her face in the mirror. But I'm beautiful, she thought; I'm five feet and eleven inches high, but I'm still a beautiful woman. If anything, then that. "Don't look at me like that," she snarled into the mirror at Beaton.

"It's time to go," said Beaton coldly. "Get up. Your people are waiting."

Heralded by shrieking pipes and cornets, Mary ascended into the chill morning air and smiled graciously at the silent dignitaries assembled on the quarterdeck. The bagpipes assaulted her ears. In France, such a noise would hardly be considered music. The sky was plated with thick, metal-colored, chilling clouds. Below, on the quarterdeck, a tall, lean man in sad gray garments looked up at her, moved forward, and dropped to his knees. As if by signal, everyone else kneeled. Then the man rose, and the others rose too.

The tall man took a parchment from his worn doublet, unrolled it, and began to read in a somber voice. "We bend the knee to Mary, Queen of Scotland and the Isles, and beg grace of her, reminding ourselves of the wisdom and fearfulness of God—"

"Brother James!" she cried and ran down the taffrail and threw her arms around his neck. Caught off guard, James blushed and looked down helplessly at her.

"You've grown a bit," he said roughly. His light blue eyes scanned her face, blinked, then shifted past her head.

She stood back and studied him. James was six foot three, at the least, sturdily built, well proportioned. If only he didn't look so sad, so grim. And she had expected him to look older. After all, he was thirty-one, twelve years older than she, but there was a youthful quality about his face. She had been prepared to treat him coolly, but when she saw him standing a head and a half higher than those behind him, when she saw the shabbiness of his clothing, and the dignity with which he wore it, her resolve had weakened. He was her brother. And even if he were a Presbyterian and the leader in the overthrow of the Catholics, he was a man of principle, who surely must have believed in what he did. Saints can be wrong, her grandmother had said, and still be saints. Even his enemies often spoke well of him. The ire of her French relatives had always been directed toward John Knox, the Queen of England, the others, never James.

"You look well, brother," she said.

"And you, sister." He turned stiffly and introduced her to a mustachioed gentleman in a bright Spanish half cape.

"William Maitland," said Mary, crinkling her eyes. "I've heard of you, Michael Wiley." Maitland the chameleon. Weathervane. Machiavelli of the north. He'd served the Queen of England; he'd served Mary's mother; he'd served France, and he'd served James. He'd been a Catholic twice, a Presbyterian three times, and once—during a stay in England—an Anglican. Supposedly, one could always tell whichever side was winning, in any dispute, by William Maitland's whereabouts at a given time.

"*Ah*, Your Grace," said Maitland, his thin lips curving into a smile. As he bent to kiss her hand, Mary caught a whiff of an attar similar to one Beaton used. She stifled a laugh. Machiavelli of the north perfumed his mustaches!

Mary followed James down the line of nobles, barons, and burghers. For the most part, they were attired in mustard-color and gray; some had had the effrontery to wear pieces of armor. The faces seemed all the same—the women's faces as well as the men's—vacant, coarse, piratical. They gave her insolent, mocking looks, bent their knees, and brushed their mouths against the ruby and sapphire rings on her fingers.

"John Stewart," said James, stopping before a happy-looking, freckled youth with unkempt, sandy hair.

"Sister!" he cried, throwing his arms around her waist and kissing her sloppily on the cheek.

Mary pulled away and stared at him: he was as old as she, but seemed so young, so guileless.

"Sorry," said the boy, his face turning red. "I don't know what to say now." Suddenly, he broke into a sunny smile and announced, "You, St. James here, and I are family, Sister Mary. Dad was a lively one, you know. Dear God, but you're high."

Mary smiled. She would like John, she decided. She started to say something, but James took her by the arm and led her further down the line.

"The Earl of Bothwell."

"We have already been introduced, Stewart," said Bothwell. He seized Mary's hand, fell to his knee, and made a loud smacking noise.

"I know," said James, calmly returning Bothwell's look. "The Earl of Huntly. Lady Huntly. Their son and their daughter."

Huntly was a thickset man of about fifty, with a flowing white mane, huge, bulbous forehead, and bulldog mouth. His dress was one of barbaric splendor; chains of beaten gold and silver were strung across rich wool plaids; his purple velvet leg-of-mutton sleeves were studded with crudely cut precious stones. Though Huntly was the one surviving Catholic power in Scotland, the Presbyterians had never dared make war against him. The man owned the Highlands—all water rights, rents and fiefs, monopolies, minerals, and clan loyalties. His influence, however, did not extend to the more civilized Lowlands, where the Presbyterians had established their stronghold. Lady Huntly had been a friend of Mary's mother.

"Much happiness," said Lady Huntly wearily. "Your mother would be pleased at the bravery you have shown in returning to this Godforsaken country." She sighed heavily and stood.

"Say the word," Huntly declaimed in a thick burr, "and we'll take men and restore the Mass." He settled his bulk slowly onto the deck.

Mary was aware of the sudden silence. Everybody was staring at her. "We cannot press the conscience of any man," she said nervously. "We can only hope our sub—"

"My son, Sian," interrupted Huntly. He clapped his hand about the shoulder of a muscular, outrageously handsome young man and shoved him forward. "Alas, Your Majesty, twenty-four years and *still* not wed and bed. Sian, show Her Majesty what a fine leg you have. And speak something in Latin for Her Majesty. There's a bonny boy."

Sian Gordon began delivering one of Cicero's orations.

"Lord and Lady Morton," said James, moving on.

"God damn your bastard heart," bellowed Huntly, clasping his hand against the hilt of his sword and drawing it halfway from its scabbard. "God damn your soul!"

"This is Edinburgh," James said, quietly, without turning. "This is not the Highlands. Take care, Huntly."

Mary watched Huntly's face fill with blood. Lady Huntly smoothed the back of her husband's neck and whispered something in his ear. Still shaking in rage, he sheathed his sword and stood back.

"Lord and Lady Morton," repeated James as calmly as if nothing had happened.

Half an hour later, Mary walked down the gangplank and stepped onto the wharf. She looked around her. Crates and broken boxes. A cat crouching on one of the low tin rooftops. Deserted netting troughs. A crowd of thirty or forty nondescript poor people in ragged gray broadcloth and homespun, mouths tight, eyes blankly staring.

"The reports said you would not be here until next week," James said brusquely. "They have some entertainment planned in the capital, but not what you're used to, I suppose. Get up."

"Surely you don't expect me to ride this," said Mary. Under the red and yellow caparisoned livery, her mount was thin and sway-backed.

"She's a gentle nag," said James. "You! Over there. Sound horns."

Mary rose on the saddle. The horse turned its head and mournfully regarded her with one sad brown eye. Mary scratched it gently behind the ear. To the screech of horns and swirl of bagpipes, the procession straggled through the narrow, stench-filled streets of the little harbor port. Men and women in brown and blue peasant's clothes peered at Mary from windows and doorstoops. What hurt her most was the wide, frightened eyes of the children.

"God bless an' bless Yer Machsty," a voice shrilled from over her head. A wizened grandame leaned from a second-story window, hunched her thin shoulders, and threw down a yellow cicendia blossom. "Queenie's back," she cackled, "Queen-queen-queenie's home again! Guid King Jamie's sweetheart dotter!" The grandame winked slyly and made the sign of the cross.

"Queen-queen-queenie," yelled the children, running after Mary's horse and trying to touch her skirts with their little hands.

A man's voice rose above the noise: "God bless that sweet face!"

Mary started throwing copper coins to the children. The adults began to run after and holler, "God save the Queen!"

After a few minutes the street gave way to a wide dirt road surrounded by stubble fields. "Everything's so bright," Mary said to no one in particular. "The colors—blinding. They hurt my eyes."

"The heather," said James.

"Halloo, Sister Mary, an' how do you like your country?" cried John Stewart, riding up alongside her.

"*Braw,* Johnny!"

"D'you hear it, James! Sister Mary's Scots again already. Hurrah for Queenie!" He grasped her reins, leaned forward in his saddle, and whispered, "I *love* you, Mary, Queen of Scots. We'll have times together!"

"Edinburgh," said James, pointing ahead.

The city rose high in the west, bordered in front by the yellow fields and behind by vast rolling hills of green and purple. Capped with high towers and arched red roofs, freestone buildings rose three, four, and five stories along the ridge that ran the length of the city. The side streets were filled with close and poorly constructed clay and wattle houses; even from this distance they seemed disease-ridden and dirty. Edinburgh struck

Mary as faintly resembling an arm—an arm pinned down by some invisible charm, but the hand free, stretching defiantly into the sky. The hand consisted of a black citadel rising from a jagged crag on the city's northernmost point, above a broad river flowing into the sea. The drop from all sides except that facing the main street was sheer and deadly. The riverway glinted in the sun and Mary raised her hand to protect her eyes.

"Somewhat like Prague," James was saying. "High-seated, clean air, warm-water springs—"

"Bothwell! Where's Bothwell?"

"Here, Your Majesty."

She pointed at the citadel and he nodded his head yes. James waited patiently, then resumed speaking.

Cannon boomed from on top the city gates. On the distant hills, bonfires sent thin lines of smoke into the sky. Mary straightened her shoulders and entered her capital.

"Fresh-print ballads," a boy screamed. "Queen Mary's Wondrous Homecome Compared to Deborah Prophetess Israel—Huzzah! Twopence." People were pushing back and forth attempting to get a look at her, but there was little clapping and cheering. "Hot oatcakes!" screamed a bakerwife. Beneath the low-crowned blue hats and white coifs, the faces expressed disapproval, even hate. But they don't know me, Mary thought to herself. They can't know I'm as much afraid of them as they may be of me.

A cart filled with squealing children dressed in angel's wings rumbled toward her and came to a halt directly beneath a wooden gallery. A little boy of five or six, whose sausagelike arms and legs were wrapped in white bunting, was lowered above the wagon. The other children sang a rousing hymn, and one of them handed the boy a purple cushion, upon which rested the keys to the city. The boy steadied himself and cautiously handed the cushion to Mary. The bunting loosened somewhat and he hitched it up again.

"Greetings to Queen," he said solemnly. "And long life to Yer Majesty. They think it well, and they the Pope do name the Anti-Christ and the Mass—"

One of the children in the wagon grabbed at his feet and started him swinging haphazardly back and forth. The bunting unraveled and floated down to the cobbled street. Tears streaming down his cheeks, the boy was wrenched upside down and pulled back onto the gallery.

Laughter broke out here and there in the crowd. Mary saw the small red face peering at her from behind the railing and cried, "Oh, young man, that was an excellent speech. I swear I never heard so good a speech!" She took her purse from her girdle and threw it up to him. A thin, sallow woman—probably his mother—caught it and deposited it in her blouse. "That's for sweets and nothing else!" Mary yelled. The woman made an ugly face and said something, but the words were lost in the crowd's roar of approval. Mary lifted an eyebrow and rode on.

After another block the procession was stopped again, this time by a procession of girls singing, "Jerusalem, Rejoice for Joy." Clad in plum-gray velvet, the Lord Mayor and an assemblage of councilmen knelt at the conclusion of the psalm and presented Mary with the Protestant Bible. Huntly grunted obscenely and rode to her side. The crowd grew silent. James had his eyes fixed on some point in the sky. Mary leaned over in her saddle and kissed him on the cheek. He looked at her in surprise and horror. She took the Bible, brushed her lips against its leather covering, and handed it to him.

"It is fitting," she said in a loud voice, "that this holy book be possessed by the head of my Privy Council, James Stewart." Impulsively, she threw her arms around his neck and kissed him again. His face turned red. The mob roared louder than before. "God save, long live, King James's daughter!" some people shouted. John Stewart rode between Mary and James, clasped both their hands, and, cheeks streaked with tears, laughed out loud, "Oh, brother! Oh, sister!" Close by, a woman's voice pealed, "Stewarts! Stewarts! Stewarts!" Huntly swore and rode back to his lady.

The swarm was thickest at the Merkat Cross, in the city's main business square. A figure draped in purple priest's vestments jutted in front of Mary. A rotted watermelon stuck on a pole served as its head—eyes two green apples, mouth a carrot, weeds pasted on the watermelon for a beard. Mary laughed, then stopped laughing. The makeshift priest danced in front of her, rosary beadings swinging from its neck, vestments whirling.

"Get that away," James said in a low voice.

The man who bore the pole backed off and slowly began to lower the priest image.

A steel blade flashed through the air. The melon splashed open, its red meat splattering Mary's face. "Traitors," roared the Earl of Huntly. "Heretics and traitors!" He raised his sword again and smote the man over the head with its flat.

Mary heard someone scream, turned, and saw a group of women carrying a small stage on their shoulders. A caricature of the Pope, blood dripping from its fanged mouth, swayed from the top. The stage inadvertently bumped into Mary's horse, which hissed, reared, and almost threw her. Chanting a fierce hymn, the stage-bearers marched to the center of the square and, shouting hosannas, dumped the Pope into a cackling bonfire. Huntly, his sword flailing, charged after them. Mary turned and saw Lady Huntly—a thin, elegant woman who had been a friend of her mother's—smile proudly as her husband scattered the women. Fleeing Huntly's sword, the women rolled toward Mary, screaming, "Jade! Doxy! Babylon! Rome! Whore!" They grabbed at Mary's reins and attempted to pull her to the cobbles. The balconies surrounding the square suddenly filled with sheriff's men, who lifted archaic-looking hagbutt guns and fired into the sky.

For three or four seconds there was absolute silence. James lifted his hand. There was another blast of hagbutt fire. James grabbed Mary's reins and led her across the cobbles to the other side.

She smiled nervously at the cluster of men and women who were solemnly inspecting her. A child reached out of its mother's arms and caught playfully at Mary's skirts. The mother slapped it across the face. Mary turned to James, but he had gone back into the confusion of the square and was attempting to restore order. A cold, sick despair crept over her and she knew that in a minute she would start to cry. There was another round of shot. "Jezebel," muttered a man in carpenter's attire. He spit.

Mary raised her eyes wildly to the sky. O God, she prayed, don't let me die. Suddenly, her heart shuddered convulsively and her spine turned to ice. She slowly lowered her eyes to the second-story balcony directly opposite her. A wild-visaged, heavy, middle-aged man with a long, tangling rust-colored beard leaned over the balcony rail. His enormous black eyes regarded her with savage contempt. With his starched black robe and voluminous sleeves, he looked like a woodcut Jehovah on the verge of signaling hell upon some wicked, luckless city. He folded his huge red hands over his breast, straightened himself, and began moving his mouth in some silent incantation. Mary smiled stupidly and waved. The huge head seemed to snap forward.

"Master Knox," said James. Mary noticed that Bothwell also had removed his cap. She giggled.

After an hour the procession passed under a small ironwork gate surmounted by lions and unicorns, and dismounted in a rectangular brick courtyard. They stood in front of a large brownstone building with two squat red turrets on either side. "This is Holyrood Palace," said James, leading her up a broad ruined staircase covered with patches of moss and tufts of brown weeds. "This is where you will live."

"An' here we have yer kitchens," said Geilles Reres, mistress of the palace staff. "They're the clean part, Ladyship; no rats, neither." Later, Geilles Reres said, "An' here's where Yer Ladyship be borned, but it's all cracked plaster and mildew now." The odor of must and decay was everywhere. All the rooms were small and dark, with the exception of the Great Hall, which also served as the feasting room, the Privy Council meeting room, the eating room, and the throne room. There was no throne—the Presbyters had melted it into coin the previous year. What little furnishings there were consisted of wooden stools, benches, and tables. There were ghosts. "Specter dogs," whispered Mistress Reres, "ay. And fairies that dance in the air when all are asleep. They never harm, though. But we've an incubus, and it's awful, awful. Some say it's your dad, King James. An' we got an old monk, a nigger monk—"

"Surely you can't believe in such things," said Mary, amused.

"Maybe there aren't these things in the country of France, Yer Ladyship, but this is Scotland. You'll accustom to it."

That was what Bothwell had said the night before: Scotland isn't France. Mistress Reres left Mary in one of the narrow halls while she went to get another candle. Mary sat on one of the dusty benches and thought bitterly: This is my land, this is my father's land, this is the land that gave me birth and made my blood, the coarse, wretched, bloody country God set me to rule over. It shames me.

The candle beside her guttered out. Mary sat in the cobwebbed stillness, thinking of France.

Mistress Reres returned. "There is not enough time to show you more," she said hurriedly. "It grows late. I have a supper being prepared for you and yer women. We'll serve it in the antechamber next to yer bedroom."

Mary sighed. "I think I should invite those who accompanied me into the city this morning. At least, James, Bothwell, Maitland, the Huntlys—"

"I'll not serve Huntlys," spat the old woman. "They'll not partake of my food—"

"You will do as I command you to do," Mary said fiercely. She raised her hand in a threatening gesture. "You are my servant, and I am not your servant. Remember that, Mistress Reres."

That night Mary sat in the glow of the fireplace and stifled a yawn. She was tired, very tired, but did not want to sleep. The Huntlys sat to her left conversing pleasantly with two lesser Catholic nobles. James, the Lord Mayor and his wife, Lord Morton, and Sir William Kirkcaldy of Grange sat to her right, saying nothing at all and plainly uncomfortable. Maitland sat opposite her, at the center of the table. Beaton and John were leaning against one of the faded tapestries laughing lightly and whispering to one another. Mary gazed lazily at the remnants of mutton, bacon, and stewed carp that lined the supper table. She wondered why Bothwell hadn't come. "Do you sing, brother?" she asked John.

"I can—and shall." He took a mandolin from the corner, sat cross-legged at Mary's feet, and tested the strings. "A ballad from the Auvergne. In free Scots."

Lady Huntly smiled indulgently. Mary stole a look at James. His face remained gloomy and impenetrable. Sian Gordon laughed out loud at something, and Mary raised a finger to her lip. He gave her an insolent smile, let his eyes rest on her bosom, then poured himself another cup of beer from the tin pitcher on the table. He was certainly one of the handsomest men she'd ever seen, and even his arrogant flippancy had a certain amount of charm in it.

When John had finished, he lay the mandolin on the floor and sighed, "I *like* you, Sister Mary. Who else do I know that could get St. James and the Huntlys together at table?" He got up, picked up the beer pitcher, and poured it over Sian Gordon's head. Sian Gordon roared, swung his fist, and caught John on the shoulder. Then, laughing like children, they ran from the room.

Lady Huntly shook her head and gave Mary a look of long-suffering.

"They're friends," said Maitland, patting Mary on the hand. "Nothing to fear, madam. All is well."

"What is that dreadful noise?" moaned Lady Huntly, lifting her hands to her ears. She stood and wearily cranked open the lattice window. Mary looked over the other woman's narrow shoulders.

Down below in the brick courtyard, a group of perhaps fifty men and women huddled together for warmth and shouted psalms to the off-key accompaniment of rebec and fiddles. Bonfires sent straggling wisps of smoke over the dark countryside.

"They're apologizing for today," said James, rising for the first time all evening. "Show yourself to them. Send down a message."

Mary moved in front of Lady Huntly and cried down, "Another song, good countrymen, for sweet dreams tonight!"

The men and women cheered. This time they were twice as loud and twice as bad.

Mary scribbled a few sentences on a sheet of linen paper, handed it to James, then rang for Mistress Reres and ordered a barrel of beer sent down with some cups.

"My dear," said Lady Huntly, "perhaps you do not realize it, but those people down there are the Presbyterian Mr. Knox's people."

Angry at the tone of the other woman's voice, Mary turned and snapped, "They are *not* Knox's people. They're *mine*." She returned to the window. Beyond the psalmists, she saw James striding toward a pile of rubble in the center of the courtyard. What a graceful man he is, she thought. He cast a lighted torch into the rubble and walked away. The night sky exploded in fireworks. What a graceful man he is.

"Ugh, they've gone and started singing another one," John called over to her. She glanced over her shoulder and saw him and Sian Gordon standing arm in arm at the entrance. "I love these men as much as brother James, but, Sister Mary, I'm not made of martyr's meat. My ears!"

Mary laughed and shook her head. "Tomorrow, at Mass, I'll send up prayers for you." She felt him standing behind her. "What is he like?" she said almost in a whisper.

"Brother James? I don't know." He scratched his head. "I've known him my entire life, but I'll wager that you, who have met him today for the first time, know as much about him as I do." He was quiet, then said in a low voice choked with emotion, "He's my brother James, and I love him. He's the greatest man in Scotland, even greater than John Knox."

Mary turned around. "You mean to say you consider this Knox a 'great' man?"

"Why, yes," he said uncertainly. "Doesn't all the people?"

Out of the corner of her eye, Mary saw Lady Huntly observing them with an amused expression.

When everyone was gone, Mary went into her bedchamber and allowed Mistress Reres and two kitchen girls to undress her.

She slipped into a clean linen chemise, walked to the bed, and drew aside the thick wine-colored curtains. "I don't understand," she said, shrinking back. "This—this—"

"This is a bed," said Mistress Reres. "Is something wrong?"

Mary pointed at the log pillow, rough-woven yarn coverlet, and tattered straw mattress. "I can't sleep in this. Look at it."

"It's the best bed," said the old woman with an imperious toss of the head. "I used it m'self, an' now I have none, an' must sleep on cold stone." She threw a sheepskin and some woolen shreds on the floor next to the chamber pot. "If you become cold, these will warm you."

"My furniture won't arrive until next week," Mary murmured to herself.

Mistress Reres stopped at the door. "If you see the specter dogs, or Patch, Pinch, and Grim, you need only ring for me. If you see a cobweb man at the foot of your bed, that one's the last King James. The nigger monk—he's harmless. But the others—"

"Get out!"

"As Yer Ladyship commands. Guid night."

Mary walked to the casement and looked down into the city. The smoke from the fireworks was spreading along the High Street in the direction of the Castle of the Maidens. A few yards beyond the gates of Holyrood, a man and woman strolled hand in hand. Thick waves of mist lapped at their feet. Mary pressed her face against the cold glass and said desperately, "I love you. I do love you."

She thought she heard somebody open her chamber door and quietly enter, but when she turned around, the room was empty. She rested her hand on the straw mattress a minute, then cautiously got under the yarn coverlet. She rested her head against one of the woolen shreds she'd rolled into a ball.

There was one thing she'd liked. That was the "limanga," a private passageway running three floors down from her bedroom. It opened in a garden behind the kitchens. It was like stories of Launcelot and Queen Guinevere. Her household furnishings would arrive in a few days. Unless the English seized them.

The court of a king must be splendid. It was fitting that God's representative— Was someone standing by the bed?

Slowly, she rose and pulled at the half-shut bed curtains. "Father?" she whispered. "Father, is it you?" No one there. Groaning heavily, she threw herself back on the mattress and pulled the coverlet over her head to shut out the sounds of her own crying. She cried all the time. Only little girls cried as much as she did. Men were brave, like James, or Bothwell, and never wept.

Christ hung on his cross, the crown of thorns pressed deep into his skull, nails piercing his alabaster hands and feet. Votive lights weaved wearily before niches containing broken saints and threw shadows against discolored squares of wall where the Stations of the Cross had once been suspended. The priest raised the jeweled chalice. *"Hoc est enim calix sanguimus mei!"*

Mary bowed her head and knelt at the altar rail. The face of Jesus erupted in mud. A brick sailed through the air, struck the priest, and knocked him backward against the tabernacle. The chalice flew against the wall, splashed red, and clanged to the floor. John Stewart appeared, pulled Mary to her feet, and rushed her to a small room to the left of the altar.

"What is it?" said Mary, trembling.

"A misunderstanding," said John. "James is out there. He'll take care of them. Hello, Mr. Maitland," he spoke to an adjoining door.

Mary wondered if he'd gone mad.

"Oh, Sister Mary," he said, smiling at her expression, "you've been in Scotland nearly two weeks. By now you ought to have learned that Mr. Maitland, like God, is everywhere."

"Not quite," said Maitland, opening the door and smiling. "Your Majesty is safe, I trust. Terrible. They came from Master Knox's sermon. Madam, it's been so long since I've seen levantine and silk pieced in such an exquisite manner. Magnificent. My own tailor—"

"Knox," said Mary. "Is he responsible for this outrage?"

"Master Knox has, shall we say, madam, a certain manner of expression that tends to inflame, to—"

"I will see him in an hour."

"Madam, let me illustrate the man," Maitland said affably. "When Queen Elizabeth was in the Tower of London during her sister's reign, she carved the following on her cell wall: 'Much suspected of me, Nothing proved can be, Quote Elizabeth Prisoner.' Quoth Master Knox as well."

"Bring him to me."

"Madam, Master Knox—"

"I will not command you again, Maitland."

Maitland bowed and left.

"Is it safe to go back into the chapel?" she asked John.

He opened the door a crack and nodded his head.

Mary walked past the altar rail, took out her kerchief, bent over, and picked up the dented chalice with it. When she stood, the bottom of her white gown was dark and wet with the blood of Christ.

Mary paced before the fire in the dimly lit throne room. "It's so dismal," she said to Maitland.

"Holyrood *is* dismal," he said. "Sacked and burned by the English in '42, '48, and just last year. Seized as a barracks for the Presbyterians in '59. Occupied by the French on numerous occasions. It hasn't a pleasant history. But once it was exquisite. My father said it was."

"Lord James Stewart," announced a page. "Master John Knox."

Mary stared at the stiff black Geneva robes. The man's nails were neatly cut, the fingers callused and thick as sausages, the hands huge and swollen with distended blood vessels. Master John Knox. She was surprised at the richness of the full red lips. Master Knox. Even the vast red and gray flowing beard had an oriental voluptuousness about it. The Presbyterian Monster. That was the way her relatives in France referred to him. He'd been a priest once, a serf before that, on the lands of Bothwell's father. According to someone or other. She did not extend her hand because she knew he would not have kissed it, and also because she would not have known what to do when he refused.

Avoiding his eyes, she said, "You are informed as to what occurred in our chapel?"

He nodded.

"Do you know that those involved were your parishioners, had, in fact, just come from your service?"

"Yes, Your Majesty," he said in a thick burr.

"We have heard much of you, Master Knox. You have ideas as to the governance of this realm, it seems."

"I am a subject in this Commonwealth—"

"And as a subject you are commanded by God to obey your sovereign."

"It may please Your Majesty to hear me speak. It has pleased Lord God to make of me His instrument and to show unto this realm the vanity, deceit, and tyranny of the papistical religion. I can do no other, for to do so would be to deny God, and that cannot be done, when He moves inside you."

"If God has personally appointed you to the Heavenly Council," she said lightly, "I fear I'm unaware of it. But you must forgive my ignorance, Master Knox; I've been away." There. That was good. That was splendid. She looked in Maitland's direction for approval, but he was examining his reflection on the window glass. James gave her a pained look.

"If this country finds no inconvenience in your rule," said Knox, "I shall be as content to live under Your Grace as was Paul under Nero."

This was insufferable. Nobody had ever dared to speak to her with such disrespect. She looked at him in amazement. "God commands men to obey their kings," she said angrily. She walked over to him and stared down into his broad, unblinking face. That was what was wrong with him: he never seemed to blink. "Do you think," she said quietly, "that subjects, having power, may resist their sovereigns?"

Maitland turned from the window and regarded the two of them with wonder.

Knox was silent, then said slowly, "There is no greater obedience to be given kings than God has commanded to be given a mother and father. But suppose, Your Grace, that a father is stricken with a madness in which he would destroy his children. Now, if the children rise up against the father, take his weapon away from him, bind his hands, and put him in prison until the frenzy is past, do you think, Your Grace, that God will be offended with them?"

Oh, it would be easy, Mary thought, to order his arrest: his words are circumspect, but in France the same words would be treason, punishable by death. But if I ordered his arrest, who would arrest him? What would the people do? What would they do to me? It would be easier to be clever with him, make him a fool before everybody. But I've heard his tale. He rowed in the galleys. Once, he'd been strapped to a stake, gunpowder bags hung around his neck, and he'd burned, burned until the mob set him loose and murdered his executioners. "The interview is ended," she said gently. She thought: Perhaps I can make him my friend. "Forgive me for taking you from your duties. I'm sorry."

Knox hesitated, then said in a dull monotone, "God grant that you be blessed with right knowledge in all matters."

"Oh, Master Knox, that would require the wisdom of Solomon."

"If Your Grace follow goodly counsel—and there is no more godly man in this Commonwealth than my Lord James Stewart"— Knox looked tight-lipped at Maitland—"then you will be pleasing to God, which will be more profitable to Your Grace than all the armed power of Rome and France." He walked toward the door.

"Master Knox," Mary called after him. She stood under a tattered cloth canopy with faded green and violet orphreys, resting one hand on the chipped wood chair that served as her throne. "We brought no armies with us into Scotland. There wasn't any need. We are the Queen."

The next morning Mary rode through Edinburgh to attend the opening of Parliament. She took the lectern and made a short, pretty speech. The applause, if not overwhelming, was at least polite. The lords voted adoption of a proclamation of welcome to the Queen, then reratified Presbyterianism as the religion of all the people. Mary and her staff, however, were to be permitted free exercise of their faith. Mary presented a list of her appointments to the Privy Council: James was to act as head, Maitland was Secretary of State, Huntly was restored as Chancellor, and the Earls of Bothwell, Morton, Erskine, Atholl, Glencairn, Argyll, and Marischal were given various other titles. She then proceeded to name James and Bothwell co-lieutenants of the border, awarded them four hundred men, and gave them instructions to destroy the great robber barons of the south by the Kilkenny section of the seacoast. It was a safe and popular move, though some questioned the advisability of dividing the command between two men known to be enemies.

That night, James made his way across the misty courtyard and strode angrily up the palace steps.

Mary was sitting in her antechamber with a map spread on her lap. She looked up in surprise when James entered, then smiled and said warmly, "Come sit, brother. Where is Kilkenny?" She ran a finger along the jagged west coast of Scotland and across the winding border the country shared with England.

"Bothwell," he said impatiently. "Bothwell and the border. You did not ask me."

"Ask you what?"

"In the future, you will consult me before making such decisions."

"I thought it would be good if you and Bothwell had an opportunity to know each other. Besides, he knows the area Maitland said—"

"There are others who know the area better than Bothwell," said James. "This will not work, madam."

"In the future," said Mary, her voice rising, "you will ask to be announced before entering my private chambers. And you will remember exactly who and what you are, and who I am. You are excused."

Outside, the mist was so thick James could not see two boot lengths in any direction. He leaned wearily against a peeling tree trunk and closed his eyes. She might as well have said the word. The languorous pluckings of a Spanish guitar wafted from the palace and mingled with the sound of the slowly rising wind. He had never flattered, never begged. He was still a bastard. Bastard born and bastard begot. He thought to himself: If I'd been the King, so many things might have been accomplished. And what was Mary?—a high-strung, lightheaded girl of nineteen, a pawn of popes and foreign kings. Why had God given over the scepter to her and not to him?

She doesn't even love Scotland, he thought mournfully. She's more French than Scots. As a Catholic, if the Pope commands her to introduce French or Spanish troops and begin an Inquisition, she will cry, and then she will do it. He wiped the thick drizzle from his face and stared at the thick sheet of white winding itself around him. The guitar music came to an abrupt halt. James slowly beat his fist against the tree trunk.

Two days later, he and Bothwell marched south.

The robber barons were easy. They were brave when burning cottages, destroying bridges, and converging upon small groups of unarmed merchants and travelers, but when the news reached them of the force from the capital, they panicked, scattered, and hid in the purple sandstone hills. There were no battles; the whole affair consisted in the main of ferreting men from caves, locking them in wheel cages, and bringing them to Justice Court in Dumfries.

It surprised James that he and Bothwell worked so well with one another. The one disagreement they had was over the matter of the executions. James thought all the captured robbers should be hanged. Bothwell said only the barons themselves. James was adamant. Then Bothwell took him to the shacks and hovels where the wives and children of the robbers lived. "Who'll till soil for them?" Bothwell asked. "Who'll father and husband them? These here—they're parents of some of the thieves; it's a bad thing to have your son die before you die." James had not thought Bothwell capable of such feelings. It touched him. He did not like Bothwell any more than he had before, but only the barons were hanged. James realized that he was making a mistake, that within a year or two the men they had released would have banded together once again under new leaders. If he had not seen the faces of their mothers and fathers, wives and children, he would have hanged them all. Having looked at those faces made that impossible. James knew he would have to return sooner or later. And the next time he would not bring Bothwell with him, and he would look at no faces.

When they returned to Holyrood a month and a half after they'd left, they found it vastly changed. Brilliant tapestries depicting mythological scenes lined the cracked walls. The stone floors were covered with gorgeous-colored carpets. The rooms seemed wider, lighter, and smelled of lemon oil and lady's perfume.

"Your sister's taste seems much in evidence," Bothwell said.

They stood before a blazing tapestry showing the goddess Diana surrounded by a pack of Cerberus-toothed wolves. Incomparable innocence and calm were woven in the round virgin face; this despite the fact that one of the wolves had his fangs clamped over her left breast and another was drawing thick jets of maroon blood from her thigh.

"I like the teats," said Bothwell. "Big, pink, rosy. I've known some like that."

"The blood's not convincing," said James.

"This ball your sister's giving for us . . . when is it?"

"In three or four hours."

"Fine. I'm going to see Johnny now. I suppose he's at Ainslie's Tavern. We've done our job, Stewart; no need to be nice with each other any more."

"No need," James said.

"We've got time yet," John said. "Drink up, Bothwell. Prepare yourself. You're to be one of the guests of honor."

Bothwell downed the last of his ale and banged his pewter mug against the table top. "Where's that God damn slut?" he yelled. "Annabel!"

"I got other customers to tend," said a buxom young woman

with bright red hair, red lip paint, and rouged cheeks who was making her way across the crowded tavern. She smiled warmly at John as she gathered the mugs together. Bothwell reached out and smacked her bottom. "What's that supposed to mean?" she demanded. "At least my Lord John here gets drunk like a gentleman." She leaned over and began wiping the table with a wet cloth, then straightened up and wrung out the cloth.

Bothwell sniffed loudly. "Smell that!" he roared. "The ale at Ainslie's is like no ale found on earth. They call it Lift-Leg. It's cursed—"

"You drink enough of it," Annabel said. She gave John a wink and trudged back through the crowd.

"Annabel!" Bothwell called after her.

She pretended not to hear him but returned a few moments later with their refilled mugs.

"I called to you, Annabel," Bothwell said. "I wanted to ask you something."

"Well, here I am."

"Would you like me to escort you to the Queen's ball tonight?"

"Is that what you wanted to ask me? Oh, I'll wager on that, all right."

"Just answer yes or no."

"Oh, it's a lie," said Annabel. She hesitated, then slid onto Bothwell's lap and kissed him on the nose. "It's a foul lie to trap and shame a poor girl, isn't it?"

"You haven't answered."

"You wouldn't dare take me to such a thing, with all the lah-de-dah ladies." She paused, examined his eyes. "Or would you? Would you really?"

"You've got fifteen minutes," Bothwell said. "Get dressed."

Annabel looked at John. "He's not lying, is he? He never lies, does he? He's an animal, but he's never once lied to me."

"Get dressed," Bothwell said.

"Oh, I love, love, love you, Jimmy Bothwell!" She kissed him again and ran off through the crowd.

"You're a braw fine fellow, Bothwell," John said, crinkling his eyes. "You are. I think I love you more than anybody. Except my brother and sister, of course."

Bothwell squeezed his hand. "You're a nice boy, Johnny boy. You're joyous. But please don't think I'm a nice man. How has Her Right Royal Queenliness been doing in our absence?"

"It's amazing the way she handles them. In the beginning, everybody was saying, 'Hang the priest.' But she was always saying, 'Conscience, my lords, conscience; it's a sore thing to constrain the conscience.' And she was so sincere, and now they all bow and scrape. Amazing."

Bothwell stared at him, his face blank.

"Some think she might be converted," John said. "Well, not to Presbyterianism, but Anglicanism—like the Queen of England."

"The Earl of Huntly might have something to say about that," said Bothwell after a long draught of ale. "He wants Rome back. He wants to get the fires burning. I heard him remark once that he'd light your brother James personally."

"There's no cause for the way he treats James. Huntly has no respect, calling him 'bastard this' and 'bastard that.' I'm a bastard, and I don't mind, but James—"

"Your brother James has expressed considerable interest in Huntly's lands. After the last rebellion, he ended up with half of Mar, which was Huntly's and not his. I can't see why so many people are so fond of your brother. He's the most unlikable, self-righteous man I ever met."

"He's a loving man," said John, starting to get angry. "He's pure!"

"Let it pass," said Bothwell. "You love him. I don't."

"Sister Mary isn't overfond of Huntly," said John.

"Your sister is a Catholic and, as such, will do as the Pope commands her to do."

"They say she might marry Huntly's son," said John.

"She'd be a fool. It'd cause another rebellion. Marriage is the only lever she's got to play with. She won't marry Sian Gordon."

"The son's not the father," said John. "Sian's an excellent fellow."

"Scotland's had enough hell for a while."

"Am I the most fabulous lady in Scotland!" shrieked Annabel, settling in Bothwell's lap again. She was dressed head to foot in scarlet, her breasts uncovered to the nipples, an orange periwig with bright crimson feathers swaying on her head.

"In Scotland?" laughed Bothwell. "In the world! Come! We're off to Holyrood to see the Queen! Halloo! Hallah!"

Boar's head, steaming capon, kain geese, mutton, chicken, and ox feet filled the lace-covered trestle table that had been set in the Great Hall. James picked a shiny red apple out of a silver bowl and lifted it to his mouth. A gilded fountain had been constructed in the center of the Great Hall and red wine gurgled and plashed from the mouths of painted Cupids. James bit into the apple.

"Why, James," said Maitland, "you've changed." He indicated James's Italian suit.

James had found it on his bed when he returned that evening. It consisted of a blue slope-shouldered coat which opened at the throat to show the square cut of a linen blouse. The hose were a slightly darker German blue, a bit tighter than he would have liked. But the cod, in contrast to the decorated French and English forms, was of a matching color. Earlier, in his mirror, it made him look dignified, even handsome. "A gift from Her Majesty," said James, slightly embarrassed.

A small orchestra of mandolin, harp, fiddle, and clavicytherium was playing a solemn court dance. A short, ugly hunchbacked man with a dark complexion was singing from a makeshift stage in the center of the hall. He had a beautiful voice. James noticed Mary Beaton a few feet away.

"Signor Riccio, from the Duke of Savoy's staff," said Beaton, extending her hands.

"I don't know dancing," said James.

Beaton handed him a goblet. "Will you drink, my lord?" she said softly. "It's canary. It is sweet, very sweet, and leaves a pleasant taste."

James took a sip. "Good," he said awkwardly. "And sweet. Yes." He emptied the goblet. "Yes. It doesn't taste like any of the wines I've had."

"There's Lord Huntly over there," said Beaton, leaning against him, "and he's giving you such nasty looks. Sian Gordon is Adonis, but his father—the Ogre of Britomant! He even picks his nose. They're playing *L'Amour de moy*. Put your hands on top of mine. There. Women don't expect their men to dance well. It makes them more manly when they miss a step." She wore little paint and her face was round and creamy-complected.

Cornets interrupted the music, and the Master of the Household announced, "The Queen's Pavane."

Mary entered the room on the arm of Sian Gordon. With long cadenced steps, they danced a processional to the makeshift stage in the center of the floor, parted, and selected new partners. Sian Gordon selected his sister. Mary looked about the room, saw James, then danced over to him and took his hands in hers. She wore white slashed sleeves tied with pink ribbons and a low neck covered with chiffon and pinned into her gown with ruby clasps.

"Splendid," she said, running a finger down his chest. "I love the material. And so light. James, I saw you dancing with Beaton. She'll love you next. Now she loves John. When we first arrived she was infatuated with Bothwell. She said, 'He's rough, as a man should be.' Then when the ships with my furniture arrived from Calais, she loved Chastelard." She indicated an effeminate, blond young man sipping wine in a corner. "He was one of Ronsard's pupils. Beaton said she loved him because he was weak and gentle. What do you think of Signor Riccio's singing? Hasn't he an excellent voice? Chastelard is sulking because the Italian has taken all the attention away from him. Poets are such a temperamental lot. James, some people say Elizabeth is balding. Is that—James? James, you're not even listening!"

"True, true," he said, closing his eyes and laughing soundlessly.

"You're a beast."

"And you are a big green lass. It makes no difference what you say, Mary; I just like to watch."

"You called me Mary," she said, a trace of wonder in her voice. "It's the first time. Have you been drinking canary?"

"Two," he said, raising three fingers. He stared at his hand, then laughed again. He wiped the water from his eyes, then took Mary's hand and drew her to the banqueting table. She had such soft blue eyes and such a guileless, friendly face.

Mary smiled impishly and filled his goblet with grain whisky. "You must drink to me," she said. "I've had a marvelous thought. I will meet with my cousin Elizabeth next spring. We shall be the best of friends."

"There might be some difficulty . . . But leave off politics." He lifted the glass and let the warm brown whisky burn down his throat.

"What difficulty?"

"There's your claim that you, not Elizabeth, are the rightful Queen of England."

"I am the rightful Queen," said Mary. "But I'm hardly in any position to drive her off her throne."

"It would take one blow in the dark," said James. "No more, or less. The Queen of England learned that early."

"Do you think she is the only one?" said Mary. "In swan meat. I was ten years old, and they put it in swan meat. Claudette stole a piece off my plate—you never met her—she was the most splendid dancing bear, lovely, kind, generous. She died half a minute later. In front of me. And she'd never harmed anyone. I was glad when they told me the man who'd done it had been drawn, quartered, and hanged." Mary lowered her head, examined the table, then poured herself some of the grain whisky. She watched a damask hobbyhorse thread its way among the revelers, then clasped James's hand. "Once, at Amboise, I was playing in the gardens, and suddenly there—in the sun— there were three men who were running toward me—so fast. They had daggers and they wanted to kill me. They were Protestants—Huguenots—and I was a Catholic, and it was as simple as that." She rested her head on James's shoulder and laughed. "It was not funny then, but now—I can still see the expressions on those faces."

The young man with long blond tresses falling to his shoulders timidly approached them, gave James a mournful glance, then touched Mary lightly on the back of the neck.

"James, this is the illustrious Pierre de Chastelard, poet. Will you mind if he carries me off for ten minutes?"

The Frenchman was about twenty-five, but he had the stale smile of a much older man who had seen everything and been disillusioned. James watched them join the other dancers.

He poured more whisky. Feeling very lightheaded, he started searching the floor for Mary Beaton.

"The Queen of Scots is an excellent Queen," he overheard the English ambassador say to Lady Huntly.

James liked to watch Lady Huntly. There was an elegant beauty about her. He watched her languidly examine her face in the tiny steel mirror she kept attached to her belt. She turned slightly and noticed him staring at her.

"Why, Mr. Randolph," she said to the ambassador, "unless I am mistaken we have your highest-priced informant in our midst. The poor fellow is definitely staggering."

"Who?" said the ambassador. "Lord James? We've no business with him. Nonsense."

"At least, no legitimate business," said Lady Huntly, turning her back.

James lifted his cup to the mouth of a fat Cupid.

"Have you seen Jimmy Bothwell?" someone whined in his ear. "He was to of been with me." He turned in time to see a pretty young woman slide to the floor. She was dressed in a fantastical scarlet gown, an orange periwig with ostrich feathers half covering her forehead. James helped her to her feet. She stared at him, backed off, then broke into a broad smile and clapped her hands. "Is this the manner in which you spend your nights?" she laughed drunkenly. She pinched him on the cheek. "Don't just look at me like that. Tell me, is my beautiful Jimmy Bothwell about?"

"I—I don't know."

"Oh—he must of run off—the drunken dog!" She hurried away into the crowd.

James frowned. He remembered who the woman was. Once, while sitting on Justice Court, he had voted to close her tavern. It was a vile place, a center of prostitution, gambling, and drunkenness. The woman's name was Annabel Farquarson. She'd appeared in court that day and threatened to expose important members of the Congregation as her clients. Defiantly, she reviled the judges, himself included, as lechers and hypocrites. Finally she spit on the floor, announced her tavern would be open next afternoon regardless of the Court's decision, and left the court-room. The judges voted unanimously to shut down Ainslie's Tavern. Three days later the decision was quietly declared null. James never discovered who it was that had wiped it from the ledgers. The woman's father had died the month before, but she'd come to court in a red and yellow gown.

Mary and Chastelard joined arms and began to lead the other gentlemen and ladies around the hall in a solemn pro-cessional. The music quickened. Mary sprang forward, took five steps, then leaped backward into Chastelard's arms. Her hair, loose and gold in the candlelight, whipped furiously back and forth. Chastelard placed his hands on her waist, bent, and lifted her into the air. Arms outstretched, hair streaming, she circled slowly above the reeling dancers. James watched the corners of her mouth curve into a lazy smile. The hall stank of smoke and hot tallow. He thought of the women who attacked Mary's mount the day she entered Edinburgh. They'd cried: "Whore. Jade. Babylon. Rome."

Clutching his head, James stumbled past a blaze of torches and out into the night air. He gazed up at the moon. Its light was blinding. He sat on a stone bench by the garden wall and tried to think.

Mary was young, very young, but sometimes it seemed as if a hardness, a cynicism . . . He didn't know. He couldn't under-stand her. He understood everything, everybody, but he couldn't understand her. Was it because she was his sister, because they were too close, as if their different mothers were insignificant in light of what they had both inherited from their same father? Once he had been convinced that he understood his brother John too, but now he was no longer certain of that either. John was a good person but weak, and he had thrown himself to the Devil's ways. Other people sinned, everybody sinned. That was original sin, or youth or human frailty or ignorance, or perhaps even simple existence. What Master Knox preached of sin and punishment was proper and undeniable. Still, when James tried to picture his brother John in hell, the vision repelled him. And then he saw an image of Mary in her white, circling lazily above the sulphurous pit, slowly descending into the crackling, lapping flames, her gown suddenly ablaze, features melting into cream, then turning black. She was as sinful as John, but it was ignorance on her part. Surely God would understand that. It was being brought up in France at the wickedest court in Christendom; it was being Catholic and believing all the erroneous tenets of that discredited faith. Would she burn, or John? Would *he?* If all men were depraved before God, what was the use? If God could kill their souls, was God just? He was too close to his sister and brother, that was the trouble. Human love was vanity. But he didn't want them to burn in hell; he didn't even want them to be sad.

"Ohhhh, it's you out here, is it? Wild, wild head!" The woman Annabel sank down next to James, pulled a feather out of her periwig, and began absent-mindedly twirling it in her lap. "It's cold here," she said.

"Yes. Cold." He moved slightly away.

"And I've been deserted," she moaned. "I can't find that wretched lying Jimmy Bothwell anywhere."

James said nothing.

"I've seen you many times," she said, studying him. "You always frown and try to look fierce, but your face is naturally kind-looking, and you can't. You have a handsome face." She rested her hand on his arm.

He turned and looked at her.

She shut her eyes. "Go ahead," she whispered. "I can't see you looking. You can all you wish. Is it nice what you see?" She ran her tongue over her lower lip.

James paused, then said weakly, "Why do you . . . do what you do?"

"Because I'm a slut."

He stared at her, shocked, and ran his fingers through his hair. It was soaking wet.

"What do you want me to say?" she said, opening her eyes. "I am what I am. Many others cannot say as little as that. Shhhh. Over there."

A white figure glided down the staircase onto the brick yard.

It was Mary. She fluttered her hands about her face and wiped the back of her neck. Lifting her skirts with one hand, she went through a series of elaborate dance steps, then laughed to herself, raised her arms, and stretched. From where James sat, it looked as if she were balancing the moon in her hands.

"I like her," said Annabel. "She's good."

Mary walked back up the stairs.

"Poor baby," said Annabel, kneading the back of his neck. "My dad used to hate you, and so I used to hate you as well. Until I saw you close, that time in the court. I looked at all those high, godly faces that I would see in my tavern two and three nights every week, and they disgusted me. But your face was pure and good. Since that time, I know all you have done. You're so wrong in all, but it's only because you want to be right in all. When Bothwell speaks ill of you, I tell him it's not true. My lord—"

James leaned over and kissed her on the mouth. After a minute she got to her feet. "You know Ainslie's. I live in the top, in the first room over the stairs. Come in through the alley."

James rested his head in his hands. People sinned, everybody sinned, and that was original sin and to be expected. He was thirty-one years old. It had been so long . . . and she wanted him to do it with her . . . and the drink, the drink—he'd had so much of it.

Suddenly he bent forward and vomited. He stared with amusement at the glistening pile of food bits and bile. He'd never done that before.

An hour later, James quietly shut Annabel's door, made his way across the darkened room to her bed, pulled her into a sitting position, and pressed his mouth over hers. "Wha—" she gasped, half awake and struggling for breath.

"I love you," he groaned. He forced his tongue between her teeth and squeezed her breasts.

"Where you been?" she laughed. "Do you know the hour? Stop it! Pack your cod and go this instant. Master Knox will hear of this."

He pulled off his coat and shirt and unfastened his hose. "Ah, that's *nice,*" she sighed. He pushed her down and pressed his weight on top of her.

When he was done, he rolled on his back and stared at the black ceiling. Something wet rolled down his cheek. He caught it with his finger, gazed at it until it dissolved into the flesh, then closed his eyes.

"Such marvelous dancing," Beaton said, untying Mary's sleeves.

"Let me finish it," said Mary, "or I'll forget. I have to say it the way Bothwell said it." She straightened her shoulders, creased her brow, and resumed her imitation of Bothwell's flat drawl. "And after the sheep lad's done humping, he moans to old Aggie—she was fifty, if a day—the sheep lad says, 'S-sorry, ma'am, they say nine inch will please a lady, and here I've g-given you but five.' And old Aggie chuckles and gives him a kiss on his *gear* and—" She buried her face in her hands and started tittering. "Oh, Beaton, dear Beaton, please, please forgive me. I never heard *gear* before. Everything's so funny!" She sat down and began wildly fanning herself.

"Johnny has the right word," said Beaton. "He calls you 'Madcap Queenie.' Stand so I can unfasten the bodice."

"Oh, Beaton, I shall be a magnificent Queen of Scotland. Did you see that woman Bothwell brought with him? I cannot understand why men—"

"Finish the tale," said Beaton.

"What tale?"

"Aggie and the sheep boy."

"Oh. Well, Aggie says, 'God's blessing on thee, my baby! I have had more flesh inside my pot afore, but I canna say I ever had more gism. Nine inch, bairn! You mourn your five! When a lassie's Aggie's age, she thanks the good Lord Jesus if she makes but three!' And with that, she takes hold of him again, and by midnight of that day the lad was dead of old age and Aggie was purring like a new-laid virgin." Mary pressed her hands against the side of her head and drew them down over her face.

"All of which must have a moral," cried Beaton, lying back on the bed.

"Don't deny, shameless slut," said Mary, wiping at her eyes. "You love my brother John, pure and simple. Confess."

"Simple, but hardly pure," said Beaton.

"Marry him," Mary said earnestly.

"I'm pledged not to marry till you have. But, madam, you must hurry. Sian Gordon asks you daily."

"There's the matter of his father," said Mary. "I fear my good Presbyterian subjects would misconstrue such a match. Though I will admit Sian has a pleasant way about him. If he is not the most intelligent of men, he does—"

"Have a glorious body," said Beaton, rising from the bed. "But I think he pads his cod."

"Oh, Beaton, he doesn't!"

"Now who's the slut?"

"*Touché*," said Mary. She hiccoughed.

"Chastelard was attentive tonight," said Beaton. She pressed her fist against her forehead and staggered to the fireplace. "Burn, fire, burn," she said dramatically. "You do not rage as the fire in my heart, which is currently"—she coughed consumptively—"currently consuming me." She dropped to her knees. "He writes badly when he writes of love. Why don't you marry Chastelard, madam? Then Knox will have material for twenty sermons."

"Leave off," laughed Mary.

"I must, madam," said Beaton, resuming her pose as Chastelard, "since you will not let me lay on—! Though my weapon be ever drawn and ready."

"You suffer valiantly, my gallant Pierre," said Mary, her eyes running. "I swear I never saw such good suffering. Oh, Beaton, enough, enough, I cannot bear it!"

Laughing, Beaton got up and stirred the hearth fire. "Were you as true a lover as I," she said, "you'd bare it soon enough."

A knock startled Mary, and the wall next to the fireplace slid open. Archbishop Hamilton stepped into the room from the passageway, followed by a tall gaunt man of about sixty. The man dropped his voluminous black cape to the floor, revealing a black cassock with a red sash. He had thin white lips, gray eyes, and a sharp chin.

"Cardinal de Gouda, Jesuit, papal envoy to the kingdom of Scotland," announced the archbishop.

Mary kissed his ruby ring. De Gouda nodded and sat down.

"Please excuse me, Your Eminence," she said, "for not receiving you with greater honor. But you know of the disturbed state of affairs at the moment."

"I have studied the situation extensively, my child. Let it suffice to say that conditions here are a source of grief and alarm to the Holy Father."

"To save a spark of the old religion, I have been obliged to bear many things which I would not otherwise have borne."

"My child, I know that you are devout and would not wish to displease either the Pope or God, but there are many things which God asks of us. They sometimes seem cruel, but they are just and necessary."

She looked at Hamilton. He shrugged his shoulders.

"I am empowered to offer Your Grace fifteen thousand Spanish troops," the cardinal said, "and as much gold and arms as you wish." He indicated a decanter of wine on the table, and Mary motioned for Beaton to pour him a glass.

"Very good," he said pleasantly.

"I hope to follow the dictates of my conscience in all things," Mary said.

"As interpreted by Holy Mother Church," said Cardinal de Gouda, "the one mediator on earth between God and man."

"When I was Queen in France," said Mary, "there was an uprising by the Huguenots. They attempted to kidnap both my husband and myself. We barricaded ourselves at Amboise, sent for troops, and defeated them. Then the executions began. The leaders of the Huguenots were not good men, and deserved the punishment they received. But the others—they were peasants, illiterate, hungry. They could not trust in Christ because their priests had taught them nothing of Christ. Do you know what I mean?"

"The Council at Trent will reform such things," said De Gouda.

Mary waited a minute and then said, "It was at Amboise; it seems so long ago. They executed three thousand the first day, five thousand the next. The leaders were of the nobility and so were hanged with golden cords and beheaded with swords. But the peasants . . . Do you know what it means to be 'hanged, cut, drawn, and quartered'?"

De Gouda nodded his head.

Mary continued. "They would hang there, kicking and screaming. The executioners would pull their trousers down, the knife would flash, the victim would scream even louder. Then they would be cut down. If they fainted, buckets of water would be poured over their heads until they revived. Then came the disembowelment. Then the fingers would be cut off, then the hands. Sometimes the legs. And often, if the executioner was particularly skilled, he would be able to hold the still beating heart of his victim in the palm of his hand, while the victim lay gasping for breath on the scaffold. The victims were not only men; women and children were killed also, 'to save the Church' and 'to save their souls.' I was the Queen Consort and I watched until I had to be carried away. I was seventeen, but I did nothing to stop any of it. I thought that I was bad for even wanting to stop it, thought I'd burn in hell. My uncle was Prime Minister then—the Cardinal de Guise—and he was, to me, the best and holiest person I ever knew. I know differently now. But . . . these people—and they did love God, I'm sure of it—they would cry out, at the beginning, for Jesus to be with them. And they would end in the foulest language."

"Sit down, madam," said Beaton.

"Affairs of state are pressing," said the archbishop to De Gouda. "You must forgive the girl. Not twenty years old and she stands alone, absolutely alone, without a single Catholic adviser or friend of importance. From the precautions necessary for your visit here, you must realize the agony this child suffers every day of her life."

De Gouda gave the archbishop a withering glance and said, "As I said, I have given the situation extensive study." He leaned over and handed Mary a parchment. "The apostolic brief," he said, without emotion.

When she had read the letter, she looked up and said, "With respect for delegates to the Council at Trent, I will consult my bishops. But I'm afraid I have little hope of success, under the present circumstances." She looked anxiously at the door.

"I have letters from His Holiness to your bishops," said De Gouda. "Could you send for some of them and give them the letters yourself? Or should I visit each in turn?"

"Your delivering them is out of the question," she said. "It could not be done without causing a great deal of disturbance."

De Gouda moistened his lips. "I have had the opportunity to speak with the Earl of Huntly, a most devout man, who may be depended upon in any—"

"Huntly is a fool," said Mary.

"He is a true son of Rome. Though he lacks the polish you are accustomed to, madam, he is zealous."

"The zeal of a reformed drunkard."

De Gouda drew open his valise. "Whatever the man's shortcomings," he explained patiently, "he is a useful man. He is loyal to the faith of his fathers." He handed her a packet. "Members of our order have penetrated the Queen of England's secret service. This is a list of Scots nobles now on the English payroll. It is reliable. And, I might add, impressive."

Mary tore at the seal, leaned both elbows on the table, and read: Wm. Maitland of Leithington, £400 per quarter, Earls of Arran (£175), Morton (£300), Calderon (£25), Ross (£50), Ennii (£30), Argyll (£50), MacDonald of Sleat (£25), Glengarry (£25), Mackinnon (£25), Montgomery (£25), etc., etc. Three thin sheets filled with the names of burghers, merchants, gentry, aldermen, Mary's own kitchen staff. Mistress Reres received a stipend of five pounds monthly. Mary would dismiss her the following morning. But what could she do about the others? And Maitland. She'd trusted Maitland, even liked him.

"Now, of all men of importance in this country," the cardinal said, "there are only three names which do not appear on that paper—the Earl of Huntly, your brother John Stewart, and the Earl of Bothwell. Your brother John's assistance must, of necessity, be private. He has no funds, no land, no men. But Huntly is the most powerful man in this country."

"And Bothwell?"

"The Earl of Bothwell is a strange man. I do not pretend to fathom him. I believe he may be counted upon for personal service, but he is poor, his clansmen ill trained and unreliable. Furthermore, he is an enemy of His Holiness and may not be trusted in any matter of religion. The Earl of Huntly, on the other hand, is eminently suited to aid in the re-establishment of the true religion."

"I will consider your suggestion," she said.

"It is somewhat more than a suggestion. I speak for Rome." He paused. "Except for your annuity from France and one third of the state revenues, you are virtually bankrupt. This is a poor country; you are a poor Queen. His Holiness knows you have borrowed heavily from the Exchange in Amsterdam. Because of the religious conflict there, His Holiness wishes you to know of his displeasure. Especially at the secretness of your negotiations."

"The court of a king must be—splendid," said Mary. "For the people's sake as well as the king's."

De Gouda drew a small leather bag from his sleeve. "A gift. Two thousand English crowns, plus"—here he handed her a small yellow piece of paper—"a note for twenty-five thousand Italian marks. Redeemable at Paris, Madrid, Rome. The Spanish ambassador will handle the transaction for you. I have already discussed the matter with him."

Mary sank to her knees and kissed the old man's hand. He waited a minute, then said, "Of course, we expect repayment in full."

"But when?" said Mary, standing up. "I cannot promise—"

"His Holiness does not expect repayment in moneys, but in the uprightness of your life, your devotion to him, and your active endeavoring for the salvation of your wretched kingdom."

"It grows late," she said weakly, looking at the door. "If you were to be discovered . . ."

"Lord Huntly—"

"Yes, yes. But Your Eminence, please, must leave. I'm watched constantly. You must leave the country. After December, the harbors freeze over, and there can be no chance to sail until March."

"Perhaps I might have an interview with your brother, Lord

James, so he will not suspect me of any designs against himself or any of the great nobles."

"I will ask him, of course, but I do not think he will see you. It grows very late, Your Eminence."

"I would like a safe-conduct pass for the rest of the time I remain in this country," said De Gouda.

"I cannot do that," said Mary. "No one will harm you in public. And what good would it do you against a secret attempt on your life? If I gave you one, it would be the same as betraying you, because greater danger would confront you if your presence were known. You are safer unknown. Please, forgive me, but you must leave now before you are discovered."

"Have you any message for the Pontiff?" said De Gouda, rising slowly to his feet.

"Yes. Tell him the misery of this country grieves me, and I would give my life for it, and for my faith, too. Tell him that I shall always be a Catholic, and would rather burn in hell forever than harm my religion in any way. Tell him that the times here are evil." She burst into tears.

De Gouda sank to his knees and kissed her hand. "My daughter, if only you knew the pity in my heart for you. I will leave as soon as possible, but someday I shall return and all will be accomplished. *All.*" He raised his hand in blessing and retreated into the dark passageway.

The wall panel slid shut.

Mary fell back into her chair and sobbed, "No way away. None. And he'll come back someday." She closed her eyes. "The moneys are appreciated. Oh, Beaton, *I* should be on Elizabeth's payroll."

Beaton rested her hand on Mary's shoulder.

"Marry John. Soon. While there's time."

"I'll marry when you have married."

"While there's still time, Beaton. For the two of you—for *someone*—to be happy."

"Good night, madam." Beaton slammed the door.

A flap of red velvet fell and dangled before the cackling flames in the fireplace. Mary stared vacantly at the royal Stewart crest:

a Lion, imperially crowned, gules, in one paw a scepter, in the other a sword. The lion was dancing between two unicorns, against a background of blood. James I had been stabbed to death at thirty-six. James II was murdered with the consent of his son, James III, who died in a blast of gunpowder at the age of thirty. James IV was the Stewart who lived the longest— till forty—he was smothered to death on an English battlefield by a monk administering the last sacrament. James V died at thirty, apparently of brain fever. *Nemo me impune lacessit,* said the armorial motto. *In defense.* Of whatever Scotland was.

De Gouda had said he'd return.

She absent-mindedly unfolded the second packet and looked through the thin sheets of paper. She saw Bothwell's name and stopped.

> Twenty-six. Possessed of a reckless, hazardous disposition. His father was a madman and a suicide . . . amoral, but no bastards recorded . . . reared loosely by Marie de Guise-Lorraine . . . speaks three languages fluently . . . has been sought out numerous times by English agents but refuses to be of service to us . . . vehemently anti-papist, but no loyalty to Protestant cause . . . rumored atheist . . . land-poor, poor in all respects . . . no friends of influence.

It had surprised her that Knox's name wasn't included in the list of English pensioners. And, though it hurt her to admit it, she was not surprised to find James's.

> James Stewart . . . thirty-one . . . illegitmt. son James V . . . wealthiest, most influential of all Scots lords . . .

The night was pearl and ivory. James trudged back from Ainslie's through the spinning mist toward Holyrood. "It's hard," he muttered. "Hard. God, please." When he reached the palace, he noticed that the light in Mary's bedchamber was still burning. He stood and looked up at the yellow glow for a minute, then went inside and up to his own room. He tried to sleep, but could not.

≈ CHAPTER FIVE ≈

Winter. Edinburgh's warehouses were rich with salted boar, calf, sheep, and capon meats, peas, barley, corn, fish, and seafowl. Goodwives unlocked crates packed in autumn and poured gleaming apple, pear, and berry jams into pewter pots. Husbands and sons churned gallons of ale into thick golden jellies.

In the mornings, boys and girls with picks and axes skittered across the city's snow-encrusted southern plain and returned home later that afternoon with barrows of black stone and peat for the hearth fire. Bagpipes were spread over tables, the pipes removed and polished, treacle smeared inside the sheepskin bag to make it airtight and pliable, then hung on the wall, over the fire. The winds were rough, numbing, but there was no soreness to them. At times, Edinburgh's bleached environs, suddenly grown still, would flood with a subtle, a poignant, warmth. Everything—rivers, trees, hills, streets, and houses—was shrouded in a milky white.

The nights James did not spend with Annabel he spent kneeling at his prie-dieu. Until now, he had believed implicitly that his work was God's. Presbyterianism was the God-given means by which the abuses of an old and morally rotten system would be overthrown, wrongs would be righted, and men might find dignity at last. James had learned the doctrinal tenets of Calvinism by rote. Now he understood them, *felt* them as he never had before. Man was depraved according to nature. Good works were nothing. Man was not cut off from God by individual acts of will. No. Each and every man that ever lived was cut the moment mother married father. (*If* mother married father.) God was unyielding, vengeful, and just. Previously, James had considered himself one of the Elect. Now he knew that he was not.

After the first few times, he never left Annabel money; he brought presents instead—lacework bed coverings, a Venetian hand glass, a peacock-feather fan, cloth pieces of levantine, brocade, and silk, delicately wrought colored glass roses from Italy. When they loved with each other, they did not speak. Hands entwined, they would wring up and down the crying mattress. And afterward, clutching each other's sweating bodies, they would sleep.

One day, shortly before Christ's birthday, when all the late flowers and low bushes were smothered by the snow, James felt compelled to visit Master Knox, whom he had not seen for a month. Knox's wife opened the door.

"Come sit down," she said. "He'll be back. He's at the church." She went into the kitchen to warm some milk.

Everything was in order. No dust anywhere. A large manuscript lay on Knox's desk beside a sheaf of writing paper and an inkstand. "Historie of the Reformation in Scotlande" was written in elaborate script on the first page, "Booke Three, Part First" on the next.

James flipped a few pages and soon was reading:

But the lord James (the one the godly did most reverence) took it upon himself to keep them outside the chapel door. His best excuse was that he would allow no Scotsman to enter into the Mass (the Queen's first such act of idolatry in this Commonwealth). But it was sufficiently known that the door was kept so none should trouble the Priest, who after

the service, was committed to the protection of the bastard
Lord John Stewart of Coldingham.

James sat down in a chair and stared absently into the hearth.
Even the tongs were gleaming. Knox's wife brought him the milk,
then went upstairs. One of the children was ill. James drank the
milk slowly.

He turned to the last page:

John Knox's judgement being asked by some, What he
thought of the Queen? "If there be not in her (said he) a
crafty wit, a proud mind, and an indurate heart against God,
my judgement faileth me. I have not found such genius and
such craft in such age."

In the presence of her Privy Council, she kept herself
most grave (for under the widow's weeds she could play the
hypocrite in full perfection): but how soon her French
courtezans, poetry-writers, and fiddlers filled the court! In
this was she aided by her brother Lord John Stewart, with
whom she showed more familiarity than is termed proper
between brother and sister. We call her not whore (though
we have heard more than we will write), but she was brought
up in France in the company of the wildest whoremongers
(of such as no more regarded incest than honest men regard
the company of their lawful wives); in the company of such
men was our Queen brought up. What she was, and is, herself best knows. But she is a Stewart, as well as a Guise. She
and the Lord John are of the blood of the father, the last
King James, a murderer and dreaming man steeped in crimes
of flesh. His howling blood is theirs, as well.

James was on the verge of picking up the manuscript and
tossing it into the fire, when the hall door opened and Knox
entered the room.

"I was disappointed," said Knox, "in your vote to suspend the city provost. He was duly elected."

James stared at him. He realized his hands were shaking with cold.

"Shall I tell Marjory you will stay and eat with us?"

"I read a section of your History, Master Knox."

"I see that."

"How could you write such things?"

"They are the truth."

"They are *not* the truth," said James.

Knox placed the manuscript in the drawer and latched it. "God has given me to see the truth and to speak it and live it and set it down."

"What you wrote . . . is vile!" James felt as if his heart was cracking, as if the next sentence from Master Knox would cleave it entirely.

"You voted for dismissal of the provost," said Knox. "Why?"

"Had his rulings been enforced, it would have meant the arrest of everyone my sister brought with her from France, of all the papist ambassadors, of my sister herself."

"Which would be law. The Mass is forbidden by act of the Lords Assembled."

"Which would be madness. What would other countries say?"

"I have heard of your project for securing food for the poor in Leith," said Knox.

"Master Knox—"

"And, whether it be gossip-talking or whether it be truth, I have heard of your interest in one of the Queen's ladies, a Miss Beaton."

Despite himself, James laughed.

"I see the dancing at Holyrood grows hot," said Knox in a tone of grim horror. "My lord, you love this country, do you not?"

"You know it," said James.

"A man cannot serve two masters. You do not know that now, but I think, with God's grace, you will know it later, and then you will decide—for longer than a year, or two, or three— which master's servant you will be. A man who serves the truth is always in the majority. There was a thought once, and the pagan Greeks called it 'democracy,' and it disappeared a long time in the past. The hour of that thought has now come full circle, and it has no space in its meaning for kings, or queens, or sycophants."

James paused at the door. "Master Knox, I do not think that I will see you for some time." He closed the door behind him and walked into the white, whirling street. A pail of frozen milk sat on the doorstoop. James's clothing was damp and heavy against his skin. Once, not so long before, he'd loved and feared John Knox as a father, when everything was blood flowing, and that stocky little man in the stiff Geneva cloak was the one man who always stood straight and never was afraid.

The one law Mary suspended from the statute books upon her return from France was that which forbade the observing of holy and secular holidays with entertainment and masquing. On the day before Christmas, a program was drawn which included singing, wassailing, pantomimes, gaming, and morris dancing. Copies were made and posted through the city. Holyrood glistened with holly, plump red berries, and colored spangles of paper. A gaily painted stage was built in the center of Holyrood courtyard, and six huge bonfires built around it to keep the townspeople warm. As in Mary's father's time, the revels were under the titular direction of a Lord of Misrule, selected by the vote of Edinburgh guildsmen. Master Knox roared against this idolatry from his pulpit, but three quarters of the guildsmen cast votes in the mock election.

At ten on Christmas morning the revelers converged at the Merkat Cross. The Lord of Misrule—a baker—fitted a papier-mâché ass's head over his shoulders, brayed loudly, and, dragging the Yule log behind him, lurched forward in the direction of Holyrood. Dressed in green and yellow flowing robes, with bells jangling about their naked legs, a horde of boys chased him down the High Street, stopping every now and then to sample the custards and cheeses goodwives offered them along the way. Girls shouted encouragement from balconies and threw down sprigs of evergreen tied with yellow ribbon. Many of the balconies, however, remained empty.

Mary stood atop the palace steps, surrounded by her ladies, a sprig of holly in her white, heart-shaped coif. She watched the boys tumble, beat drums, and somersault in the snow.

Puffing heavily, Balaam's ass lay the Yule log at her feet. He removed the head and held it before Mary. She kissed it reverently on the snout. The Lord of Misrule lifted the silver bowl, drank, and turned to the cheering crowd. He cried "Wassail" three times, then faced Mary and said happily, "Waes hael hlaford Cyning. Be of good health, Lord Queen." He handed her the bowl of spiced ale and bowed. Mary put her hand around his neck and kissed him on the nose. The crowd cheered and clapped their hands.

"Good cheer," Mary said in a loud voice. "When the angel appeared to the shepherds, they were afraid. But the angel said: 'Don't be afraid; be glad, because Lord God has given you His baby boy.' That is the only speech we have for you. Be kind, be generous, love everyone. And, above all things, always be glad! We're late in setting out the sack kegs, but give us half an hour. God be with you, and peace in every house and heart."

The courtyard erupted with noise of viol, horn, cithern, pipe, and flute. Mary gave her arm to James, who led her down the staircase and to the wooden viewing platform that stood opposite the performers' stage.

At noon the crowd numbered approximately five hundred. By eight that night the number had quadrupled. James made his way toward Annabel. Somebody pushed him forward and he found himself crushed against the poet, Chastelard.

"Pierre Chastelard," laughed James. "Are you smiling? Have you had overmuch wine today? I never saw you smile." Somebody tugged at the orange sack James had on his back, and he turned around and yelled, "Off, you Prussian!"

"Earsplitting," said Chastelard.

"What's the occasion?" said James. "You look a fine fellow when you smile." He was shoved forward again and knocked to his knees.

The Frenchman dropped beside him. "This is the day of my

destiny," he said. He slipped his hand around James's neck and kissed him on the mouth.

James pulled back, but Chastelard forced his head forward and kissed him again.

"God damn you, you—"

"Mmmmmm. Almost as good as your sister," said Chastelard with a sad smile. "A pity. I always liked you best. Now, of course, it's too late."

James raised his fist, but the Frenchman stood and was swept away by the mob. Someone grabbed at the orange sack again. James snapped about and cursed brutally. A little girl stared at him in bewilderment, broke into tears, and ran off. He reached after her, but it was too late. Somebody blew a long-necked rebec in his ear. A blizzard of evergreen, shreds of colored paper, and silver spangles rained down on his head. With an effort, he got to his feet.

"My lord," said Annabel, giving him a bear hug.

He drew back.

"There's so many people," she laughed, "that we could make love right here and no one would see."

"Happy Christmas," he said gently. He put his arms around her and held her against him. Then he drew open the orange sack and showed her a silver nightingale in a gilded cage. "Touch the spring," he said.

The bird tinkled "Greensleeves."

"I love you," said Annabel.

> "Spite asketh spite, and changing, change,
>   And falsed faith must needs be known;
> Thy fault so great, your case so strange,
>   Of right it must be blown abroad;
>   Blame not my lute."

Chastelard stood on the firelit stage, his light yellow hair lifting in the icy wind. As he sang, he kept his eyes fixed on Mary. His voice, above the din, was high, angry, rude.

"Madam," said Maitland, sitting at her feet, "I am enslaved."

She was glad not to have to look at Chastelard. He must be drunk, she thought. He's never behaved in such a manner. "Speak plainly," she said to Maitland. "You wish to marry my lady Mary Fleming. Granted."

"Madam, I could never repay—"

"Yes, you could. It would be nice if you stopped accepting the Queen of England's moneys." She put her hand over his mouth. "Now," she said briskly, "I know the value of money. And there is really no way I can keep you from Elizabeth's. But you don't have to tell her *everything.*"

Maitland muttered something.

"I know, William, that you would like to be remembered in the chronicles as the man who united two kingdoms. But it grows increasingly plain that Elizabeth will marry no one if she cannot marry Robert Dudley, and she cannot marry him, no matter how much she thinks she loves him. He is hated by everyone. Even worse, he is mistrusted. Especially since the circumstances of his wife's death, as we all know, were so mysterious. Elizabeth would be driven from her throne if she were so foolish as to marry him. No: Elizabeth can never become Queen of Scotland. But I may someday be Queen of England."

"They call *me* Machiavelli," said Maitland.

"Continue to accept the moneys. But play the game with Cousin Elizabeth, Mr. Maitland, not me. Also, I shall be happy to accept your gift of twenty-five per cent of your monthly allowance from England."

"But, madam. Twenty-five per cent!"

"I would accept even more, but, of course, you will have a wife to support."

Maitland sighed and nodded.

"I like you, Michael Wiley," said Mary. "You're not as honest as Bothwell, but you're more dependable, for all your diplomatic game-playing. All Bothwell seems interested in these days is drinking and street brawling. I may have to put some restraints on him if he refuses to behave in a more proper fashion."

"Bothwell's a madman." Maitland said. "It's useless to talk of him in terms of restraints and proper behavior."

"But he'll be with me if I need him," Mary said. "He takes no one's money, not even mine." She smiled and gave Maitland a peck on the cheek.

Chastelard had risen from his stool, descended from the stage, and walked toward her. The courtyard was still. He thrummed his fingers across the lute strings and sang bitterly:

> "Yet have I found out, for thy sake,
>   Strings for to string my lute again.
> And if perchance this foolish rhyme
>   Do make thee blush at any time,
>   Blame not my *Lute*."

Before she knew what was happening, he seized her head with his hands, bent, and kissed her brutally on the mouth. With a wild gesture of despair and triumph, he leaped from the platform and disappeared into the crowd.

"Drunk," she said, wiping her mouth. She stared at the shocked expressions around her. "Inebriate. I never gave him cause."

Signor Riccio lifted his arm as a signal for the fiddlers. Mummers danced about the makeshift stage performing the story of Maid Marian and Robin Hood.

"Shall I not die in Araby for him?" said the boy playing Marian, "I've sung him songs of passion in the greenwood, pleasure on the sandy beach."

The moment Mary lay her head against her pillow she was asleep. She dreamed Chastelard kissed her. She dreamed she hid her face against the silken sheet as he moved his hands across her breasts and down onto her belly. She dreamed she was dying. She dreamed she was air. Her eyes fluttered open. Chastelard stood by her bed, naked.

He sat down beside her. Then he leaned over and brushed his tongue lightly across her lips. Her hands trembled down his back and up again. Chastelard made a fist and smashed it into her face.

Mary screamed and scratched at his eyes. Blood streaming down his cheeks, he lifted his arms and began raining blows on her head. She heard the door burst open and saw James, blood vessels straining from his temple, pull Chastelard off the bed and send him banging to the floor.

James aimed his sword at the Frenchman's throat. Chastelard gasped and squeezed his eyes shut.

"Kill him," Mary shrieked. "Kill, kill him!"

He told the guards to take Chastelard to the dungeon prison in the Great Castle.

Infuriated, Mary jumped from the bed and attempted to wrest the sword out of James's hand. He sent the steel clattering against the wall and slapped her across the face. "Here, you," he yelled at Beaton, "cover her before she shames us any more."

Mary realized that the bedroom was crowded with people. She allowed Beaton to lead her back to the bed. As she passed Chastelard, she leaned on his arm and vomited.

"Take him," James was saying. "Not to the Tolbooth. Take him to the castle. And clear this room. John, await me outside." He turned to Mary. "He'll have a public trial. As public as possible."

"I hate, hate him," she sobbed. Her hair fell disheveled about her shoulders and her face was blue with bruises.

"It will, of course, be necessary that you attend his execution."

"Execution!"

"Five minutes past, you cried out for me to kill him on the spot. I must warn you, Mary, if you attempt to aid that man in any way, you will be doing yourself grave harm. Now go to sleep."

"James . . ."

"I said sleep."

"James . . . please. Stay with me . . . awhile?"

"You have your ladies," he said harshly. He shut the door.

At his trial before a special session of the Lords Assembled two days later, Chastelard was condemned to head-cutting. He showed no emotion, said nothing in his defense, and requested only that the executioner use a sword rather than an ax. Mary did not sit in attendance. She kept to her private chambers and refused all visitors. It was, however, expected that she would attend the execution on February 22. To do otherwise would be construed as an admission of complicity.

On the night before Chastelard's execution, James followed a jailer through the darkness to the prisoner's cell.

The jailer unlocked an ironwork door, pushed it open, and fitted his torch into a wall bracket. Chastelard sat on a pile of matted rushes in one of the corners. His long yellow tresses had been cropped.

"Why did you send?" said James.

"Because I wish to tell you something," the Frenchman said in a cracked voice. "But that other man may not be here when I say it. It is necessary that he leave."

James nodded at the jailer.

"There are many things which are permitted down here," said Chastelard, "of which people above know very little. Or do you?" He smiled ironically, stood, and opened his gray prisoner's gown. James stared in horror at the scars, bruises, and congealed blood that covered his body. Chastelard shut his robe and sat down again. "You must pardon me, but it is difficult—simply standing is difficult. But that is not what I wished to tell you. What I wished to tell you is: I have done what I was sent to do. And now there is no Catholic prince in Europe who will take her to wife. And now there is no possibility of an Inquisition here in this country, as there was in France, or Spain." He turned away and faced the wall. His voice, when he spoke again, was deep and far away.

"I had a sister once. When your sister was Queen of France, she attended some executions at Amboise. Just *Huguenots.* Protestants. Nothing out of the ordinary. I believe they executed six hundred the first day, a few more the second. Your sister the Queen was watching from a high balcony—canopies, cloth of gold, ladies with fans, jeweled noblemen eating oranges and pomegranates, a lutanist. I was on the balcony too. We all became ill. Even Catherine de Medici became ill. That night I searched for my sister's body down below. But there were so many bodies." He groaned and wiped at his eyes. "The executioners at Amboise were magnificent. They could cut a man's heart and hold it in their hand while that man was still struggling for air at their feet. They were magnificent at burning, magnificent at dismembering, castration, disembowelment, strangulation, drowning. Your sister the Queen fainted, which was good of her. But, since she was the Queen, she might have done something more. Tomorrow morning she will faint at my execution. But I shall still be executed."

"You are a *Huguenot?*" said James. Of course, he was a Huguenot. Stupid. His brain was cold, blank.

"No," said the Frenchman. "But I am not a papist. But, you see, my lord, she was my sister, and I knew some of the others. Later, after Amboise, I fell in with some of Admiral Coligny's men. They were good men—as my sister was a good woman— and they were *Huguenots;* they believed in that cause. They never wished anyone ill, and their lives were virtuous. When some of them were killed in a later purge, I offered my services. Because of my association with the Queen, I was given instructions: destroy her. I have done so. Not because I believed in a given set of dogma, but because I knew good men who believed. I was never a good man. And I know that—for a particular reason, because of a particular curse I have—I shall never see the face of God. There are many, many good men in the world, even in Scotland. Through my death, I will have given them life."

"Is there nothing—"

Chastelard smiled angelically. "I don't know. I'm not dead until tomorrow."

James stared at the other man, unable to speak. With his close-cropped hair, red eyes, and thin dirty face, he looked like a water-color picture of some early saint, wronged, innocent. Finally, James said, "It is possible some sort of escape might be—"

"Thank you, my lord, but I must not accept."

"But, man, you can't want to die."

"It is necessary. That was part of the arrangement."

"With whom? Surely, they wouldn't—"

"It is necessary," said Chastelard. "As for 'whom,' I don't know any names. I asked for no names. If I had, they wouldn't have been given me."

James crouched down beside him and whispered, "There's no need. There will always be doubt in men's minds after you are dead. They'll say, 'If she was in sin with him, she'd not have had him executed.' But when you escape, they will think it was she arranged your escape, and they'll accept that as proof of a liaison." James lowered his head. What he was saying was good and practical. Mary would always be the possibility of more death, more blood. There would be no peace until she was gone. But this way, with her reputation gone, perhaps she would be able to stay, perhaps there could be peace under her rule. There were two Marys: Mary of Rome, and Mary his sister. He could kill the one and save the other. It was logic. But he was ashamed. "Did she . . . lie with you?" he said.

"No," said Chastelard. "She has never lain with any man. Her husband, the Dauphin, was incapable. But she is one of those women who . . . how shall I say it . . have a way of sending invitations which they do not understand."

"Let me help you escape. I give you my word you'll be safe. I have connections with Admiral Coligny's men. I can give you a paper for them. You've done your work."

"Pierre Ronsard is the greatest poet," Chastelard said dreamily, "and no one can be a greater poet than Ronsard, not Du Bellay, not Wyatt, certainly not I. But my death will be more beautiful than anything Ronsard could ever write. I sent for you tonight because tomorrow, when I mount the scaffold, I would like to be able to look up and see a human face which knows why it is that I am dying. I wanted that face to be yours because you are the greatest man." He shuddered. "I'm beginning to be afraid, and it is necessary that I do not become that. Take care for Lord John; he's not as strong as you—or her. But to get at you, there are those who will do him grave harm, and, because your sister loves him as well, there will be those who will hurt him to punish her—"

"What have you to do with John?" said James, standing up.

"Nothing. I like him. He's been a friend. I wrote things for him to sing. Nothing more than that. He has no knowledge of what I've done. None. There is one last request I have of you," said Chastelard rapidly. He seized James's hand. "You can't refuse a dying man the last request. . . ."

"What is it?"

"Tomorrow," he whimpered, "I don't want to die in rags. Not rags. But good clothing—gay, bright colors, cap and cape, bathed. It's an awful thing . . . the most wicked thing of anything . . . to make a man die in rags."

Mary was lying fully clothed on the rumpled quilt of her bed. "Oh, it's you," she said when James entered the room. "I was going to say it is customary to be announced when one enters the presence of one's sovereign. But you never have yourself announced, do you, James?" She stood and stretched her arms. "For a while, James, I'd thought you'd changed. You'd laugh occasionally, every now and then, sometimes, here and there." She sat down again and pressed her fingers over her eyes. "I've been drinking brandywine. I've had too much. I had to stop awhile, because it makes me sick if I drink too much of it, but as soon as I feel better, I'll drink some more. After all, brother, if I'm to be a whore I may as well be a sotted whore. It's more fitting."

"Nobody believes you to be—that," said James.

"Wonderful! Then all's well. Good. Splendid. I love it. *You* believe me to be a whore. Don't deny what God knows, James. Finally, you have proof. Are you content now, James? Everything Master John Knox has ever said is true."

"I never said—"

"You did. You did! The other night you did! In front of everyone. It never occurred to you that night that perhaps Chastelard might have tried to take me by force. Despite the fact that I screamed and cried for help. You never, never knew me. Never. You never will. How I hate you sometimes. How I wish you'd never existed! Do you think I'm mad? You look as if you do, Brother James. But if I'm mad, then I have an excuse for my special sin with Chastelard. Madmen are God's children. He protects them because they haven't any wits. My physician told me he thought the Scots air conducive to madness. He recommended annual visits to my French estates at Poitiers, where the air is clean, and warm. After you left that night, I sat down and wrote a three-page letter to my mother. I knew she was dead, but it didn't matter. I used my best penmanship. I told her that what she'd written me about the snow here is true. How it's sometimes so thick and dark, other times so light, with all the lost sunlight filtering through, and everything grainy one minute, everything clean the next. After I was done writing, I folded the papers into quarters and tore them in half. *Jesu,* when I lived in France, when I was a girl, everything was ordered, and everything was proper and expected, no surprises. We had parties all the time, and everything we wished to have we had. We were all so safe and warm then, but now—nothing is expected, nothing is sensible. I thought you were my brother, James: I thought that would make the whole world well. But you never loved me! You never cared."

James raised his hand and slapped her across the face.

She stared at him in disbelief, then burst into tears. He saw the same expression on her face that their father had had the night he died at Falkland, when he had cursed the man who brought him the news of Mary's birth, when James, a child, wide-eyed, watching his father die, had asked his mother, innocently, "Am I the King now?"

Suddenly, James told her everything that Chastelard had told him. It was an agony for him to say the words. It filled his heart to say them.

"What are we?" she asked hoarsely.

"Two dangerous people," he said. "I love you."

Mary threw her arms about his neck and kissed him. Her tears burned down his neck. He led her back to the bed, set her down, and wiped her eyes. She told him of Cardinal de Gouda's visit. He cradled her in his arms.

He sat holding her hand until she slept, then attempted to rise and go, and realized he was sleeping too. He dreamed he saw

King Arthur's evil sister Morgan le Fay and all her fairies, half in, half out of the tapestried walls. Legend had it that the great sin which killed Camelot was committed in the castle, that there King Arthur and Morgan le Fey did incest together and made the bastard Mordred. The demon fairies' faces were remorseless. "It's the blood," they droned, struggling to pull themselves free.

Morgan le Fay fluttered about the ceiling. "And Mary too," she light-laughed, "and your brother John, the blood in her, the blood in him, the blood in you, your dad's blood come to catch you up. Each. Every one. Stewart blood. Hallo, hallah!"

I was eight once, and they ordained me a priest, because I was a King's bastard. And God was light then, and everything was lovesome, and God was like a fairy elf to me, with lightning belts between his toes, a smile, a great laugh, and nothing but good, and kind, and happy, and all-love. Eight. One year past the age of reason. And I loved him.

I love her. Love her.

He gazed at their reflection. In the window glass, they were transformed into wraiths, rising against strange, twisting lights, then spinning down again. The snow. But who would have thought that white, or gray, could be so many colors, or that so many colors could all be one color.

Clothed in bright red, with a yellow wool cape and white plumed cap, Chastelard walked slowly across the market square at St. Andrew's to the scaffold. He was singing Ronsard's *Hymn to Death:*

> *Je te salue, houreuse et profitable mort,*
> *Des extrêmes doulours médecin et confort.*

His voice was strong, young, beautiful; it rose and fell and merged with its own echo and with the low moaning sound of the wind. He mounted the snow-encrusted steps and smiled at the crush of people that filled the courtyard. His face was flushed, radiant.

The executioner bent his knee and begged forgiveness, which the Frenchman granted. With a gesture of infinite grace, he extended his hand toward Mary, who was standing next to James on a balcony above the scaffold. Chastelard brought the hand to his lips and blew her a lover's kiss.

The people who jammed the courtyard looked up at Mary, but her face was without expression.

Chastelard knelt. The executioner raised his sword. Suddenly Chastelard jerked back his head, faced Mary, and cried, "Farewell, *cruel mistress!*" Shaking uncontrollably, he clasped his hands together and muttered a few indistinguishable words.

In the courtyard, the shuffling feet made harsh crunching sounds in the snow. A number of women wept openly. A man's voice said loudly that it was an injustice since it was *her* sin as well.

On the balcony, James gave the signal once more.

"Sir, you must kneel very straight," said the executioner.

"Yes," said Chastelard. "Straight. Very straight." Tears were streaming from his eyes.

The executioner raised the sword and swung. Chastelard screamed, a thick jet of blood shot upward, and his head flew through the air, missed the catch-bucket, and landed in the snow. The body twitched convulsively on the scaffold.

Mary raised her hands to her neck, screamed, and fell.

CHAPTER SIX

Everyone ought to have known what he was doing, but he was James Stewart; he was the man "the godly did most reverence." In late February, he and Annabel traveled to his holdings near the west coast. They stayed in a small cottage and went on walks in the snow together. While Annabel cleaned and cooked, James hunted. For miles around there was nothing but the white hills and the low moaning sound of the wind. On the second night they made love on quilts James placed on the dirt floor in front of the hearth.

Afterward, Annabel said, "Do you love me?"

James sat up and stared into the fire.

"I didn't think it could be that," she said, a note of irritation in her voice. After a minute she said, "I'm with child. Your child."

James stood, looked at her, averted his head, and sat down on a stool near the bed. He picked his shirt off the floor and held it over his lap.

"Don't cover it up," Annabel said ironically. "That's the thing did it."

98

"There were others," James mumbled. "How do you know it isn't from them? Not mine."

"It is no other man's," she said, getting up and seizing his hands in hers. "Touch it. It's not ready to begin kicking yet. You hardly can tell that it is there. But it is. Part of me is part of you now."

He pulled his hands away, rose, and struck her across the face. He stared uncomprehendingly past her head at the bright red and yellow shreds of flame in the hearth.

Annabel slid to her knees and bowed her head. "I won't tell," she whispered. "If you're afraid of that, I'll never say it was you. There's no need that you love me, my lord; I ask only that you do not mind my loving you. It is not easy to love, my lord. It's hard . . . until you do. Please . . ."

As if under an enchantment, James kept his eyes fixed on the devouring flames. He felt her wet cheek brush lightly against his hand. He felt he was standing at the bottom of the sea with sandy water dark all around him.

Early next morning, they left for Edinburgh. The next week he married Agnes Keith, heiress of Dunfermline, and there were three days' banqueting at Holyrood.

One morning in the beginning of the month of March, James stretched before his casement window in Holyrood. The white skies had slowly turned blue and the countryside was moist and beautiful. He'd spent the night before drafting a Poor Law which he intended presenting for approval when Parliament reassembled in April. It would be a good session. He had so many plans. He took pleasure in the bright patches of green which were slowly stretching across the city's southern plain. The High Street swarmed with citizens. Merchant galleys from France, England, Italy, and the Netherlands crowded the harbor at Leith.

Down below, Archbishop Hamilton was running across the brick courtyard, looking for all the world like some great, flocked bird. James smiled. At first, he'd thought Mary's interest in Hamilton might have an element of danger in it. The other prelates from the old, Catholic days had either fled or been killed, but no one had ever thought to end Hamilton. He lived in town now, with his concubine of twenty years and their brood. Mary liked him because she was lonely for people who were witty and could speak French. Unlike the other prelates, Hamilton, in his time of ecclesiastical sway, had never shed the blood of Protestants. Apparently, De Gouda hadn't bothered with him during the course of his secret mission. He was, in short, safe and unimportant. A peaceful time was coming. Vengeance was no longer necessary. Seagulls flew noiselessly about the town.

James splashed water under his arms and over his face and chest, then dried himself with a linen cloth. He clicked his tongue. There would always be the Huntlys. Old Huntly had had the effrontery to offer Mary his son in marriage. And Mary, even though she had no immediate plans to marry, genuinely liked Sian Gordon. I even like him, thought James. But give him ten years—he's soft now—but give him some years and he'll be the image and likeness of his father. He wondered: In ten years will I be mine?

Mary had spent the winter planning one elaborate masque after another, and reading French and Italian romances. The Italian bass, Signor Riccio, had become one of her favorites. It amused James to see the misshapen Riccio following Mary everywhere, his huge doe eyes soft with admiration and attention. The man provided companionship and kept her from boredom. He would sit at her feet in a heap, strumming his guitar. James was proud of his sister. He was assured that she would make an excellent sovereign. Her nature was docile and gentle; she loved familiarity, little kindnesses, and grand ideas; she hated hypocrisy and cruelty.

The day before, she'd come laughing to him, her arms full of wildflowers she'd picked in the gardens. "Oh, brother," she said, fixing a blossom in his cap, "I'm *glad* spring has come. Pall-mall, archery, tennis, jousting, the hunt, the sun every day, and everything good. No more artificial flowers. Birds. Blue air. And everyone falling in love with everyone!"

But there were times when, for no apparent cause, she would give way to violent fits of weeping and hysteria, be driven within herself, and refuse to see anybody but her ladies and Signor

Riccio for days. There were times when she would not even see them. "I don't understand," she'd told him after one outburst of tears. "It comes and it takes me. Then it goes." Her mother had died of an ascitic dropsy, but these were different symptoms. It was because Mary, despite her lively spirits, was sensitive, James told himself; it was because she was sensitive and unused to the rough Scots climate.

He picked up the correspondence that had been placed under his door and put it on the table. There was a banishment case pending against two minor burghers for butter profiteering, two or three divorce hearings, and an evasive missive from the Queen of England's secretary concerning the proposed visit between the two Queens that fall. The city cleansing station was in need of funds.

He tore the seal on the last missive and read: *I would not have had him stay here if he could, but it was a thing that happened and I did not cause it. Do not come; you did not come before. Your bastard is dead. . . .*

James stood in the night air outside Ainslie's Tavern and watched the procession of revelers come and go. Annabel sat by her window on the second floor and looked down at him. He watched her press against the window until her breath on the glass transformed her face into the face of a ghost. Then he returned to Holyrood.

In June, Mary decided to accept the Earl of Huntly's invitation to travel on a progress through his counties in the north.

Two days later, Sian Gordon, the Earl of Bothwell, John Stewart, and a number of other young lords were involved in a drunken brawl on the High Street. A man was accidentally wounded. James moved swiftly. He issued a warrant for the arrest of Bothwell and young Gordon and confined John to the palace. An example had to be made. Bothwell was captured and confined in the Castle, but Sian Gordon had gone north to the Highlands. James persuaded Mary to issue another order: if Huntly's son did not give himself up to Queen's ward within the month, he would be put to the horn and banished, under pain of death, forever. He explained that, yes, of course, the man would give himself up, and then he and Bothwell would be fined and let go. Nothing more, or less. It was essential, in the beginning, to prove that she favored no party and that her power touched upon all factions, papist or Protestant, great or little. Mary reluctantly agreed.

But Mary could not decide, because of Sian Gordon's refusal to commit himself to Queen's ward, whether or not to go on her progress to the Highlands.

"You should go," James told her. "But I would advise you to take a sizable contingent of men."

Though possessed of little imagination, the Earl of Huntly had been Chancellor of Scotland for sixteen years and filled the office well. In the old time, Archbishop Hamilton had once termed him a "wild ass of a man," and the appellation had driven Huntly to a characteristic outburst of rage. The archbishop retreated in horror and immediately apologized, but afterward Huntly would recall the prelate's words with, first, amusement and then pride. "I'm a wild ass of a man," he'd bellow to his comrades. His wife, Lady Huntly, would always reply, "Surely more than sinply that, husband George." Her husband would say, "Truly, for I am that, and King of the Highlands, and Jeannie Corrichie's husband, to boot." It was a game they played together.

James studied the map on the Council wall. He'd been to Huntly's territory several times during the campaign against Marie de Guise. He remembered the shacks like dog kennels, the pinched peasant faces. Squalor everywhere. No law but Huntly's law, which was the same as no law at all. The barbaric splendor of the old man's fortresses, where he kept court like a king. Filthy streets piled with refuse and children starving in the streets and deaths by the thousands from disease, starvation, constant clan quarrelings which Huntly did nothing to stop. The worse thing, though, was the sight of children with the eyes of old, dying men. There was also the fact that Lady Huntly kept witches. James stared at the map. He decided he would have it spread about in the north that Mary intended granting him the Earldom of Moray, to which Huntly laid claim.

Lord and Lady Huntly bent their heads and bowed at the great gates to the College of Aberdeen. Huntly offered his hand to the Queen to dismount.

"Where is your son, Sian?" said Mary.

"I do not know, Your Majesty. Will you come in and dine?"

"We have received a report that your son is in Aberdeen," said Mary. "Is he here to give himself up to our just authority?"

"The report is false," said Huntly.

"We have asked you a question, sir."

Aware that something serious was going on, the townspeople had quieted down and were jumping to get a look. Lady Huntly rested her hand on her husband's shoulder.

"Your Majesty," she said graciously, "we have fresh clothes, a bath. My daughter Jean will see to your pleasure." She indicated a plump young girl in the shadows of the college gates. The girl executed a clumsy curtsy.

"Thank you," said Mary. "When we have had the answer to our question."

"He is not here," said Huntly.

"He's rash, madam," said Lady Huntly. "It's youth, nothing darker. Forgive him."

"He is past the age of reason," said Mary. "In the eyes of the Church, he bears responsibility for his sins. In the eyes of the law, he must bear responsibility for his lawlessness."

James, who was by her side, cleared his throat and said, "I have a warrant for the arrest of three women in the service of Lord Huntly."

"Your Majesty, please come inside," said Lady Huntly.

"We do not think we will spend the night in this place," said Mary, jerking her reins.

"Your Majesty, come in. You promised you would come with us to Inverness," said Lady Huntly. "Inverness is awaiting your—"

"Inverness," said Mary. "Inverness. I've heard that name."

"Macbeth murdered his King there," said James. "A Pict stronghold once. Now, of course, my lord of Huntly's."

"Perhaps I will come," said Mary to Lady Huntly. "Perhaps
not. That is up to your son." She slapped her riding crop against
her horse's flank and began riding away.

"Blind!" Huntly bellowed after her. "Blind in the Bastard's
pocket! D'you dare think——"

Mary turned, rode at him, and struck him across the face with
her crop.

"Do you know who I am?" said Huntly.

"A subject like all these men around me. Nothing more or less."

Huntly spit on the cobblestones. "You're not in the Lowlands
with your Presbyterian friends now, Lady. You'd best think on
that. I've given you no safe-conduct, Lady, to travel through my
lands."

"*Whose* lands?"

"Mine." He spread his arms toward the townspeople. "I am
lord of all of these, and they know it! Who are you?"

"We shall see," Mary said furiously. She yanked at her reins
and faced the crowd. "I hereby and now declare if Sian Gordon,
son of George Gordon, does not deliver himself up to Queen's
ward by twelve noon tomorrow, he shall be outlaw and traitor
and banished forever from all this country. Further, if any choose
to aid him they shall suffer the supreme penalty—in despite of
rank or position. And that if any having information of the
man's whereabouts does not come forward with that information,
he also shall be declared traitor." She spun around and faced
Huntly. "Not one word from you, m'lord. Not one."

"You have no rights here to——"

"Arrest him," said Mary. Soldiers leaped from their horses,
surrounded him, and wrested his sword away.

Lady Huntly dropped to her knees and pressed her lips against
the hem of Mary's skirt. "Madam," she said, "I have never
begged. Your mother knew as much."

"My quarrel is not with you," said Mary.

"That man standing over there is me," said Lady Huntly,
pointing to her husband. "Give us one day."

"Very well," said Mary. For some reason, she felt tremendously relieved. "Unhand him." She watched as Huntly marched quickly into the college, slamming one of the gates behind him.

Lady Huntly searched Mary's face for a few seconds, then said, "You tolerate heresy, Your Highness. If you wish to do that, then you must tolerate the errors of men, especially those who join with you in the true religion. My husband is a plain, blunt man, but I think he is a good man, as well."

"Your husband has caused much blood in the past," said James. "The massacre of the presbyters at Farnum, the pillage at Finlater—"

"I am not in the habit of addressing bastards," said Lady Huntly.

"Damn you!" said James.

The color washed from Lady Huntly's face. She raised her hand to Mary, then dropped it helplessly by her side, beckoned weakly to her daughter, and went inside the college.

"Long live the Earl of Huntly," someone cried in the crowd behind them.

"And Jeannie Corrichie. And Siannie Gordon," a number of other voices yelled.

James snapped around and cried back, "And so they shall. As long as they serve their Queen—who is God's appointed representative to you in this kingdom, who is King James V's lawful daughter—who is the servant of all those who serve her in this *one* nation!"

"Long live the Queen," the bodyguard of soldiers cried in unison. No one shouted back. The crowd began to break up.

Mary tried to catch the expressions on the passing faces. She smiled and waved at a small group of children who were staring sheepishly at her. One of them started crying. She looked back at the stone walls of the college and saw Lady Huntly, her face half hidden by a curtained window on the second floor.

"You have forgot the warrant for the witches," said James.

Mary looked back up at the window. It flashed orange with the descending sun. "I cannot believe Lady Huntly believes—in witches."

"There's nothing here to make light of," James said. "The Huntlys are dangerous people."

Mary nodded, and waved to the few people remaining in the square. She felt sorry for Lady Huntly. She even felt sorry for her husband. He was insufferable, a boor; ten minutes before she would gladly have struck him dead; now she had to fight down the urge to leap from her palfrey, hitch up her skirts, run into the college, throw herself before him, beg forgiveness for shaming him. It was insane. She was the Queen. Huntly was even more insane. They all were. Except James. Seagulls screeched past her head. She looked at James. "Let us continue," she said.

"God bless that sweet face," someone cried. The monk lifted the wood cage and starlings flew high into the clear blue sky over Mary's head.

She gazed at the birds until they were specks. The villagers cheered and cast heather, cragberry leaves, and rosemary in her horse's path. Mary dipped into her purse and threw a handful of coins at the rocking crowd. A bouquet of cicendias tied with pink string struck her on the arm and fell to the ground. Mary attempted to catch it, but the string had come undone, leaving a trail of bright yellow behind her. She pulled the reins and leaped off her horse. She ran back and scooped the flowers up in her hands. In the crowd, men and women screamed delightedly.

Lifting the flowers above her head, Mary cried out, "I have received things of beaten gold from princes of France, Morocco, Spain, from the Americas and India. They were rich and shining, good people, but you are more rich and shining. You are *my* good people and you are *good!*" She buried her face in the cicendias and breathed deeply.

They surged forward and surrounded her and, shouting exultantly, extended their hands to touch her. Mary laughed and lifted her hand. The crowd fell back obediently.

Mary remounted and fixed the blossoms in her saddle. "Who am I?" she suddenly cried.

"The Queen! The Queen!"

"Queen of what?" It was like drunkenness. And lightning. Everything was swaying. The sky rose and fell, breathed colors.

"Of Scotland! Scotland! Scotland!"

"Who was my father? What was his name?"

"King James! King Jamie! The Good Poor Man's King! Scotland! Scotland!"

"And the pipe music!" cried Mary. "Do you hear the old bagpiping?" She cupped her hand against her ear.

"Yes!" they squealed.

"No, you don't."

They laughed, too, and cheered.

"Pipers, play," she yelled back. "Play Scotland loud and noisy!" She pulled the ribbons from her hair and let it fall down her back. Even the harsh grate of the bagpipes was wonderful.

The cortege ascended and left the village.

Several clouds flew overhead toward the rolling green hills. The clouds joined, billowed, and the green seemed to leap forward. Mary yanked at her reins.

"You'll become accustomed to that," said James, pulling alongside. "It's the wind levels. The clouds magnify the altitude and cause the color changes."

The clouds lifted and were carried farther north. The hills retreated. Now, instead of green, they were purple and gold. The clouds rushed overhead again and the hills, speckled with shadow and sunlight, seemed to break into fragments, and rock, undulate back and forth like the waves in the sea.

Mary rode back to John, seized his reins, and pulled him after her. "A conference," she explained to James and Beaton as she passed them. When they were several hundred yards ahead of the others, Mary slowed her pace. "Have I offended you?" she said. "Have I—"

"Have you?" John said sullenly.

"We used to sing and laugh. But—it is very unfair of you to be angry with me and not give me a reason." She reached for his hand, but he drew it back. She squinted up at the hazy sun.

"There are many things which are not fair," said John. "Bothwell in the castle is unfair. Putting Sian Gordon in Queen's ward is unfair. Chopping Pierre is unfair. There's a ballad the Picts sang about these Highlands. If I had my mandolin I'd—I'd—"

Mary turned and saw him wiping at his eyes.

"If I had my mandolin—why, I don't think I'd sing it for you anyway. There now, don't you begin brimming in tears. That's your special trick, isn't it, Sister Mary? Are you blind? Are you a fool? Don't you know what is going to happen up here? Can't you see what is going to happen? Are you mad!"

Mary slapped her riding crop against her horse's flank. Slate and sandstone rocks jutted in bosses on the rolling hills. Gigantic slabs of quadrangular sandstone rose at ninety-degree angles out of the crests and ridges. Through her tears, Mary saw a herd of red deer pause briefly on the summit of the highest hill.

They loved her here up north. In France, they'd worshiped her. Down in Edinburgh, most merely clapped their hands politely as she rode by, or ignored her completely. In Edinburgh, if an individual might cry out, "God save the Queen," those standing close would turn and regard him as if he'd broken some moral law. But in the Highlands everybody was Catholic, and everybody loved her. Bright blue streams swept down the green and purple.

"There is a Power in the Highlands," Bothwell had told her once, in one of his pleasant moments.

"Indeed," she'd said, amused. "God?"

He'd laughed that laugh he always laughed and said, "Not the one you know." And that laugh again.

A flock of Hebridean wrens flew overhead in V-formation. Mary watched as the wind changed direction and scattered them across the sky. They circled helplessly in the whirling currents, screaming in terror. Mary realized she was halfway to the summit. She looked back and saw her caravan at the base of the hill. For miles around, great spongelike masses surged restlessly in a westerly direction, toward America.

A cold wind gushed past Mary, knocking down the cicendias she'd attached to her saddle. She watched the bright yellow petals fill the air and wheel away over the precipice. She had reached the summit.

From here she could look east down to the sea. Waves crashed against massive, jagged rocks. White sand dunes spurted and bloomed inland. Far out to sea, a flat stone island glistened under the sun. Mary leaned forward and breathed deeply of the sea air. Her horse threw back its head and whinnied. Mary turned and saw, a few feet away, a large gray dog. The horse snorted in terror. The dog growled.

"What's your name, fellow?" said Mary. The dog was standing on the remains of some sort of stone fireplace covered with roughly carved human and animal figures. Here and there in the grass were signs of recent fires. Mary reached into her saddlebag and drew out a *petit four*. The dog cocked its head.

A pistol shot cracked the air. The dog leaped forward, caught the cookie between its fangs, and scampered off. Mary's horse screamed, reared, and sent her hurtling into the soft, springy foliage.

James helped her to her feet. "You're not to go off like that again," he said.

"Who—how dare—it was a dog—"

"A wolf. Give thanks I had my eye on you."

"But he was a dog, he was gentle—"

"Gentle like Chastelard, perhaps? He was a wolf. It's a trick they learned. But they're thieves and cowards; they eat their own when they're hungry. We're in Huntly's land now. Don't ride apart again." He strode over to the westerly side of the summit. After a minute he motioned for her. "Down there," he said, pointing. "It's luck we thought to bring men with us. I warned you about Huntly. Warned you. Now mount up. And now you will see what it means to be a sovereign, to hold and bind a country."

Mary looked down and saw an army, Huntly's banner flying at its head, marching in their direction.

The smoke in the full sun downward drumming. Barrage and fusillade of grapeshot, canister shot, iron balls flying, and the hiss of arrows. And the rapturous-loud clan cries of her men killing. She remembered passages she'd memorized in Malory: "What will ye do?" said Merlin to the little kings; "ye were better for to stynte, for ye shall not prevail here tho ye be ten times as many." During the course of the battle, some of Huntly's couriers were taken. The man had meant to seize her, force her into wedlock with his son, then march south into the Lowlands and restore the Catholic Church in Scotland.

"Her Majesty is an intrepid horsewoman," said James proudly as they rode past the field of green corn.

"Will you inspect the field of battle, my lady?" said the captain of her guard.

James nodded his head.

Escorted by James and the captain, Mary made her way through the thick carpet of ripped ensigns, metallic debris, and dead bodies. Mary liked the feel of the sword at her side, the swinging of it, and the pressure of the French pistols under her belt.

A group of foot soldiers hallooed at them. One of the men jogged over to James and reported, "Huntly's body here."

"And the son?" said James.

The foot soldier said, "Not yet, sir." Mary watched him glance up at James and smile, then blush and drop his head.

James thought a minute, then said, "Mary, look at it. For them —the men."

The captain of the guard didn't think it was necessary; it was nothing for a woman to see.

"I want to see it," said Mary.

They picked their way through the piled bodies. James motioned for them to turn the corpse over.

Mary felt very cool.

"There's no marks," said James, bending over and examining the thing.

"It must have been apoplexy or his heart or the sun," said a soldier.

"Oh, it must have been the sun," said John, walking toward them. *"You'd* like to think so, wouldn't you, Sister Mary?" He knelt beside the carcass. "You flew high, old man. You ought to have known better than to let your foul fish pride interfere with other men's ambitions. Oh, God, what am I doing—talking to a dead man! It's a bit late really. Happy Christmas."

"Get up," said James. "I asked you to inventory his castle at Inverness."

"Do you actually think— Never mind. Where's Sian?"

"He escaped," said Mary.

"James is too neat a fellow for that," said John. He hiccoughed and a grin slowly spread across his face. "James, why was it Huntly had to die?"

"They were traitors," Mary said harshly.

"Sian Gordon was my *friend*," said John. "He might have been yours. He might even have been your husband once upon a time. But neither he nor his dad were Brother James's friends, and so—happenstance—they're *poof* now." He threw his arms up in disgust and walked away.

James snapped his fingers. "Here," he said, indicating the corpse. "Take it and hang it from the walls of Inverness."

Nearby, a troop of her men were passing in disarray. Their commander let them rest a minute to look at her. "Halloo," they cried, "hallah, Queen Mary!"

She let her kerchief flutter in the breeze above her head. They liked that. Splendid, wonderful men!

"You have given me joy of life to drink!" she called to them.

The troops cheered and cheered. A boy of about fifteen broke from the ranks, ran to her, took her hand, and brought it reverently against his lips. "You *ray*, you!" he whispered. He ran back to his fellows.

"Have you found the son?" James asked another man.

"No, sir, we have not."

That night, Mary adjusted her blouse and her long Highland cloak, then walked from her tent to the seat of honor at the banqueting table. The rough people of the district were leaping and tumbling around bonfires to the screech and swirl of pipes and fiddles. James gave her a look of stunned disbelief, turned red, and faced the other direction. Every other head but his was turned toward her. She smiled her Mona Lisa smile.

"Wrong wi' th' ribbons," said a dour chieftain's wife in checkered phrygian. She ripped the thin pink lengths from Mary's hair, and exploded into such an infectious, wrinkle-kindling grin that Mary impulsively took her in her arms. The woman chortled it was time Mary knew the fling. "Donalbain McCreath," she yelled over her shoulder, "David or Columba or Patrick or Sian McCreath come show our Queen what dancing is. They're all sons of mine," she said proudly to Mary, "and though they were pledged to Huntly, they led their men for you today."

"Well, perhaps I should watch them dance awhile," said Mary, "and then I could attempt it."

"That's not the way to learn," said the chieftain's wife. She pushed an awkward giant forward and announced, "My Columba!" The man took Mary in his arms, led her around the table, then dropped and clacked his knees in the dirt. He smelled of sweat, rabbit grease, and ale. There was a great deal of sly laughing.

"Forward and backward, *click*," he panted through his heavy whiskers. "Here, maybe we should have the swords." He bent his burly frame and crossed two rusty swords on the dirt. Then he took her gently in his hands and taught her to leap.

"Now put your hand on your side, Machsty, and yer other hand there a little more slanted above yer head."

Mary skipped, whirled, jumped, and leaped again. *Hoc est enim corpus meum,* she thought wildly. She could hardly hear *that* above the blur of lively, burring language, hands clapping, and the noise of the bagpipes, sheepgut filled with air.

"She *is* the Queen of Scots," Mary heard someone say.

Someone else said, "An' yes, you can see King Jamie's face and his limbs in her."

Another voice said, "And Lord James, also."

Finally, she fled back to the table in front of her tent and sank into her chair of honor. The Highlanders swarmed around her.

"Oh, madam," laughed Beaton. "Your most magnificent performance." I know a little secret, the other girl's face seemed to say, but when she spoke again her voice was low and sad. "Speak to John. He won't come out."

Mary patted her on the hand. John was sulking in his tent. He was the only man Beaton had never fallen out of love with. Oh, what, what have I done, Mary thought; why has he changed so? She thought with horror: At the moment I don't particularly care.

"I don't know why it should be," James was saying to a cluster of chieftains at the end of the table, "but I believe the Earl of Huntly's treason was foiled by God Himself. How else—"

"The Queen has given you one of Huntly's titles. She's made you Earl of Moray, my lord," said one of the chiefs.

Hours later, Mary walked carelessly from the circle of tents toward the open field where the battle had been fought. The air was crisp and whiffing. Her soul slowly filled with a wonderful sweetness and calm. She watched the moon pass from behind a purple cloud. For a minute, the earth turned light yellow, then the sky was gray again. It began to rain. Oh, if I were a man to sleep the night in fields and pass the time of campfires. The moon was dripping like apple butter behind the twisted sheets of cloud.

From up on top of that hill over there, I watched the battle. On that low hill opposite, during the fight, women in black writhed their arms and screamed incantations. James said they were Lady Huntly's witches. I said: Surely, you don't believe in such things? He said yes, he did. Well, if those deluded crones were truly witches, why did I win, and not Huntly? But he seemed not to hear. Dead: theirs, 578. Dead, ours, 107.

Mary's heart was pounding; thick beads of sweat rolled down her forehead. Who am I? she asked herself. She answered: I am Marie Regina, Queen Regnant of the state of Scotland, sovereign by the fundamental right of primogeniture and succession, which no dogma, no law, no fault nor forfeiture may alter or diminish. My title does not derive from the people but from God. The high grasses whipped at her bare legs.

She rested a minute and watched the widening arcs of wind blizzarding across the field. The earth rocked with a thunderblast. Down past the area where the enemy dead had been piled, a flash of red caught her eye. The rain suddenly stopped. The sky was one vast, bright white sheet. The wind was gone. The red flashed again, then glowed warmly and began extending its rays against the sky. Mary stared, fascinated. The sky was a hundred miles high. The rays were ninety-nine miles high. The sky was a thousand miles. The rays extended nine hundred and ninety-nine miles. Then the white sheet gleamed red, shook, and burst. Moon, rain, lightning, thunder, black and green pounded into the earth. The wind careened, battering bodies, grass, and her.

Mary whimpered. Lightning split the sky in half. A body lay stretched across a mound of rocks splashed with red, glowing paint. Its ankles and wrists were tied with garlands of rue. A thin red line extended from the head and neck, down the shoulders and arms to the sides and legs, then up the corpse's other side and back to the skull again. Mary shuddered and drew back. His chest was torn open, a gaping, raw cavity of wet red muscle and bone ends. She stared at the stones. They were covered with the same runic drawings she'd seen earlier at the deserted campsite where she'd given the dog who was a wolf a *petit four*. With a shock, she realized they were the inscriptions carved on her father's tomb. A twisted crucifix lay between the corpse's feet.

"You sorry bitch," Bothwell said.

It was a devil-dream. It was the witches. Those demon mermen tigers serpents barking hiss me, Virgin Mary ever Virgin, St. Denis fold me away, God! She brushed the wet hair from her face and, without thinking, grabbed the crucifix from the dead feet and held it out in front of her.

Bothwell slapped her across the face. She screamed.

"Close your mouth," he said flatly. He took her arm and smeared its blood across her face. "Now we look *honest!*"

"You!" said Mary, her teeth chattering. She bit into her tongue and her mouth filled with blood. "Are you going to kill me!"

"I said to close the mouth. Huntly's dead. His son's an outlaw. Huntly was a fool, but he was the only papist fool big enough to check your brother James. You're Pandora!" He clapped his hands. "Congratulations. You let the Bastard out of the box. Magnificent." He slapped her again. "That's for being a stupid, cowardly, murderous cunt." He unbuckled his belt and threw himself on top of her. "This," he said, twisting her arms behind her back, "is for being—what you are. Period."

Mary screamed and sank her teeth into his cheek. Bothwell

loosened his grip, and she rolled over and attempted to crawl away.

"Bitch," groaned Bothwell, knocking her back down into the muddy grass. He forced his tongue against her teeth and one of his hands was tight on the back of her head and the other hand was pushing the kilts past her hips.

Mary kissed him clumsily and dropped her hand on his back.

Bothwell suddenly stood up and fastened his buckle. He was quiet a minute, then said, "It was the witches. In their own kind, foolish way they thought they'd protect him with this—stuff!" He turned back to her. "You let the Bastard lock me tight. If you strike me, then"—he slapped one hand over the other—"then I strike you back. Without a thought. That is me. You locked me tight and you had no cause. You put me in the power of a man who is not my friend. Did you think you could keep me locked up forever? Did you think I'd be puppy enough to sit there waiting upon the pleasure of my gracious Queen, praying that she would one day, in her compassion, deign to give me my freedom again?" He paused, breathing hard. "I would say that I am sorry for what I have just done. I know that it was wrong. But I am not sorry for it. Farewell."

Mary slowly nodded her head. After a minute, there was no sound left but that of the wind.

"I'm lonely," she said out loud. "Lonely."

She got up, wiped her eyes, smoothed her kilts, and started back to the encampment. She wished she might meet Bothwell tomorrow morning, early, for the first time again, and that he would be different and that she would be better, and that they might . . . she did not know what.

CHAPTER SEVEN

For two successive years, the corn and wheat harvests had failed, but the resultant famines were minor. Edinburgh's warehouses were always full, and James supervised the carting of peas, turnips, and salted meat goods to the south. The seas in the north, as always, were alive with fish and seafowl. Mary met three more times with Knox. His last visit had been almost pleasant.

"I understand," she said to Knox, "you have been appointed to go to Dumfries in a few days for the election of the presbyters."

"Yes," said Knox, "those quarters have great need."

"But I heard the Bishop of Athens would be superintendent."

"The vote has not been taken, madam."

"If you knew him as well as I do," she said, wondering if he was going to take offense, "you would never promote him to any office in your Church."

"What he has been, I neither know nor will inquire; for we were born in a time of darkness, and what could we do but grope as the darkness carried us?" And on and on for a full fifteen minutes.

"Well," she said, while Knox rested his tongue, "you will do as you see fit, but the Bishop of Athens is not a good man." She added, "I may be wrong, but that is what I think."

"You are not wrong," the old man sighed. "There will be no concord with him."

Mary smiled to herself. Since she'd come to Scotland, that was the best compliment. They walked along the garden path awhile longer, and she asked him if he would help solve the difficulties between James and his wife. "She visited court last month, and I could see there wasn't any happiness with them. But don't tell my brother I asked you to intervene, because he'd be angry."

"I have been troubled with that matter before," said Knox, stopping before a yellow rose. "Nothing can be done."

"It's worse between them than I believed possible," said Mary, bending over, breaking off the rose, and extending it to him. "For your wife. They have to have at least eight leaves taken off with them. They live longer that way."

Knox nodded his head.

Sometimes, Mary missed Bothwell. He was gone, and she had no word of his whereabouts. Despite James's protestations, she'd lifted the bans of outlawry against him. She knew that wouldn't bring him back. But she knew that if she needed him, he would come back.

There was also the question of an appropriate marriage. Sian Gordon had been executed a few months after his father's death. The King of Sweden was syphilitic. Don Carlos of Spain chewed rugs. The King of France, aside from being her former brother-in-law, which was within the realm of prohibition, was thirteen years old. Elizabeth had offered Mary her male whore, the Earl of Leicester. There was one other possibility, and he was ideal: Mary's cousin, Henry Stewart, Lord Darnley, the son of the traitor Lennox. He was a Stewart, a Catholic, and a citizen of England, whose claim to the throne of that country was second only to Mary's. Maitland, whom she'd sent to London to investigate the possibility, wrote back that Darnley was tall, handsome, and charming. Unfortunately, Elizabeth caught wind of what was going on and confined the young man to the palace at Whitehall.

Maitland returned to Scotland the following week. Mary was on a progress south and she consulted with him at Dunbar Castle. As they walked up and down the brightly lit promenade deck, the odor of the fresh mown hay strewn across the floor caused her nose to tingle.

"Tell Elizabeth you wish to negotiate a marriage with Leicester," said Maitland.

"You must be mad. Marry the Queen of England's horse-keeper!"

"Madam, madam," said Maitland, fingering the pearl in his right ear, "do you think Elizabeth would ever consent to Leicester marrying anyone? I have it on the best authority she loves him. A sympathy of stars, you might say."

"Then why the idiot farce?"

"Game time," said Maitland. "Skip-and-jump. Runaround. You trick me and I trick you. The human mind at full speed. Wheee."

They left the promenade and ascended a staircase to Mary's private chambers. The light cadences of a virginals floated from one of the rooms below.

"Diplomacy," Maitland was saying. "She has her plan; we have ours. She's given old Lennox a passport to Scotland for reinstatement of his lands, because of the general amnesty you decreed last year. Now, madam, young Darnley has got to be brought to Scotland, and he needs Elizabeth's signature to do so. With marriage negotiations between you and Leicester going at full speed, Darnley will not be so suspicious a character, and there we are—Darnley in Scotland. Diplomacy. I have not yet been able to ascertain Elizabeth's reason for offering Leicester in the first place, but give me time."

"What is Darnley like?" said Mary.

"Politically, as an heir to the crown of England, he's marvelous. Personally, he's charming, madam, charming. I can think of no other word but charming. Do I have your permission to go ahead with the Leicester negotiations?"

"Yes," she said.

When Lennox visited Scotland the following month, Mary was impressed with his youthful appearance. He was a handsome, strong, silent man, not one wrinkle, line, or scar on his skin. James refused either to attend the reinstatement ceremonies or to speak with the man. Mary was shocked at the vehemence that took hold of James if Lennox's name was so much as mentioned. He shook convulsively and acted as one would expect a madman to act.

"Why?" she asked him.

"He murdered our father!" said James.

"He didn't. He betrayed him, but—"

"*Oh*, is that all. Forgive me, Mary; you must forgive me. He only betrayed him. That's good; that's rare."

Mary neither liked nor disliked Lennox.

More and more, she missed Bothwell. If she wished, she might command him to return, but, no, she wouldn't do that. Sometimes, the best thing was—nothing. She allowed Beaton to help her into a light summer gown of pink-ash. "No collars today," she said.

"Summer at last," sang Beaton. "Suck in more. Cuckoo. Jug-jug. Pu-wee, tu-witta-woo. Let me comb out your hair, madam."

"Ah, after the Italian style," said Mary, smiling at David Riccio, his small, hunched body curled up on a couch by the window. "Oh, that's good. Mmmm. Harder."

Riccio brought his hand against his guitar strings and sang:

"Behold the skies with golden dyes
    Are glowing all around;
The grass is green, and so are the treen,
All laughing with the sound."

"Of hey tantara tee ree!" Beaton joined in. "Jug-jug."

"Davy, did you write that missive for Spain?" said Mary, reaching for a bottle of rose water. She gargled, spat into a little bowl, and began lining her eyebrows.

"Yes, signora," said the Italian, lazily strumming the guitar. "I think you should shave your brows."

Mary peered at her reflection in the mirror. "No, no, Master

David, your advice on matters of state is invaluable, but the Queen of Scotland's appearance is exempt. My forehead's high enough as it is. Where's the tooth cloth? And I need some kohl."

"Madam, leave off the jewelry," said Beaton. "It spoils everything."

"Such a hurry," laughed Mary. "We've an entire hour. The tourney will still be there. John will still be there. And, eventually, we will be there."

Beaton giggled and fluttered her hands across her face.

"My little fool is gone to play," Riccio half sang, half laughed, "hey-ho, frisk-a-jolly, under the greenwood tree."

"Pu-wee, pu-witta-wee," said Beaton, dancing over to the cabinet and selecting a peach-colored cap with a pink plume.

The grass was green, the sky was blue, no clouds. The hours of the Huntly rebellion had been dear, dangerous, and critical; no such hours since. Beaton was in love with John; this irritated Mary. She could not help herself. It did more than irritate her— it infuriated her. She wanted to love and to be loved in return. Mary wanted to have a husband who was a man with a face and a first name. Not simply a titled parcel of lands, goods, and coin.

Mary turned to James, who was riding alongside her. He noticed her looking and smiled wearily. With a shock, she saw a few gray hairs on the side of his head. Suddenly, she felt as if she was going to weep. James was only thirty-four. It was unfair. She never, never wanted him to be old. It was a shame he hadn't been able to join the lists. Once, she'd seen him throw the caber thirty-three feet, six inches. He was very slim, but he was a powerful man. John had promised Beaton he would win every match for her and crown her Queen of Hearts. He'd regained the sense of fun he lost after the Huntly affair.

They passed through Edinburgh's south gate to the tournament ground, a broad fenced-in meadow. Mary raised her hand in salutation to the throng of men, women, and screaming children straining against the fence. Others sat on mounds of dirt that had been piled up to afford spectators a better view of the field. Far off, away from the crowd, she noticed a youth and a girl lying in the honeysuckle, their arms entwined, faces hidden. Mary smiled, frowned, then smiled again.

She dismounted at a richly panoplied gallery with seats covered by carpets and yellow cushions. On the opposite side of the fenced-in area was a raised throne decked in heather and red roses. This would later be occupied by the woman the day's victor designated Queen of Hearts. Mary sat down, with Beaton on a small stool in front of her. James sat to her right, Lennox on her left. Neither man took notice of the other.

"Jug-jug," giggled Beaton.

The Lord Mayor rose to a wood podium and announced the first event: the caber-throw. The contestants, John among them, lined up in a row before Mary and bowed their heads. The crowd settled down. Mary raised her kerchief.

The jousting academy had been James's idea. He'd said, "Sports take a man's mind off the troubles, and make any woman, even a nagging woman, proud of the most worthless man." Today was a graduation of sorts for the academy.

Mary let her handkerchief flutter to the grass, then sat back in her chair and watched the games begin.

"It used to be the best way to get logs across streams," whispered James. "Watch how they balance in the legs. When I was a lad, I liked cabering."

"Thirty-three feet, six inches," said Mary. "And 'when I was a lad'! You're only thirty-four; I think you have a year or two left on earth." She poked him in the rib.

"We're missing it," he said, turning away, a mixture of embarrassment and pleasure playing about his face.

Four youths mounted the fifteen-foot caber in the first contestant's hands. "Now!" the man groaned. The boys ran to the fence and sat down. Slowly, the man moved across the green, broke into a run, leaped, and heaved the hundred-and-fifty-pound log into the air. The crowd applauded politely. A thin woman in a checkered dress jumped the fence and ran, arms outstretched, across the field. "That's my Somhairle," she cried happily. "My Somhairle! Somhairle, laddie boy of mine!" The man picked her up, threw her over his shoulder, and ran out the entrance gate.

"So-so," said James.

"Oh, excellent," laughed Beaton, clapping her hands. "Excellent man!"

"He'll fall down as soon as no one can see him," whispered Mary, "and then she'll have to carry him."

Beaton gave her a surprised, then a concerned, and finally an indifferent look. She returned her gaze to the field, and John.

"Twenty-eight feet, seven inches," announced the Mayor. A herald chalked the spot where the tip of the caber had landed.

The next contestant scored twenty-nine, eleven. Then a drunkard was shoved toward the starting mark and the log lodged in his hands. He looked unsteadily about him. "Say now," yelled someone from the fence. The crowd took up the cry. "Now," moaned the drunk. The youths scampered off. The man's neck muscles strained and swelled, and the log crashed down on his foot. Lord Mayor's score: Minus one half. Mary clapped her hands. Score: twenty-nine, nine. Score: thirty, one. Mary was positive John would win.

"Oh, look, look," Beaton cried as he cupped his hands to receive the caber. "Oh, there's a gallant head for you! John! Johnny!"

"Now!" yelled John.

"Very good," said James, smiling like a father.

The Lord Mayor mounted the podium and announced, "Thirty-two, five."

"Huzzah," screamed Beaton, jumping from her stool.

"There's another contestant," said Lennox, staring vacantly ahead.

"Pooh, it's won and done," snapped Beaton, "and my Johnny's won."

Lennox folded his hands and smiled vacantly.

A tall figure in homespun, with bright yellow hair, advanced to the starting mark. He took position, allowed the log to be settled in his hands, cried out, ran, lifted his arms, and loosed the caber to the sky. It bounced into the grass several feet ahead of John's chalk mark. The people who had been sitting on the piled turf stood and cheered.

"Thirty-four feet, nine inches."

The stranger raised his arm in a token of victory.

"Who is it?" Mary asked James.

"I don't know." He yelled down to one of the heralds, who shook his head. "Whoever," said James, "I haven't seen such a throw since . . . I never have. Never."

Beaton examined her fingernails.

"Courage, sweetheart," said Mary, rubbing the back of Beaton's neck. "This is only the first trial."

Beaton rested her head on Mary's lap.

John won the archery match with a bull's eye. The stranger was third.

The stranger won the hammer-throw. John was second.

The wrestling matches began. This was Scotland's favorite sport, and because of the large number of entries, the preliminaries had been held the previous day, reducing the number of contestants to ten. To Mary's relief, the tall stranger had not been one of them. Stripped to loincloths, greased bodies glistening in the sun, the contestants grappled, fell, rolled about and tried to strangle each other to death. Men have so much hair, Mary thought, especially on the legs, chest—some of them even have it on their backs. She wondered if Bothwell had it on his back. Chastelard hadn't. John's skin was smooth. Did Henry Stewart? Oh, those arms, legs, fronts and backs glistening in the sun! John won. But only barely.

The scores so far were: John: 39, the stranger: 37, someone else: 30. The jousting would determine the outcome. There was a ninety-minute rest period. Mary walked to a small tent where the Lord Mayor and his lady had prepared a small lunch for certain dignitaries.

Afterward, on her way back to the gallery, Mary saw James talking with a street woman. Mary was at first shocked, then she grinned to herself, slipped behind a canvas tent and made her way to a spot behind the crates of fireworks and powder James and the woman stood before.

"I know you know," James was saying. "You've been running

about telling everybody you know who he is, that he slept with you last night. Who is he?"

"A crown would be pleasant, my lord," said the woman. James looked at her as if she'd struck him.

"I said if you want to know, give me money."

Exasperated, James dipped into his purse and handed her a coin.

"Jesus' blessing on thee," laughed the woman. "He said his name was Creagan Sgairbh. They often have odd names when they visit Ainslie's."

"Who is he?"

"Creagan Sgairbh. Peter Pisspot, for what I know. *He* didn't know how to do anything. He pretended, but he didn't. He was almost crying. He was getting married, he said, and he'd give me six crowns if I taught him everything. The rest is one more crown, my lord."

"No."

The woman turned her head briefly in Mary's direction. If she'd worn less paint and looked less unhappy, she'd be pretty. Then she laughed maliciously and turned back to James. "He was nice, but, you see, he'd never done it before. I liked him. The next morning, old Lord Lennox made inquiries. He's an evil man. He asked me to describe the night in detail, but I said I didn't know what he meant, and he left angry." The woman's voice softened and she put her hand on James's arm. She said something Mary couldn't understand, then said, "But the way he was on the field today and the way he was last night, he might as well have been two separate people. Watch Lennox, my lord, please."

James stared at the woman, then suddenly fished through his purse and handed her another coin. "Is there anything else?"

The woman threw the coin into the dirt. "Yes," she said, "he had the biggest cock I've seen in my life; I think I even bled a little, it was so huge. And it felt good. And I didn't think about you once all the time it was crammed up inside of me. And *that* felt good!"

James turned to go. The woman reached out and pulled his sleeve. Then something happened which Mary could not believe.

James looked at the woman with loathing and disgust, then his face went blank and he looked down at the ground. A second later, his arms were around the woman's back and his face was half hidden in her hair. The woman was crying. Then James said something to her and she said something back. They kissed, and then they left, going in separate directions.

Craig-an-sgairb, Mary thought wildly to herself: that means the Cormorant's Rock. The war cry of the Stewarts. Who was that man? And James, in Jesus' name, what had happened to him? The woman was a whore. Hail Holy Queen Mother of Mercy Our Life Our Sweetness and Our . . . She wished she knew more about men and women, or more about whores. If Bothwell were here, she could ask him. Bothwell was outright. He told what he knew and said what he thought and admitted the things he believed, no matter what anybody else believed, knew, or thought. Bothwell was an honest, honest man.

She wondered if Beaton and John had done—it. Beaton had been wandering about lately with a glazed look in her eyes and a sly way of smiling, bumping into tables and chairs, singing to herself with her eyes closed, and suddenly laughing for no reason at all. They must have. At any rate, sooner or later they would. But it was only natural that sooner or later they would; they were in love. But they weren't married, and it was a sin. But sooner or later they would be married. It was confusing. François, Mary's first husband, was so young—sixteen when he died—and he'd rubbed up and down over her a few times, but that was all.

Of all the men she'd met, Bothwell was the one who must have had the most women. But he'd never had a child. Was that because he was committing a sin? That was asinine. At the French court, unmarried ladies were always having babies. Her father had committed sins. There were James and John: sins. Was it possible that James and that woman— It horrified Mary to think the thought, disgusted her. But the way they'd held each other—why, if they had, it couldn't have been lust; it couldn't have been anything but love. But James was pure; James was good.

Back in her gallery, Mary lifted her kerchief and watched it float to the ground. The trumpets sounded. The joust began. John won; the stranger won. John won; the stranger won. Three times each. The final time, they faced each other.

The two men resaddled on fresh mounts for the final contest and faced each other from the opposite ends of the lists. The galleries of the nobles, benches of the gentry, and heaped-up turf piles where the commoners sat were hushed. At the tourney's start, the yeomen had favored John. They knew him; he was likable; he was King Jamie's last bastard; and, most importantly, his performance suggested he'd spent long hours of hard and diligent preparation. But, at the same time, they admired the stranger because he seemed not to be working at all. The two opponents bent and took fresh shields and lances from their squires.

The cornets blared. Mary's handkerchief fluttered to the ground. The ground pounded with the sound of hoofs. There was a loud cracking noise, shattered fragments of wood flew into the sky, and the horses reared backward on their haunches. The spectators shouted out, waved scarves, and clapped hands. The two men got up and led their horses back to the end of the lists, saddled again, and waited for new lances.

The cornets blared. Mary's handkerchief fluttered to the ground. The horses sprang from their stations. John aimed at the center of his opponent's shield, made a hit, and sent the other man reeling in his saddle. The stranger struggled, regained his balance, and slowly rode back to the end of the field.

"Almost," said Beaton, catching her breath. "Three's the number." She crossed herself.

The cornets shrieked. Mary watched her kerchief go to the ground again, then leaned forward and grasped Beaton's hand. John struck the other's shield again—Mary winced at the flying sparks—but, in the last second, the stranger had aimed his lance high, at John's helmet. He scored a direct hit. John exploded from his horse.

Beaton stood and screamed, "No!"

The tall stranger leaped from his mount and ran to the spot

where John had been thrown. He bent, pulled off the cracked helmet, and unfastened the breastplate.

Mary swayed, reached out to grab hold of one of the streamers fastened to the canopy, and regained her balance. The streamer snapped and she fell against Lennox. Heralds and marshals scurried across the field.

John got unsteadily to his feet. Lennox sighed deeply. The victor took John's hand in his and lifted it high. The yeomen burst through the fence, hoisted the two men on their shoulders, and shouting and singing, carried them around the field. In the excitement, the stranger's helmet was dislodged and fell into the rush of heads. The sun streaked across his mane of bright yellow hair. He threw back his head, laughed, and cried, "Bratach Bhan nan Stiubhartach!" The pipers filled their sheepskins with air and played "The White Banner of the Stewarts."

Mary turned to James, but he was gone.

The yeomen circled the field once more, then brought the yellow-haired champion to the foot of Mary's gallery. He waved at Lennox, then smiled and blew Mary a kiss. "Eanruig Tearlach Stuibhartach," he announced, "at your service, most lovely of Queens." He pulled off his gloves, tossed them over his shoulder, and unfastened his arm irons and let them fall and clang against the heads of the men whose shoulders he straddled. "May I introduce my son, Your Majesty," said Lennox. "Henry Charles Stewart, Lord Darnley."

"But Elizabeth refused his visa—"

"My son," said Lennox.

"Where is it?" shouted Darnley impatiently. "I've come to crown the Queen of Hearts and where's the crown?" He yelled at the crowd, "Don't you want a Queen of Hearts?"

They cheered, yes!

The Lord Mayor took a spear and lifted the garland of daisies from its crimson cushion and stretched it down from the gallery to Darnley. He took the spear and slowly extended the garland toward Mary. She formed the word "no" with her lips and indicated, with a sidelong look, that she wished him to give it to Beaton. Darnley looked at his father Lennox, then back at Mary.

"I have a fair lady that I see," he said loudly, raising his free arm for silence, "and she is fairer than any lady here, save one. That one is a valiant theme of honor, good works, and brave deeds. But, good fellows, since that lady has a crown—of sorts—already, the other needs be served. But I'm not the man to do the honor." He leaned over and passed the spear to John. John rested his eyes on a few faces in the crowd, then blushed, took the spear, and presented the garland to Beaton. The yeomen huzzahed, stormed the gallery, and dragged Beaton onto their backs. Darnley smiled at Mary, then leaped to the ground and disappeared in the crash and sweep of color.

Mary sank back into her carpet-covered chair. She loved his outright smile. And yellow hair. Suddenly, the empty section of the field immediately in front of her seemed very, very green. Bright as fire. She blinked.

"Skag beastie, ye played me false," screeched Judy, legs akimbo. "Ye were the falsest knight that e'er bestrad horse!"

"Nay, m'heather," cackled Punch, "I plowed to satisfy yer monster, an' ye would have it so, heat-pony." The wooden puppet dropped to the little stage floor, its mitts drawn over its shiny black head. Judy banged her heels against his buttocks. The paper curtain jerked down.

"They'd never have had such words in public before you came to Scotland, Sister Mary," said John, imitating Punch's cackle.

"Queen of Hearts," said Mary, leaning against Beaton.

"Queen of Scots," said Beaton. "They almost rhyme."

Punch and Judy bowed to a quick flute finale.

"Ah, blithe," said John. "Blithe! Will ye serve me so when we're wed and bed, my lovely?" He kissed Beaton on the neck, then dug his fingers into her ribs. She doubled up, screaming with laughter. "Should I marry this witch?" he asked Mary.

"Why not?" she said, trying to sound cheerful. A few hours before, for a few seconds, she had thought he was dead. It was strange looking at him now, looking at him laugh and kiss Beaton on the neck.

128

"We'll marry as soon as you marry," said Beaton. "Not until. Where's the handsome hero?"

"I don't know," Mary said listlessly.

"Thank the Holy Apostles Peter and Paul and all the saints," said Beaton, "thank the Lord in heaven that Lord Darnley's not a thing like his father Lennox." She winked at John.

"What are you saying?" said Mary angrily.

"Nothing," said Beaton, taken aback.

"In general," said John. "Where's Davy? Or James? Or even Lennox, for that matter?"

"It would have made Davy sad," Mary said. "To sit and have to watch. To have to sit. Just watching. He plays tennis, but he tires so easily. If there were something I could do for him, I would do it. Davy has a handsome face; his body is not that bad, the hump itself is not large, but—" A burgess bumped into her, fell to his knees, and crawled hurriedly behind the puppet stand. Mary stared blankly at his shoes. A minute later, he leaped laughing into view, lifted a tankard to his mouth, and staggered off. Beaton pointed excitedly to the dunking booth and dragged John away. A group of kilted youths—she recognized one of them from the wrestling match—swayed past her, arms encircled and singing drunkenly:

"That, that; thair, thair,
Yallow hair, yallow hair,
Hippis bare, hippis bare,
Lang swak, lang swak—ly aback."

Mary hummed along in accompaniment. Brilliantly flamboyant fireworks drew rough pictures on the desolate sky. They were English fireworks, a gift from Elizabeth. Even Elizabeth had someone—Maitland had written that he had it on the best authority that she and Leicester slept together on New Year's night.

Mary walked about, smiling whenever anybody looked in her direction. Everybody looked and they looked and looked and mostly out of the corners of their eyes, but they never approached her and never said anything to her, even God be with thee. Suddenly, she wanted to be away from them all. She made her way to the secluded spot where she'd seen James and the woman talking.

"Yellow hair," she sang softly to herself. "That, thair, yellow, yellow hair." She rested her head against some wooden crates. He had beautiful yellow hair, like the sun. The genial, full pink curve of his lips—bright blue eyes, ruddy cheeks. Close, he looked country, innocent. Mary's spine froze and she jumped.

"Whoa, dear heart. I didn't mean to give you a start."

"You rhymed," she said slowly.

"A spur to poetry, as well as brave deeds," he said.

Mary shook her head and focused her eyes. "My lord, forgive me, I was dreaming. I imagined—"

"That I was part of the dream," said Lord Darnley. "I've done that lots of times." He offered her his arm.

They walked along looking at everybody looking at them. They stopped and watched the dancers dance. She was silent, because she was afraid if she said anything it would be stupid. He was wearing a peach-colored satin doublet lined with sarcenet, white hose, no belt.

"Dance with me," he said.

"The visa—Elizabeth refused to give you one. How—"

"Give Bess a rest. That *almost* rhymes. Now—dance with me."

"But how did you—"

"Very well," he said, rubbing his palms. "Bess shut me in the Tower. I met an acquaintance of yours there—Jimmy Bothwell."

"Bothwell!" Mary said, jerking up her head.

"The two of us were chained, scourged incessantly, nothing to eat but black bread and Châteauneuf du Pape. Eventually, we grew bored and decided to break our chains and fight down the guards. It took a nonce. That, despite the fact there were two hundred and fifty-eight thousand one hundred and forty-seven guards. We won. Bothwell went to Denmark and I came up here to visit Father. And now it's time to dance, Mary, Queen of Scots. And now we dance." Darnley put his hand on her waist and moved her into the dancing area. The other dancers moved slightly away and whispered to each other.

She didn't care; it had been so long since she'd enjoyed herself this much. But Bothwell—she couldn't keep that separate. It kept intruding. "Did you two really escape? Did he really go to Denmark?"

Darnley bent down and gave her a light kiss on the forehead. She moved away, and he pulled her back into his arms. He was tall, taller than she was, taller even than James. "I must confess," he said pleasantly, "that it's all a tale. I was never in the Tower, and neither was Bothwell. They merely confined him at Tynemouth Castle until his ship left for Denmark."

"Why did he go to Denmark?"

"Perhaps because it was far from England, far from Scotland. Do you know, I like the way you laugh, Queen of Scots. In London, you never hear an honest laugh. And you get so tired, after a while, of all those *great people* at the court! You start thinking nobody's left that's common any more." He stopped a minute and fanned his face with his hands. "Whoo, but it's hot; I'm hot. Do you like to fish?"

"No," said Mary. "Well, what I mean is, I never have."

"Good Lord," he said. "She's never gone fishing. Fishing's everything! Now, I am going to call you Mary. And you'll call me Harry."

"Harry," she said.

"Mary," he said.

Around and around. Everything blurred and blurring, except him, because she was dancing with him. It was madness, wonderful, and he said faster. He tightened his arms around her waist, bent backward, and her legs flew from the ground. The moon streaked the night sky yellow. Her head fell to her shoulder and she looked sideways above the rushing heads at the sky. Her shoes scraped the ground. Elizabeth flew a sieve across the restored circle of the moon.

"Mary, you ought to be up there. Hunting with Diana."

"I prefer Scotland," she said, and added, ". . . now." The coyness in her voice surprised her. "Whew, I'm blinded, can't see straight." She leaned against him. He put his arm over her shoulder and led her to a bench. Everybody was staring, but she was the Queen and would do as she pleased.

"No," she said softly. "If I sit down, I'll—"

He took her hand and led her through an opening in the fence and out into the meadow. Here and there, lovers whispered in the high grass.

"You can hear the sea breakers up here," said Harry.

"Yes, loud. Of course, it's impossible for you to return."

"Return?"

"To England."

"No, I suppose not," he sighed. He let go of her hand, picked up a stone, and hurled it at the moon.

"What will you do?" she asked.

"Stay here, if you allow it." He took her hand again. "Will you allow it?"

"There's no question," she said. "Stay."

He smiled beatifically.

"I *want* you to stay," she added.

He bent and brushed his lips over hers. "Thank you, dear heart."

She lowered her head. "I know what it is to be away from your home. And . . . after a time . . . even if you might go back to that place you left . . . it's senseless to think about it, but sometimes you will still think, I want to go home."

"Dance with me," he said cheerfully.

"Out here. In the grass."

"Diana won't mind," he said, taking her by the waist. "She doesn't exist."

"But she does," said Mary, going round.

"She doesn't."

"She does. I'm the Queen and say so, therefore she does exist."

"Doesn't!"

"Does! Does! Does!"

"She doesn't," he cried. "You do." Suddenly, he bent down and kissed her on the mouth. Around and round in the meadow under the moon.

"I love you," she said.

"Who?"

"You," she said. "You."

"What is my name?"

"Harry. Harry, Harry, Harry."

"Marry me," he said, pressing his lips against her eyelids.

"Yes, no, yes. It takes—we're cousins—a dispensation. Papers, Riccio would. A day. I don't know, I've only just—"

He put his hand over her mouth. "Shh," he said. "Hear the crickets?"

"So suddenly. Too sud—"

"Shhhh. Shh. There now. Listen to the crickets. They're merry tonight. Look at the moon. Beautiful. No, not at me, at the moon." He pressed his lips against her ear.

"You know nothing of me," she said.

"I do. From Maitland, Bothwell, everyone."

"Bothwell," she said, staring at him. "What did he say?"

"He quoted Ronsard. '*Ainsi qu'on voit demy-blanche et vermeille, naistre l'Aurore.*' He said you were dawn and the morning star; those are your colors. At the lists today, you were beautiful. You're twice as beautiful now. It's true. Have I made you angry?"

"You told me you loved me," she said, moving away. "Was that honest, my lord? So soon. How does one love someone they've only just met the first time? Love. At first meeting?"

"There are precedents," he said. "When I tell you that I love you, I mean only that I love you. I've no explanation. Perhaps tomorrow I will not love you. Perhaps—a hundred things. But I love you, Mary Stewart."

"If you loved me," said Mary, "you wouldn't have listened to a thing I've said; you would have taken me in your arms and kissed me again."

He stared at her.

"Well," she said, dropping her head. "If you . . . did love . . ."

He kissed her again.

"Madam," cried Beaton, "I can see you! It's time to go. You have thirty seconds."

Mary rested her hand against Harry's cheek and kissed him on the tip of the nose. They walked back to the tourney grounds. Tu-witta-woo. Hello, half-moon, you lemon slice!

"In the name of heaven, shut those curtains," Mary moaned from her bed.

"Sun is medicine for the skin," said Beaton, pulling open the other set. She walked to the bookcase, snatched a volume, and began flipping through the pages.

"Has anyone been here this morning?" said Mary, wiping the sleep from her eyes.

"Eat," said Beaton.

Mary stared at the eggs and pushed the breakfast table away. "Has anybody been to call?" she asked nonchalantly. She reached for her hairbrush. "Beaton, answer me!" Two days, Tuesday, Wednesday, two days and not one word from him.

"I found it," said Beaton, pulling a stool next to the bed. She read: "'Alas, said the Queen, where is that false knight become? Then the Queen was nigh out of her wit; and she writhed and weltered as a madwoman. She was nigh wood and out of her mind, and for anger and pain wist not what to do. She cried upon her Creator—'"

Mary slapped the book out of Beaton's hands. "That's more than enough from you," she snapped.

"Why, madam, you seem 'nigh wood.' Is it possible—"

"Close your mouth," said Mary.

"But here I've word of—"

"I warn you, Beaton."

"I've word of Lord Darnley!"

"What?" said Mary, climbing out of bed and upsetting the breakfast table.

"If you did not sleep till noon every day," laughed Beaton, "you'd be better disposed. Lord Darnley has measles. They didn't want to start an epidemic in town, so they moved him down here to Holyrood."

"They moved him here!"

"It was Davy's idea. Lord Darnley was staying at Ainslie's

Tavern and it's so noisy there, and you-know-what there. We've no available space here, but Davy put him in with John, and John will double with someone or other." She walked over to the fireplace, slapped her hand against a brick, and watched the wall open. "Shall we go, madam? The limanga goes to John's room, the Great Hall, and the back gardens. May I hazard a guess?"

"My kohl," said Mary. "And the Persian gown—the yellow one." She sat down at her dressing table, soaked her toothcloth in mulberry water, and rubbed her teeth. "They'll never be white," she cried. "And my skin. Too much sun—I'm as black as an Ethiopian." She snatched at her lip-paint vial, reconsidered, and let it drop to the floor. She pulled the tangles out of her hair, bit her lips until they were a rosy red, slapped her cheeks, rubbed a wet cloth down her throat and breast, and ran a stick of cinnamon wood across her tongue.

Beaton pulled Mary's chemise over her shoulders and went to the clothes chest in the antechamber.

Mary gazed at the reflection of her body in the steel mirror. Her breasts were large, perhaps too large, but—what was the word?—they were "globular." Neither high nor low. Waist: twenty-eight inches. A little too much flesh around the belly. Legs: good, dimpled, a bit long. A bit! Mary Stewart *in toto:* chestnut hair to the small of the back, round smooth shoulders, light blue eyes, high forehead, heart-shaped face, large breasts, long legs, five feet eleven and three fourths inches high. There, she'd said it. Before, she'd always said five feet ten. But Harry, he was—

"Stop admiring yourself," said Beaton. "Lift up now."

"Beaton, be honest. Am I—pleasant—to look at?"

"Such sheep eyes," said Beaton, tying Mary's stays. "You might lose a little thigh, but now that summer's here, we'll have sports, so no problem. You're too tall, which you know, but now that Lord Darnley's here, no problem with that, either. Don't look so sad; go downstairs and see the man."

"Is anybody—"

"Only Davy. There's a hole in the false wall that you can

peek through. I must warn you he might stink somewhat, but, then, he's just been taken out of the meat-pickling vat."

"Beaton?"

"What is it now?"

"Nothing. . . . Jug-jug, Beaton dear." She realized her hands were trembling.

Beaton ran across the room and embraced her. "We women," she sighed. "It happened to me, and now it is happening to you; and we all think we're the only one it's ever happened to. Godspeed, sweet lady."

The wall slid shut and Mary stood alone in the black.

She picked her way down the narrow, creaking stairs. Hello, Cardinal de Gouda, are you here? Still? He said he'd return. At the proper time. At this moment, he was probably sitting in a naked Italian drawing room. Waiting. She walked the remaining steps, fumbled along the clammy wall, found a lever, and pressed it sideways. A tiny square opened in the wall. Davy sat at a mahogany desk, writing. Darnley lay on the bed, tangled in a white sheet. She stepped back, slapped her cheeks, put her hands in front of her mouth, exhaled, and smelled her breath. Her heel caught on something and she almost lost her balance and fell down the musting continuation of stair. Reaching blindly for something to hold onto, she caught at the lever and pulled it down. The wall sighed open.

"Madam," said Riccio, getting up and pressing a finger over his lip, "he's sleeping. Shhh."

"Oh, Davy, is he well?"

Riccio smiled wisely, gathered his papers into his valise, and tiptoed to the door. When he was gone, Mary walked to the bed.

Wet ringlets circled the red-specked face. She sat down and wiped at his nose with her kerchief. He stirred, moistened his lips, and said, "Daddy?" She wiped the glaze off his forehead. "Daddy," he murmured, "I want home . . . tennis balls, ah, fish and water wet . . ."

"Harry," she said gently.

He turned on his side. Ah, Eanruig Tearlach, me . . . Shhhhh . . an' would marry me, Eanruig, Daddy . . . bark, bark . . .

mmmm, sun an' sky on 'em . . . an' marry mummy moon moo-
cow, tears, tearlach . . . Mary might . . ."

He looked like an angel-baby. She rubbed her little finger
against the back of his neck. Suddenly he sat up, looked around
the room, then fell back onto his pillow and closed his eyes
again. Mary smiled, soaked a linen cloth in the water bowl at
the foot of the bed, and placed it on his forehead. He jerked
his head to the side and the cloth slid onto his bare shoulder.
"Aughh," he cried, sitting up.

"Eanruig," said Mary, laughing. She poured him some water.

He hugged his knees to his chin and wrinkled his nose. "I'm
so dry," he moaned. "I've never been so dry." He indicated a
tankard on the table Riccio had been working at.

"Thank you," he said. "Boiled ale mixed with aristolochiaceae,
angelica, celandine, mithridate. Echh. But it's not bad, after it's
down." He squeezed his eyes shut and poured the chunky liquid
down his throat. He set the glass down and tousled her hair.

"You talk in your sleep," she said.

"Oh. What do I say?"

"You talked about fishing, tennis . . . the moon, your father."

He wiped at his eyes and lay back. "Could you open the
curtains a little?"

"No, it's not good for you. Later, if you like, I can come and
read to you."

He rested his hand on hers. "I'd like that, dear heart. Very
much."

She stood to go. "Perhaps I'll come back after supper."

"Excuse me," he said, smiling, "but the door is in the other
direction. Unless you walk through walls."

"I do," she laughed. "Observe." She pressed a brick by the
fireplace.

"Marvelous, beautiful witch!" she heard him call after her.

During the next week Mary read aloud from *Gargantua and
Pantragruel*. She, Harry, Davy, John, and Beaton played cards,
diced, told anecdotes, and exchanged dreams. Davy played his
harp and sang.

"Scotland's good," Mary said to Harry. "To see the fields on a summer morning . . . Edinburgh is not Paris, granted, but it's picturesque, a charming city. The people are not half as dour as they might seem at first glance. Don't stop, Davy, please go on."

"What you like," said Riccio. "One more song, and then I rest."

"I like every kind of music," said Harry. His spots were almost gone, but he was still weak. "More wine, dear heart. You said from Gascony."

"Yes," she said, handing him a silver goblet. "I like it best. Rhineland is much too light, almost tasteless. The ale they make in Scotland is better than any I've had. I never liked ale till I came to Scotland." She realized Harry had fallen asleep.

"I talk and talk," she said, turning to Riccio, "but I say nothing. Tonight we'll have lobster. Spitchcock eel and fallow-deer pastry. He'll like that."

She set the wine down and straightened the sheet over Harry's legs. He looked like a little boy. O you who dwell in gardens. She walked to the curtains and parted them slightly. He'd have to be gotten something lighter than these; they were too heavy, kept out the fresh air. Perhaps a lemon color. You couldn't see the city from this section of Holyrood. Fields of long grasses throbbed westward in the spring breeze. Farther down, east toward the sea, driftwood fences and crumbling stone walls were speckled with hopping wrens. He was hot and naked on top of her. Screaming like shriek owls, seagulls flew haphazardly from the sea. Blood churning, breasts pressed flat under his chest, his hands sprawling alongside her engorged, grinding hips. O you that dwell in gardens.

"No marriage is more to Your Majesty's interest than this," Riccio was saying. "It is ideal. However, because of the fact that it is ideal, there will be difficulties. Number one, the Queen of England must be appeased. She's been made a fool of, so I would suggest a small concession on some minor matter. Number two, we'll need assurances of support from Philip of Spain in the eventuality of civil disturbances. Number three, because of your kinship with Lord Darnley, I've taken the liberty of sending a letter in your name to the Pope, requesting a dispensation. Number four, and most important—"

She walked back to the bed and looked at Harry's face. He was the most beautiful man she had ever seen.

"Lord James is a special problem. Until now, you've been Queen and he's been somewhat more than head of the Privy Council. A King will change that. The change, I think, will not be pleasant."

"Regardless of truth," said James, pacing back and forth across the empty Council chamber, "the Italian is suspected of being the Pope's pensioner. You say you grant him favors and positions of influence because he is a brilliant man. That is true. But what was such a brilliant man doing as bass singer in a small orchestra?"

"Waiting for someone like myself, perhaps, to recognize his brilliance."

"The Italian forwards Darnley because Darnley's Catholic. The Italian dreams of a Roman restoration."

"It isn't true," said Mary. "I've given you my word."

"What people say," said James, "is often more important than what is true. Because people act on what they think, and not on what they don't know."

"You sound like Maitland," said Mary sarcastically.

"The Italian puts on insufferable airs. He's arrogant, impossible, dangerous. He is a foreigner, and you have entrusted him with the most important matters of state. Everyone in Scotland is turned against him."

"No more, James."

"You're mad," he said, ignoring her. "Mad over that popinjay Darnley. With your usual disregard for consequences, you are presently—"

"I've had enough!" she said, suddenly losing her temper.

"—presently destroying everything I've worked for. You cannot marry Darnley, and that's an end to it."

"Damn you," she screamed, "you bas—"

His mouth dropped open and he stared at her. Then he left the room.

Elizabeth wrote:

> . . . as Lennox and Darnley are my subjects, father and son, they are commanded to return postehaste into this realm. If not in London by Wed. the 18th of this month, all estates, lands, revenues will be deemed forefeit to the Crown. A marriage with this man is deemed unfit, unprofitable, and perilous to any amity between my realm and yours.

Mary threw the letter on the floor and looked at Riccio. "What shall I do?" she asked.

"Marry Darnley," he said.

Later in the day she asked Harry what his opinion of the letter was.

He said he needed a bath.

Outside, the sky was calm, lovely. Mary watched the green wheat fields in the north, and the blending of the sun with them.

"Be my wife, dear heart."

She felt she could move her hand through the glass, out across the wheat field, and over the wrens and seagulls, farther than the drifthood fences. She felt she could catch the sun and balance it in her palm.

"Yes," she said.

In Aberdeen, a cow gave birth to fifteen dog whelps, then went mad. A man in Glasgow had been found guilty of murdering his father and his mother. An Arbroath farmer accidentally killed his son with his plow, then hanged himself. Last week a dragon, two and a half miles long, flew back and forth over the Shetland Islands for half a day.

"Today is the seventeenth," said James.

"Why do they send me such things?" said Mary, dropping the dispatches onto the table. "They're ridiculous. Dragons!"

"If it is possible for a man to kill his mother and father," said James, "or for a man, even accidentally, to kill his own son, then it is, I think, entirely within the realm of possibility for a dragon—two miles long—to fly over the Shetland Islands."

"Tell me what you think of this," said Mary. She picked up a sheet of linen paper and read: *I am truly amazed at my good cousin's dissatisfaction at a choice made in accordance with her express wishes. I have rejected all foreign princes, and have found in the person of Lord Darnley an Englishman who is of the blood royal of both kingdoms, and is, as far as England is concerned, on his mother's side, the eldest male descendant of the House of Tudor.*

"You can't mean to send that," said James.

"I already have. This is a copy."

"You're a fool."

"James," she said, "I'm a woman. I love him."

"Love is madness."

"Would you have me marry Elizabeth's horsekeeper?" she said, getting up and standing in front of him.

He shook his head.

"Or Don Carlos? Or the King of Sweden? Or—who else is there? I can't marry you. There's no one."

"But not Darnley," said James.

"There's only Darnley," she said, pressing his hand. "Why won't you be happy for me, brother?"

"He's not a man," said James. "You're more a woman than he's a man. This isn't love you feel; it's infatuation."

"If only Elizabeth were a man," sighed Mary, "then I could marry her and there'd be no problems."

"If only you weren't a woman. Sister, I shall oppose this marriage."

"Fact is not reflection," she said hotly. "It's more real; it can't be seen!"

"And what does that mean?"

She shook her head. "I don't know. I just . . . don't. But,

I warn you, James, I will brook no opposition from you in this matter. That is all. You may go."

Tick-tock-tick, and the honeysuckle blossoming from the red Chinese vase on her dressing table. Everybody who commits sin is guilty of lawlessness. The round Antwerp clock Harry had given her chimed twelve midnight. Is love a sin? Mary read the creased note again:

Love crowns and pageants us—but Love can be the sharpest deepest pain—when, skill-less as a baby, it hopes an act, ventures a posture, attempts a move. Dear heart, come to me tonight.—Harry.

Is love a sin? Can rhubarb and senna, penance and prayer, morning and evening . . . Bone of my bone, flesh . . . and they *knew* one another. Tick-tock-tick. Mary saw herself suspended in the round watery scape of the Antwerp clock. Is love a sin?

The source, purchase, and distillation of love, the benefit, issue, and common sense of love is a more glorious work of God than His creation of the entire material universe. Love is what we have in *us,* and us as good as God. Because He loved us first. Mary buried her face in the honeysuckle and breathed deeply. And honest love can never die. She brushed her hair and slipped into a robe of pink cobweb.

Mary descended down the pitchy limanga. Cardinal de Gouda hung upside down from the ceiling, flapping his musty wings in disapproval.

Harry was sitting in a cushion chair looking out the lattice window, his feet propped on the sill. He turned when he heard her enter.

She moved into the half-light, unfastened her robe, and let it fall to the floor. After a minute Harry stood up, drew his nightshirt over his head, and dropped it on the chair. She reveled in him: shadow of the eyes, shadow of the mouth, chin, throat, broad expanse of shoulders and chest, swelling of the muscles of the upper arm, silhouette of slim hips, long legs.

"Dear heart," he said, his right hand on the back of her neck, his left hand on her waist.

Shaking uncontrollably, she lay back on the satin pillowcase and wrapped her arms around his back. His finger caressed the cleft of swollen flesh beneath her belly, then gently drew aside its moist lips. "I love you," she whispered. She felt herself open, stretch, fill. Harry drove, flat on top of her.

"Let me go," she moaned. "You hurt me; it hurt." She wiped her eyes and attempted to stand.

He rubbed her belly and brushed his tongue lightly across her lips.

"I'm afraid, afraid," she said.

"Lie back, Mary. Help me. I love you. Lie back."

Ly abak, ly abak, lang swak, yellow, yellow hair. As he moved over her, she opened her eyes and stared past his chest and down toward his legs. "Oh, God, no," she cried, "it can't, won't—too—no—it's so—"

He knelt, rested his hands on her hips, and spread her knees with his elbows. "Dear heart, relax . . . reach down and make friends . . . there . . . there . . . it's only part of me . . . oh, that! Hold onto my shoulders now . . . hold tight . . . put it . . . there. . . . Shhhh. Now slowly . . . you do it . . . Slowly. Shhh. It always hurts the first time, it always hurts."

She bit down on her lip to keep from screaming, and dug her nails into his shoulders. Gar me greet, amhuinn na naither. Fhir, fhir tun, Stuibhartears, as her hands moved about his neck, arms, back. Mairi, mara, muir, mhara, marina, mary, mer. He stretched his weight full across her and began moving his hips.

Ah, I love, ah, Eanruig, uh, belly, yes, hands moving, air on air, oh. Eanruig na Mairi. Light. Like a leaf. Amhuinn.

I'm not lonely now.

"Tell him I *beseech* him to come," said Mary.

"He won't," said John. "Sister Mary, the archbishop's waiting."

The bridegroom is waiting. Everybody's waiting. Don't let James spoil it."

"He was to have presented me. How can he do this? How can he! Tell him I command him to come." She picked up her white lacework skirts and started for the door. "Where is he now?"

"He's invisible," said Riccio. "Madam," he said softly, "this is not only your happiest day. It is the happiest day for all of us." Tears rolled down his cheeks as he took her hand and kissed it.

Weeping, Mary hugged him. "Davy, Davy, I love you. And you, dear John. And Beaton, oh, Beaton, it *is* the happiest day." She smiled. "I love you all. My friends . . ."

"Madam," cried Beaton, untangling Mary's train, "the ceremony!"

Mary watched the play of stained-glass shadows on the face of the alabaster Jesus of Prague. *"Dominus vobiscum,"* intoned Archbishop Hamilton. *"Et cum spiritu tuo,"* she murmured. She glanced up as Harry knelt beside her. The archbishop raised the jeweled chalice.

Husbands, love your wives. Wives, honor your husbands. This is a great mystery.

"Te Deum laudamus," Riccio cried out. "It is done and cannot now be undone!"

Mary and Harry stood on top the sun-drenched palace steps. The people who thronged the courtyard yelled their approval: "God bless, long live, King and Queen!" Women stood on tiptoes, straining for a look.

"I shall be leal and true to my Princess," Harry proclaimed, "honest and honorable in all things to my Sovereign Lady, Queen, by God's grace, of all Scotland and the Isles, Queen, by God's grace and right of birth, of all England and Ireland. I shall be husband, fellow, and humble servant. I shall never fly from my Princess in time of danger or of need." He turned to Mary and whispered, "And I will love her, and love her, until I die."

James had left a note: *What is a Prince without a people?*

CHAPTER EIGHT

Three weeks since the marriage.

Tu-witt. Tu-witt.

Not yet.

James leaned against a peeling oak and bit his thumb. Above, a solitary cloud rushed across the sky and disappeared beyond the brooding hills in the distance. What was taking them so long? He watched a squirrel dart across the winding forest path below. This was dangerous business. But it was Mary's doing, not his. James turned and regarded the oaks and maples crowding the steep incline behind him. Even he couldn't see his men. Five hundred would be more than enough—for now. The Queen of England promised ammunition, more men, as soon as the plan was carried out. When Henry Stewart, Lord Darnley, and his father Lennox were safe in English hands. When Riccio—who James was certain was a papal agent—was gotten rid of. When Mary had been brought to a realization. How could she have done it! How could she make all this trouble! Hadn't the lesson of Huntly been enough? She'd told James she hated De Gouda, hated everything he stood for, everything he wanted. Mary wasn't a fool. She must have known that Darnley and Riccio wanted the same thing as De Gouda. But Riccio was witty and smooth, and Darnley was—lust, sensual lust. Presbyterianism, Presbyterianism, Presbyterianism—what was it? It was hateful because it was true. God was hateful, but He was true. The Presbyterian religion was—what had Knox called it?—democracy, yes. *Tuwitt.*

Did he hear laughter down below, close by, beyond the curve of avocado-colored leaves and birds singing? No.

Though waters roaring make, we will not be afraid.

James looked at his fingers. Bitten to the bone. And his hand —he could feel the cold skin that covered it, the blood, meat, bone inside it. Mary had called him Bastard. She married in a marriage blessed with Rome's blessing, even though it had taken place before the papal dispensation arrived; and Rome was home again. In Scotland. He wouldn't have that. He remembered the blood. Blood, blood, blood. Oh, Annabel. It's been a week since I was with you last, but it seems a longer time than that. God, give me the strength to see this through. You always did before. And I was always all nerves before. And I always won before. I drove out Marie de Guise time and again. I drove out the French when they came. James heard horses' hoofs coming along the forest path, stepped behind the oak, and raised his hand to the men concealed behind him.

Pooh-wee, Pooh-wee, whistled a sentry.

Damn, thought James. We'd be dead, buried, and gone if we depended on such as him.

"The Queen is coming! Coming!"

The voice came from the path below, not from the trees above. James dug his fingers into the oak.

"The Queen is coming! The King and Queen are coming with eight hundred horsemen!"

James's men dropped like pine cones from the trees, scrambled to their feet, and scurried up the incline.

"Mount!" James shouted. "We double round to Edinburgh and sound a call to arms."

"For Scotland's sake," he cried from beside the Merkat Cross to the press of people that filled the square.

They stared at him. A few cried out "Long live" and "To arms," but most simply shuffled about and stared uncomprehendingly at him. Then someone hollered, "God save the Queen!" Almost everyone cheered.

James yelled passionately, "You know me, and I know you. You followed me not so long past, when we beat the French into the sea, beat Pope Pius back to Rome. Are you blind to let—"

"That was years ago," cried a woman. "Before the Queen came. She'd have led us had she been here." There were cries of approval.

James wiped the glaze from his forehead. Were they insane? "For true religion's sake," he yelled.

"The Queen lets us have our religion," spoke someone near him. The voice belonged to a man in a cobbler's apron. He looked at James, then dropped his eyes. The woman next to the cobbler sighed and clicked her tongue. There was a sudden shrieking.

James's eyes widened and he stared straight ahead in stark amazement as Bothwell, sitting on a brown mare at the edge of the square, lowered the trumpet he'd just blown, nodded his head, and raised his hand for quiet.

"I've a message for Sir Golden Tongue," Bothwell announced loudly. "A message from his liege lord the Queen." He unrolled a scroll of parchment. " 'You are not satisfied,' " he read, " 'to heap wealth upon wealth, honor upon honors; you want to have ourselves and our kingdom altogether in your hands that you may deal with them as you will, and compel them to act wholly in accordance with your desire. In a word, you want to be King yourself, and leave us with nothing but the title of nominal ruler of this kingdom.' " Bothwell leaned from his horse, took a nail from his doublet, and hammered the parchment into the crevice of a brick wall with his fist. He straightened himself, faced James, and said slowly, "A bastard cannot be a King. A bastard may not rule."

A pistol crack rang out, there was a stunned silence, another crack, and Bothwell slumped in his saddle.

"Who fired that?" cried James. "Who fired that?" His words were lost in the screams and shouts and clatter of running feet.

A fisher-wife wrenched the reins out of his hands, and a crowd of youths grabbed at his clothing and tried to pull him from his horse. James struggled to unsheath his broadsword. Someone yelled, "Edinburgh Castle's trained her cannon on us!" James lifted the broadsword and crashed it down onto the heads beneath him. He fought his way clear and drew his horse beneath the balcony of Ainslie's and looked back at the square. Was Bothwell dead? He saw one of his lieutenants shooting blindly into the crowd. Spears glinted in the sunlight, the skirmishing in the square grew hotter, and men were fighting hand to hand. An explosion rocked the square and there was a sudden silence. "The castle!" someone cried. "The castle's cannoneering!" Fire erupted in several businesses. James heard someone scream out his name, turned, and looked above his head.

Annabel leaned over the balcony and threw down a rope she'd affixed to her window railing. "I've a horse in the wynd," she yelled. "Hurry. The sheriff's men are barricading the streets."

James caught hold of the rope. There was another explosion, a sudden flash of red, a scream, and the sound of cracking wood and stone. James was hurled into the middle of the street. James crawled back toward the flaming ruins of the tavern.

He opened his eyes. Dusk. He realized he was still clutching the torn rope. White-robed nurses with medical cases and pallets were moving wraithlike along the High Street, stooping over inert forms, and either dropping to their knees or moving on. James searched through the charred tavern, found nothing, looked about helplessly for a minute, then made his way to the wynd. The horse was, miraculously, still there.

James whipped his horse across the plains leading down from Edinburgh. He clattered through Sandelbraigh-on-Zester at one in the morning, tied his horse in front of a fisher's hovel, cut loose a skiff, and poled his way across the river to Foulaway. He found another mount outside one of the scattered shacks there, laid a crown on the entrance stoop, and set out for Tratores. Tratores at three-thirty. Dingstrath at four. Twenty miles to Berwick on the English border. He slept in the woods.

He awoke at sunset, foraged for berries and mushrooms, ate,

and remounted. He crossed the Tweed River and arrived in Berwick at four in the morning.

"Decent folk are abed this hour," said the proprietor of the Harry Bluff Inn. He led James upstairs and into a small room. "The pet's under the bed," he said, setting the candle on a table. "The ladies are asleep now; perhaps you would like one in the morning? That will be one pound, sir."

"No ladies," said James, handing the man a pound. He lay back on the soft bed.

James woke up, raised his hands to shield his eyes from the sunlight streaming across his face, blinked, opened his eyes full, and watched the club come cracking down on his skull.

James woke up, raised his hands to shield his eyes from the barred sunlight, blinked, and sat up on a bed of matted rushes. He looked at the dirt-gray walls around him.

A clean-shaven young man in a red and yellow uniform unlocked the door and entered the cell. "It is good to see that you have finally risen," said the young man. "What would you like for breakfast, sir? Or would you prefer to bathe first?"

"Where am I?" said James.

The young man laughed. "Why, sir, this is the Tower of London."

"Impossible," said James. "I just . . . just . . . but Berwick—two days up—"

"You were recognized and seized at Berwick," the youth said amicably. "You have been unconscious for a few days. You are being held in protective custody. At the moment no complaint has been officially lodged. Perhaps we may talk as you breakfast. Excuse me, sir; my manners are intolerable. I am Captain Edward Drake. I am the captain of the Tower. I can assure you that there is nothing to fear. There shall be no foul play. We are a civilized nation."

"Very civilized," said James, rubbing his forehead.

"That was most unfortunate, sir," said the captain. "However, the farther south one travels in this kingdom, the more civilized one's circumstances, pleasures, acquaintances."

"Therefore," said James, "as Wales is farther south than London, Wales is more civilized than London."

"Oh, sir, you are too quick for me. Allow me to order you breakfast. Or do you wish to bathe?"

"Food," said James. "Food.

"I want some more," said James, scraping the egg yellow off his plate with a piece of bread.

"Well, that is very irregular, sir," said the young captain, "but it does, I am happy to report, fall within the realm of those irregularities we are permitted to commit. Since you are a privileged prisoner—"

"And what is a 'privileged prisoner'?" said James.

"A privileged prisoner is a gentleman—never, never, I might add, a lady—in whom the Queen takes great interest."

At that moment James hated Elizabeth more than anyone he had ever hated in his life. More than even Bothwell. Bothwell had ruined his plans, had defeated him, but Elizabeth had done something worse. She had used him. She had cajoled him with promises, provided him with information on Darnley and Riccio, sent him copies of letters damning to the Italian—letters to the Vatican. She had urged him forward in his rebellion against his sister and her papist consort, assuring him of its success. And now, having lost, he was clapped tight in her Tower. So as not to be an embarrassment. And there was another reason that he hated her. Don't deny, he thought, what God knows. Elizabeth was a bastard. Elizabeth wore a crown.

When the captain was gone, James rested his arms on the stone pane of his cell window and looked down into London. A vast concourse of merchant ships from France, Spain, Amsterdam, Germany, Sweden-Denmark, Africa, India, and America lay at anchor in the peaceful blue and gold boulevard of the Thames. He shifted his eyes to the west and royal city of Westminster. Queen Elizabeth's palace sat under a glare of afternoon sun, surrounded by massively built rich brick mansions, the houses of what writers from other land like to call "the new nobility"—amalgam of lawyers' sons, merchants' and churchmen's sons, King's mistresses' sons, the sons of the butcher, the baker, the candlestick maker. James liked the water gates and landing stairs. They looked nice against the Thames. Farther down sat the royal palaces of Whitehall, Greenwich, Richmond, and Hamp-

ton Court. What we've got in Scotland is the Firth of Forth
and two hundred thousand peasant shacks and sheep grazing,
corn, peat, cattle, ghosts, and the Presbyterian religion. How
could my country live or survive if this country got up an army
and went north with it? Then James thought: But we've fought a
thousand wars with England, and they never won, not once, not
with all the trade and munitions and arrogant pride. Not once.
There's no land on earth as wild and big as Scotland! Suddenly, it
was nightfall.

"Supper, sir," said Captain Drake. "And candy apples for
dessert. I've also taken the liberty of bringing you some books."

Day after day. Night after night. James read Tottell's *Mis-
cellany,* Caesar's *Commentaries,* and Thomas More. Sometimes
he would play cards with Captain Drake. He learned that Drake
had been in the employ of the Lennox family—his family had
been their retainers for years—and that Lady Lennox used her
influence with the Queen, who was her cousin, to get Drake
named captain of the Tower. Since Darnley's marriage to Mary,
however, Lady Lennox and the Queen were at odds. Drake felt
he soon would lose his position. It was only a matter of time, he
explained, before Lady Lennox ended in the Tower. James asked
him what he planned to do. "I believe, sir, that I should like to
travel to America," he said. "Or perhaps to Muscovy. There is
an expedition planned. But one never knows, does one, sir?"

A few nights later, as James lay on his bed, he heard Captain
Drake's voice at his cell door. "I shall miss you very much,
sir," said the voice. It was the first hint of genuine feeling James
had ever heard in him. It made him feel good, but he didn't
answer. Instead, he yawned, rolled over on his side, and fell
asleep.

The next day Drake was gone.

James stood at his window gazing at the forest beyond London's
north wall. The leaves were turning red, yellow, brown. He
looked down at the Thames. There was some sort of festive day
in progress. He watched the gaily painted barges splashing down
the river. Cornets blasted, scattering the thousands of swans
swimming in the wakes. Citizens cheered wildly from the banks.
Then he saw the Queen of England. She wore a cloak of black-

silver tinsel and emerald plush, a mantle of gold and orange taffeta folded across her lap. Her hair was bright red. The royal barge pulled alongside St. Edward's wharf, almost directly beneath James's cell window. Down below, the crowd roared and showered the boat with flowers and colored spangles. Elizabeth stood and said something to the crowd, but James was too high to hear anything but the cheering. The barge pulled away from the wharf and Elizabeth sat down next to a dark-complected man. James guessed that it was Robert Dudley.

Elizabeth suddenly rose again, shielded her eyes from the glare, and looked up at the cell window. Involuntarily, James moved back into the shadows. When he looked out again, the barge had resumed its journey.

England was Elizabeth, he thought. Scotland was . . . ghosts in the night.

A day and another day. More nights. Weeks and months of days and nights.

CHAPTER NINE

And God said. And God said. Bothwell was alive. Mary was glad. *Let there be a firmament in the midst of the waters. Let there be a firmament in the midst of the waters.* It was amazing the way he'd recovered from the wounds he'd received during James's revolt. He'd been in bed three days, then he was up and walking about again. Mary had asked him to stay in the capitol and join in the celebration with her and Harry, but Bothwell said no, his lands needed tending. During his exile, they'd gone halfway to ruin. *The waters from the waters. The waters from the waters.* He'd returned to Edinburgh the week before. They were talking in the council chamber when he collapsed. Mary's physician, Dr. Lusgerie, said it was part infection of the bullet wounds which Bothwell hadn't cared for, and part acute dysentery. Mary stared at the sleeping man. *And then there was morning and evening, and a second day.*

The midmorning small-bell of the chapel school next door ting-a-linged. Fifteen minutes, young gentlemen, then the generations of Noah. And our grammar work.

But they have no Latin! thought Mary. No myths, rhetoric, hardly any history at all. Just nouns, verbs, psalms, hosannas,

Enoch, Amos, Methuselah, Lamech, Jabel, Jubal. She heard horses in the High Street and got up and looked out the window. It was Harry. She walked back to the bed, hesitated, then touched Bothwell on the shoulder. "Bothwell, wake up. Wake up." The walls were so unbearably thin. Couldn't the chapel masters simply sound the bell once to announce the midmorning recess, and then once again to announce its end? Instead of letting it scream—yes, scream—incessantly for the full fifteen minutes. Bothwell sat up against his pillows and stared uncomprehendingly into her face.

"Good God," said Harry, slouching onto a chair in the corner of the room. "Mary tells me you're the bravest man in the country, and all you do is sleep. Well, Jimmy, nice to see you."

"Don't pay attention," said Mary. "He's jealous. For a time, Dr. Lusgerie didn't think you'd live, but I told him you were the Earl of Bothwell, and he said, 'In that case death is no consideration.' I brought you some apricots, probably the last of the season."

"Excuse," mumbled Bothwell. "It's hard to concentrate. The doctor saved my life, but my stomach is gone for good with that—what is it?—celandine liquid . . . foul . . ."

"I think he's asleep again," said Mary. "Look at his face, Harry. Have you ever seen a face like his?" He'd appeared out of nowhere, equipped with information of James's plans which he'd stolen from nowhere. He'd saved her crown for her, just as he'd probably saved her life that time on the sea when the pirates attacked her ship on its journey to Scotland. But he'd changed. During his brief stay in Edinburgh, she realized that Bothwell had somehow matured, grown less reckless, more reserved. Except when joking, every word he said seemed carefully thought out, cautious, measured. He did not seem sure of himself any more. And he seemed incapable of looking her, or anyone for that matter, in the eye. It was as if he had done something terrible and black, and he was ashamed of it.

"I've just the remedy to wake him," said Harry, getting to his feet and walking to Mary's side.

"It's too early. Let him sleep."

Harry bent and pulled Bothwell upright against the bedstead. "Sit up and be a man now," he laughed. "This will make you feel like ten men." He drew a flask from his doublet and held it up to Bothwell's mouth.

"Can't," said Bothwell deliriously.

"Nonsense," said Harry. "There we are. Now we look fine. I'm afraid I spilled a little." He handed Bothwell the flask.

Bothwell nodded and took another sip.

"It's too early," said Mary.

"No, it isn't," said Harry. "Have some?"

"No," she said, turning her attention to Bothwell. "You're alive," she said happily. "Alive."

Harry unstrapped his mandolin, sat cross-legged on the floor, and started singing "Lord Randal."

He's drunk again, thought Mary. Drunk. At midmorning recess. *The King of Scotland is polluted,* recited a heavenly assemblage of choir children. *The King of Scotland is polluted.* She squeezed Bothwell's hand and said, "Davy's decided—"

"Davy, Davy, Davy," said Harry angrily. "I get tired of hearing his name. I know you like him, and I know he's a nice clever humpback dwarf that sings better than I do and advises you on matters of state—also more than I do—but I get sick of him, of hearing you go on about him constantly to anybody who's willing to listen."

"David has served me well. His advice is honest and impartial, and he understands Scotland better, I sometimes think, than those who have lived all their lives here, fighting with each other the whole time. Besides," she added, "he beat you at tennis yesterday."

"What's that got to do with it?" said Harry. He strummed his mandolin. "Besides, he cheats."

"He did not!" said Mary. "You did! I saw you. You cheated and still he beat you."

"What's wrong with you?" he said, banging the mandolin onto the floor. "You have to see, know, and say everything." He uncorked the flask. "Do you want some more?" he asked Bothwell.

Bothwell shook his head.

"But it'll drown out the taste of all that awful celandine inside you. When I had the measles I had to take—I can't even pronounce the name—but it was awful. This always helped. *Aqua vitae.*" He walked to the bed. "Here, Jimmy, open up."

"Uhmmm, good," Bothwell muttered. He wiped his mouth. Harry lay his arm across Bothwell's shoulder. "As soon as you're better, we go fishing. Fishing's the only decent thing there is about this Godforsaken country."

There was a knock on the door, and John Stewart entered the room. "Jimmy Bothwell," he said, advancing to the bed, "I'd heard somewhere that you still existed. In one form or another." He grasped Bothwell's hand and plopped down on the mattress.

"He's acting properly indifferent," said Mary, taking out her embroidery and laying it across her lap. "But he came to see you every day."

"Sorry," Bothwell said. "My mind's all over. I can't remember it."

"You were always asleep," said John affectionately. "Tossing and turning, sweating and snorting about—"

"John would rush in," said Mary, "and he'd moan and say, 'He was so pale today,' or 'His pulse was so weak today,' or—"

Harry cut in, "Do you remember, Mary, we were at Privy Council that one time and John came in—"

Mary laughed. "John came in, face white, limbs shaking like palsy, and cried, 'Sister Mary, Sister Mary, he went and pissed his sheets today.'"

Harry smiled and gave her a buss on the cheek.

"I love you," she said fiercely, as if there wasn't anybody else in the room.

"Enough, enough," said Bothwell. He forced a smile. "I love, honor, and respect both Your Majesties, but if you . . . you're shaking the bed, and my stomach—"

John jumped from the bed. "He's threatening to do dysentery on us, Bothwell is," he cried.

"Naughty man," said Mary, threatening Bothwell with her needle. "You have to have all the attention. Just like Harry." She drew her fingers through her husband's yellow hair. "Who can I trust?" she suddenly said. "There's you, Harry, and then there's John, and Beaton, and Bothwell, and there's Davy."

"I understand everything," Harry said affectionately. He stood up. "Well, I'm off. The fish won't wait all day. Come, Johnny."

"Husband, stay a little longer."

"Impossible," he laughed. " 'By, dear heart, give us a kiss and send us on our way."

After they'd left, Mary sat next to the bed silently plying her needle.

"Your brother," said Bothwell. "What's happened to—"

"John? Nothing. He's gained weight. I'm afraid he's losing interest in Beaton, but I don't really know. Otherwise, he's the same as the last time you saw him."

"Not John. The other one. Your brother James."

"John is now my only brother."

He was quiet a minute. "May I?" he said finally, reaching over and lifting the heavy fabric from her lap. *"En ma fin est mon—* It's incomplete."

"Commencement," she said.

"In my end is my beginning. That's strange."

"Yes," she said icily. "Isn't it?" She pulled the embroidery from his hand, rolled it up, and thrust it into her bag. *After the flood, Noah lived three hundred and fifty years. All the days of Noah were nine hundred and fifty years; and he died.*

"It was good fishing today," said Harry, pulling off his shirt. He threw his boots and trunk hose onto a cushion chair and blew out the candle. "Ah, here we are," he sighed, sliding under the sheets next to her. He stretched and kissed her on the cheek. "Good night, dear heart." He turned on his side, away from her.

"Don't sleep," she whispered.

"It was a long day," he yawned. "Pleasant dreams."

"I love you," she said.

"Me, too."

She snuggled behind him and rested her hand on his hip. "Harry?"

"Is that all you ever think about?" he said angrily. "I said I was tired." He lowered his voice. "I'm sorry; forgive me. But I'm exhausted. I couldn't. Tomorrow."

"You're beautiful," she said. She licked the back of his neck. "Every part of you is beautiful. Oh, that's good. I love you."

"What am I?" he said furiously. "What do you want of me? Stop it! It's all you ever think about. You'd think you were the one with the prick, and not me. Mary of Scots—with a prick three feet long—to beat us over the head with when we're bad." He climbed out of bed. "I'm going downstairs to sleep with Johnny. Then maybe I'll have peace."

She heard the secret passageway slide open and close, and the sound of bare feet slapping down the hidden stairs. The Antwerp clock chimed twelve. She waited for him to come back.

The clock struck one. Mary opened her eyes, sat up, and ran her hands along the icy sheets. It was her fault. Harry was young, very young, only twenty, three years younger than she. It was Scotland; he wasn't used to her. She hated Scotland. Drawing on a gossamer nightdress, Mary pressed her fist against the brick and ran down the limanga.

"Here, there, rest here," she heard John whispering. "I know she loves you. Kings and queens don't usually love. Is her loving such a tragedy?"

Wonderful John. Mary sank down on one of the steps and pressed her ear against the false door.

". . . be like other wives? Then we could be friends."

"You must love her . . . a little," said John. "I know you must."

"I do. It's impossible not to. She's got so much spirit; she's so completely human. But she holds on too tightly; she's grasping, grabbing, always grabbing. My mother and father told me everything, but they didn't tell me she was like that. My mother and father are amazing people: they—"

"Why do you drink all the time?" said John. "Put it away."

Mary heard something hit the floor.

"They're amazing. Thank Daddy for Harry's prick and Mother for his golden hair. She's mad because her hair got dark—maybe mine will, as well—but hers was dark very young. And I remember taking the baths with Daddy once and I was bigger than even him. But he kept looking at me down there with that look of his, and, clearly, it was a disappointed look—disappointed."

"If it makes you unhappy," said John, "then don't think of him."

"He's my father. He said they have a song in Scotland called 'Nine Inch Will Please a Lady.' He said, well, nine inch will saturate the fiercest whore, son Henry, but that's as far as it goes. But you, you'd outfreak them all. I felt like a monster. But before this marriage business my mother and father never paid me much heed. At Elizabeth's court, the ones who always paid me heed were the ones who wanted something. I liked their attention. It made me feel as if I was important. I'm not bright. I know I'm charming—everybody has always said so— but there has to be more than that. I'm tired and can hardly keep my eyes open, but I don't want to sleep yet. Have you ever had her?"

"Who?"

"Beaton."

"Of course," said John lightly.

"Did you like her?"

Silence.

"It feels good," murmured Harry, "but not enough. Kissing, feeling—that's good. No, I'm wrong: not the kissing part. I don't like the kissing. But I like the rest. Mary's good. Doing it with her. She does everything. She was pure the first time I had her; it must be instinct, the way she learned things. I didn't think women did such things. I like doing it with her while we're doing it, but after—it's empty. I lie there. The minute I pour into her I'm alone, and I feel I've done something I shouldn't have done, committed some horrible sin that can never be forgiven. But with men, with some, the afterwards part—the skin touching together on the sheets, holding and breathing after . . . just the quiet. And I think that's the best part of it . . . the part I do just to get to . . ."

"It's a lie," said John. "I never had her. I never had any woman. You make me want to cry."

Mary reached forward and pressed the iron lever on the wall sideways. Through the round circle, she watched the sheets crumpling to the floor. She raised her eyes. John was kneeling over Harry and Harry had pulled back his thighs and was resting the calves of his legs on John's shoulders.

Mary pressed the lever shut, sank to the dusty staircase, and stifled a groan. She put her hands over her ears to shut out the harsh sounds from the bed in the other room, then got to her feet and stumbled up the limanga.

"Rise and shine," said Beaton, drawing aside the damask bed curtains. "It's almost noon. Come, sleepyhead, up." She pulled the pillow from Mary's face. "Madam. What is it? Oh, my God, you've messed your bed."

Mary pulled the pillow back over her head. "Get James," she moaned. "Get James."

"James? Lord Moray is in exile. Madam, let me get Lusgerie."

"No. I want Davy. Get Davy—now!"

Riccio's usual easy smiling way had deserted him. He stood by the window casement of her antechamber, pretending to look at someone or something in the courtyard below.

Mary drummed her fingers on the dressing table. Soon it would be winter. All the birds gone again. She shifted in the chair so she could see Riccio's back in the mirror. "It's not simply sodomy," she said listlessly, "it's incest. John is my brother." She chewed at her thumbnail.

Riccio sighed. "You were to give Signor Harry equal power with you at the opening of Parliament next March. I do not think that advisable now. The Crown Matrimonial will have to wait." He looked out the window again.

Mary waited, but he said nothing else.

Suddenly she turned around in her chair and stamped her foot on the floor. "Davy, you tell me: handle Elizabeth in such and such a way, submit this law to the Parliament and withhold this one, reconstruct this letter to the King of France or Spain in this way or that. You're brilliant. I depend on you as I depend on no other individual. Can't you tell what to do about the one thing that is most important to me?"

"There," said Davy, rubbing his hands together and smiling again. "You love him. That is to say the battle is half won, signora. He is only twenty. This action with Signor John may be no more than the idle curiosity of a boy. In Milano, the son of Duke Alessandro was a scandal, but now he is wed for years and his offspring crowd the city streets."

"I *do* love him," said Mary. "He's everything to me; *everything!* The day I made him my husband was the happiest day of my life. But you're right, of course, Davy; it probably is nothing more than boyish curiosity. The drinking, too—it's because he's not used to Scotland." She covered her face with her hands and burst into tears. "He's young, very young. And he was right when he said I'm a grasping woman." She wiped at her eyes and looked at the sky outside the casement. "Harry will never change," she said, almost in a whisper. "Not judging from the things I heard him say last night. But do you think *I'll* ever admit it, Davy?"

"I came back to apologize," said Harry, from the doorway. "Up all night, and I didn't get a wink because of you."

Mary didn't turn around, but remained staring out the window.

Harry moved behind her and mumbled, "I'm sorry. I don't know what happened to me last night. C-can't you say something, Mary?"

"I love you," she said thickly. Outside, it looked as if it might rain.

"I know, Mary. You don't have to tell me. I know." He bent and timidly kissed her on the back of the neck. "I've got to go over some papers now, then Johnny and I are going to visit Bothwell." He started to leave.

Mary turned around. "Harry?"

"Yes, Mary."

"Why not ask Beaton along?"

He stood awkwardly at the door a few seconds, then smiled and said, "I doubt she'd want to go. It's just men talking, you know."

"Beaton could curse Bothwell under a table if she had a mind to it," said Mary. "At any rate, it will give her an opportunity to be with John. Since your coming to Scotland, Harry, she's hardly seen him. You'd think you were the one he was marrying."

From his position on the day couch, Riccio moaned loudly.

"I'll see," said Harry. He shut the door slowly behind him.

"I see Lord Lennox down below," said Riccio, now at the window. "He's talking with the Lords Morton and Ruthven."

Mary stood beside him. "It's chilly out," she sighed. "Morton? Ruthven? I know those names."

"From the southwest," Riccio said. "They were of some importance during your father's reign. Now they are antiques. Ruthven is the thin, sepulchral one. It is said that he is dying of consumption. The fat one is Morton. I wonder what they are up to." He coughed and cleared his throat. "I have completed a draft of the Act of Toleration. Does signora wish to see it?"

"Freedom of religion," she mused. "That means Catholic freedom. It will not please many people."

"There is nothing to fear," said Riccio, drawing the draft papers out of his valise. "Our enemies are in exile in England. They will still be in England four months from now—March 12— when the Parliament reconvenes and passes the first edict of universal religious toleration in the history of Europe."

"Why did I do it?" said Mary.

"Signora?"

"What I said to Harry. There was no cause. It was cruel."

"That, signora," said Riccio, "is something you must answer yourself."

Mary went to visit Bothwell a few days later. His room was empty. She sat down and thumbed through a collection of Ronsard's *Poésies,* which was lying on the bed trunk. That morning she'd received a letter from James, requesting that she pardon him for having taken up arms against her. The letter was cold and formal, and it left her uncertain of her own feelings. She resented the fact that Elizabeth had imprisoned him; despite his treason in trying to deprive her of her crown, James was still her brother, and she still loved him. He was also a Scottish citizen, subject to the liberty laws of Scotland, and not subject to the whims of the Queen of England. But at the same time Mary felt that it might do James good to cool his heels for a while, to have time to reconsider his allegiances. There was no danger that Elizabeth would harm him; he was too important. Besides, Elizabeth had been his co-conspirator in the rebellion. Every country in Europe knew this. Were Elizabeth to execute or deal too harshly with James, she would be held up as an object of contempt.

After March, Mary thought, I'll demand his return, forgive him, and restore his lands. What was James's betrayal when put side by side with John's? Or Harry's? And what, who was anybody else when put side by side with James? He was the best man she'd ever known.

The door opened and Mary looked up.

"Excuse me, Your Majesty," said a plump, freckle-faced young girl with curly red hair.

"Are you the girl here?" asked Mary.

"Oh, Queen Mary, don't you remember me?" She wiped her forehead and smiled weakly. "Your Majesty doesn't remember. I'm Jean Gordon—the Earl of Huntly's daughter."

Mary asked the girl where she'd been, what she'd done, why hadn't she written. Mary's quarrel hadn't been with Jean but with her father. Well, she'd try and make up for whatever sorrow she caused. Even if it wasn't possible.

"When my father died," said Jean, taking Mary's hands in hers, "I was young, frightened. I ought to have thrown myself on Crown's mercy, but I couldn't—not then, Your Majesty. I made my way on foot to the south, near Corrichie, my uncle Ruthven's territory. He took me in and cared for me. Ruthven's hard as stone. But he was good to me at a time when no one else would have been. I'm grateful for that. Your Majesty has changed since the last time I saw you."

"And you, Jean. You're a young woman now. Are you married?"

Jean blushed. "No, Your Majesty. But soon I hope to be."

"And whom have you chosen?"

"I mustn't say, Your Majesty," she murmured. "Not until after he does. *If* he does. It took me half the morning to clean this room. Impossible for any man to mess things the way Jimmy does."

Mary stared. This girl and Bothwell? No. Impossible.

The first day of Christmas. The most desperate, the saddest, loneliest time of the year. Snow everywhere. Smiling strangers, gifts, suppers, and masques.

Mary took her place at the chair of honor and smiled at the hundred or so faces in the torchlit dining hall. Roast pig. Boiled burgundy. Red potatoes cooked in Indies sugars. She loved the odor even better than the taste.

"No, thank you," Harry was saying to one of the pages. "I'll have some of the licorice drink, though." The page reached across the table and poured from another pitcher. Harry sipped at the drink, then turned to Mary and said contritely, "I haven't had anything to drink for a week."

"Shall I have a proclamation posted at the Merkat Cross?" she said.

"Mary, I'm trying. . . ."

"What?"

"Don't you love me any more?" he said brokenly. A number of the guests seated at their table looked up.

Mary turned away and said something to Beaton about the potatoes, and weren't they wonderful with the sugar. Bothwell rose from his seat at the next table, bowed before Mary and gazed into her eyes for a few seconds. "Everybody shut their mouths," he cried, turning to the room. "I have an announcement."

From her seat next to Bothwell's empty chair, Huntly's daughter Jean Gordon raised her eyes and smiled.

"Let me come to you tonight," whispered Harry.

"Shhh!"

"Mary, talk with me."

"I haven't seen you for two weeks," she said in a low voice. "It was your decision to move into John's room. Not mine. I was always forcing myself on you. Even John, who's everybody's friend, seems to have offended you, since the two of you never speak any more. Of course, John's—"

"Mary, I can't bear any more of it. They walk away when I enter the room. They won't address me as King. They laugh at me and mock me behind my back. I can't live like this."

"You live in a flask," she said. "There's nothing you care about—except yourself, your *aqua vitae* and your—*boys*."

Harry's eyes widened, flickered, then shut.

"Stand up, Jean," Bothwell was saying.

His wife, thought Mary. Mother of his babies. She's fat, plain. How could he make love with her, feel love for her?

"Oh, Mary," Harry said, staring at her, "if you were going to say—it . . . here like that . . . did you have . . ." He pushed his chair away from the table and accidentally upset his fine, imported glass, which spilled and crashed onto the floor. He got to his feet, swayed back and forth and looked at all the faces that were now looking at him. "All this time," he said in a dull monotone, ". . . the things you'd say that'd . . . frighten me . . . that was cruel."

"He's polluted," Mary heard someone say. "As is his custom," Ruthven added. The banquet hall was silent.

Mary clenched her fists and stood. "I have an announcement to make," she snapped. "The King and Queen of this country are expecting a child, a son." She took Harry's arm. "Eat," she cried. "Drink. Speak of us. Ridicule and laugh." Her eyes shot around the room. Riccio sat very still with his eyes shut and his lips moving. Ruthven trembling under his cloud of gloom. Morton sitting on his grease fat. Fat Jean Gordon's face all red. Beaton hiding behind her hands, Bothwell openmouthed and staring, John's back turned toward her. Crocodiles. Monsters. Who were any of them to laugh at Harry and her? How she hated them all. She would have liked to insult them, to strike each one in the face. She stared at the cut-glass bowl of hot wine on the table. It crashed to the stone floor.

Mary pulled Harry after her through the hall, past the lackeys and kitchen staff, the pages, guards, and coachmen. Harry begged her: "My rooms, not yours."

He lay down on his bed and stared blankly at the plaster ceiling. "I've done you great wrongs," he said. "So have others, but you've pardoned them. I'm young. You've overlooked much before. I never knew that you knew about the—men. There, I said it."

Mary pulled off his boots and hose, then unbuttoned his shirt.

"I'm naked now," he said. "If I said that I loved you, would you believe it?"

"Yes," she said, snuffing out the candle and lying beside him.

"You can't see the bruises in the dark," he said. "A slight mishap in Caithness. He didn't know I was the King. He beat me when I asked him."

"I'm sorry. I'm sorry." She rested her face against his. His cheek was wet.

"Don't be sorry, Mary. If I was what I should be, it would never have happened. Sometimes they're angry with me, but when they know I'm the King, they like it. Except the one in Caithness. I had him beaten. I watched them do it. If you like, I can give you a list of names—perhaps twenty, fifteen names."

She cradled his head in her arms and rocked it slowly back and forth.

"But there might be one name I won't—"

"I know," she said. She started humming a lullaby that her mother used to sing to her a long time ago, when she was a child, and they were always running. Until now, she'd forgotten it.

"What a pretty, pretty song, Mary."

"Rest, my baby, rest."

"Uhmmm. You're jealous about Jean Gordon. Don't deny it. I could tell tonight. I was jealous of your being jealous. In spite of everything, even if . . . I love you."

"It's me," said Mary. "It's not all you, your fault. I say and do things. Things that are cruel. I have a genius for cruelty. I strike out. Blindly. I break the flesh and draw blood. And while I'm doing it, I love doing it. After, I'm ashamed, but only after. If I promise to forgive you, then you must promise to forgive me."

"When did you first know?" he said.

"The night we fought, and you went down to John's room. And I went down, and I listened."

"Now I'm ashamed. Do you hate me?"

"No," she said, kissing him on the nose. "Tomorrow, if you like, we can ride off from Edinburgh and find a stream and fish. You said you could break the ice and that the fish lived under. You said once you liked to do that." There wasn't any moon tonight. She was thinking how, even in France, her life had always been moving from one place to another. Faces would become familiar, then their bearers would fall from grace, new faces would surround her, then they, too, would disappear. She'd known her mother only through letters. Her father was a name in histories. James was gone; James would always be cold. Harry was the only home that she owned.

"Poor Johnny," he mumbled. "I hurt him, as well—even more than I hurt you. He was—"

"I love you. *I* love you. Me!"

"We're a hundred miles from everywhere," laughed Mary. "Well, ten miles from Edinburgh, at least. But alone, alone, and together." They broke open the thick ice with picks, spooled their reels, sat down and huddled together.

"This is good weather," said Harry. "Clean whiffing weather. It tells your limbs they're limbs." He settled his arm around her shoulder. "Are your limbs limbs?" he asked.

Mary smiled at the icy water.

"Brrr, it's cold," said Harry, snuggling closer. He waited a minute. "Look, Mary, the ice is on fire."

Mary smiled again, lifted her ermine muff, and hit him affectionately in the face with it. Harry gasped, clutched his skull, and fell back dead.

"Oh, *you,*" laughed Mary. "Get up!"

"Where's the tackle box?" Harry chuckled, sitting up. "I wish spring would come—football, jousting, tennis, pole vaulting, and the sun—but winter has its advantages. Shall I show you something amazing?" He jumped to his feet, threw off his overcoat, tugged out his shirt, pulled off his trunk hose, and skidded naked across the ice to a place where the river water flowed. "Watch, Mary," he cried happily. He straightened his long white legs, bent, and dived into the gray water. After splashing about awhile, he ducked under the ice.

Mary clapped her hands. He didn't come up. "Harry," she called out suddenly. "Harry!" She stood and crossed herself.

Beaded with water bubbles, Harry tugged his red and white splotched body onto the ice. His thick blond hair covered his eyes, nose, mouth, and chin. "I didn't see any mermaids," he said, "and all the fish were sleeping." He smiled dazzlingly, took a deep breath, and slapped his sides. "The best thing about rivers is that you don't have salt sticking all over you when you come out. When our son is born, I'll teach him how to swim."

He recalled little details about their courtship. She hung on his arm and listened. When it grew toward dark, they rode back to Holyrood.

The next day they went tobogganing on a hill immediately outside the capital. The white slope was filled with people. Mary patted a boy on the head and told Harry she hoped their boy would be as lusty. The mother, a burgess's wife, talked with them awhile. Then, in a low timid voice, she asked if the two of them might, if it please, come to supper that night.

Mary looked from the woman to Harry.

"Why not?" he said.

Out of the corner of her eye, Mary saw the woman's rough face bloom, then drop into the checkered phrygian fabric of her shawl.

They had a marvelous time at the burgess's that night. Afterward, they returned to Holyrood, went to Harry's chambers, and made love together. She asked him about John. He spoke openly. He said it was a thing that had happened; there was no other explanation. He said he was sorry about John. John was good and kind. There had, of course, been others. The first time was when he was fifteen, at Hampton Court. "But it will never happen again," he said before he dozed off to sleep. "It doesn't have to, now."

They both believed they would be happy.

Early one morning the following month, after Mary had gone back up to her own rooms, the Earl of Lennox entered his son's sleeping chamber. "Your father," he said, "has a matter of some urgency to discuss with you."

"Later. Come back then." Harry sighed, turned away, and pressed his face into the pillow. He could smell her smell on it.

"Now," said Lennox.

Harry crawled out of bed and drew on a red silk dressing gown. He looked briefly at the little gold mermaid rising from a block of black marble which sat on his desk. It had been a gift from Mary. "What do you want?" he said mildly. "I know you must want something, or you wouldn't have come." He splashed water on his face and drew his razor out of its case.

"The Italian has persuaded the Queen to deny you the Crown Matrimonial, joint sovereign power which is yours by right as her consort. The Italian, and no other man. In exchange for some favors, certain lords in this realm will see to it that you are granted the Crown Matrimonial by Parliament this March."

"Leave off. I don't want to hear." He scraped the razor up his chin. Blood trickled down his throat.

"Listen, Miss Nancy, and—"

"You will not call me that," cried Harry, cutting himself again.

"I planted you inside your mother's gut. I shall call you what it pleases me to call you. First, Miss Nancy, you will sign James Stewart's pardon and restore his estates."

"James Stewart? What have you to do with him?"

"Secondly, you will aid us in preventing the Toleration Act from being presented to the Parliament."

"You will have to discuss these things with the Queen, not me."

"Thirdly, you will aid us in dealing with the Italian."

"Are you mad?" said Harry. "You must be." He rinsed and dried his face with a hand towel. "I know many people hate David, but I think that's because he is intelligent and they aren't.

Some, like Lord James, suspect him of being a papal agent, which is ridiculous. Many people think *I'm* an agent of the Pope."

"There is more to this than politics," said Lennox. "It is generally believed that the Italian has dishonored your marriage bed."

Harry chuckled and ran his fingers through his hair. "Davy! Oh, that's funny. You *are* mad."

"The influence which he has with the Queen is unnatural," said Lennox calmly. "He has been seen coming out of her chambers as late as two in the morning. He, a foreigner, rules all in this kingdom. He possesses more power than you, Maitland, or any other man, more power than even Lord James had when he was at the court. Why do you suppose that is?" Lennox clapped him on the back, then said amicably, "Of course, Henry, you may be right. It may be ridiculous. I must go now, but we will discuss this later, and at length."

Harry sat down and rested his head against his hand. He was thinking about the day he and Mary went fishing. Water pouring. He looked up. A young boy handed him a goblet of wine.

"My name is Jeremy," said the boy, taking off his doublet and neatly folding it on the desk.

"What's this? Where did you come from?"

"I'm English, sir," said the boy. "I'm from Highgate, sir." He untied his ruff and placed it on top of the doublet.

"Put those things back on. What do you think you are doing?" Harry stared at the boy, fascinated.

"Here, drink now," said the boy. "Earl Lennox said it was the best burgundy. I stole a sip before I came in. He said you would be hesitant, at first, but there's no need, sir."

Harry reached the goblet off the table, smiled ironically at his reflection in the red, then drank it down. It tasted terrible. "More," he said.

The boy sat on Harry's lap and put his arms around his neck. "You are so good, sir," he lisped, squirming and licking at his ear. "You are such a handsome man, my lord. You're marvelous and nice. Oh, you are good, sir."

Harry seized the boy by the armpits and threw him backward

onto the floor. "How could he possibly think I'd . . . that I could possibly . . . My father is a monster. . . ."

The boy lay on the floor with a puzzled expression on his face.

"It's not your fault," said Harry. "You didn't know. You're only a little boy."

Smiling seductively, the boy got to his knees and attempted to unfasten the belt of Harry's dressing gown.

Harry raised his hand and slapped him across the top of the head. "Get out! Now. I'll see your father knows of this, and I hope he whips your bottom till it bleeds."

"I haven't got one," snarled the boy. "I don't need one. I'll leave the wine bottle. When you're finished drinking, you can use it to hole yourself." Suddenly, he rushed forward and bit Harry on the hand. He darted for the door, opened it halfway, and then turned around for a second and burst out with such a hideous and malicious laugh that Harry half expected to see flames burn from his eyes and smoke shoot out of his mouth. The door slammed shut.

Harry rubbed his hand. "If a child . . . if a little boy . . ." He sat in the chair, staring at the bottle of wine.

"You couldn't leave it alone, could you?" said Mary. She slapped him across the face and ripped at his nightshirt.

He opened his eyes.

"Look," she said furiously, holding a hand mirror to his face. "Look. *You* demand the Crown Matrimonial! Look, damn you!"

His eyes were glassy red, lower lip purplish and swollen, hair matted over his forehead. The chalky stubble of his beard made him look like old men he'd seen lying on doorstoops in the night in London. He lowered his feet to the floor, straightened his shoulders, and stood. "Don't you laugh," he said threateningly.

"I'd rather be dead than laugh at you," she said. "Why do you do it?"

"Why do I do what?"

"Destroy yourself with drink."

Infuriated, he said, "Why did you have a stamp made bearing my name and give it to Riccio? Why is it coins used to say

'Henricus et Maria' and now they say 'Maria et Henricus?' Why is it Riccio stays up with you until all hours of the night in your bedchamber? Tell me that."

Mary walked to the limanga. "For the past month I've been in this room, with you, until all hours of the night. In your present stupor, it is understandable that you have forgotten." She pressed the brick, the secret door slid open, and she left.

Harry caught at a bottle on the desk and raised it to his mouth. Empty. The bottle on the mantel was empty as well. He searched under his mattress, through the wardrobe, in the drawers of the desk. He was tired. It must have been about six in the evening. The days in Scotland, especially the winter days, were short. Mary had torn the top of his nightshirt, drawn blood. He went to the wardrobe and took out another.

In the floor-length mirror, his body was pale green. Like the color of the underbelly of a dead fish.

"But I'm the King of Scotland," he said, winking at the reflection. "A charming fellow, quite handsome, in fact, and, as you can plainly see, a most amazing fellow. All in all." He waited for the reflection to wink back.

When he spoke again, it sounded as if his voice was coming from behind the glass: I'm unclean. I hurt. I'm nothing.

"It's not true," said Harry, lying back in bed and stretching the linen sheet to his chin. "Being a King is murderous business. (As for the other matter?) Soon I shall be a father; surely that's a proof of something. A camel can't pass through the eye of a needle. (Is that all?) Yes; I'm young. (And her?) I do love her, but sometimes I hate her as well. (Why?) Because at first she seemed merely gentle; she was meek, always so attentive. But you couldn't see what she really was like. (What?) Strong. Clutching. Cruel. (But the other matter?) It's a hard thing to be a King, especially in Scotland. (Would you rather be a shepherd?) No. That's only in poems." He lifted his hand to the leather belt that hung from the ceiling over his bed and rang for more wine.

Later that night he woke up and, on a sudden impulse, made his way up the secret staircase. Inside Mary's room a clock struck one. Harry pressed his ear against the wood and listened.

What was David Riccio doing in his wife's bedroom at one o'clock in the night?

Harry and John and Mary rocked over the confused city. The breeze dipped and they tumbled down past the gabled roofs and shiny windows. The Italian sat in his room at Holyrood, chewing on the tip of his rusty pen quill, stamping *Henricus Rex* on papers of state, laws, grants, and bloody ballads of faithless wives and grotesque hobgob fairy lovers.

Mary's eyes dimmed and she drifted toward the Italian's window.

Harry's arm grew long and longer. The window glass gave way like spit and he seized the gnome by its curly black hair and yanked it outside and up into the night.

"Sign here," Lennox said. "Sign it."

"Oh, Daddy, I couldn't do *that*."

"Sign," Lennox said.

David's fisheyes plopped and popped. Harry dropped him. In London, ladies of position lounge, play cards, have affairs, and powder their threadbare faces. Jaws dripping, the bat whirled into the snowy currents. What have I done? What have I done!

Harry squeezed open his eyes, reached up for the bell cord, but instead caught hold of something thick and damp that slithered down his arm and wrapped itself around his chest, hissing, tearing. "Jesus, Mary, murder!" He screamed again. His rib cage heaved, splintered, and burst. Mud bubbled from his lungs. Before it reached his eyes and blinded him, he saw Mary, Beaton, John, Bothwell, and David rush out of the wall. But he'd just killed David. Shrieking exultantly, the bat sank its fangs into his throat. Harry tore at the sheets. Suddenly a pair of arms encircled him.

"Do something," he heard Mary scream. "Where's his father Lennox?"

"Get her to bed before she sees any more," said Bothwell.

Mouth. Bowels. Bile. Suddenly he thought: I'm going to be dead. He did not want to die. If he died, he would burn in hell forever.

Bothwell, not too far above his head: "I've seen this in lots before. But not as young as him."

John, holding him tight: "Give a hand, Jimmy; he's strong. At the tourney last spring—get his legs! Dear God, but he's powerful. Last spring . . . what's going on inside that body? She and I should know. I think he's calming down now."

Bothwell: "How can she love him?"

John: "When you love someone, they can do anything."

Ah, that's good. It's pleasant—most pleasant thing of anything—to fall away asleep in someone's arms. O my God, I'm heartily sorry for having offended Thee and I detest all my sins because of Thy just punishments, but most of all . . .

In early March Maitland returned from his embassage in London. Mary received him in her audience chamber. His shoulder welts were stuffed with an enormous excess of rolled cotton, his twilled sarsenet hose were padded, and his head seemed suspended above the wide starched ruff. "And how does our lord the King?" said Maitland.

"Well," said Mary, indicating a chair.

"If I might bring up the matter of Lord James, with whom I had the opportunity to speak recently?"

"You may not."

Maitland spoke of the proposed trade pact between the Edinburgh merchant guild and the guild of London. Elizabeth was said to be contemplating marriage with the Holy Roman Emperor. It was a game, though: except for the Holy Roman Emperor, who was in financial straits, nobody believed she would do it. If it were not for the scandal surrounding the death of Robert Dudley's wife, Elizabeth would have married him, of that Maitland was certain.

"Oh, Maitland, how is he?"

"Why, Dudley's Dudley."

"I mean James."

"He miscalculated the significance of your marriage. He feared it would be used as a wedge by which the Inquisition might be introduced into the country. He realizes now how ridiculous it was to think that. I spoke several times with him in London." Maitland played with the tip of his thin forked beard. "He's getting gray. He's sick for home, madam. Will you allow him to come home?"

Mary paced back and forth. She said, "Yes."

"Very good, madam," Maitland said pleasantly. He cleared his throat. "Now I should like to speak with you concerning Master David. He has enemies, madam."

"Even you have enemies, Michael Wiley."

"That is true, that is true. But, with the exception of Your Majesty, Master David has no friends—of importance. I know the man for a good songster, an excellent wit, and an intelligent fellow. But he has made too many enemies in Scotland. Ruthven and Morton hate him passionately. The Earl of Lennox is incensed with your refusal to grant the King the Crown Matrimonial, and he lays the blame at Master David's door. I myself, while engaged in the most delicate of negotiations with the English government, have twice been superseded by Master David's directives. The Queen of England does not care for what I say— or, for the matter, what you say—she wishes to know what the Ital—what David says. Now, madam, David is a foreign subject, a commoner, and yet he wields more power than the natural-born nobles of Scotland. It is said that he is an agent of the Pope. Now, madam, you know that to be false. I know it to be false. No man of sense could believe it. But, madam, how many men of sense do you know in this country?"

"Needless to say, you have a solution, Maitland."

"Send him away. A ship sails shortly for Italy from Leith."

"No."

"Not even for a short time?" said Maitland urgently.

"No. I'm adamant, Maitland. He's one of the few people I trust implicitly. I need him here."

"Madam, perhaps you do not fully comprehend the situation. David is a hated man. Ruthven and Morton are not his only enemies. I've heard, on the best authority, that your husband the King has made certain accusations."

"I also have heard the accusations," Mary said impatiently. "Because they are not true, they do not disturb me. You are dismissed, Maitland. Now."

The ship bound for Italy left without Riccio, two days later. On the following night, Mary held a small supper in her private chambers. Riccio glumly surveyed the buffet board. He sipped at his ale tankard, saw Mary looking at him, and smiled wanly. Beaton and Jean Bothwell were engaged in an animated conversation on the merits of overseasoning kidney pie. Lord Livingstone, a captain from the border who'd arrived with dispatches earlier in the day, tore contentedly at a leg of mutton and listened to the chatter with detached amusement. He was a friend of Bothwell's: they'd grown up here and there together. Very quiet, tall, attractive in a raw-faced sort of way.

"Davy, Parliament won't vote for three days," said Mary. "Let's not worry about toleration till then."

"No worries," said Riccio. "The act will pass. Scotsmen will hate it and hate me for making it, but let that pass, the act will pass."

"Especially the capon with the pea stuffing," said Jean Bothwell, wiping a streak of butter from her chin. "Though carrot would be delicious."

"Mmmmmmmmm," laughed Beaton. "But I'm afraid I don't know anything about preparing foods."

"Things take so long," said Jean, "and, next thing off, they're gone. You should have seen the way my husband ate when we first married. But you let me teach you some cooking if you ever want to be a good wife to Lord John. Lord John is a favorite of my husband's but, Mary Beaton, you've been engaged too long!"

Beaton blushed, then looked uncertainly at Mary.

Outside, it was lightly snowing. The last snow of the season, Jean had said earlier.

It will be good to see the green again, Mary thought.

"Madam," Riccio was saying, "I want—so badly—to go home."

Mary stared at her plate. Everybody hated him because he

was loyal to her. She could tell Davy was afraid. Well, she was afraid too. That was something one got used to after a while. And she knew the feeling of being far from home, away from one's mother. She had no choice: if he wished to go, he would have to be permitted to do so, eventually. For a little while, at least.

"You're from Turin," said Jean, breaking the silence. "Scotland must be dreary after all those olive trees."

Riccio smiled. "No, no, signora, the olives are farther south. We're near the Alps, Milano." He turned back to Mary. "My mother is old. Does Her Majesty understand?"

"Yes," said Mary.

"Your Majesty would love Turin. All the streets are straight and intersect at right angles. At the Cathedral Giovanni Battista you could see the Sudario—the Holy Shroud with our Saviour's imprint," he explained to Jean. "Beautiful! Your Majesty understands: I must see my mother, who is very old. For a little while. The sun is always a circle, ripe. The heat, swimming in the Po, just sitting doing nothing in the Palazzo Madama . . ."

Yesterday, she'd asked him how it felt to be the most important man in a country that wasn't even his. When he was young, he replied, he'd pray before the Sudario that he might hold office in a state. He said God gave men brains to serve and care lovingly for other men, to think God through them. He said that he was proud beyond expression to have written the first act of religious toleration in Scottish history. He knew the law would not make men kind, but he also knew that it would cause them to think before they were unkind. And in certain cases the thinking would cause other thoughts. The act was certain to pass, as its chief opponents had left the country, except for Master Knox, who had lost his sway forever. Davy said his mother and father, who were poor, would be proud of him.

"Edinburgh's so twisting, narrow, and confined," sighed Jean, stuffing a roll into her mouth. "I miss the country. It doesn't seem as if they've erected a new building here since Robert Bruce."

"They age quickly," said Beaton. "Instant—" She rose and curtsied. "My lord."

"Your Majesty," said Lord Livingstone, getting up from his chair.

Harry sat down next to Mary and bussed her on the cheek. His breath smelled of cinnebar wash and brandy. He was very pale. "You look well tonight, sweetheart," he said unsteadily, without looking at her.

Clank.

Mary turned in her chair and saw Lord Ruthven swaying in the door entrance. The old man caught hold of the knob, steadied himself, and walked slowly toward the couch. "Your Grace," he rasped, grabbing hold of an arm and sinking back. Jean got up and went to him. "Uncle," she said, "you should be in bed." As she attempted to straighten his fur-trimmed nightrobe, the damask material fell back from his knee and Mary saw that he was wearing a suit of black armor underneath. The room was suddenly very cold.

"I was going to visit you later," Mary said hurriedly, "but they told me you were sick, and now you—"

"May it please Your Grace that yon man, David, come out of this chamber, where he has been overlong."

Mary looked at Riccio. He was staring at the plate of mutton on the table in front of him. "What has he done?" she said. Out of the corner of her eye, she saw Beaton rise and move slowly toward the door.

"Madam, he has offended your honor," said Ruthven. "Mistress Beaton, get away from the door."

"How has he offended my honor?" she said.

Ruthven raised his hand and pointed to Harry.

Mary heard movements outside in the corridor. She moved in front of Riccio, who was still staring at his plate.

Livingstone got out of his chair and stood beside her. "My lord," he said to Ruthven, "this man is unarmed."

"Uncle," said Jean, kneeling beside him, "if he's done anything wrong, he can have a trial." She put the palm of her hand over his forehead. "You're burning," she said. "Let me take you back to bed."

"What have you done?" Mary said dully, turning to Harry. She heard the door open.

Helmeted men with armor breastplates rushed into the room with broadswords and cocked pistols. The buffet board overturned. Porcelain plates, pewter mugs, water ewers, and food clattered to the floor. Beaton caught a candle as it fell and held it—the one light in the room—above her head.

"Justice," cried Riccio, jerking to his knees and grabbing hold of Mary's skirts, *"giustizia, madama!"* Mary put her hands over his head and moved backward toward the window bay. A knife rose and fell in the flickering candlelight. Riccio coughed and twisted his arms around her waist. The knife chopped forward again. Mary saw Livingstone grip the wrist of the assailant and knock him to the ground. There was a low thud, Livingstone's eyes suddenly widened, he made a sucking noise, tottered, and slid to the floor. Whirling about, Mary threw open the lattice window and screamed down below into the snowy, deserted courtyard, "Murder! Bothwell!"

A hand folded over her mouth and pulled her inside.

"Giustizia, giustizia," sobbed Riccio. *"Madonna, io sono morto!"* They were beating his fingers with the butts of their pistols to loosen his hold around her waist.

A sharp pain burst from the pit of her stomach and swept upward to her heart. She bent over. Riccio's thick curly hair brushed across her cheek as he let go of her waist and was wrenched into the center of the room. "God damn you!" Mary wailed. "If you—uh, God!" Her spine buckled and she fell backward into the torn curtain.

Through the water in her eyes, she saw Riccio crawling through the mass of gleaming armored leg-covers. They tripped into each other and clanged to the floor attempting to catch hold of him. Mary raised her hands to wipe her eyes. If James were here . . .

Then Riccio screamed.

Her stomach rocking with cramps, Mary lifted herself onto the bay and beat her fist feebly against the cold glass. Outside, two men scurried along the moonlit, snow-encrusted palace wall. One of them lifted a cudgel and smashed it against the tocsin. She knew, even at this distance, he was Bothwell. Hands pulled at her arms. She pressed her body against the window glass, cleared her throat, and tried to scream. Nothing came out except a hoarse, rattling sound. The hands dragged her back into the room and pushed her against a wall. Someone pressed a pistol into her belly. She screamed: "My baby!" In the fluttering light and dark, she saw six or seven men drop to their knees in the center of the room, raise the daggers they had in their mailed fists, and bring them down, raise the daggers and bring them down, and again. And again. Somebody spit in her face. No, it wasn't spit; it was blood. On the other side of the room, Beaton fell, and the candle fell.

Turin is a city in the Piedmont on the river Po in northern Italy. In the summer, boys like to swim in the river and their mothers and fathers come to sit on stone benches along the river wall and watch them. He said God gave men brains to serve and care lovingly for one another, and that his mother and father would be proud beyond expression. The Holy Shroud of Our Lord and Saviour Jesus Christ is exhibited in the Cathedral of John the Baptist.

Mary slowly opened her eyes and Harry turned away. As Beaton's face came into focus, Mary whispered, "My baby." She touched her stomach lightly with her little finger. He was still there.

Wringing the water out of her kerchief, Beaton nodded, tried to smile, then lay the wet cloth on Mary's forehead. A trail of dark blood glistened on the floor from the overturned table to the doorway.

Mary looked at the back of Harry's head. "Traitor," she said vehemently. "Son of a traitor." The back of his shirt was ripped and soaked through with blood. If it was his, she was glad.

Ruthven, Morton, and three other men entered the room. Because they had to step in the blood when they came in, they left a trail of muddy brown footsteps behind them. Shaking uncontrollably, Ruthven lowered himself onto the couch and poured himself a glass of water.

"Is this your sickness, my lord?" said Mary, sitting up on the bed.

"God forgive Your Majesty had such sickness," he groaned, squeezing his nose.

"Stand in my presence! Get up, Ruthven, up, up. I am the Queen. Oh, God, I swear—"

"He's sick," said Harry in a little voice, turning, and looking slightly past her head.

"You're responsible for this," she said, turning on him. "I am no longer your wife."

"That is a sin," said Ruthven, coughing into his handkerchief. "He is Your Majesty's husband. You must do your duty to each other." He poured himself another glass of water.

Mary remembered Jean mentioning Ruthven's marital difficulties. When Lady Ruthven did not say her prayers at night, Ruthven beat her with a riding crop and locked her in the bedroom closet. "Why can't I leave him," she said sarcastically, "as your wife left you? Stand up in my presence, damn you."

"I am ill," said Ruthven, getting to his feet. "I think I will go."

"I've not given you permission to leave. You'll pay for what you've done tonight, Ruthven. I warn you."

Ruthven observed her calmly. "You are in protective custody, Your Majesty. That is not a position for warning or permission-giving." He moved slowly to the window. "The rabble's still outside," he said. "You must say something to them, Your Majesty."

Mary swung her legs over the side of the bed.

"Not you," said Ruthven.

Mary stared with disgust as Harry flung open the windows and told whoever was down there that everything was fine, the tocsin had been rung by traitors, and the Italian was dead. As King of Scotland, he'd decided the opening of Parliament would be delayed. Go home, countrymen, sleep in peace, and good night.

"What cause have I given you to use me like this?" she said. "I made you a King, and this is my payment."

"Good cause," said Harry quietly, but avoiding her eyes. "David dishonored my bed."

She looked at him in astonishment.

"Night after night, you'd have him in this room until one and two in the morning, and in the past two months I've never once been alone with you; he was always the third person. King! David signed the King's name on state documents, not me. I've never been the King."

"No," she said. "Only a man can be a King."

"There was a time when you thought I was a man. I just had to touch you and you'd have a bliss on."

"My lord," said Ruthven, "there is no need—"

"Shut up, you," said Harry. "You said this was to make me King in fact, Ruthven. Now I'm the King, and now you shut your mouth. I think sometimes I had her more times before I married her than I have since."

Ruthven went into a violent coughing fit, got up, and left, the other men following behind him.

"What are you waiting for?" she said to Harry. "Get out!"

"Dear heart . . ."

"I have no heart."

He moved slowly to the door. "You thought I never wanted you," he mumbled. "You thought I only wanted—men."

"Her Majesty said to get out," said Beaton in a low voice. "Davy's dead, you almost killed your baby, and you almost killed your wife."

"Someone put a pistol to my belly—to my baby—your baby," Mary said.

"That was Fawdonside," Beaton said. She turned to Harry. "If I had a dagger, I'd stick it in your heart." She twisted her mouth into a smile. "You sorry man."

"I'm sorry about that too, Miss Beaton," Harry said. "But you'll find someone else. Mary, do you want me to leave?"

She could feel the child moving inside her body. What were their plans? Would they lock her up, kill her, kill him, too, as soon as they were done with him? At the moment there was one thing that mattered: the baby. "Go, Beaton. Please."

"Leave you with this—"

Mary motioned for her to come close. "Find out everything," she whispered. "Find friends. Dear Beaton."

After Beaton had gone, Harry started a fire in the hearth. He crouched in front of the yellow flames a few minutes, rubbing his hands, then said in a low voice, "I was drunk. I didn't even know I'd signed the thing. What could I do? I'll stay with you tonight. If I hadn't joined, they would have hurt you too."

"Yes, husband."

She tugged at her buttons and pulled off the sleeves. "Could you hand me a gown, please? Thank you." He looked like a twelve-year-old. She sighed and lay back on the sheets.

Harry came and sat beside her on the bed. "Don't worry," he said gently. "I'm in complete command. I've told them they're not to touch you. I didn't mean for him to be killed. They said there would be a trial. We tried to get you to get him back to Italy; we tried, but you wouldn't. Maitland said you said—"

"Did Maitland know, Harry?"

"Yes. He came in late. He didn't want it in front of you, though."

"They have everything now. Not only me and the baby, but you too, Harry."

"They're my friends . . ."

"You can't trust them," she said in a remote voice. "They're going to kill both of us."

"Daddy said . . ."

"They're going to kill him too."

"Nobody can kill my father."

"Harry, I have a pain where the baby is." She bit her lip. "Is there . . . some wine . . . yes, there should be a bottle on the cabinet . . . just a sip . . ."

She watched him walk over to the cabinet and come back with the bottle and a glass. "You have some too," she said.

"I don't think I should. I haven't had anything for five days." He eyed her uneasily, as if to see if she believed him.

"Harry, you've been so good. Five whole days. That's *good*. You're entitled to one drink for all that. It's selfish of me to think only of myself. You've been through a lot tonight too. I believe you when you tell me you didn't want him dead. I do believe you." She filled the glass halfway and placed it his hand.

"I don't think I should," he said, looking at the glass.

"Just one. It's only when you do it by yourself that it's bad. Now you're not alone. I'm here. The two of us."

He drank. "Mary, I do love you."

"Sometimes you do not act as if you . . . loved me."

"It wasn't until you stopped wanting me," he said, refilling the glass, "that I realized how much I wanted you. I started having a nightmare. Over and over. I'd be alone in a dark place, and I'd look through a door and see all the great people laughing and dancing. I'd know you were in there with them. And I couldn't come in, but had to stay outside and wait for you to come out every now and then. In that dream, all that mist with this heavy sound—the sound of no sound—yes, the sound of nothing at all. Nobody came out to get me. For some reason, it occurred to me that all the great people were going to die. Then I knew that you were dead. I was glad, then terrified, because I realized that—whatever it's been between us—if you were dead, I could never live to be old. Good God, empty already." He got up, strode to the door, and threw it open. "Wine," he said to someone outside.

Mary stared at his silhouette in the rectangle of light. If it weren't for the baby she'd kill him. With her hands, if she had to. He crawled back in bed beside her. She listened to him drink.

Suddenly, she could have wept, because once she'd loved him completely, and now he'd murdered Davy and almost murdered their child. And because she hated him now, but she still loved him the exact amount she hated him. She was sick with her love and hate of him. "Dear heart," he sighed, curling around her. The bottle dropped to the Turkish carpet.

When she was certain that he was sleeping, she got out of bed, sat at her dressing table, rimmed her eyes with gray kohl, and hurriedly applied a thick coat of powder to her face. The Antwerp clock struck eleven times. She whispered a prayer. Outside, something hung from the wall that faced Edinburgh. Mary watched the black, mangled form as it swayed in the wind and snow. Inside her, the baby moved.

She lay down on the mattress again. Her hand moved along the carpet until it found the wine bottle. She poured the few drops that were left down her throat, then counted ten, and screamed.

"Mary," said Harry, shooting up. "Oh, my God, is it the baby? Mary, straighten up!"

"Dr. Lusgerie," she groaned. "Hurry—Lusgerie. Get Beaton. The pain." She screamed again.

He called down the corridor and she heard the sound of footsteps running, and of people moving about the room.

She slowly opened her eyes. James leaned over her. "Oh, James," she wept, throwing her arms about his neck, "if you'd been here, you wouldn't have allowed it."

His light blue eyes shifted past her head.

"Clean linen," the physician yelled. "The blue vial. Madam, how fast are they coming?"

What was James doing here? she thought wildly. It was only two days since she'd told Maitland she would pardon him. Not enough time to— Had he known? Had he— Sitting up in bed, she gave him a blank look and whispered, "One more thing . . ." The last words her mother had said to James before she died. A cough, then she rolled her eyes and fell back on the pillow.

"No!" said James.

"Is she dead?" Harry asked, like a child who'd only heard of death.

"You let them do it in front of her," James said hoarsely. "In front of her, you sotted bastard."

"I'm the King," Harry stammered. "Not you. You're the bastard. Not me."

"You let them do it in front of her! If she dies, I swear, by God, you'll die."

"We shall send for Master Knox," said Ruthven, "to settle Christ Jesus in her heart."

Mary sat up, seized James by his collar, and pleaded, "Get them *out!*" She bit the inside of her cheek. Blood trickled from the corner of her mouth. "I have my own religion," she snapped. She turned to Dr. Lusgerie. "Send for my confessor."

Ruthven hovered at the end of the bed. "That man is also sent to sulphur," he rasped. "Pope's spy, Pope's idolater priest, all are sent—" He stumbled to his knees, grabbed hold of the bedpost, and slid to the floor.

Lennox pressed his ear against the old man's chest, then said matter-of-factly, "Ruthven's dead."

"What?" said Mary, rising from the bed. She stood over the body. Even in death, the man looked malignant. A curl of spit glistened on the cracked lips. "He's not dead," she said hysterically. "*I* have to be the one to do it. Get up, Black Man, Black Man, get up!" She kicked him savagely in the head. It snapped back and forth, mouth opening at each jolt, glazed eyes staring up. Lennox caught Mary by the arm, and she spun around and struck him in the face. Her bare feet stuck in Davy's blood. She dropped to her knees. *Oh, God,* she thought, *the pains—they're real now.* The room was like a giant kiln. The bones in the small of her back blazed and her stomach heaved. She muttered, *"Jesus, Mary, Joseph,"* then opened her eyes, bent, and spit in the dead man's face.

James caught her in his arms. As he lowered her onto the sheets she saw Beaton leaning against the wall, pretending to cry and trying not to smile. The pains ceased abruptly.

"The room must be cleared," said the physician. "Everybody but the King must leave."

Lennox sat down on the day couch and folded his hands in his lap.

Mary clenched her fists and screamed as loudly as she could. The baby kicked her fiercely in the stomach. She bit her tongue.

"Lord James," said Beaton, "I appeal to you as Her Majesty's brother, with equal blood from your father— Madam, lie back."

"From our father," gasped Mary, "who's in heaven, looking down. James, please get them out, oh, God, my brother James." She started giggling.

"He does look down, you know," said James in a thick voice. "It's true. It is. It is. There's a bridge." He turned around. "Out. Everybody."

Mary listened as they dragged Ruthven's body over the threshold.

"Is she going to die?" asked Harry, but the physician ignored him.

"Marvelous, madam," laughed Beaton. "For a second, it was

almost too real. It was Bothwell and John who sounded the tocsin. Bothwell's gone to get men and match them at Dunbar."

"Get me water," said Mary. "I'm dry."

"When the Parliament meets," said Beaton, "Lennox expects defeat for the Toleration, legal protection for those lords controlling the old church lands, and the Crown Matrimonial to that Judas skulking in the corner over there."

"What's happening?" said Harry drunkenly. "I don't understand. And you, remember your place, and address your King with the respect due a King."

"The guard?" asked Mary, ignoring him. She tore off her nightdress and threw it to Beaton. "Strip, dear. For the next hour, you're the Queen of Scotland."

Beaton started unfastening her gown. "After the town was quieted, they relaxed the guard. Outside, the corridor's swarming. But there's only two men at the limanga now. And there's three where it lets out. And," she announced, dropping her petticoat and squeezing her breasts, "one of them is a fellow I happen to know quite well. He told me not to worry about the others. Bothwell's man, Paris, is waiting outside the kitchen walls with horses. Oh, Madam, look at the King; you'd think he'd never seen a naked woman before." She laughed and pulled Mary's nightdress over her head.

"What's happening?" said Harry, moving toward the door.

Mary pulled on a pair of men's trunk hose she'd gotten from her trunk. She fastened a doublet tight across her chest, then tied her hair into a knot and pushed a flat, wide-brimmed hat onto her head.

"You can't leave," said Harry, grabbing at her arm. "They're my friends. They only—"

"Only plan to end you tomorrow morning," sneered Beaton. "Ah, yes, I have ears, my lord the King, and the walls have ears, and the traitors have plans." She slipped under the bedcovers and loosed her hair over her face.

Mary took her husband's hand in hers and said gently, "Harry, other than me, Davy was your one friend. He played tennis and went fishing with you. He would always say of you: 'How brave he is, how handsome, what a prince, how good.' It was

Davy who secured our marriage. Now he is dead. James, who hates you so much he led a revolt against you, is back in Scotland. The Toleration Act, which would have assured freedom for our religion, is dead. I am supposedly dying. Our child is supposedly dying with me. Now why, in the name of logic, should you live to trouble them?"

"I know my father wouldn't—"

"Madam," said the physician, "it grows late."

Harry sank back on the day couch.

Mary sat next to him, took his hand, and placed it over her stomach. "You have known your father Lennox many years longer than I," she said softly. "But—do you feel it?—this—right here—this is his grandson. This is the same flesh and blood as you."

"But he's my father," said Harry in a weak voice. He hunched his shoulders.

"I had a father," Mary continued, after a minute. "And your father Lennox was his half brother by marriage. My father loved your father, and he trusted him. Do you know what your father Lennox did to mine, once, at a place called Solway? Do you know, Harry?"

"But that was politics," Beaton purred from the bed. "Why, our King's 'daddy' loves him; he's always speaking of our lord the King. Of our lord the King and your brother John. Of our lord the King and various assorted page boys, fisher boys, apprentice lads, soldier men, blacksmiths, perfumers, glass blowers, fiddlers and on, and on."

"He never said things like that," said Harry.

"Walls have ears, my lord the King," Beaton said vehemently, "and I hug the plaster now, since you left me nothing else. And I've heard old Lennox now for months. Though I'm not naturally inquisitive, it's one of my duties. He delights especially in telling folk about the time he accidentally discovered you with some dark fellow with a strange predilection, even among your type, for—"

"That's enough," cried Harry. "Not one more word!"

Beaton sank back under the shadow of the canopy.

The Antwerp clock struck twelve. Shaking uncontrollably,

189

Harry knelt and wound his arms around Mary's hips. "Beat me," he sobbed, digging his fingers into her back, and twisting his head. "I didn't mean for him to die. My father tricked me. I didn't even know I'd signed the bond. I *liked* David; I did. Beat me!"

Mary looked down and ran her hand carelessly through his thick yellow hair. She felt she was going to cry. "No," she said, crouching beside him. "No. But please, husband, do as your wife *begs* you to do. For all our—" She stood up. She couldn't finish the sentence.

He lifted his head and searched her eyes, then looked away again. "Dr. Lusgerie over there must think all men and women are . . . I don't know."

"He took my betrothed from me," hissed Beaton, "and when he was done with his *sin,* he cast him by the wayside and went in search of something fresher, less tainted by him. If he'd loved my Johnny, there'd have been some pardon. I loved him! But our lord the King of freaks and—"

Mary ran to the bed and slapped Beaton across the face. If Beaton said another word, if Harry said another word, if anybody even moved, she thought she would die. "This isn't the time, *ma chère,*" she said softly. "It's time for a good scream."

Beaton screamed and screamed, then lay back on the pillow and covered her face. There was some movement in the corridor outside the door.

"Excellent," said Mary. "Splendid. Now business."

The heavy clock cradled in her arms read twelve-seventeen. Harry placed himself in front of the corridor door. Beaton screamed. Dr. Lusgerie flung open the limanga, cried for one of the guards to get boiling water from the kitchens and asked the other to come in and help hold the Queen's legs.

Mary raised the Antwerp clock and burst it over the man's skull. Together, she and Dr. Lusgerie bound him with a curtain cord, stuffed a kerchief in his mouth, dragged him across the room, and pushed him under the bed.

Mary grabbed an iron bookend from her bookcase and hid against the limanga again.

"Boiled water," announced the second guard, rushing by. Mary watched the water ricochet against the ceiling and splatter to the floor. Harry and the physician bound him and shoved him under the bed with the other man.

"Give us one hour," Mary said to Beaton. She kissed her on the mouth. "Then get you down that passage over there. And, lady love, don't go hoarse on me."

"Godspeed, madam. Careful for the baby. When you pass down below, tell the guard—his name's Alex, madam, and he doesn't know a thing that's happening, except his head is going to pay when they find out what he's done—tell him Miss Beaton sends her love. He can have the rest later."

Mary kissed Dr. Lusgerie good-by, then took Harry by the arm. The dank stairway smelled as Ruthven had when she bent over his corpse. The baby thumped against her heart. They passed two dead men.

A soldier slumped lazily against the bolted door. He undid the bolt, tipped his steel helmet over his eyes, smiled, and kicked the door open.

Mary grinned, threw her arms around him, and kissed him lightly on the chin. "Miss Beaton sends best wishes," she said.

Harry pulled her outside. "It's fine for you to do knights and ladies," he said, "but it's me whose throat they'll slit, if they ever catch hold of us."

The snow drummed against her face. The rest of her was numb. Harry held onto her reins as their horses careened across the snowy plains to Dunbar. Behind the thick sheet of clouds, the moon glimmered like a puddle of yellow mud. "Too fast," she cried. The swigging clouds whirled about, pouring down.

"Faster," he yelled against the blasting wind.

"I'll lose the baby if—"

"We can have another!"

The wind almost spun her from her horse. She yanked at her reins.

"If they catch us," he cried, "they'll kill both of us."

"Then save yourself!"

"Mary, please!"

"Let go my reins," she said. "I have to rest. A minute." She slipped from her saddle into the snow. It crunched up halfway to her knees. Her face was wet.

The snow melted down into her eyes, momentarily blinding her, and when she opened them again, she realized she was alone.

"Harry," she wailed. *"Harry!"*

Nothing but the sound of the wind.

She wound her arms around the thick neck of the horse and pressed her body against its side for warmth. Our Father Who art in heaven hallowed be Thy name Thy kingdom come Thy will . . . That was useless. No sense in that. She shut her eyes again. God must sleep all the time, she thought—how else could He bear it? The snow was warm and soothing. She'd never seen so much snow before. At the cruelest moment, when Nature has us in her grip entire, she relents. Death is so easy. . . .

Mary shook her head, placed her foot in the stirrup, and raised herself up. She jerked at the frozen reins and the horse moved forward a few feet. "Don't be afraid," she whispered, nuzzling him behind the ear. Far off, the wind roared like ten thousand drums and harps struck at once. The horse wandered aimlessly. Mary started singing to keep from falling asleep. She bit savagely into her lower lip and sat straight. The baby's weight pulled her down again. Suddenly, the horse broke into a gallop. Mary hung onto the reins, then something—a branch?— struck her across the skull and she flew from the saddle into the snow. It was soft; it didn't hurt; it was almost warm. She struggled to her feet, lifted her left foot, and planted it firmly in front of her right. She waited a minute, then pulled her right foot up out of the ice and carefully moved it in front of her left. She steadied herself and took another step. "I will not die," she said out loud. She laughed. *"I* will not die. I *will* not die. I will *not* die." She rubbed her hands across her belly, then stopped. Had she heard voices? Mumbling to herself, she broke into a run.

"She's alive! Alive!" someone hallooed. Or was it the wind, playing tricks?

She fell into something.

"Here," Bothwell cried. "Over here!" And then, settling her down in the snow and holding her tight in his arms: "Was it bad?"

"It was bad," she moaned, resting her head on his shoulder. "Is the baby safe?"

"I can't feel him any more. Only weight. I can't feel him moving any more. They killed my Davy. Killed. I'm cold. I'd cry, except they'd freeze and that'd make it colder." Her face stung. Like a thousand bee bites. "I can't feel him move, Bothwell."

He rested his hand on her waist. "We're a mile from Dunbar. Two hundred men, more coming." His hand jumped, then he laughed slightly, and said, "I felt him."

"Are you sure?"

"Yes."

She heard movements through the snow, and voices all around them. "What did he feel like?" she said suspiciously. Bothwell was lifting her up.

"He felt—odd," he said. "It made my whole arm tingle." He adjusted her foot in the stirrup and eased her onto the saddle.

"You must promise, Bothwell, to be with me when he's born. You must promise, promise. Do you promise?"

"Yes," he said, settling down behind her on the horse.

She turned her head and kissed him.

"Your Majesty is exhausted," he said. "Come, let's go. Johnny, throw me a fur."

"Is he here? Oh, Johnny, brother, where are you?" She bent slightly from the saddle and rubbed her hand through John's sandy hair.

"Nothing can kill us," he laughed, throwing a fur across her lap. "Nothing. We're remorseless, Sister Mary."

"They killed him," she said thickly. "Then they hung him from the wall. They stabbed and stabbed him."

"Dear God," said John, clasping her hand, "Davy's in heaven now. God's fixed his legs and straightened his back forever. And when we laugh down here, he'll laugh up there. And God will only let him see us when we're happy." He wiped at his eyes, then ran off through the cascading snow.

"It's our blood," Mary said to Bothwell. "We're all Stewart.

We'll take so many with us. Even James is a Stewart. We'll take so many. Do you think we will?"

"Yes, I think," said Bothwell.

"Did you really feel the baby? You weren't simply saying it?"

"I really felt him."

After perhaps twenty minutes, she saw the black shadowy form of Dunbar Castle rising from the hills. It looked like something out of a nightmare. In Paris, she'd seen copies done from Bosch's *Hell*. That's what it looked like to her. The entire ribbed-stone citadel was brightly lit. Smoking torches scurried along the walls and turrets. Mary rested her head against Bothwell's doublet and closed her eyes. In the distance, she could hear them cheering.

Bothwell sat her on the mattress and motioned for one of the women to come and undress Mary. "She delivered me," he said. "She's good."

"He was a hard one, too, Your Machsty," laughed the woman. "He was shy to come out. Hardest one I ever had and here he is now."

"You can have only a few hours' sleep," said Bothwell. "We must march as soon as it is possible. This is Magridge Bundy." He went to rise, but Mary caught at his hand and held him.

"I love you, Bothwell," she whispered.

The old woman looked at Bothwell, then at Mary, then at Bothwell again.

He stared at her. "If you ever say that again," he mumbled, "I'll take you."

Mary sat up, smiled brightly, and smoothed the thick black hair from his forehead.

Bothwell got up, walked to the door, looked at her, then left.

"Best lay back, Machsty, give babby his rest," said the old woman, easing Mary back onto the straw mattress and unbuttoning her blouse. "I don't think it will happen if you rest."

"All the babies you've delivered, Magridge," sighed Mary, arching her back to ease the pain. "And Bothwell was the hardest! His poor mother—did he hurt her very much? I want to know everything that will happen, so I won't think anything wrong is happening. What was his mother like?" A sharp pain traveled up her spine. Magridge sat next to her on the bed and rolled her hands along her back.

"What was Bothwell's mother like?" That felt good. She was almost asleep. Her eyes felt as if they were full of sand. "Magridge . . . ?"

"I only seen her oncet."

Oh, that was very, very good. Lennox would pay dearly, Morton and Ruthven would pay—Ruthven was dead. She'd forgotten. How could she forget? "She *died,*" Mary cried suddenly. "She died having him! He killed her."

"There, there," soothed Magridge, "there, my lady, she was tiny, I remember, she didn't have hardly no hips at all, her. But you're big—it'll slip right out."

"It hurts," moaned Mary. "I'm afraid. I never had a baby before." She buried her face in the woman's lap. It smelled of cold, fresh air and old wool.

"It hurts because you had a fright tonight, my poor lady. Sleep. Your time has not yet come, but you must sleep for the bairn and for so to go back to Edinburgh tomorrow and take back what was took from you, and have your bairn then, when its time comes."

"Yes, that," said Mary.

Bothwell nudged her into wakefulness. She stared blankly at the bowl of thick brown nettle broth.

"Eat, and then we march," he said. "Are you all right? Magridge said you're not quite ready to deliver yet."

She nodded and scooped at the broth.

"A surprise for Your Majesty," Bothwell announced. "A magic surprise." He pointed toward the opened doorway. Outside, in the corridor, Maitland was leaning against the peeling yellow wall. He saw Mary and smiled broadly.

"Magic," said Bothwell. "Michael Wiley out there says the traitors tricked him. He says he had no idea."

"He's lying," said Mary.

"What shall I do with him?"

Mary thought a minute. "Tell him," she said quietly, "to leave Scotland. Tell him that if he ever comes back I will cut off his head."

"And your husband, Your Majesty?"

"Is he here?"

"They found him half an hour after we found you. He was half dead with the snow."

Mary lifted a spoonful of broth to her mouth. "You should have let him die," she said.

"He will return with us now to Holyrood," Bothwell said.

Knox preached: "After his condemnation by the cardinal's ecclesiastical court, Master Wishart was bound to a stake in the Merkat Square, but the people did not cheer. In the midst of the flames, the man was heard to say, 'Though death is bitter to the flesh and fearful to the eye, it is the entrance to eternal life.' The cardinal laughed and asked George Wishart if he would recant. But he said no, and so died." Knox, overcome by emotion, rested his arms on the gleaming oak pulpit and waited.

James sat alone in the choir loft and surveyed the congregation below. Maitland was gone. James knew where he was.

Knox continued, "That is twenty years since, but marvel not that I speak of such an event today. For there are some who mourn the death of one David Riccio, who is known to have been the servant of many cardinals. His end was a deed worthy of all praise. His end was ordained by God."

The stained-glass windows sent shimmering colors against the rafters. Crimson and gold and green caressed the dust. Clever Mary. Still, she'd only been gone a matter of hours and it would take two days at the least for her to gather sufficient force together. Then what? The Italian was dead; there was no need for further turmoil. It would be disastrous. There was a bond with the King's name, Morton's name, Ruthven's name, Lindsay's and Lennox's and Argyll's names—but his name wasn't on it. He had known, but he had not said, "Do it." They were fools to have done it in front of her. Suddenly, he was aware of the scattering, shouting congregation.

"God damn it, Stewart, come down," Morton called up from the frenzy down below.

James sat back and looked at the gigantic mahogany cross which hung suspended above the empty pulpit. At Whitehall, Elizabeth's palace in London, there were elaborately cut hedges depicting griffins, mermaids, dragons, centaurs, unicorns, and all matter of mythic beasts.

When Mary's escape was discovered late the night before, they'd pried open her private drawers and found letters from Rome. The letters spoke of Catholic restoration: the Queen of Scots had delayed too long. His Holiness was beginning to doubt the Queen of Scots' fidelity to Holy Mother Church. When could De Gouda, the papal nuncio, return to Scotland and see her? It was time to begin a great venture in the name of Christ Jesus. Difficulties in the realm might be obviated if justice were executed against a small band of dangerous men: the heretics James Stewart, Maitland of Leithington, the reformer John Knox, etc. Madam, His Holiness grows most impatient. Etc., etc.

George Wishart tied to the stake. Wishart, that most gentle and beloved minister, who had converted Knox, among many others, to Presbyterianism. Tied to the stake and burned to embers. That was almost twenty years ago, in an age when there were many George Wisharts.

He sat in the choir loft a long time. Now that he had returned from his exile, he would never leave Scotland again, even if it meant his death. He would never leave. How unbearably sad and lonely the whole world was. Then it was night.

The next day, James presented himself at Holyrood. He slowly approached the canopied throne, then knelt. Mary's face was sculptured, without expression. Harry Stewart, hardly looking like a King, sat next to her, letting his eyes circle and recircle the room and fall here and there on everything except faces.

"Do not kneel," said Mary. She was big with child, her belly like a mound.

Would she kill him? Why did he think that she would kill him? He was her brother. But he thought that she might do it.

Mary got up and kissed him on the cheek. "Brother," she said, "in my presence, you need never kneel."

He thought he detected a note of hatred in her voice, but when she backed away, James saw nothing in her face but a friendly smile. Darnley was staring at the ceiling.

 CHAPTER TEN

Bothwell watched the hazy sun bob up and down in the sky as he and Jean rode up the steep ascent of Ramsey Lane to the Castle of the Maidens.

"Fifty crowns is much too much," said Jean as they reached the level ground of the esplanade. "There's no need for half the staff we have."

"Money, money," said Bothwell, reaching out and affectionately chucking her on the chin.

"We've so little," said Jean.

Bothwell shook his head no and Jean lapsed into silence.

They'd told Bothwell that the pains were now four minutes apart but that Mary would be safe.

"Beaton showed me the will," Jean was saying. "She leaves a great deal to her servants, and to her relatives in France if she and the child should die. But she left you her three Arabian horses and some of her books. She even remembered me—some clothing."

Bothwell waved up to the governor of the castle, then he and Jean clattered across the drawbridge. Inside the portcullis gate, the vast quadrangular courtyard was filled with helmeted men. Bothwell pulled at his reins.

"What's wrong?" said Jean. She put her hand on his forehead.

"I don't know. Nothing," said Bothwell, brushing the hand away.

Jean said something so softly that he couldn't hear it.

"She won't die," she said again.

"I know," he said.

"Soon, husband, I hope to be with child," she said in a little voice. When he didn't say anything, she said brightly, "How many would you like, husband? I want a stable."

Bothwell laughed and turned his head away.

They rode to the main building, where, six years before, Marie de Guise had died. What I am most afraid of, Bothwell told himself, is that she will beat the Black Man bloody so as to save the baby, but that after the baby has been born, she will let herself die. They alighted and waited for a guard to unlock the heavy iron door, then walked along the sloping carriage corridor to a flight of stairs. At each wind in the staircase, a soldier stood at attention.

Beaton met them at the top. "It's begun," she said. "Lusgerie says it will be a difficult labor. Archbishop Hamilton's in there with her. And the King." She squeezed Bothwell's hand. "Please, Bothwell, she doesn't want him there when it happens."

On the way to Mary's room, they passed a dark young gentleman sitting on the embroidered couch. He wore the bright red and yellow livery of the house of Tudor. "Elizabeth's courier," Beaton explained. "He wouldn't stay downstairs with the others, and, well, the Queen of England *is* the Queen of England."

The young man waited until they had gone into Mary's chamber, then poured himself some wine from the platter on the little table next to the couch. The door opened and Harry entered the corridor.

"My lord," said the courier, falling to his knees and presenting a letter.

Harry looked at him with something approaching disbelief, then took the letter and tore it open. "It's only from Mother," he sighed. "I thought it might be something exciting, like another threat of death. I haven't heard from Mother in months. She still maintains her suite in the Tower, I see. Last week, she bought some land in Kent. She's always buying land. Your name is Ned Drake, she says, and I'm to get you a position." Inside, Mary screamed deafeningly, and Harry winced and muttered, "How can women take it?" He sat down on the couch and patted one of the cushions. Drake poured him a goblet and sat beside him. "Mother says you've been to Labrador, but you're such a dark-looking man. I thought Labrador was all ice. But forget that. What do you want, Drake?"

Drake bent his head. "My family has been in your family's service for some time. It is now my turn to serve. And, if Your Majesty will please pardon my boldness in saying so, you are much in need of service. As the Queen of England's courier, I am instructed to return with news of your wife's childbirth, but if you ask me to stay, I shall."

Harry gave him a curious look, then stood up, walked to the door, and pressed his ear against the wood.

"As a favor to Your Majesty's mother," said Drake, getting up and walking to Harry's side, "the Queen of England made me captain of the Tower. I was a very good captain. But when your mother was sent to the Tower, I was—quite understandably —dismissed from that position. But the Queen had seen me a few times and she thought me well mannered, efficient, and possessed of a good leg."

Harry looked at Drake's legs.

"She made me a chamberman. I met important people. I was allowed to go on a sea voyage to Labrador and I lived through it, even though a majority of the crew did not. I made my mind up not to die, and so I survived."

"Tell me about Labrador," said Harry. Harry liked the man's voice. It was generally without expression, like Bothwell's, and there was an undertone of sadness and wonder in it. Unlike Bothwell's voice, however, it never seemed to rise above a respectful murmur. It was a quiet, extremely pleasant-sounding poor man's voice. "Willoughby froze to death in Lapland," Drake was saying, "but the vessel sailed on. The storm still went on, and we could not see any land, Your Majesty. There were hundreds of floating ice mountains, some as high as fifty feet. I was in the topgallant crosstrees, under the lookout, and they towered above me. The ice scraped against the bulwarks and the main jib cracked and—"

Inside the room, there was a resounding *smack!* and a baby's howl filled the night.

"I suppose I should go in," said Harry. He grabbed hold of Drake's hand. "Wait for me. You see, Drake, everybody in there *despises* me."

"Then you will give me a position, Your Majesty?"

"Yes," said Harry. He stopped at the door, and added, "I need even one friend."

Mary was propped up against two thick pillows, holding a small white bundle in her arms. Dr. Lusgerie, Beaton, John, James, and Bothwell and his wife were standing around the bed and smiling. Everybody was smiling. Archbishop Hamilton muttered something in Latin, then trickled drops of water down the infant's forehead. Mary's face was pale and streaked with sweat, her hair damp and colorless against the pillows. Down below, in the courtyard, cannon exploded into the night.

"He makes me to laugh," said Mary, her head swaying back and forth. "There, little old man, oh, Bothwell, James, he's so red. Look, Eminence, look."

"James Charles," said the archbishop, beaming. "What a beefy little lad!" He clapped his hands. "Splendiferous, madam. Excellent well done."

Mary saw Harry and lost her smile. "My lord," she said solemnly. "God has given you and me a son. He is your son and no other man's. He is so much your son, I'm afraid for him."

To hide his burning face, Harry bent and kissed the baby on the head. "Dear heart," he mumbled, "is this your promise to forgive and forget?"

"I've forgiven everything," she said, covering the child, "but I can't forget. What if Fawdonside, the man who held the pistol against me that night, had fired?"

"These things are past."

"Then let them go." She looked at Bothwell. "I hope this child will be the first to unite England and Scotland as one country."

"Not the first," said Bothwell. "The second. After Your Majesty and his father."

"His father has broken with me," said Mary. She lowered her head and laughed. "I'm still famished for radishes and iced cream. Even now. That must be why he's so red. All those radishes, all that pink iced cream inside me. In honor of the event, Maitland can remain here in Scotland. Tell him that, James; I know you're close to him. He may remain, but tell him I won't trust him again. But there's no reason why—never mind. . . ."

John sat down in a chair and ran his fingers lightly across his lute. *"Ben venga Maggio,"* he sang, *"E'l gonfalon gentile . . ."*

"That was one of Davy's favorites," said Mary to no one in particular. "I never think of him. I try never to think of him. Poor Davy." She motioned for Bothwell to come close. "You see here, Bothwell, the one who will unite the kingdoms. You saw him safe to Dunbar after that night at Holyrood, and you saw to it that he was safely delivered in this castle. Wherefore," she said, clasping him by the arm, "I make of you his servant."

Bothwell drew aside the baby's coverlet. Harry watched, his face rigid.

"He's beautiful," Mary said sleepily. "Isn't he splendid? And I made him inside me. He'll be tall, I know he will . . . like James and my father. Don't stop, John. Davy would never stop in the middle of a song. I didn't think I'd want to hear it, but, please, go on."

John strummed the lute strings. *"E quindi uscimmo a riveder le stelle."*

Mary lifted her hand and ran it carelessly through Bothwell's hair. Jean turned away and looked at John.

"Bothwell, you take James Charles . . . no, no, let his uncle James take and show him at the window. Where's James?"

James lifted the child in his arms and went to the casement, walking past Harry, who stared at him dully.

Fireworks were zooming in great arcs across the black sky, crisscrossing and flaring down upon the chunky towers and gabled roofs of Edinburgh. Down below, outside the castle's walls and beyond the moat, hundreds of men and women stood cheering.

⚙ CHAPTER ELEVEN ⚙

Mary, James, and Maitland walked about the palace garden;
the odor of some dying flower moved about their feet, mingling
with the morning mist.

"Dr. Lusgerie's orders are explicit," said James. "It's been
four months since the Prince's birth. You need fresh air, a change
of scene. A progress to Alloa would be ideal. You can attend
the assizes along the way, if you like." He watched Mary bend
and clip a yellow rose from its stem.

"The air's good in Alloa," said Mary, lifting the yellow petals
to her nose. "Summer's short in Scotland. Autumn already."
She turned to go.

"The christening is scheduled for December 17," said Maitland. "The King of France has appointed Monsieur du Croc as
his proxy. We have as yet no word from King Philip of Spain
as to whom his representative will be, which is most irregular."

Mary smiled languidly.

"Your Majesty," said James, "the Presbyterian superintendent
for Lothian, Master Spottiswoode, has come with a deputation of
ministers from the south to pay his respects to the Prince."

"I'll see him after breakfast."

Mary stooped by the garden gate, picked up one of her toy terriers, and walked across the courtyard and up the palace steps.

On her way to the dining room, she saw Spottiswoode and his delegation and invited them to eat with her. She liked Spottiswoode; he was a good old man, not at all the typical Presbyterian. He laughed, his eyes crinkled, and he knew Ronsard's poetry. Afterward, she took them upstairs to the nursery. On the way they met Bothwell, and she asked him to come too.

"Braw," said Spottiswoode, his white beard dangling over the baby's cradle. He looked up at Mary. She nodded her head. The old man cautiously lifted the child from its cradle. It gurgled and grabbed at a strand of his beard. Spottiswoode laughed gently.

"Look, Bothwell," said Mary, "he's going to be a Presbyterian for sure now." She felt proud because her child was beautiful, and because upon her return to Scotland five years before, Spottiswoode had been as outspoken against her as Knox, and now he was acting like an old grandfather who'd come to visit his first grandson. He'd even brought a Bartholomew baby and a rattle gift with him.

"There's some business I have to do," said the old man, raising the child affectionately against his chest and patting him on the back. He winked at Mary, cleared his throat, and proclaimed, rather summarily, she thought, "We, the assembled ministers of the district of Lothian, most humbly request Your Right Royal Majesty that the Crown Prince, James Charles, Duke of Albany, be baptized according to the solemn rites of the Presbyterian religion. As the country is Presbyterian and Reformed, it would be justice." He winked again.

"I may not do that," said Mary. She rested her hand on Spottiswoode's arm, bent, and kissed her baby on the head.

The old man smiled warmly. "Alas, madam, but what is, is. In any case, you must at least allow me to pray for the little fellow."

"Granted," said Mary.

"There, there, little boy," said Spottiswoode. "Don't cry. Prayer is just good talking with God."

It had been such a long time since Mary felt so much at ease, even happy. She looked up, saw Archbishop Hamilton at the door, and motioned for him to come in.

"Now say 'Amen,'" whispered Spottiswoode, chucking the baby's chin. "Amen. Ah-mmm-ehhh-nn."

The baby cooed and grabbed at the old man's finger.

"By God, Your Majesty," laughed Bothwell, "he said it. I actually heard him say it."

"Wonderful," laughed Mary. "Master Spottiswoode, from this moment on, I dub you Master Amen." She embraced the old man, then stood back and said confidentially, "When he's old enough, he'll need good tutors and you'll be one."

Spottiswoode looked past her head at the archbishop and lost his smile.

Hamilton examined his fingernails. After a minute of awkward silence, he raised his head and said, attempting to sound jocular, "I never expected to see old Spottiswoode again, old Archie. We were little boys together. We had great times fishing together. Splendiferous times. But that was—oh, Your Majesty, let me see —that was a long time back."

"A very long time back," said Spottiswoode quietly. He lowered the baby in the cradle.

The ministers in his delegation stood alongside the wall with blank expressions on their rough, country faces.

"The weather's fine," said Mary. "All the clouds are down in England. Why don't you both go fishing?"

"I do not think that possible," said the superintendent. "I have some business with the presbyters, but . . ."

"Oh, Your Majesty," said the archbishop, fingering his crucifix, "Archie and I are *enemies*. We can't go fishing together. What would people think?"

"Times change, but friends are friends," said Mary, drawing Spottiswoode and Hamilton to a small door that led to an adjoining chamber, "Now, under pain of the Queen's displeasure, I command both of you to make arrangements for a fishing excursion to the Firth. Ten minutes. That's all I give you."

Spottiswoode's face went slack. He avoided Hamilton's eyes and looked back at the other ministers who were staring at him in amazement. Mary drew them to the antechamber.

"Excuse me," said Harry, tottering at the opposite entrance-way.

"My husband," said Mary, closing the door on Hamilton and Spottiswoode. The ministers bowed gravely.

"The King, by God," said Harry. "Tell me, gentlemen, even in the Protestant Bible, does it not say a wife shall cleave to her husband and obey him? Doesn't it?"

"It also says the husband shall honor his wife," said Bothwell, from a corner.

Ignoring him, Harry said, "I was told you heretics came here to request my son be baptized in heresy. I say no. Now you've had your answer, and now you can leave."

The ministers looked at Mary.

Finally she said, "They'll leave shortly, husband. Sit down. You look tired. *Please.*"

"I've given you permission to leave," said Harry, holding the door. Mary turned her head to the wall. The ministers stood in the corner of the room. "Could Your Majesty inform Master Spottiswoode that we're going now," one of them said.

Mary jerked around and faced Harry. "They will not leave until *I* have told them to leave," she said. "*You* will leave."

The door slammed shut.

"Your Majesty," said another of the ministers, clearing his throat. She had to bend down because he was so old and his voice so thin. "In our religion, a bill of divorcement may be obtained before a tribunal of presbyters empowered in such matters. It would affect the Prince, your son, in no way."

"Oh, friend, it's really the funniest thing. Everybody knows, don't they? Everybody! There's nobody who doesn't. Thank you very much—very, very much—for coming, and you will come again, I promise, and there's nothing to fear from me on religion." She walked to the antechamber door, opened it, and saw Archbishop Hamilton and Master Spottiswoode kneeling on the floor, clasping each other's hands. She shut the door again.

There's no other way, she was convinced, none whatsoever.

The Reformation in Scotland is a fact, but now we have to think about ourselves.

"Even in the Anglican faith," said another of the ministers, "divorce is permitted. Anglicanism is similar in many respects to Your Majesty's own religion."

"I'm a Catholic," she said. "I can't be anything else." It amused her to think that, had Henry VIII succeeded in kidnaping her twenty years ago, she'd be a Protestant now anyway—she might even be Queen of England—and none of the troubles she'd been faced with since her return to Scotland would have existed.

"We're going—together," announced Hamilton, returning with Spottiswoode from the antechamber.

She took their arms and walked them to the door. She kissed both Hamilton and Spottiswoode on the cheek, extended her hand to the ministerial delegation, and asked Bothwell to show them through the garden on their way out.

Mary sat down and rocked her baby in his cradle. About half an hour later she heard a noise at the door and turned around and saw Harry.

"I thought you were a Catholic," he said.

"Go find a corner somewhere and drink," she said, bending over the cradle.

"There is no church but the Catholic Church," he said like some small boy rehearsing for a morality play. " 'Thou art Peter and upon this rock I—' "

"Splendid," she said, walking toward him and folding her arms. "He can spout the Bible. The man can't stand up straight, but he can quote God with the best of them. What do you want? Have you come to complain again?"

"I've enough cause," he said. "You've deprived me of all my authority—I can't even sign documents any more. All the nobles avoid me and make fun of me behind my back."

"Is that my fault?"

"Yes! They do it because they know it pleases you."

Mary sighed. "If you want them to like you, then you'll have to learn how to behave."

"Drake said—"

"Is Drake your latest?"

Harry raised his hand.

"Hit me if you like," she said, shrugging her shoulders. "I'm not pregnant now."

Harry started to say something, caught himself, and said smoothly, "That is really none of your business, my dear. I don't ask you who—"

She slapped him. "I've *never* been untrue to you, and you know it! That baby over there—he's as much you as he is me—he's your son, and God knows it. But you, by your conduct, have made him a *bastard* in the eyes of the world." She moved away and said calmly, "I don't even hate you. But I don't want to see you . . . hear you . . . think anything of you . . . until—"

"You said 'until,' dear heart." He walked behind her, started rubbing his hands up and down her breasts, and kissing her neck and shoulders.

"Have we run out of page boys?" she said, trying to pull his fingers away. "Is Drake so dull?"

"I'm going to make love to you on the floor," he said desperately.

She realized with a start: Oh, God, I want him to! "Shall I call the guard?" she said in a thin voice. "You wouldn't want me to embarrass you in front of them, would you? I know how much the opinion of other people means to you."

"I dismissed them. And I'm used to being laughed at. You wanted me once, Mary. Now I want you. Oh, dear God, you feel good. Please. Let me."

Stop talking, she thought to herself, stop fumbling and do it! His hands were under her bodice and he was pressing his body against her back and running his tongue along her neck. In a minute she would turn around, put her hands on his shoulders, and kiss him. "I don't want to," she said weakly. He folded the pink chiffon material that bordered her breasts in his fists, tugged, and ripped her gown to the waist. In a minute they'd be lying on the floor. They'd be naked and he would have that gigantic thing of his up inside of her, and she would have her legs twisted around his bottom. And everything would be well after they were done. But she had no intention of making it easy for him. She reached back and tore at his hair with her finger-nails.

The door of the nursery opened and Mary spun around in time to see Harry land on the floor and cover his face with his hands. She raised her eyes. Bothwell gave her a look, then kicked Harry in the side.

"What—what are you doing?" she said.

Harry jumped to his feet, folded his hands, lifted his arms, and smacked Bothwell across the skull. Bothwell fell against the couch. Harry rushed at him, raised his foot, and crushed it in his groin. Stifling a cry, Bothwell twisted his leg around Harry's, causing the other man to lose his balance, fall, and bang his head against the iron doorstep. Bothwell dropped to his knees and began methodically pounding his fists into Harry's face and throat.

"You'll kill him!" cried Mary, pulling at Bothwell's shoulders. "Stop! He's my husband!" He shoved her away. His hands were covered with Harry's blood. His hands dropped to his side, and he slumped to the floor and leaned back against the wall.

Harry gasped, dragged himself to his feet, looked at Mary and Bothwell, opened the door, looked to see if anybody was outside, and left.

The door opened again and she looked up.

"Whore," said Harry. The door slammed shut.

Mary fastened the lock and looked at Bothwell. She realized her breasts were exposed from where Harry had ripped her gown. She tried to cover them with her hands. Bothwell got up, took a cloth napkin from the table, and fastened it over the torn bodice. "The baby's crying," he said, moving toward the cradle. She watched him pick up the baby and rock it slowly in his arms, then lower it slowly back into its cradle. He sat down on the couch. "He only shames himself," he said bitterly. "Your husband."

Mary drew the blanket up to the baby's chin and wiped the dribble from the corner of its mouth. "He also is capable of shaming my son, and me. But you must remember that he *is* my husband. And you must understand that I am my husband's wife; I love him. He's young. He can change. Maybe he won't

become a different person, but I know he has it in him to become
. . . better."

"I understand that you're a fool when you say such things."

She sat down next to him on the sofa. "Bothwell," she said,
touching his hand, "there's little I can do for you now, but
someday, when I'm Queen in England, I'll give you more than
anybody else—except—"

"I know," he said without emotion. "Except your brother
James."

"You're like James," Mary said softly. "You won't admit it.
Neither will he. But the two of you are the two most solitary,
sad-looking men I've ever known. And the two of you care more
for Scotland than anyone." She sighed and sat back. "Harry never
loved me. He only wants me now because he can't have me. But
he doesn't love me, Bothwell. That night Davy died, we were
out in the snow and he said—he left me and our baby to die. He
doesn't even love our son. That night Davy died—"

"Madam," said Bothwell wearily, "that was March. This is
October. Your baby's alive now. Your husband's nothing now. If
he issued a proclamation on his own authority tomorrow morning
that said cows give milk, nobody would believe it."

Mary looked up at the clock. It was ten-thirty. "I should go and
read my Latin," she said, not moving.

"Hablo, habla, hablas, hablais, hablamos."

"Oh, my lord, that's not Latin," said Mary, a giddy feeling
rising from her stomach and fluttering upward to her brain.
"That must be Gaelic. Or Swiss-Mohammedan."

"Just bad Scots," said Bothwell, a smile wrinkling his face.

"Hablaba," sputtered Mary. *"Hablabamos. Hahh-bug-aboo."*
She poked him playfully in the ribs.

"No more," he said hoarsely, "Oh no, no, no. It's too much.
Oh . . . it's wonderful to . . . laugh!"

She sat next to him on the floor and whispered in his ear,
"Es un elephante en mi vaso de vino." Giggling uncontrollably,
she covered her face with her hands.

"There's an elephant in my wineglass!" he guffawed, lifting his
hand and resting it over hers. She pressed it against her lips.

"Don't do that," he said, pulling his hand away.

"Did . . . I'm late for my Latin," she said, attempting to rise. Bothwell caught her by the ankle. "Don't go. Talk with me. A short while."

"I'm not in the mood for Latin anyway," she said nervously. "Did you see Spottiswoode and the archbishop when they left? Amazing. Splendid. Poor John. How long has he been gone now —three, four months? And where?"

"John can handle himself. He's probably up north. That's what your dad used to do. Whenever he had a disappointment, he'd run up to the Highlands, and half a year later he'd come down again—out of nowhere—refreshed."

"Am I mistaken, Bothwell, or has Jean been putting on weight lately?"

"You're mistaken," said Bothwell, shifting uneasily.

"She *has* been gaining weight. After all, the two of you have been married almost a year now. I must say it's about time. You'll have only boys, Bothwell. I'm sure of it."

"Don't say it. Please."

"Don't say what?"

"It! God damn it, *it!*" He got to his feet.

Oh no, Mary thought. Not that, please God. Impossible. Bothwell's file in De Gouda's report had contained the remark: "Totally amoral—yet no known bastards recorded." She wanted to cry because Bothwell was her friend. She respected him, trusted him. As Queen, she could grant him lands, revenues, titles, any number of favors, but she could not command his wife to bear him a son.

"I know many women who didn't have children until years after—"

"Jean hasn't. And Jean won't."

"But you never know," said Mary. "That's all I ever learned. You never know what will happen."

"Right," he said.

"Jean loves you."

"Right."

"The love's the most important thing. If you have somebody who loves you as much as she loves you, then anything else you want—isn't necessary."

"I don't love Jean. And I never will. Don't look so shocked."

"But she loves you . . ." Mary turned her head away, so he couldn't see her smiling. He *didn't* love Jean, after all. She was glad, *glad*.

"You loved your husband," he said cruelly. "Did that make him love you? I think not." He stood up and moved to the door. "The world's a baby. You want him and can't have him. She wants me and can't have me. And I want you."

"What?" she asked, still averting her head to hide the smile. She wanted to hear him say the words again.

"I want to *lie* with you." He hesitated a minute, then unlocked the door.

"I love your Aegean eyes," she whispered.

"Aegean?" he said, dropping to his knees, wrapping his arms around her waist, and laying his head in her lap.

Her hands glided down his calfskin back. "At the Louvre, there was a statue they found in the Aegean sea. Bluish bronze covered with sea wrack a thousand years. It was about six feet. A charioteer—"

Bothwell lifted the napkin from her torn bodice.

"It was a Greek statue," she said. "They found it in the Aegean. They cleaned it, but they couldn't clean it altogether. They used to paint on the eyes. The statue was under the sea a thousand years, but the paint hadn't corroded. They put the statue outside my apartments in the promenade deck. Sometimes I'd get up early in the morning and sit and watch the sun edging its way along the gold walls from the window, until it touched his face."

"Oh, you're good," he sighed, running his hands along the back of her dress, unfastening the clasps.

"His eyes were so white. With gray circles and black circles painted inside the gray ones. They were such sad eyes." She knew that when it was over it would have been bad and she would be sorry it had happened.

James Hepburn, Earl of Bothwell, Lord High Admiral of Scotland, thirty-one years old, five feet six inches tall, perhaps one hundred forty pounds, copper skin and muscles, short black hair, Aegean gray eyes, a nose that looks as if it might have been broken. His smile brings his face to life. His smile is the diamond point of him. Mary stared at the cracked plaster ceiling.

"I love you." He hunched and heaved. "Oh, *you!*"

She scraped her fingernails along his buttocks and squeezed her thighs against his hips.

When he'd finished, he raised himself on his elbows and looked at her. His face was red and puffy. He lay beside her and took her hand in his and kissed it.

"It's late," she said, sitting up, holding her petticoats to her breasts.

"Let me come to you again, tonight," he whispered.

She drew the petticoats on over her head, stood, looked about the room, then went to the mirror and began adjusting her hair. Bothwell lay on the the floor, not moving. The thick blood vessels on his brown arms disgusted her. From the waist down his body was a sickly white, except for that part of him that had just been inside her. She noticed a blemish on his right shoulder. When he sat up, she saw the two ugly purple scars from the bullet wounds he'd received during James's rebellion. "You have a wife," she said hurriedly. "I have a husband."

He said nothing, but bent over and began pulling on his hose.

"It's four-thirty," she said. "I'm dining with Archbishop Hamilton tonight." She dropped the torn pink gown over her shoulders.

"When you're fucking," Bothwell said suddenly, "it's easy to forget you're God's representative on earth. You speak in Gaelic —something none of the other whores I've had could do—you speak in the old Gaelic, too, that nobody uses any more, which sounds like no language you can hear on this earth, unless you've seen some of the blacks the Portuguese bring up from down in Africa."

"Everything they say is true," she said in outrage. "You're an animal. Mad—like your father."

He strode across the room, wrenched her arm behind her back, and smashed his fist into the side of her face. Blood rolled thickly from her nose and over her mouth. She swayed, then yanked her arm free and backed off.

"There's a window over there," she hissed. "Go do what your madman father did!"

"There's a couch over there," he said in a strangled voice. "Go lie down and do what your father did. If my father went mad it was because he was too much your father's good friend. You Stewarts are such fairy-tale fools. You love drowning in your own blood. Lie down and die of a broken heart—"

"You'll pay—"

"I can see you twenty years from now. What an ugly little picture. Sitting by the hearth. You'll be knitting stockings and wearing rouge and powder and false hair and you'll be dreaming about how young you thought you were once and how maybe you could have danced with elves when there was lightning in the sky. But never did. And Darnley will be sitting by the hearth holding your hand, and looking twenty years younger than you. Right. And like every night, that night you'll be thinking maybe he'll be good to you and maybe he'll shove his glorious slug up your glorious dried-up gash. And you'll look into the fire, and never think of me at all. And you'll go to bed alone again that night and you'll hear the rain and lightning thumping off your window, and suddenly you'll get an urge—"

Mary picked up a Chinese vase and hurled it at his head. Bothwell ducked and the vase smashed against the cupboard and shattered the glass front piece.

"Very good, Your Majesty," he laughed.

She reached for a book, threw it, and hit him square in the face. He stopped laughing. "When you die," she said coolly, "since there won't, of course, be any heirs, I think I'll confiscate your lands and give them to my brother James."

"Twenty years from now," he said furiously, "you'll be in bed alone again, and you'll remember something that happened between your legs once. And the Queen of Scotland and the Isles will roam like a ghost through the halls at night, old, wrinkled, clicking her rosary beads, looking for page boys, soldier boys, clerk boys—anything your husband may have neglected. Who's—"

He sighed and fell back on the couch and looked blankly at the bits of glass lying on the floor in front of the cupboard.

The sun was on one side of the earth and the moon was on the other. Mary watched the sky slowly darken. Down in Edinburgh, smoke began curling from the chimneys. She moved behind the couch and put her hand on Bothwell's shoulder. "I was the cause of what happened," she whispered. "I was, not you. But if we ever made love again, it wouldn't be love, and we wouldn't be friends."

"Harry will never change, you know," said Bothwell. He got up and walked to the door. "He doesn't need you to live. Do you know that?"

"I'm sorry," she said. "There's nothing else I can think to say. I'm sorry."

Bothwell closed the door behind him.

Mary sat in the darkening room, her hands folded in her lap. She rested her head on the back of the couch and gazed out the window at the rising moon.

Yellow. Bright yellow.

Like that yellow rose she'd plucked this morning in the gardens and handed to James because she could not bear to have put it in a vase and set it on a table and watch it die. Not simply fold into thin paper. They don't do that. They fade and brown, then curl and rot, then stink, turn rank, rancid.

That night she dined at Archbishop Hamilton's house. As was her custom of late, she dismissed her escort upon her arrival. It was only a short distance back to Holyrood and she liked walking alone in the night. There was no danger involved. The streets were usually empty and they were well patrolled. Besides, she was the Queen.

After supper, as she walked along the High Street, she marveled at how much Edinburgh resembled a fairy city. The moonlight made it look clean, neat, compact. As she walked, the thin mist wafted about the hem of her skirts. In the distance the night watchman jangled his bell and called out the time. On an impulse, she turned down a narrow side street.

The walls on either side rose five and six stories and were

caked with mud and clay. The odor was oppressive. Mary listened as someone threw open a window a few yards behind her and emptied a chamber pot. A tear ran down her cheek. She wiped it away.

I know for a fact, she thought, that there is much good in that man my husband, almost as much good as there is hurt. But I've stopped loving him. I can no longer love him. It is impossible for me to love him, no matter how much I tell myself that I should, I must.

In her mind, she envisioned the naked width of his shoulders, and his yellow hair. Despite the drinking, he was powerful. The way he'd thrown Bothwell—if he hadn't hit his head against the doorstoop, he could have beaten Bothwell easily. And Bothwell was not a weak man. . . .

The alley opened into a cluster of wooden hovels. The cobbles came to an abrupt halt and were replaced with dirt and scattered stone. Women lounged at the windows of the shacks, talking animatedly with each other. Small groups of men prowled about the muddy square. Light rankled from a tavern door, to which a number of men had flocked, showing, however, no inclination to go in. Mary moved back into the shadows of the alley.

An unshaven youth burst from the tavern, dragging a woman behind him. The woman shrieked, pitched backward, then hurled herself on top of the youth and thrashed him about the skull with her fists. A number of women crawled out of their windows and joined in an earsplitting clangor. The woman darted her head into the young man's groin. He collapsed in the mud, drawing his arms between his legs and spluttering curses.

"Tear him 'a," shouted the chorus of women, "bloody, tear 'a his poxy eyes!"

The woman kicked him savagely in the buttocks, then held out her arms and allowed a burly fellow in a carpenter's apron to escort her back to the tavern. The young man gave off an outraged scream and jumped to his feet.

Mary's hand closed over her mouth. A trickle of icy sweat wound its way down her cheek and onto her neck.

The noise rose, then stopped abruptly. There was dead quiet. Mary opened her eyes.

The carpenter, his knee bent in the other man's stomach, raised the youth's head and slammed it onto the stones. There was a dull thud, coupled with a cracking sound. Something black and wet dribbled down the side of the young man's face.

Mary ran back through the black alleyway to the High Street. I'll go back and command the carpenter to stop, she told herself: I'll say "In the name of the Queen—" She continued running until she was perhaps a block from the Netherbow Gate, which separated the city proper from the area around Holyrood. Her breath was coming in quick, short gasps and she sank down on a doorstoop. The youth was dead. She knew he was dead. And she had done nothing. To thee do we cry, poor banished children of Eve—send up our mourning, our weaknesses—turn then thine eyes of mercy toward us—O clement O loving O sweet. A rectangle of light suddenly appeared in the middle of the street, revealing two dark figures. Mary moved against the door. The two figures retreated against a wynd on the opposite side of the street. A woman's voice drifted out into the night air: "Mama's here, sweetheart. She won't let the Black Man harm you. Did you say your prayer tonight?"

"But I heard him down below," came a small, shaky voice.

"Silly little boy. That was the angels whispering. All that white swirling air down there is angel's breath."

There was a long pause, then the child said, his voice brimming, *"Really?"*

Mary smiled to herself. Up above, the window creaked shut and the light went out.

The two dark figures moved from the wynd and into the street again. They were women. "The evenings are lengthening now," said one of them. "Much cooler, too."

"Ah, the years an old man now, an' little than a month before the snows again."

"It's easier to get tired now," said the first woman, whipping her shawl haphazardly in the air. "An' the moon—real fat, real round, real yellow."

They were speaking in a low womanly tone that was comforting. As a child at the Louvre, Mary always loved going to sleep with the sounds of voices filtering through her door from the brightly lit promenade deck outside her apartment. As a child, if she heard no voices, she would invariably wake up screaming, only to be soothed to sleep again by one of her ladies. It was always the same nightmare: She was picking gilliflowers on a sunny green hillside. She would be alone. A friendly, wiry-haired dog would appear and playfully chase her. At some point during her flight, she would realize that she was going to die.

"Like apple butter," said one of the women. "Dear Jesus, why don't someone come? The child had turnips today. His face is so thin an'—"

"Poor girl, you. If I had more than I do, you know—"

"I do, Joadha, saint, you. Hark—shhh."

Down the street, laughter echoed between the high-storied buildings. The women moved toward the sound, nervously running their fingers through their thick dark hair. Before they disappeared in the gradually rising mist, Mary heard one of them say loudly, "Dear Jesus, what I would not do to warm my puir body."

Mary thought: Her voice is different now; it's not honest, human any more. She squeezed her fist between the legs. She would have done anything to be one of those women, to be able to take a different man up inside her every night, and not care.

> "'Leven o' the clock, look well to your lock,
> Your fire and light, and so guid night."

Mary lay in her bed thinking. What about Bothwell? She didn't know. Her skin felt moist and heavy over her bones. Her body was tingling.

But if she went to awaken Bothwell, she'd awaken Jean too, since, after all, Jean was his wife and she did sleep with him. In the same bed. Mary wondered how many women Bothwell had slept with, would sleep with. She couldn't bear the thought. Don't men ever tire of it? But that was being hypocritical, wasn't it?

Pressing the goose-feather pillows under her chin and breasts, Mary rolled on her belly, crossed her feet, and tried to sleep. Bothwell was an accident. Bothwell was a mortal sin.

The sweet pungent odor of dying roses filled the garden. Two green pumpkins, flecked with strips of orange, lay among a tangled curl of vines. The last cicendia had died the night before. I must learn to be like Elizabeth, thought Mary. The Queen must gather her senses for the sake of her God-given mission: the good governance of her kingdom. Bees hovered above the weltering crimson blossoms of the berry bushes. The twelve thousand pounds the Lords Assembled had voted for the christening was an act of great good will. Except for an occasional outburst, the Presbyterian ministers no longer railed at her from their pulpits. Davy's death had shamed them. In fact, what religious struggle there now was centered, in the main, between the Presbyterian lords and the Presbyterian ministers over the matter of state revenues. The Kirk was getting half but wanted more. The Lords Assembled was getting most of the other half, and wished to keep it. Mary had remained aloof from the battle, saying that her religion prevented her participation. Thus, by doing nothing, she'd won the good will of both sides. That was the thing Elizabeth did best: nothing. Even Elizabeth's constant teeter-tottering on the question of marriage was ingenious. As long as she was unmarried, Philip of Spain would be solicitous, Catherine of France would be solicitous of England's welfare.

As Mary saw it, Scotland was faced with only one problem of any import: Harry. In the previous years, Mary had been besieged with missives from Rome: *The Queen of Scots has delayed too long. When may the nuncio return? It is time to begin a great enterprise in the name of Holy Mother Church. Madam, His Holiness grows impatient.* Finally, all such correspondence had ceased, and the papacy seemed to have accepted the fact that there would be no Inquisition in Scotland.

Justice and mercy, thought Mary as she wandered past a row of fading bluebells. Magnanimity. Good counsel. Kindness. Hope. I must learn to be like Elizabeth, only better.

"You're up early," said James, walking toward her.

She gave him her hand. "I've decided we should leave for the assizes as soon as possible. Tomorrow, if it can be arranged."

"We'll need three days," said James. "I suppose you'll want Bothwell to go before as lieutenant. He'll round up some of the thieves. I warned him last time what would happen if they weren't all executed."

"Must it be Bothwell?" she said casually.

James seemed surprised. "If you wish someone else—"

"No," said Mary, sitting back on a bench. "Bothwell is fine."

"He'll ride on ahead of us with his lines," said James, rather pleased for some reason.

"They say all the cragberries are in bloom." Mary was laughing. "When I was little, at Inchmahone, there were cragberries everywhere, all over the isle, and I'd hide in the bushes and stuff myself. I'd get sick constantly. I'd promise never to touch the berries again, but next day, well . . . The birds ate the berries too, when they first bloomed, and they'd become inebriated. I used to love to sit on the sand and watch them skidding across the top of the water. Sister Regina used to scold me all the time for making such a pig of myself, but she was as bad at it as I. Lately I've remembered so many things that I thought I would never remember again. Winter's too close for a trip to the Highlands, but it would be nice to ride up some mountain and look at them. But I've never been south to the border. I must have documents on former assizes, local customs, and traditions." She stretched her arms and threw back her head. "I love to get up early in the morning. It's invigorating, fresh. I love to watch the sun come up."

James smiled, almost as if he were in some way suddenly proud of her.

CHAPTER TWELVE

A breeze was winnowing down from the distant hills and through the fields of yellow corn that filled the plains of East Lothian, fifty miles south of Edinburgh. Mary rode at the head of a procession of courtiers, musicians, soldiers, and local dignitaries. This was the fourth day of the progress. They'd attended justice courts in twelve towns and been greeted courteously and with a mild sort of enthusiasm. The crimes consisted mostly of organizing monopolies, selling at unfair profit, minor infractions of minor laws—like singing on Sunday, blaspheming, couples arguing, drunkenness—and cases of adultery. The important assize would be held tomorrow at Duns.

"A storm's coming," said James.

Mary sighed and let her eyes glide along the variegated fabric of the landscape. Beyond the corn fields, sheep grazed in open meadowland. Far, far off, the heather-colored hills eased above the plains.

"If Bothwell meant to seize the robber barons this morning, we ought to have heard from him by now," she said.

"We'll be at Duns in an hour," said James. "He should arrive shortly thereafter."

Two horsemen galloped along the narrow road toward the procession. Mary glanced up at the clouds that were stretching themselves across the gradually deepening sky. The earth turned a light grainy color.

The horsemen were riding too fast, she thought; they were whipping their horses bloody. Her heart froze.

"Your Majesty," said one of the men, slipping from his horse and grabbing hold of her reins. He fought to catch his breath.

Mary turned to James. She heard the soldier say the word "dead." James's face drained of color.

"—Surprised by the Armstrongs at Cornon Pass. And riding in the lead as he was, he got the first volley. They took him to Hermitage Castle, but even as we left him there was no hope."

Mary turned and stared at the kneeling man. It was Livingstone, who'd tried to save Davy that night at Holyrood. "Take me there," she said.

"Madam—"

"Now!"

"The storm's almost on us," James said. "I never thought Bothwell would die. What good will—"

"He was my friend!" said Mary. "The one true one."

"My lord, my lady," cried Livingstone, "for God's sake, Your Majesty can't mean to ride through that storm that's coming—"

The sky was like an ocean, clouds foaming across the grizzled plains. Thunder boomed in the distance. "How much farther?" Mary cried up to Livingstone.

"Thirty minutes by the road."

"Is there a faster way?"

"If you cut through the heath," he yelled. "But in this rain, all mud. Dangerous to attempt."

"We'll cut through, then."

"Too dangerous—madam!"

Mary struck her heels into her horse's flanks and galloped off the road. The rain splattered furiously against her face. He will not be dead. He will not be *dead. Will not!* A sharp and narrow blast of wind seized her cape and hurled it over her head. She struggled to undo her neck clasp, almost lost her balance, and watched the cape reel away across the black, rain-soaked stubble. A large white square building loomed in front of her. Lightning cracked the sky, the horse reared, and Mary tumbled from the saddle and struck her head on something sharp and hard. Weeds flapped wildly from the rooftop of the ruinous house. The window-rod door creaked open and three men with lanterns swayed onto the entrance stoop. The wind pulled at their long black robes.

"Will you help me, please?" she said, extending her hand.

One of the men moved forward a few steps. Mary caught at his black robe but he moved away again. "You may not touch us," he said in a deep but kindly voice. He lifted the lantern to his face. The first thing she saw was his eyes—light, sad, almost beatific under the thick black eyebrows. He lowered his hood and she looked at the part of his face where his nose and lips should have been.

Mary moaned and rolled over in the warm mud.

"It's over," someone said.

Livingstone said: "She's still breathing."

There's a fire, Mary said to herself. I can feel it. Warm. My eyes are glue.

"Is there nothing?" asked Livingstone.

The other voice said no.

But there is. Mary tried to raise her right hand. Then she tried to raise her left hand. A door was opening, then closing. Voices trailing off. One of them was an angry woman's voice. Mary could hear the sound of the sea. Then she couldn't hear even that.

I'm drifting. I've gone back a bit. A gust of wind—gusting me—is tearing cicendias from off my saddle. Ah, and they dance such yellow swirling above the sandy sea cliff, down past the confused beach, the frightened, twisting rocks, across the rumpled sea. I remember I watched them until they were specks on the tide line and then I turned and looked at the hill and saw, standing on the ruined runic fireplace, the wolf I thought was a dog. He's never frightened me—not even then, not in the dreams I've dreamed of him since. Before then, though, at Paris in the Louvre, at Chenonceaux, at Amboise, when I picked gilliflowers on the sunny hillside, I'd dream; he was always a nightmare. But not since I saw him on the way to old Huntly's death. He had gray-green Aegean eyes like my charioteer. Bothwell was a beautiful man. He was my friend, Bothwell was; my mother's friend, too. When I have dreams . . .

I have dreams with a thousand people in them. I fancy sumptuous masques and costume balls. I fancy barges going down the Firth of Forth with parties on board, oars splashing on the gold water. I've dreamed Edinburgh burning to the ground countless times, all red and black. And every man and woman and child I've ever seen in Edinburgh is burning.

This desolate land.

Almost one hundred years since my great-grandfather, one of the Jameses, said there were to be no more serfs; since coming back to this country I've seen nothing but bonded men. I used to dream of Harry all the time. I never dreamed of Bothwell. In Paris I overheard my uncle the cardinal say that the difficulty with my family was that we were unreal—until reality killed us dead. Then we were something else. Because, he said, we dreamed too much. My father, his fathers, my brother John, me, and my brother James. Ronsard wrote a poem

now my body's lengthening   now breaking and   I'm a hundred parts   I'm a thousand indistinguishable shreds   I'm a million colored dots

"So nice of you to come and stay awhile," said Sister Regina, legs crossed under her white robes, and sipping cherry *aqua vitae*. "But I see you're weary and would rather sleep. If you've made up your mind to go, there's really nothing I can do about it, though I used to wipe your bottom and take a stick to you when you gorged yourself on marmalade and berries. But I liked us anyway."

"What happened?" Mary asked. "Where did you go? Where are you now?"

"I suppose I'm dead, or old somewhere. But I had some blithe times." The big dog whimpered and ran back and forth across the sand, meaning for her to follow after. Then he tucked his tail between his legs and slunk away.

Sister Regina bussed Mary on the cheek and danced off with a sapling.

Bothwell is dead.

Did I say I was the Queen? I wonder what made me say that?

"He's mad with grief," someone said. "For God's sake, Lord Livingstone, get him out from here."

"If God were here right now," said James, "he'd crack you on the skull. Get me more rope, and I want fire."

I think I'll leave now. *Ohhh, God!*

"Did you see?" said James. "Again—pull!"

"Halloo-hallah," yelped Livingstone.

Mary opened her eyes, raised her arm, and looked blankly at the black swollen flesh and purple rope burns.

"Mary," said James, bending over.

"You should have been the King," she murmured. "You be my baby's Regent. Be kind to those who are Catholics. . . ."

"She's asleep again," she heard James whisper.

It was the middle of the night. Beaton was curled in a large leather chair next to the bed. Mary attempted to reach her, but it hurt too much and so she closed her eyes and slept again.

Beaton was reading Rabelais to her. She shut the book and took off her spectacles. "I saw you smile three times," she said. "Do it again."

"There's not enough room for four smiles," said Mary, lying on her back and staring at the ceiling. "Where are we?"

"Jedburgh Castle. One of Bothwell's strongholds. We're on the sea."

"Oh, Beaton, I can't bear lying here much longer. But I can't move an inch without such—hurt."

"A courier from Edinburgh brought, among other news, word that John Knox had prayers said for you at St. Giles. Is it bad again, madam?"

"It's always bad," Mary said with a grimace. "And Bothwell?"

"I must have told you a dozen times. But you keep asking me to say things again and again."

"I remember: you said Bothwell was alive. I just didn't believe you at first."

"He seems to be recovering even faster than you. You had a terrible fall. Do you remember that?"

"The fall. I remember the fall. The storm. How long have I been lying here like—this?"

"Two weeks, madam. Most of the bruises are almost gone now. They did everything they could to save you. They tied your wrists, knees, hands, everything, with rope cords and pulled as hard as they could on them. I shrieked when I saw them doing it, but they said it was right, it was the only treatment for shock and blood loss. Then Lord James burned you with coals. Livingstone said your pulse was gone for an hour, but they saved you. The treatment worked. Only then they were worried because of the Lazar Hospital."

"Lazar Hospital?"

"Lepers," Beaton explained. "Don't you remember? After you fell. That's where the parish puts them. Hopeless cases, all of them, but none of them touched you."

Mary lay back and listened to the seagulls outside her window, and Beaton began reading Rabelais again. After a few minutes Mary said, "I remember when I met Monsieur Rabelais. My uncle, the Cardinal de Guise—Rabelais dedicated his *Sciomachie* to him—my uncle took me on a progress to Metz, and I met Rabelais there. He was the merriest fellow imaginable. For all his wisdom and learning, how he loved to laugh."

Beaton had gotten up and was standing by the casement looking down at the beach.

"What are you staring at?" Mary asked.

"He's down there now. I don't see how he takes the cold. They gave him up for dead too—just like yourself—and you're still lying here in bed and he's down there in all that chill."

Mary hesitated, shaken by a sudden clutch in her chest. Then, unsteadily, she lowered her feet to the floor and padded over to the casement. It was a dull, cold, overcast day. Down below, a jagged ridge of rock extended out to sea, forming a speckled border between the ashen clouds and gray water. He *was* there. Bothwell: walking by himself along the waving outline of the shore. He was alive. Beaton had been telling the truth.

"Madam," laughed Beaton. "You look as if you've just seen the Ogre of Britonmart. Madam!"

Harry's hair was longer than she remembered it and fell in loose yellow curls down the back of his neck. "Dear heart," he said, leaning forward and pressing her hand. "I would have come sooner, but they said you were dead. Our son cries and cries, missing you. You won't recognize him when you see him, he's gotten so big."

She said nothing.

Harry waited a minute. "I think you want me to go. Is that it?" There wasn't any reproach in his voice; he might as well have asked her what she wanted for supper.

She shook her head yes.

He raised her hand to his lips and gave it a light peck. "Very well," he said amicably. "You're half asleep, so I'll leave now. Would you like me to go back to Edinburgh?"

"Yes."

His face was clear, with an expression of self-confidence about the mouth and eyes; it was the same expression he'd had the first time she met him, at the tourney. Maybe he'd stopped drinking. That surprised her, but what surprised her even more was the fact that it made no difference in her feelings toward him. If Harry no longer drank, well, that was good—wonderful —for him. But it had nothing to do with her.

When he left, Mary slipped out of bed and walked to the casement. At some distance, a dark figure moved along the water's edge. Mary smiled. Her pains were almost gone now.

Tomorrow morning, perhaps, she would take a walk along the beach.

The wet sand crunched beneath her boots. Close up, she saw that the rocks were filled with numerous caves and clefts, and cave upon cave of nestling sea birds. She made her way through a narrow passage in the cliff to a section of the beach that couldn't be seen from the castle. Seagulls whirled across the white sky and filled it with their shrieking. The wind rushed through the rocks, sounding like timpani.

Bothwell sat against a boulder, looking at the sea.

"It's cold," she said, sitting beside him and drawing her knees up under her chin.

He looked up at the birds. "My aviary," he said in a flat voice. "Thrones. Princedoms. Powers. Gannets. They forage the sea for me."

"It rhymes," said Mary.

He sighed and rested his head against the stone. "One time I hated you. You know when that was. Had you died, I would have hated you again." He stood.

Mary folded her hands over her knees and gazed at the rock-weed lining the shore.

"I almost did die," she said, her voice breaking. "For a while, that is what I wanted. But I lay in bed day after day and I thought about everything that ever had anything to do with me, and the one thing which was left after everything else was thrown away was you."

She looked at the currents eddying about the scarred rocks. Up above the winding clouds, the sun must have been shining, because they were tinged here and there with a soft mellow light.

The water lapped about Bothwell's boots, but he said nothing, and continued looking down the narrow coast line.

She was tired, exhausted, but she couldn't stop talking. "I have no wish but to always be with you. For you, I would forsake everybody. For you alone, I want to be great."

He knelt beside her and kissed her very gently on the mouth. "I love you," he said.

She wrapped her arms about his neck and kissed him.

"Let me come to you tonight."

"I can't wait until tonight." She threw her ermine cloak to the wet sand, stood up, unfastened her gown, and drew it over her head. "It's only cold until you get used to it," she said, standing on top of her petticoats. "You were right."

"You've gotten so thin," he said.

They lay down together on the ermine cloak.

Beaton sank into the leather chair and rested her head on her hand.

"Why, Beaton, you sentimental thing," said Mary. "You're almost crying."

"Only almost. I haven't cried for . . . eleven years," said Beaton. "Always only almost. That's as far as it goes. But I never do. I always marveled at how easy it was for you to cry. On the spur, so to speak."

"You must be happy because I am happy," said Mary, kneeling at the other woman's feet.

"Madam, Elizabeth has Leicester and, in England, God's in heaven and the body politic still thrives. But, madam, you're not Elizabeth, Bothwell's not Leicester, and Scotland's not England. And the Queen of England doesn't have a King, and you do. All this is confused, and I can't see anything but . . . sad things." She threw her arms around Mary's neck. "But we women —why, we're oil when you throw us on the fire. It's all impossible, but only forever."

"He's a *man*, Beaton. I love him more than all the world."

"Those words—I remember them from some time ago, when you said them about someone else."

"I said them about a picture of a man, not the man," said Mary. She walked over to the bed, lay down, and pressed her palms over her eyes. "Do you think badly of me, Beaton?"

"I think nothing at all, madam."

"Do you still love my brother John?"

"Yes, madam."

"And no one else will do?"

"A ship can sink in the sea," Beaton said quietly. "It can

sink a hundred miles from land. And if someone's the only one
left, do you think he would fight the water and hope to be
rescued? It hurts when you fight it. But I think most people
would fight it. Should I not want John simply because it may
be impossible for me to have him? If what you felt once for
your husband was honest, then you would not now be an adulteress,
in a state of mortal sin. Will you come down and eat, or take
your supper here?"

"Here," said Mary. Outside, the gray, haggard clouds separated
slightly and admitted a few thin rays of sun into the room.

Beaton hesitated at the door, then said, "Remember, madam,
my name is Mary, too."

"I'm sorry," Mary cried, "sorry. And I'll find him for you.
Wherever he is. And I'll make him love you."

"You can't make somebody love," said Beaton, her voice
nearly inaudible. "We're both grown women now. We have to
accept the blame for . . . it all."

"God bless you, Mary Beaton," said Mary in a rich full tone.
A wild smile settled across her face.

Beaton gave her a curious look and shut the door.

Sighing contentedly, Mary moved across the thick carpet to the
lattice window. She raised her hand to brush back her tangled hair
and noticed the effect of the dying rays of the sun of the skin on
her arm. It was a soft rosy gold. She took a handmirror from her
dressing table, walked back to the window, and studied her face.
She was gold. After a minute, the sunlight was sucked beyond
the horizon and the gray clouds began rolling across the sky like
waves. She looked in the mirror again. This time she was ivory.

No, not that, she thought exultantly. Not gold, not ivory,
but a woman. Mary said out loud, "God bless all men and all
women!"

She opened her eyes and watched the blurring shadows weave
lazily against the cracked plaster of the ceiling. Bothwell grinned
and bent his head to her shoulder.

"Soft," she murmured, drawing her fingers down his chest. "I
thought you'd be hard, but you're not; you're soft, smooth."

He laughed. "You're softer," he said, lapping her breasts. "And *warm.* Have I changed so much from this morning? Was I hard then, and only soft now?"

"Come back up. I want you to kiss me like the monster again." She pulled at his hair.

"You're not soft any more," he whispered, biting her lightly on the nipple.

"And you?" she said, reaching down.

"I love you. Love you."

The next day they climbed to the top of one of the cliffs and looked out to the sea. From where they stood, the sea and sky were indistinguishable, all milky white except for a few spumy black rocks far out and crawling with breeding sea lions. The air was damp, chill. "It looks mild from here," said Mary. "Like a water color."

"It's like a mask," said Bothwell. "Like one of those French things they wear on festival days—those lacy types."

"We'll have to leave for Edinburgh soon, I think. The christening is for the seventeenth, and there are all the plans to go over, emissaries to greet, things to do. My son must have the most splendid christening this country—or any other country—has ever seen. A christening for the history tracts!" She looked past Bothwell's head at the shrieking gulls. A young goat, separated from its mother, had been trapped on one of the rocks. The birds surrounded it and tore it to pieces. They plummeted across the white sky, bits of red hanging from their beaks. Mary rested her hand on Bothwell's shoulder. "I intend revoking all exiles for the christening festivities."

"Did you say *all* exiles?"

"Yes."

"And that includes Morton, Lindsay, everyone who killed David?"

"Yes," she said "Except, of course, for Kerr of Fawdonside, who held a pistol against my unborn baby. I won't sign a pardon for that man."

Bothwell stared down toward the beach. "I've killed men in battle," he said. "Even that made me ill. I couldn't kill a man I've spoken to. I couldn't hand that man over to other men to kill for me. You must know that if the men who murdered David are allowed to return, they will murder your husband. They will not easily forget that he was once with them, and has since returned to you and abandoned them. They will want their revenge."

The rocks were hazy now: she couldn't make out the sea lions. She suddenly buried her head in her hands and walked off a few steps. "I don't know what it is with me. There are times when I become so cold, inside and out, and I say things I don't mean, want things I'd hate if I ever had them. I don't want Harry to be killed; I just want him never to have happened. And I want to be your wife, not his."

"You've changed again," he said.

"But I'll sign the pardons, anyway." She walked to the edge of the cliff and sighed. "It looks so soft and calm from here. If we were standing below, it would be like a cauldron, only cold. You said the calm was like a mask. In a position such as mine, you come to realize everybody's face is a mask. Your face is a mask. You don't like people to know what you think and how you feel. You know, and that is sufficient. It isn't necessary that anyone else know. But my husband has always been frightened of whatever he is, and so he's come to believe he's what he wishes to be. He fell in love with the reflection of his own mask. But he won't ever know what's underneath that mask—or even if there *is* anything under it."

"I don't understand you at all," said Bothwell.

"Why should you have to?" She took his hand. "I don't understand you either. Now take me to that place you told me about. And we can leave the philosophy of men to Aristotle."

They walked along the ragged cliff top in silence. Gray wiry bushes appeared and disappeared behind the floating swaths of mist. At a place where the rock sloped they came upon a series of stairs carved from stone. Mary saw a jet of foam rise and totter.

"This was where pagan worshipers would meet," said Bothwell. "They used it for thousands of years. I don't know the last time they met here, but it must have been at least before you and I were born."

They moved down the stairs and found themselves standing in the center of a huge, walled circle. A gigantic phallus, some twenty feet in circumference, was carved from one of the walls. Periodically, a blast of sea spray shot from its center into a gaping hole directly beneath.

"They worshiped this?" said Mary, leaning against him.

"Ay," said Bothwell. "They would gather here threshing days, or the start of spring seeding. They still do some places up north. They would elect a Black Man's representative and he'd strip off his breeches, spread his cheeks, and everybody kiss his arse."

Mary made a face. "And . . . ?"

"Then he'd fuck every last woman in the place."

"Hmmmm," laughed Mary. "I can't quite believe that."

"He'd use a polished stick."

"Aha, even the Devil has a trick."

"I wish I was in bed inside you now," said Bothwell.

Mary was wondering: When we're away from here, when we're back in Edinburgh, what's going to happen to us? Nobody knows about us now, but after a week, a month, even a year, it will be impossible for anyone not to know. They climbed back up the ancient steps and out onto the cliff again. It was snowing. He saw that something was troubling her, and so said nothing.

James returned a week later, and requested audience. She met him in the library. "It's time you return," he said. "Maitland tells me the christening will be magnificent. He said the French servingman of yours—Sebastian?—has drawn up the preliminary plans and that he's a genius."

"Yes, Bastian Pages. He came with me from France."

"But the emissaries are beginning to arrive; you must return posthaste."

"The christening is a month away, James."

He studied her eyes. "The King says he will not attend the ceremony."

"What?" said Mary, sitting down in a cushioned chair. "He couldn't, wouldn't— When he murdered my Davy, he threw enough doubt on my baby's legitimacy. But, if he refuses to attend the ceremonies, he may as well—and before all the representatives of the crowned heads of Europe." She stood and began pacing back and forth. "What cause does he give?"

"He learned you intend signing Morton's pardon. His father Lennox was not sent an invitation to the christening. The Queen of England's representatives have been given orders not to recognize him as King of Scotland. I think this man Drake is much to blame. I told you about having met him, and when he first came I thought he might be good for the King. But his influence is not . . . healthy."

"How delicately you say it," said Mary, kneading her fingers. "What you mean to say is that Harry is Captain Drake's wife lately."

"I never wanted any of this," James mumbled. "I never did. I attempted to warn—"

"Tell Maitland to send Lennox an invitation." She nervously arranged the small white ruff on his collar. "When Bedford and the other Englishmen reach Edinburgh, I want you to speak with them. There's no need to insist upon their addressing him as King, but ask them to, at the least, be courteous. As for the pardons, I haven't made up my mind as yet. Perhaps I will sign them. Perhaps I won't. I have to think on it. But have Maitland tell the King that if he is not present at the christening I will sign the pardons that day." She walked to the window.

James said he had to return immediately to the capital. "By the bye," he added, "your husband has struck up a friendship with Di Moretta, the Savoyard ambassador. It's curious—the two of them." He blushed. "I don't mean—well, you know what I don't mean. But why should Di Moretta seek out the company of the King?"

"Who knows?" said Mary.

As soon as James left, Mary threw on her ermine cloak and went down onto the beach. The sand and rocks were greasy with melting flakes of snow. The sea was like a maelstrom.

She walked half an hour before she found him. He was on one of the rock islands about fifty yards out, stark naked, legs pressed together, arms outstretched. Mary watched him steady himself,

then dive into the pounding water. She sat down on the wet
sand and rested her back against a smooth rock. The birds
gradually left the sky and huddled, thousands upon thousands
of them, against the cliff caves. Bothwell bobbed up and down
in the waves. Mary watched him drag himself onto the shiny
black rock and lie on his back.

She sat by her lattice window and wrote him a poem. Every
now and then she would look out and down at the beach. She
read it aloud, then opened the window. A gust of wind rushed
through the room and sent the papers flying against the wall. She
decided to translate the poem into free Scots:

> I hae known those who,
> Wounded here and grief-reeling,
> Thought drowning a' inexorable
> Sweet coral sleep and sea music,
> An easy drowsing down
> Tae gorgeous shining sea-wrack
> Ebbing warmer than the wind and air above.
> They didnae think
> The water would taste tae much
> Of salt. They ken
> The sky is na higher than itself and
> Eyes slapped shut,
> Bodies downward drifting,
> Black sand rising, soundless sighing,
> They oped their mouths
> Tae swallow the setting sun.
> There was na struggle.
> But you, you'd have an angry arm extended
> Fra' the palsied clasp and flack,
> Bloodily grabbing at a piece of wreck above,
> You would ascend wi' the full rose
> Of a blooming dawn
> And the wind would sing, bring blue,
> Blow free, lift, and whisper you.

Bothwell covered his eyes. "It's you," he said, "All of it—you, not me."

"It's us, both." She dug her fingers into his ribs. "Smile. Laugh. I didn't write it to make you sad."

He pushed her away. "You're a rakish sort of lassie-girl," he said with a wide grin. "And I like scudding up your belly —fodder, fill, feast and fat." He lifted her in his arms, staggered to the bed, and dropped her onto the linen sheets. She giggled and rolled over on her stomach. "Never could an arse so braw," he said, slapping her on the rump, "refuse to answer Nature's urgent ca'." He threw himself on top of her, slid his hands under her breasts, and sang in her ear:

"There was a Shetland laddie and to Stirling did he ride,
With sword and pistol in his belt, and his ballocks by his side,
With his fal de diddle dal dee swinging low beneath his knee,
Hey-Ho."

"Ah, that's good," said Mary, turning on her back.

"And I push him against the wall, thus. And such meikle fun."

"Give me meikle gravy. I see you have a sceptre of your own, my lord. Put him . . . uh, that's good, oh, he's good, you're good—"

"Last night, I swear—and who taught you that?—I swore you wore an inch off my fal de diddle."

"Will it grow back? Ohh, that."

"Mary's mad. Mary's thick with wet. Mary's hairy furnace gripping wheel of—*ah!*"

"And that, that, and *ahh!*"

They lay together listening to the sea plunging against the beach down below.

Bothwell was thinking: High big girl. . . . In bed, though, I kiss her on the mouth, and have my cock up inside her, and my ball-sack between her legs, and my feet are on top of hers if she puts them down. In the streets they have their nasty song: Mary, Mary, quite contrary, how does your garden grow, with

silver bells and cockle shells and— God, bright side and dark side
of you . . . God, I know if I'd never fucked her, but knew
every corner of her life except that, I'd not know Mary, Queen
of Scots, in all this life. But I know her now. She's me, even
further back. A thousand years further back than I could go.
The Stewart blood in her. Scotia was a Pharaoh's daughter when
Egypt was a baby. She was a vampire girl set adrift on the sea
by an angry mob and the sea stormed wherever she went. But
the sea would not open up to take her and so it spit her here
in Caledonia. She conquered the chieftains with her magic and
she married the best one and she loved him. They were fierce
and lovesome and got the Stewarts and the Stewarts got Scotland.
Mary wrote "bloodily grabbing at a piece of wreck above," but
they were always drowning, reaching up and drowning. The God,
gods they knew. They're always us, far off. Listen. Look how she
sleeps. Listen. Dulcimer and clavicytherium and virginals. Pretty
Mary, and she's a woman twenty-four years old. When she sleeps,
you can hardly hear her breathing. She looks like an angel. And
I'm no sooner done than hard again.

They were scheduled to return to the capital in three days.
Mary grew pensive. Bothwell sensed that something was troubling
her and let her alone. She walked along the beach the next
night and watched the sunset struggling through the vast panoply
of birds, rolling clouds, and slowly rising mist. Mary allowed
herself a daydream: Bothwell and she would stay forever in
this ancient castle above this ancient beach. Scorn, the world's
condemnation—none of that would matter. This would be the new
Eden. They would swim in the sea when the warm weather came
and laugh and dance and look at each other and make love on
the sand. But it was only a daydream, and could never be
more. She was a sovereign whose duty it was to serve her
subjects. It was fine and good to read romances, but in the
end love had to be, above all, practical.

Their love would survive—nothing could destroy it—but it
would not be the same in Edinburgh as it was here. Sooner
or later she would have to start lying, and she did not approve

of lying, except in diplomatic affairs, where it was expected and therefore permissible. Besides, she would have to see Jean in Edinburgh. She would have to see Harry. Everything would be different, and more difficult.

The beach gradually blackened.

At supper that night, on impulse, Mary told Bothwell she wanted to ride along the English border for an hour or so before her train set forth to Edinburgh. She asked him if they could inform the governor of Berwick-on-Tweed of her wish.

"The Queen of England might think you were trying to stir up trouble," said Bothwell, putting down his spoon. "Although if you only want to look, and not cross the border, it may be permissible."

"I only want to look," said Mary.

The little caravan moved slowly over the snowy landscape. Here and there, in the distance, Mary made out peasant shelters huddling together, with gray smoke wisping from slipshod chimneys. The caravan passed a high wood sentinel keep. Mary waved at the guard and he waved back.

The governor of Berwick greeted them at the end of Bound Road, then led Mary's mount to the summit of a low, sloping hill. "Berwick," he said with all the magisterial pride at his command. "This is England, madam."

Mary looked down at the sprawling port city. Merchant galleys tied at the dock rocked listlessly. A fine snow was falling, but the broad street were crowded with people. The city's cannon fired a salute.

"It's so clean," said Mary. "And big."

"We've excellent sanitation, madam. We hire beggars to clean the streets."

"Edinburgh is a dirty place," said Mary.

The governor stared at her.

Mary averted her head, then moved her horse close to Bothwell's and leaned over to whisper in his ear: "Someday this will be ours."

They arrived in Edinburgh late that night and Mary went immediately to bed. It was the first time in three weeks that she had slept alone.

~~~ CHAPTER THIRTEEN ~~~

"The Dance of the Satrys," read Jean Bothwell. She looked up, observed Mary, who was sitting in a high straight-back chair looking out the window down into the High Street, then sighed and continued reading. "A mime play of Cupid and Psyche. A play of Macbeth and Elsine his wife, on the murder of King Duncan."

"Strike that," said Mary, without turning. "Not fitting for a baby's christening. Go on."

Jean stared at the list. "Madam?"

"Yes."

"Are you displeased with the program? Or have I offended you in some way?"

"No, no," said Mary, turning around and gazing briefly at the other woman's face. "No, Jean, it's—I'm not feeling well. Nothing more than that. Forgive me. Please. I'm sorry." She turned away again. "Strike Macbeth and Elsine. It's too unhappy."

"One clavicytherium. Five viols. Two violas da gamba. Assorted theorbo, cithern, and lutes. Hautboys, recorders, a dulcimer, three harps. And here comes Miss Beaton."

"Christmas is early this year," sang Beaton, dancing into the room. "Madam, close your eyes, then open them again. Tra-la-la."

Mary stared with disbelief at the lean, tanned figure standing behind Beaton in the door-through, then stood and cried, "John, Johnny, brother, where have you been?"

"Going to and fro about the earth," he laughed, bussing her on the cheek, "and walking up and down on the face of it. That's from Job." He drew back and slipped his arm around Beaton's waist. "I came back because it gets cold up north this time of year. I also came back in order to consider your handmaid, Mary Beaton, and to ask Queen's Majesty a question."

"Granted," said Mary. "I now pronounce you."

"I never thought it would happen," blurted Jean. "Lord John has always been a favorite of my husband's, but, Miss Beaton, I never thought he'd ask you."

"Have you ever thought, Jean?" said Mary, but Jean didn't seem to have heard her.

John dropped to his knees and crossed his hands over his heart. "Miss Beaton, are you pure? Are you blameless and upright? Will you tend me in the happy times and the bad? Will you bear faith, keep hearth, fear God, and never play the shrew?"

"No," said Beaton, grinning. "But I'll marry you anyway."

"You might at least let me ask first," said John.

"It's too late," said Mary. She took John's hand and whispered, "Brother, you've gone so thin."

"And you, Sister Mary. I heard about your accident—the horse—about a month after it happened. I wanted to go to you, but by then you were already on your way back to Edinburgh. You look older, too. You look . . ." He rubbed his eyes. "It makes me sad. I can't go on talking. I feel older too. I—" He backed away, squeezed Beaton's hand, and smiled happily. "I have to tell brother James he's going to have a sister-in-law. Is he in Council now?"

"No," said Mary. "I think he's entertaining the justices in the Great Hall. Wherever, go tell him. Godspeed." As soon as he was gone, Mary poked Beaton in the ribs and laughed. "Now, at last, dear, you're an honest woman. What do you think of that?"

"Fa-la-la-la, and so on. Tu-witta-woo. That's better."

"Oh, you're smiling now," Jean was saying, "but wait until you're married, and dying from lack of sleep. My Jimmy's just back from the south with Her Majesty, and I'm exhausted already." She smiled. "Madam, I forgot to mention we had to leave the kain geese off the banquet list—they're scarce this time of year—but we can substitute capon and cock." She dropped her head. "When I mentioned that to my husband, he made one of his jokes. Lord John is a handsome man, Miss Beaton, but I think my husband even more handsome. He told me last night that if he'd never married he'd probably be as fat as Morton, that it was my 'office' to keep him well proportioned." She glanced nervously at Mary. "He's a good husband," she said, her voice faltering. "I didn't mean to give an impression . . . that he wasn't, but . . . since . . ." Her voice trailed off.

"Do you know Lord Livingstone, Jean?" said Mary.

"Certainly, madam. He's a good friend of Jimmy's, a very likable—"

"Once I overheard him make a disrespectful comment to your husband with regard to your weight. I mention it only because of what you just said about your 'office.' That was very delicate. Bothwell laughed at what Livingstone said. 'It's like having two at once,' he said. So you see, Jean, you have no one to blame but yourself if Bothwell will not let you sleep. In the short time we were gone from Edinburgh, you seem to have gained—just a bit—just a little bit really. I think it's because you eat so much. Perhaps you should try not to eat so very much. Perhaps, them, you might sleep."

Jean looked from Mary to Beaton and back to Mary again. She nodded her head, laughed weakly, asked to be excused and left.

"That was *cruel*," said Beaton.

"She has put on weight," Mary said irritably.

"Then it was doubly cruel."

Mary felt only pity for the other woman. She wondered if

Jean knew. Poor Jean. She loved Bothwell, but he didn't love her. He couldn't!

Beaton said something in a low purring voice. Mary snapped from her thoughts and stared at her.

"Don't be angry with me," said Beaton. "The King says he won't attend the christening, and I've nothing to do with it."

"It was the way you said it, Beaton."

"Sign Morton's pardon."

"What?"

"Sign the pardons so they can come back and have their revenge upon him. They'll kill him for the way he turned his back on them, and that'll be best for everyone. You talk and talk about the pardons, but you do nothing. They'll all be dead and buried by the time you sign any pardons. You'll be dead and buried. Sign them tonight."

"I've never seen you so—vehement," said Mary. "You should be happy. Don't think about unhappy things."

"I'm not happy yet," sighed Beaton, sliding back into a chair. "I'm afraid. You know what it was between John and . . . your husband."

"That's past."

"It may very well be. At any rate, the King won't attend the christening. He was angry because he requested an audience with the French ambassador and was refused—three times. That was yesterday. Since then, he's given it out that he won't come. He's nothing but trouble; he's never been anything else. I think even he would be happier if someone killed him. The first thing John asked me was 'How is the King?' "

Mary ran down the limanga staircase to Harry's chambers. She heard voices inside but pressed the lever anyway, and walked in.

Harry was sitting on a multicolor cushion chair in the center of a group of men. Mary recognized the Savoyard ambassador Di Moretta and Edward Drake, but she'd never seen any of the others before. With the exception of Harry, everyone stood and bowed. The yellow curtains she'd bought him at the time of his illness had been replaced with hangings of purple velvet. A huge ebony crucifix hung suspended above the bed and a votive candle flickered before a statue of the Virgin on the mantel. There was a polished oak prie-dieu beside the desk.

"There's no need for anyone to leave," said Harry, and the others seated themselves again. "Now, madam, how may I be of assistance?" He was clothed head to foot in mauve and Flemish ruffwork. "But you must first excuse my manners. This, madam, is Guzman Sanchez-Moro; he's from Turin. You know Di Moretta. Luca Potormo, a Savoyard. Vittore de Silva—a nephew of the artist. Cosimo Datino, also of Savoy. They are my friends," he added pointedly.

Di Moretta nodded pleasantly at Mary.

Mary forced a smile. "There is talk that you will not attend our son's christening ceremonies."

Harry gave Di Moretta an amused look, then turned back to Mary and said, "I cannot and will not attend."

"But you must."

"There is nothing that I must." He poured himself a glass of sarsaparilla and lifted it to his lips. "I have sufficient reason, as well. One: my father was not invited. The invitation, when it did come, arrived so late as to be an insult. Two: you have caused all authority to be taken from me. Three: you are permitting Elizabeth's representatives to be present at the ceremonies, even though they refuse to recognize my title as King. Four: you intend pardoning Morton and the others. Does it surprise you that I know that, madam? I may not be quite the fool you think, madam."

"If you don't attend," said Mary, her voice rising, "you will brand our son a bastard before the eyes of the world."

"They have a song they sing in the streets. It goes: 'Surely the next King will be another Solomon; his father was the harpist, David.'"

Mary rushed at him and slapped him across the face. His glass smashed to the floor. "I swear by God, Harry, by my soul, if you don't attend the christening, I'll sign Morton's pardon that night!"

"And you know exactly what they'll do to me the first chance off," he said, a tinge of hysteria cracking his voice.

"If you were a little daggered," she said savagely, "it might make you a man." Out of the corner of her eye, she saw Di Moretta cough into his ruff. "By the bye, husband," she said, trying to control her voice, "my brother John is back."

"And what is that supposed to mean?" said Harry, turning red.

"Nothing. My brother John is back. Nothing more, nothing less. Except . . ." She paused at the limanga door. "Except that there is perhaps more than one song they sing in the streets."

Harry seized her by the arm. "I think, *dear heart,* that you will not see me for some time. I may go to my father's holdings in Glasgow. Then again, I may return to England. Or France."

"I don't think you'll be welcome in England," Mary said coldly. "Please take your hand off my arm."

"I may surprise you, Mary. You think I'm a fool. You think everybody takes me for a fool, but I may surprise you, Mary."

"My lord," said Drake, walking to Harry's side. He glanced at Mary. Despite himself, he smiled. It was a sad, fleeting, half-pleased smile.

Mary turned on him in a fury. "Do you bathe, Drake?"

"Your Majesty?"

"Excuse me, Drake, but the smell . . . I do not mean to pry, but you really ought to bathe, Drake. Does he bathe afterward, Harry, or do you douse him with perfumes?"

"I think we must go now," said the Savoyard ambassador, rising from his seat.

"I haven't given you the permission," said Mary. "Sit down!" She turned back to Drake. "Have you ever had a woman, Drake?" She glanced disdainfully at Harry, then added loudly, "A *real* one?" Suddenly she seized Drake's face in her hands, leaned forward, and kissed him on the mouth. He stifled a cry and pushed her away. His face was a sickly white. He looked like a man who would desperately like to strike you in the face but knew he never would.

"What one cannot help, God understands," Harry said calmly. He let his eyes rest on hers a second, then said in a low voice, "If He can understand why I could never be as complete a man as you or anyone else may have wished—as I may have wished—He can understand why you could never really be a woman. Perhaps He might forgive both of us."

"If you do not attend the christening," Mary managed to say, "I will sign the pardons. Good day gentlemen." She rushed out, tears streaking her cheeks.

The tiny silver bell tinkled three times.

"Sanctus, sanctus, sanctus," intoned Archbishop Hamilton, resplendent in crimson silk gown and white chasuble. He placed the holy water stick in a small bowl held by an altar boy, then took the bronzed salt container in one hand and the chrism box in the other.

"James Charles," he sang, "Duke of Rothesay, Earl of Carrick, Earl of Kyle, Earl of Cunningham, future High Steward of Scotland, baptize I thee Duke of Albany, Crown Prince of all this kingdom." From high above, an organ pealed the *Magnificat*.

Mary received the infant, sat, and held him in her lap while one of the priests fastened a gold ring around his finger. Another priest folded the child's tiny fist over a coronet. The third priest placed a brown and purple mantle across his shoulders. Mary thought: His eyes are so big and wondering.

She looked around the chapel to see if his father was there. He wasn't.

Bothwell and Jean whirled past to the sound of pipe and viol. Mary lowered her head. "Time loves us sometimes," said the archbishop, reaching over and chucking her on the chin. "Perhaps Time will regulate the mind of that too boyish Prince, your husband." He said the words as if they were lines from some mystery play he'd been forced to memorize for a pageant. He flushed and let his eyes wander across the long, food-cluttered table, then suddenly exclaimed, "Ah, peppermint drops! Colored ones. I haven't seen colored peppermint drops for years, no, not once since the beginning of the Reformation in Scotland. I must show my Grizzell." Grizzell was Hamilton's concubine of twenty-five years. He must love her, Mary thought to herself: Grizzell

Sempill's the ugliest woman I've ever seen, with a face like a crocodile and so fat she can't walk except she has pain. I wonder if Jean will be like that someday. But Jean's face is soft, country. Archbishop Hamilton asked me to let Grizzell come tonight; she's never been to court before. I couldn't refuse him. Their children love her so. I've seen them hang on her at market and when I've taken supper with them. Mary watched with amusement as Hamilton scooped up a fistful of peppermint drops and scurried off through the crowd. He always looks as if he's sliding on ice, about to lose his balance. A bad priest, an awful priest, but, all in all, he's a good man, and I'm fond of him.

Must Bothwell dance every dance with Jean? Every one? What a hypocrite he was—showering Jean with affection, kissing her on the cheek in front of everyone and patting her on the shoulder, bringing her goblets of wine, napkin cups of *petits fours,* sweetmeats, and candy babies, laughing and smiling, playing the part of a well-trained, solicitous, and loving husband. He didn't love Jean. He'd always said that he didn't love Jean.

Mary had asked Maitland to pave the way in Privy Council for the re-establishment of the Ecclesiastical Court in Edinburgh, with Hamilton, as the ranking Catholic clergyman in the country, at its head. The people would complain, doubtless, and threaten, too. But her Christmas largesse to the presbyters would seal the lips of the ministers, and she would see to it that John Knox was given to understand the Court would be abolished as soon as it had served its function—the Queen's divorce. Maitland assured her a divorce could be obtained without throwing doubt on the legitimacy of the Prince. As for the Pope, he really had little choice in the matter, and would have to give his permission. After the divorce, Harry might go and do as he pleased. Mary had told herself it would be better to allow him to depart in this manner than it would be to leave him to the mercy of Morton and the other traitors he'd betrayed. But no matter what happened, it would be his fault now, not hers, because he had not attended the christening. She had warned him that she would pardon those who wished to kill him if he insisted on flaunting her. And so, if she did pardon them, and they did kill him, he would have only himself to blame.

Mary sipped at her cherry burgundy and let her eyes circle the throne room. The Italian men were all young and beautiful; they dressed better than their women. The English ladies wore huge starched ruffs that made their heads look like sides of beef on platters; they wore too much jewelry—Mary doubted the gems were true—too much face paint, bright periwigs that tottered perilously on their heads. The ceiling was decked in evergreen and pine, silver spangles, flame-color candles, and water-color angels stuffed with cotton and wool. Elizabeth had sent a large gold baptismal font as her gift; it was a magnificent bowl. For years, Mary had been hearing about her cousin's parsimony; she believed the stories and was doubly touched at Elizabeth's generosity. Bothwell was dancing with Jean again. Mary wondered what was happening between Harry and Di Moretta. The Savoyard had been chosen as the King of Spain's representative but had not attended. His absence was disturbing. She told herself there was a reasonable explanation. But Di Moretta was old, experienced, and that made his apparent courting of Harry very strange. She gazed at the gilded manger arranged above the orchestra stage. It would have been nice to have the christening on Christmas Day, but church dogma pro-hibited that. It would have been nice if her little man had been born on Christmas Day.

"Whew," said Bothwell, pouring himself some wine. "Winded. I never danced this much."

"Jean told me that you dance every night," Mary said icily, "that she never gets sleep because of all your constant dancing."

Bothwell grinned. "Begging your pardon, Majesty, but the lady is my wife. It takes so little to keep her happy."

"Then what am I?"

"You are my whore."

"You haven't come to me once since we returned," she whispered, but he was already talking to someone else.

A musician heaved his sticks on his dulcimer, the galliard came to an abrupt halt, and the dancers took seats. Flute players swaying from its top, a huge engine in the shape of a clam entered the hall on its own power. It jerked to a halt in the center of the dancing area, the flutists leaped to the ground, and miniature fireworks erupted upward toward the high-vaulted ceiling. The clam slowly creaked open. A group of about fifteen youths bounded out of the shell and began prancing about the floor. They were naked except for patches of hair tied about their waists and huge flaxen tails erupting from their behinds.

"Oh, this *is* splendid," said Mary, clapping her hands.

"Bastian's ballet of the satyrs," said Beaton, moving beside Mary. "With certain readjustments by my Lord Johnny. Look at him, brown as a berry all over. He told me it comes from running around naked with wolf packs and deer herds in the Highlands. Ah, braw, blithe, swaggering and whatever else the Scots say."

Across the room, the retinue of the English ambassador rose and turned their backs on the performance.

"What have I done now?" said Mary.

The satyrs bounded toward the Englishmen and suggestively wagged their tails.

"There's a legend," laughed Beaton, "widely believed outside England, that all Englishmen are born with flaxen asses' tails."

"Did John and Bastian know this?" said Mary. "I suspect they did." She watched the satyrs scamper from the hall. Above the fading applause, she heard an unmistakably English accent saying loudly, "Were it not for her presence, I'd stab that French knave in his heart."

Mary walked quickly to the center of the room, lifted her hand for silence, then raised her goblet. "A toast to Good Queen Bess, God bless her and hers."

The Englishmen solemnly quaffed their cups.

"There's a legend that all Scotsmen are born with horns," said Mary, smiling at the English, "but we don't believe that either." She kissed the goblet and raised it again. "God bless my little man." Then she signaled to the orchestra to play again. The French ambassador Du Croc offered her his hand and they danced slowly across the floor to a solemn pavane.

"Di Moretta is not here," said the ambassador. "He was to proxy for Spain."

"He is an elderly man, monsieur. Perhaps the cold, his bones—"

"He is not so elderly, Your Majesty, that he does not weigh

and consider what he does and does not do. Yesterday your husband requested a private audience with me. As I am instructed by my master to pay him no honor and to have no dealings with him whatsoever, I refused. An hour later, I received a note from Di Moretta urging me to meet with your husband and him together. Of course I refused again. But I feel Your Majesty would be well advised to investigate the matter between those two. I saw Di Moretta in the town this afternoon, and he appeared well to me."

"My husband is a fool," Mary said lightly. "He knows nothing of politics and cares for nothing but boys. I would not be in the least surprised if, at this very moment, he were—"

"But madam, Di Moretta is not a fool," said the Frenchman. "And, if you will pardon me for saying so, the King of Spain is not a fool. Do you think it probable that the Savoyard would risk a diplomatic breach between his state and King Philip's country? He was King Philip's proxy. Madam, my country loves you, and I say these things not to alarm you, but only because I feel you have seen and known more than enough grief." The music came to a halt. Du Croc led Mary off the floor. "Pardon me for saying this, Your Majesty. I am older than Di Moretta, but even I must bow to you. It amazes me to think that you are only twenty-four years of age, and that you have seen and known already all that you have."

"That's not happy," whispered Mary, kissing his hand. "Don't say it. Please. Let me be happy tonight."

For the next hour or so Mary was effervescent, witty, attentive, and charming. Every now and then, out of the corner of her eye, she would see Bothwell staring at her. Every now and then, out of the corner of her eye, she would see Jean staring at her. As the night wore on, she slowly began to feel tired. Somebody tapped her on the shoulder and she adjusted her smile and turned around. It was Maitland.

He asked her to accompany him to one of the antechambers, then shut the door, drew aside the thick casement drapes and pointed down below. "The King bids us adieu."

Down below, a small group of horsemen galloped across the

courtyard and out the postern gate. The snow rushed after them, covering their tracks.

Maitland and James watched Mary dip her quill and sign the documents. When she was done, she nervously gathered up the papers and handed them to Maitland, who stamped them with the royal seal.

"One pardon you haven't signed," said James.

"I know," she said. "Morton, Lindsay, and the others can return but Fawdonside held a pistol against me and could have killed both me and my baby, and he cannot return." She folded the paper and ripped it neatly in half.

Maitland started to say something.

"I will not sign it," she snapped. "It's finished." She got up and walked to the mantel.

"Why so wan, madam?" asked Maitland in a concerned tone.

"I miss the flowers. The snow's cold, so cold. I feel I've done a wicked thing. I think sometimes that there is no way out. If he'd kept to his *aqua vitae* and his boys, we could have left him in his rooms, and he'd never have bothered us. If he'd never involved himself with Morton in the first place, never murdered my Davy, never plotted . . . if he'd attended the christening. If I'd never loved him it would be easy. But once I did or thought I did."

Maitland gazed admiringly at the Venus and Adonis tapestry which hung opposite the fire. "I see you've had it cleaned. Brings out those marvelous oleander leaves." He cleared his throat. "The Court will be empowered to discover the best possible means of annulling Your Grace's marriage without throwing doubt on the legitimacy of your son. The difficulty in that is that your husband may be called to testify. He'll make unpleasant accusations. The other possibility is that we might have him arrested. Or, if you will, he could be arrested for Riccio's murder. He held you against your will, prevented you from the exercise of your royal rights."

"But, man," said James, "that would only open the case again. We just got the pardons signed."

"Morton and the others acted under Lord Darnley's authority," said Maitland. "They presumed it was the Queen's desire. They need only claim ignorance and misrepresentation on the part of the King. But, I agree, the situation might present difficulties."

Mary pressed her face into the heavy wine-colored curtains by the window. "Won't there ever be . . ."

"Madam?"

"Peace."

"Madam," said Maitland matter-of-factly, "the problem will be settled. By the end of February. Trust me."

"And how?" she said, her voice muffled by the velvet curtain.

"That will be determined later. No prejudice to you, none whatsoever to your son. Lord James is as good a Presbyterian as Your Grace is a papist—"

"That's what none of you can see," said Mary. "I'm not a papist. I'm a Catholic."

"An unfortunate choice of word, madam. Forgive me. As I was going to say, in this matter of your marriage, Lord James will, I'm sure, look through his fingers."

Mary released the velvet and, turning to James, looked deep into his eyes and said, "I don't want anything done that will bring a spot on my conscience." She thought to herself, I have done a wicked thing tonight. I have so many spots on my conscience.

James nodded his head. He looked guilty too.

"Madam, you'll see nothing but good," said Maitland. "And approved by Parliament."

She was silent a minute, then, her face dimpling with a warm, girlish smile, she turned and took James's hand. "Du Croc said my little man was so big he could hardly lift him. He is powerful—when I saw him to bed tonight, he wouldn't let go my little finger. Dear James, they say he already looks like our father."

James nodded without smiling.

"Wake up. Wake up."

Mary's eyes fluttered open and she reached for the pistol she kept hidden under her pillow.

"It's me," Bothwell said briskly. "Me. Put on a robe. There is a matter must be tended to.

Mary smiled and wound her arms around his neck.

"No," he said, pushing her back. "Put on a robe." She realized he was dressed in riding gear. His canvas cloak was wet with snow. He waited until she fastened on a wrap, then strode back to the door and ushered a small, middle-aged man in Lennox livery into the room. He fell to his knees.

Bothwell motioned for him to rise. "Tell Her Majesty what you said to me."

The man glanced up at Mary, then lowered his eyes and began to speak. "I am William Walker, Your Majesty. I am of Glasgow, my Lord Lennox's hold; I am his man. I never told a lie, never lied, not one time in all my life, Your Majesty, except unimportant things. I never did treason or thought it—"

"Walker," growled Bothwell, "to the point." He added, in a softer voice, "Do not be afraid of her. She's good."

"It was the dark one, the Mr. Drake one," said Walker. "I did dealings for my Lord Lennox in the merchant clerk's office. Mr. Drake is the evil one who started all this treason. My Lord Lennox would never do such a thing unless by magic. Mr. Drake is of the evil one. He would cause me, at table, to speak ill of Your Majesty before the King, and to mock you. The King is Mr. Drake's servant; the man has bewitched him. All think Mr. Drake wonderful, all but the servants, and who knows the character of men better than servants? Ever since his coming here, he has brought the King into habits so vicious that I cannot say them to you. He procures evil pleasures for the King, and all are so frightened of his power that none will disobey his command, however dissolute. There was a galleyman's daughter Mr. Drake—"

"No need to go into that," said Bothwell. "Tell about the English captains and the old man."

"Yes," said Walker. "He talked to the English captains. I arranged the meeting, but I swear I knew nothing of its reason." He suddenly stopped talking, clasped his hands, and bent his head.

Mary sat down on the chair before her dressing table and

looked at the blackness outside the window. "Go on," she said quietly.

Walker said nothing.

"I give you my word no harm will come to you from me," said Mary. "Or from the King. Bothwell is your witness."

Walker waited a minute, then proceeded. "I did not hear all their talk. But the end is this: they mean to close you up in a prison, kill your brother Lord James, so that the King will become the Regent for your son, the Prince."

"It's Elizabeth," said Mary, hitting her fist on the table.

"Please, Your Majesty, but no. The old man spoke badly of her. He said it would be you first of all, then she, and then this country would be the same country as England."

"Who is the old man?" said Mary. "What's his part in this?"

"I do not know his name. He spoke Scots, but he was from another country. I could tell by the way he said his words. He spoke the Scots too good. But he had no accent. He talked constantly of the old religion. Once I saw the King kneel down and kiss his finger—"

My God, thought Mary. Is it possible? De Gouda?

"He told the King it was fine for him to have his vicious habits if he could not help them. He said Jesus would understand all. He said Mr. Drake was like an Italian saint and that he would have the first place in heaven, and that the King would too. He spoke always of a 'Great Enterprise.' All of them always speaking of the Enterprise."

"When did you hear these things?" asked Mary.

"It was more than a month ago, Your Majesty," he said. "It was the time of Your Majesty's illness."

"Then why do you come now and tell me?" she said angrily.

"Please, Your Majesty, but I thought then that it was talk, and my father and my father's father and all those before him have always been Lennox men—"

"There are two reasons," said Bothwell. "Number one: Walker here had a daughter. Her name was Johann. She was pretty. Johann thought Captain Drake loved her and so she let him love her. Then he loved someone else. So she killed herself. Number Two: Walker read some letters tonight." He threw three parchment scrolls on the dressing table. "I suggest you read them."

The first letter was addressed to the King of Spain: ". . . and as Your Most Catholic Majesty knows, I am a true son to Holy Mother Church, but my wife the Queen is lax in these matters and it is to be feared overly solicitous of the heretic presbyters in this kingdom, so much so that it is openly given about that she will soon become one of them in order to secure the throne of England. As long as she holds the sceptre, there is no hope that Christ may be again born within this wretched northern clime. By the beginning of March, it is hoped that the situation, with your assistance, may be alleviated. My man in London is to be trusted in all negotiations. Your brother in God, Henricus Rex." The next letter was addressed to the Cardinal of Milan. The third was for Lady Lennox in London, requesting more information on the timetable for the Spanish troop advance into the Netherlands.

"But King Henry is a good lad," whimpered Walker. "It is Mr. Drake who has done these things."

"You have told me everything?" said Mary. "You have not lied in anything?"

"Your Majesty, I swear, on my mother—"

"That is enough," said Bothwell to Walker. "Now go where I showed you."

"I'd die for you," Walker said to Mary.

Mary smiled sadly and shut the door.

"Another conquest?" said Bothwell.

"He wouldn't really . . . die . . . for me."

"Walker told me that he tried to get to you about a week ago. That was before he read those letters. It must have been his conscience. But Mr. Maitland's secretary thought he was lying and sent him away. Don't be angry at the man—Walker told me the only way he could get enough courage that time was to drink himself into insensibility." He put his hands on her waist and rested his head against her neck and shoulder. "You can't tell when people like you or me or Maitland or your brother James lie, but you can always tell, sooner or later, when the simple people are lying. John's like that. That is why I like him.

He's in his rooms now, crying at the top of his lungs. He doesn't understand anything, I think. Or maybe he understands everything that we don't." He sighed. "Whatever Walker's credentials, the letters are true. Sooner or later, they'll be missed."

"Harry's a fool," said Mary. "We'll send them on to where they were going. He used his seal to close them. What is really funny is that he only has a copy of the royal seal and I have the original."

"Funny," said Bothwell. "The Presbyterians who love John Knox so very much have always hated you. They never knew you were the one person who was saving them from the Pope's bonfires, after all. Now you must forget the Catholic Church. It is done; and the Catholic Church is in league with your husband, with your enemies. There is you and there is me and there is Scotland. Your husband has gone up to Glasgow. You must follow him and get him back; you will lie to him; you will lie *with* him, if you must. You will do everything and anything to get him back in Edinburgh. And you will do it because you want to live, and you will be safer with your husband here, where he can be watched."

Mary sat down on the chair and stared blankly at the dwindling fire.

"He wouldn't dare to attempt anything now," said Bothwell. "There are too many important people here for the christening. The letter says the beginning of March. That gives us one, two months."

"Don't talk," said Mary.

"What—"

"Don't even think."

"I am adamant that you get him back to Edinburgh."

"Not one word," she said wearily. "Not one." She walked to the bed and lay down. "Bothwell and Mary," she sighed. "Is that all there is? Yes. That. But the Pope, the Pope would never allow . . . No, I'm wrong. He would. He's a human man. But the Church isn't human; it will always go on, regardless. It always has. Jesus tests us constantly. But I didn't think—"

"Stop it," said Bothwell, sitting beside her. "What is done is done."

She wound her arms around his neck and murmured, "You and I are alone now. Once you said that when we were alone like this nothing else had to matter, exist. Now nothing does." She brushed her lips across his, then reached back and pulled her hair over his head. "Only you and I. Now we're that, Bothwell. Bothwell and Mary."

"Ay, when we are alone."

"Always. Now come inside me. Be me. You already are. And it's true. The two of us. We're the same one. Both. I love you. I am you."

"Mary and Bothwell," he said, his voice breaking.

"No. The other way around."

"Ay, when we are alone."

"Always."

She would bring Harry back to Edinburgh. At the proper time, he would be arrested. Then he would be brought to trial for treason before the Lords Assembled. Then the Lords Assembled would deliver a sentence.

Two days later Mary set out for Glasgow with a train of two hundred guardsmen. The snow was deep and it took a long time to travel the smallest distance. On the afternoon of the journey's second day, a courier brought news that Harry was stricken with smallpox. His face and body were covered with running pustules, his eyes blinded, his throat so swollen he could not eat.

Mary liked the snow. It was cold, invigorating. She liked the way all the distant sloping hills looked dappled blue. She hoped he would die. She would cry if he died. But, at least, he would be dead.

Edinburgh. First day of February. White everywhere. White moving along the High Street like a thousand overturned buckets of unchurned butter festering, pouring into side streets, alleyways, blind wynds. Gabled rooftops covered with caking milk. At the end of the High Street, white cobwebbing Holyrood Palace like a tattered wedding dress. High above, to the west, Edinburgh Castle buried under fold upon fold of spongy winding sheet. To the south, the deserted monastery of Kirk o'Field, all white.

In the daytime, everything was white. At night, the sky was gray. That was the only separation.

Every sound was lost in the all-pervading monotone of the wind and snow. You couldn't hear the cock crowing the dawn. Suddenly, it would just be day. You couldn't hear the cows lowing in the morning. There wasn't any morning. You couldn't hear the undistinguishable children slipping and sliding along the crusted streets, or their mothers when they called them home for supper. That was how you knew when night was coming. When there were no children in the streets. When night was coming, the High Street was always empty.

Bothwell climbed up the swaying rope ladder to the parapet of the city wall directly above the broad entrance gates. Steadying himself, he looked down the slippery walkway and cried, "Paris! French Paris!" A sudden downward thrust of the wind billowed his fur greatcoat and he almost lost his balance and fell. Everywhere the wall was crumbling. Once, hundreds of archers stood here and fired into English armies. Now, Bothwell doubted it could hold the weight of twenty men. "French Paris," he cried again. He paused and watched the vacant plain outside the city, then walked on a bit until he saw a pair of legs stretching from behind a stack of broken crates.

The man was alseep, his cape bundled against his chest for warmth. Bothwell studied his servant Paris' thin, indolent face. He was so thin. It made you ache for hunger to look at him.

"Hello, Paris. Wake up. Lazy houghmagandie."

Paris stirred, muttered something, then lifted his bony hands to his eyes. He cursed, looked around, saw Bothwell's boots, and leaped to his feet. "M'lord, I must've dozed. Yes, but just one moment of it."

"You were supposed to watch for the King and Queen."

"The Lord knows I have rights to be weary," said Paris, rubbing his flat nose. "When you made me Her Majesty's valet, the thing appealed to me. Great honor, it. But I have done not one thing since but it was riding back and forth across this country carrying letters between you."

"Don't preach at me," said Bothwell.

"Me? Preach?" said Paris, in mock horror. "No, but I will be plain to you, Bothwell. All the time I've been in your service, I've seen you in great trouble, but I never saw you had any friends to help you. Now you are out of trouble, and because you have the Queen's favor, everyone great or small pays you court. But you are more of the country than the court, Bothwell. People like Lord James and Mr. Maitland and the King and the Queen eat people like you and me, Bothwell." He rested on the wall and glanced at the snow-covered hills. "Get you on your horse, he said, "Queen Guinevere is coming."

Bothwell slapped Paris on the back, hurried down the ladder, and galloped out the city gates. A gust of wind blew a flurry of snowflakes in his eyes. His horse threw back its head and whinnied. The little caravan seemed frozen against the white hills.

He rode past the double line of soldiers, the King's horse-drawn, damask-curtained litter, and the retinue of servants. Mary was riding by herself, at the end of the procession.

Bothwell turned his head and saw Captain Drake approaching them.

"We approach the city, Your Majesty," Drake said to Mary.

"Yes," she said. "I can see that."

"His Majesty would like you to ride next to his litter, Your Majesty."

"I will ride where I am. Is His Majesty ill again?"

"To be blunt, Your Majesty, the King has a fear that—"

"There is no remedy against fear," said Mary.

"Your Majesty," said Drake, "I know that my master desires nothing more than that the secrets of every creature's heart were written on their faces."

"That would be nice. Is there anything else, Drake?"

"No, Your Majesty."

"Then you may go."

Drake returned to the damask litter. Bothwell waited a minute, but Mary gave no indication of wishing to speak with him, so he rode on a little ahead. As they approached the city gates, he turned briefly in his saddle and looked back at her. The wind whistled and shrilled across the plain. The flurrying snow struck her face, but she didn't lower her head or draw her ermine hood closer. Bothwell watched the colorless flakes melt down her cheeks. He quickly turned his head.

The caravan passed under the crumbling stone gates and entered Edinburgh.

Instead of the High Street, which led to Holyrood, they turned south and onto the Cowgate road. A few women opened their shutters, waved, and yelled down, "God save the Queen." Nobody called, "God save the King." Black smoke rose from the chimney tops, mixing the white sky gray.

Mary pulled up alongside Bothwell. She had drawn the white hood over her face and he could only hear the sound of her voice. "I think he's well," she said, "but he has another week of cleansing baths before he'll be able to come back to Holyrood. He told me over and over, every day, that he loved me. You would have laughed, Bothwell, to hear him tell me that."

He watched the litter's snow-covered top swaying ahead. The soldiers and servants bent their heads against the cascading wind and snow. Nobody spoke.

They left the Cowgate and proceeded up a steep incline which ended with a high, worn brick wall. They passed through an ironwork gate and into a vast orchard of barren trees, less than a mile from Holyrood. The procession came to a halt. Bothwell followed Mary out onto a broad flagstone courtyard; there was a large garden, a ruined church, a pleasant house. This was Kirk o'Field.

Ten years ago the church had been the monastery and collegiate church of St. Mary's in the Fields. Nine years ago, with Marie de Guise and her French retainers under siege in Edinburgh Castle, John Knox had torn the host and chalice from the tabernacle and trampled them beneath his boots. The church, the poor-school, the library, free hospital, and living quarters of the monks were shot with cannon and set afire. The monks were hanged from the city walls, then thrown into the sea. The crypts were desecrated, a thousand years of corpses were torn from their resting places, loaded into carts, and burned at the Merkat Cross.

Mary stopped in front of the gutted, roofless church. Servants were untying crates and carrying them into a small two-story house with red gables. James helped Mary off her horse.

"St. Mary's was a beautiful church once," she said to no one in particular. "This spring I intend having it restored. I also intend restoring a good deal of confiscated church land back to the Crown."

"It isn't within your jurisdiction," said James.

Have you forgotten, James, that you gave your permission for the Ecclesiastical Court? At any rate, on my twenty-fifth birthday, all the holdings given away during my minority revert back to me. Customarily, they are returned to those who hold them. Customarily." She walked across the courtyard to the litter.

A red taffeta mask covering the upper part of his face, Harry swung his long white legs onto the ground, pulled down his nightgown, and stood. Drake adjusted a thick wool robe over his shoulders.

"It's snug here, peaceful," said Harry, indicating the house in which he would stay. He lifted Mary's hand to his lips. "It's a place where a man can think. Consecrated ground. There's even ghosts nearby—not one ghost, mind you, but an entire monastic order—so I'll have plenty of good company." He squeezed Mary's hand and smiled.

Bothwell thought: Those frosted dormer windows set back so deep in the stone—they look as though they were looking at us. They look as if they would like to kill us all, whisper to the stones: "Fall down, crush them dead." He realized Harry was addressing him.

"The Queen has commanded me to love all whom she loves. I wrote a letter to the King of France explaining that the reason I couldn't be present at the christening was my illness." Behind the eye slits of the red mask, he examined their reactions. "There's one of the crypts under this house," he continued. "That must be where our ghosts spend the day. But I have the key."

"My time will be divided between Kirk o'Field and Holyrood," said Mary, kissing him on the cheek. "I've had a bed put downstairs."

"And if you get frightened, you come upstairs and sleep with me."

Mary put her finger to his lips. "When the cleansing baths are done, and you've come back home to Holyrood, then we'll sleep together."

"If you haven't been infected yet, dear heart, I doubt you will be." His voice was mild, almost thoughtful.

Bothwell turned away in disgust. Here we all are, he thought, standing out here in the middle of all this snow, getting cold and wet, and talking at each other as if we were on some wooden stage on Mayday, and there were a thousand people down below, listening, wondering. He glanced up at the dormer windows on the second floor. A pale face pressed against the center lattice. Involuntarily, Bothwell's hand closed over his heart. He sighed. It was only one of Harry's valets drawing a white cloth across the oily glass.

On the ground floor, there was a tiny makeshift kitchen, a bedroom, and an anteroom. A bolted door beneath the wrought-iron turnpike stair led to the crypt below. Bothwell followed James up the turnpike, through a sitting room with two benches, and into a richly furnished bedroom. Previously, this had been the grand prior's residence.

One of the walls was covered by a thick tapestry depicting bluebirds, robin redbreasts, and sparrows tumbling above a jungle of contentedly smiling wolves and tigers. A card table with a green velvet cloth stood in front of the uncurtained window, next to three high-backed mahogany chairs. In one of the corners sat a double-seated chair of state, draped in red and yellow watered silk. Harry was propped up against some satin pillows in the gigantic bed, a brown and purple quilt across his legs. Mary sat beside him. Camphor and French attars had been sprayed about the room, but it still smelled of damp. The floors slanted.

"Your flint," said James. "They need it for a fire."

Bothwell reached the implement from his belt and handed it to him. He took it but didn't move.

Finally he said, "You're shaking, Bothwell. You might be coming down with something." He let his eyes rest on the bed where Mary and Harry were carrying on an animated conversation, then shuddered and looked over Bothwell's head and out the window. "She wants to restore that old church down there. You look on the verge of a cold. Better watch, Bothwell."

From a distance, James had always struck Bothwell as massive, tight-lipped, and colorless. But up close, there was a quality of boyishness about his face. He's tall, but doesn't weigh much more than I do. He's strong, but close he looks delicate, frail. And those eyes—if an eighty-year-old man could die and be born again, remembering everything, and, at fifteen years of age, have ninety-five years of earthly dealings behind him, I think he would look like James Stewart. I hate him, but not as much, I suppose, as I once did. Sometimes, close up, he looks like an innocent. Is it possible, after all the blood, lies, and treason, that he could be an innocent? God how much he can look like her sometimes—the same eyes, nose, hair, height, even, when I've seen him smile, which is not often, almost the same smile. It's unnatural. They both have that restless look.

"I always wondered," said James, absently handing the flint to a passing servant, "how it is that it can be so much colder inside a place than outside."

"Dear heart," said Harry. "Spend the night tonight." He touched her neck with his little finger.

Mary looked in Bothwell's direction, smiled, and slipped her hand under the quilt. Harry giggled so loudly that everybody in the room turned and looked at them.

"Better watch, Bothwell," James said again as he moved away.

Bothwell leaned on the window sill and stared into the white courtyard. It had taken the snow ten minutes to obliterate their footsteps. It's cold, so unbelievably cold.

Drake and another man brought in a tin bath and set it on the far side of the bed. They covered it with an unhinged door.

"We'll make so many babies," said Harry. "And they'll all look like you and me."

"Your Majesty," said Bothwell, walking toward Mary, "may I have a word with you?"

"Ah, Jimmy," said Harry, clasping his hand. "I'm glad we're all friends again. Next week, when the cleansing baths are done, we can go out on the river Firth and cut ourselves a hole and fish. Mary can come too, if she wants."

"Yes, that would be nice," said Bothwell. "Your Majesty—"

"Can't you see I'm speaking with my husband?" Mary snapped.

Bothwell rode through the dead orchard. He looked back at the house. The only signs of life were the lighted windows on the second floor, which cast an eerie yellow glow onto the snow beneath.

Before she left to fetch her husband back from Glasgow, she was terrified for her life. She knew there was a plot against her and that her husband was a part of it, and that her Church was part of it. Now she's sticking her hands under his bedclothes and kissing his fetid mouth, and now she's planning to restore church benefices throughout the whole country. I have heard her say she was a faithful, loyal Catholic often enough. She's always said it to everyone. What happened in Glasgow? And what does James know? Twice he said: Better watch, Bothwell. Oh, God, dear God, for a plain man who speaks out plainly, straight out, no tricks.

The wind and snow were remorseless, but he liked the feel of the snow melting through his clothes and onto his skin. That was the only thing he did like. What was anything? But he was Bothwell. Mary, Queen of Scots, should be walking on the hills outside the city, the wind billowing her white skirts and the snow following after her.

CHAPTER FOURTEEN

Three days later Mary sat by her window lattice in Holyrood and stared into the frosted panes. Outside, guards pulled their caps tight about their ears and rubbed their hands together. Fur-covered men and women trudged up and down the High Street. "Beaton," she said. "Come here. Edinburgh's been invaded by bears."

Beaton put down Boccaccio and walked to the window. "It's so glazed over, madam, I wonder you can see anything." She took a long handkerchief from her belt and wiped the glass.

"Now the bears look like people again," Mary sighed. "What an amazing woman you are, Beaton. Singlehanded, with but the aid of one red kerchief, you've saved five thousand Scots from an army of bears." She put her hands over her eyes and added, "Singlehanded, you've got my brother Johnny and you've got the man you love; you're happy. All singlehanded."

"There's not much worse than a Presbyterian bear," said Beaton.

"Oh yes," said Mary, smiling despite herself. "Nothing on earth. They say they do not care for dancing, that poetry writing and painting are idle faults, that pretty clothes are dreadful waste, holy days and holidays and you and I are tools of Satan—"

"And the wickedest sins of all involve sports: snow-sledding, woman-looking, cockfighting and, most especially, bearbaiting."

"You don't understand," said Mary, on the verge of crying. "They only want to save our black, *black,* damned, worthless souls."

"Before they eat us!"

"You are cruel."

"Madam," said Beaton, throwing her arms around Mary and kneeling at her feet, "I am honest. They wish to devour us. You see, they are suspicious that we sometimes smile and laugh. They don't know us very well, do they?" She rested her head in Mary's lap.

"Wait until the glass frosts again, and you'll see what I mean."

"There's no need," said Beaton. "They still look like bears." She stood up. "I wish I was dead. Look at that one—there; he's been running about all morning."

"I know, I know," said Mary. "It's Drake. Either he's very busy, or that's the only way he knows to keep warm. Beaton, I haven't seen my little man all day. Go get him, *ma chère,* please."

"Yes, madam." Beaton made a huge, awkward curtsy.

Mary smiled. She recognized it as an imitation of a female bear, named Claudette, that had been part of the royal children's menagerie at Versailles. "Oh, Beaton, Claudette was graceful. Why, you know, the two of us used to dance together, and it was Claudette had everybody's eye, not me. Just think, Mary, Queen of Scotland and the Isles, Queen Consort of the kingdom of France, obscured by a dancing female bear. Poor Claudette! Go out and put your ear to the dirt. If you can dig through the snow. She's growling there now. You'd never have made a proper bear, dear."

"Master Knox thinks me bare enough," said Beaton, pushing up her breasts from the low-cut border of her gown.

"You have lovely rosy breasts," said Mary.

"Not as large as yours," said Beaton, "but there's some I know that likes them."

"Do I detect bruises?"

"Johnny likes to bite. He's rougher than I thought. But I love it. And, at any rate, Master Knox thinks me very bare indeed."

"If I remember it correctly, in one of his sermons he said you had half the gentlemen here at Holyrood bare as birth. Knox has a fondness for alliteration—jangling Jezebels, carnal cardinals."

"Now Johnny's my only bare gentleman," laughed Beaton, "but I'm not at all displeased. Bothwell is downstairs again. Shall I have him come up?"

"Tell him I'm ill."

Beaton sighed. "I don't know what has happened between you two, but I know Bothwell is your friend. Don't knit your brow at me, madam. I'll get your little man."

Mary gazed out the lattice. Outside the city, against the hills, black specks sailed above the snow. She watched them hit the bottom, then wearily pull their sleds back up the smooth hills. Reaching the summits, they threw themselves on top of their boards and went sailing down the white again. Their wild laughter and shrieks of delight, though she could not hear them, were deafening, and she put her hands over ears and shut her eyes.

When she opened them again, she found herself staring into the face of a ghost. The lips were tight, eyes dull with hate. It was not a woman's face. She touched the window glass with her hands and let her fingers move over the ice-cold cheeks.

She looked past the reflection to the point where the east and south walls of Edinburgh joined. A thin wisp of gray smoke wafted into the sky from the lonely quadrangle of buildings there. Inside the outline of her face, the snow-encrusted ruins of Kirk o'Field suddenly merged together like an enormous white wedding cake.

Her baby would be a handsome man when he was big. He would be King of England. She bounced him on her knee and sang.

"Lull, lulla, lull, lulla, lullabye, sweet babe,
  Quoth the Virgin she,
  And rocked little baby on her knee,
  Lull, lulla, lull—"

The infant's huge blue eyes stared curiously at her. She wondered: What do babies dream about—other babies, milk and food, nothing, or us?

"Beaton, Beaton, take him away. I can't bear it."

She ate little supper that night, and asked the captain of her guard to ride to Kirk o'Field and beg the King's pardon: she felt ill and would not come tonight. The night before, she'd lain at Kirk o'Field, eyes open, listening.

Snow pattered against the window glass. She wished she was dead. But she didn't want to be dead. Whatever anyone said, whatever anyone did, it was better to be alive than dead. She remembered Chastelard. Going to execution in red and yellow, singing Ronsard. He'd been in love with death. Until the executioner raised his ax. Poor Chastelard.

Poor everybody.

The limanga slid open. Mary pressed her face against the cool satin pillow, closed her eyes, and murmured a prayer.

"Point-blank," said Bothwell, "are you joined with your husband and the Pope against us? Yes or no. Don't think, answer."

"No!"

He sighed and sat down next to her on the bed. "I believe you might let me think something to be true that was not, but—when everything is done and said—you would not lie to me."

"I don't want to hear, see, touch you," she said. "Go away. Go back to Jean."

"Why are you so angry with Jean? What am I supposed to do with her?"

Mary sat up and clutched his collar. "You must know, Bothwell, that you may do anything you wish to do. But there is one thing which I will not bear, and that is to share you with any other woman."

"I've told you that I love you. I do love you. What more—"

"Then you wouldn't make love with anybody else."

"I am a man," he said angrily. "I do what men do. Have you set spies on me? Did they hide under my bed? Did they tell you that in your absence I frequented certain taverns? Would you like me to present you with a list of names?"

"You must be a fool," she said calmly, "to think I'd put my husband in your power, put myself in your power, while you betrayed me."

"Is this why you have been acting this way?" he said. "Is it because of the women that you refused me audience?"

Mary looked at her hands. "No."

"Then why, in the name of God?"

"I don't know," she said. "I feel nothing any more. Nothing at all. Not even hate. Nothing. I want to go away and sleep a long time. I want everybody else to go away too. But to another place." She burst into tears. "I want to *rest*. I want it all to end. I want it all never to have happened. Not you, not Harry, not the Catholics and not the Protestants, not Knox and the Pope, not James, John, Beaton, Elizabeth, Maitland, Huntly, Hamilton, Pierre, me. I want you all to go away and never come back. I want to go away and never come back. Peace. Simply one unadulterated, simple, pure second of peace." She rubbed her eyes and lay back. "As for your women," she added in a dull monotone, "that's only another thing."

"This is stupid," said Bothwell. "You are overwrought and that is understandable. But I love you and do not want to see you die before I do. Listen, please, for both our sakes. Maitland has word there are fifty thousand Spanish troops moving into the Netherlands. An armada is set to sail from Lisbon later this month. Their purpose is supposedly to quell the heresy there. But the Netherlands are rather close to Scotland, if I may put it simply. Elizabeth is getting fidgety, and with good cause, I think. When England is gone—no more Protestants. Period. Envisage a sea blockade of the Thames. Add to that a march on London from across the Scots border and through the Catholic north counties of England. The Pope has branded Elizabeth a bastard ever since she took her sceptre. Picture a Spanish army, with a legitimate heir to the English throne at its head, marching down to London to take the she-bastard's crown away and restore Christ forever. Now, Mary, since you have never been the most zealous of papists, it is not you but your husband that I see at the head of that Spanish army. Have Maitland draw up arrest warrants for Harry and his friends, sign them, give them to me, and I will use them when the time is right."

"If I sign, will you leave me alone?" she said. "All of you? Will you all go and never come back? I'm tired, Bothwell, so tired."

"Trust me," he said urgently.

"Why should I trust you any more than the others?" She covered her eyes with her hands and rolled on her side, away from him.

"God, how I hate you sometimes," he said.

The snow pattered against the window glass.

Harry pushed his plate away, sat back, and stretched contentedly. "That was nice. Supper. You and I. Seafood goes with winter. It seems like such a long time since we've been alone together." His blue eyes, though the slits in the taffeta mask, were festive.

Mary looked at the cracked shells and greasy bits of lobster meat in front of her.

"The last cleansing is Sunday," he said affably. "You promised your man Bastian you'd dance at his wedding masque, but afterward, when you come back here to spend the night, bring James and Maitland with you, and we can have a small party. It's so lonely here. Do you promise?"

"Of course," she said. She wiped her hands. "It's late, and I'm very tired. Will you excuse me, please?" She stood up, walked behind his chair, and kissed him on the ear.

"You can sleep up here as easily as down below."

"That's all right. You need rest too." She paused at the door. "Do you mind if I take some of your books? Reading helps me sleep when I have trouble."

"I want to thank you," Harry said timidly. "You've been— the only word I can think of is 'kind.' I love you for that."

He bit his lip. "I'm young. You're young, as well, but you're older, because you know how to forgive people. But I swear to you that I will try never to be a trouble to you again. And I ask nothing but that we may be at bed and table again as husband and wife. I'm not a brilliant man, Mary, but even a fool can learn from experience, and I . . . never mind. I think you understand. You're the only one."

"Why don't you take off your mask?" she said. "Let me see your face. Is it bad? Do you think they'll be able to cure it? I wish you'd let Dr. Lusgerie examine you. I had the smallpox in Paris when I was a girl, but they lanced the sores in such a way as to leave me unmarked."

Harry took four volumes from one of the stacks by the chair of state and handed them to her. "My physician is capable," he said good-naturedly. "But thank you for offering Lusgerie. There's nothing to do here but read and count snowflakes. A party Sunday night will be wonderful. Just you, me, James, Maitland, Bothwell if you like, Beaton, too."

Mary put a robe over her nightdress and crawled under the icy sheets. She thumbed through the books—*Spiritual Excercises* of Ignatius Loyola, a thin volume of rough ballad verse entitled *Jocky Was a Bonny Lad,* Castiglione's *The Courtier,* and Munster's *Historie of the Kingis of Scotia.* The ballads were in such archaic Gaelic that she couldn't make sense of them, so she turned to the *Historie.*

She read about Macbeth murdering Duncan, MacDuff cutting off Macbeth's head, and about Robert Bruce and the spider. James I was daggered in bed, James II blown to bits by a faulty cannon he was cannoneering. James III was poisoned. James IV was smothered to death by a Franciscan monk as he lay dying of wounds at Flodden Field. James V, Mary's father, was twenty-eight years old, said the book, God grant him all grace and long life.

Mary thought she heard a noise down below in the crypt. She put the book down and listened. Nothing. She got out of bed and looked outside at the ruins of the old church in the steadily falling snow.

John was sitting against a section of the orchard's northern wall, his knees drawn up, his canvas cloak pulled up over his head and chest for protection against the cold. He held a hagbutt musket between his legs. Bothwell leaned forward and shook him by the shoulder.

John threw back his cloak and raised the musket. "It's you, then," he said, his voice shaking with the cold. "Have you come to kill him now? So early in the morning, Jimmy?" He bent his head and coughed.

Bothwell sat down beside him.

"There's too much confusion," said John. "Do you know why all these things have happened, Jimmy?"

"No. Why?"

"I don't know. I asked you the question. I think I must look ridiculous sitting out here in the snow. We both must look ridiculous. It must be about six in the morning, I'd guess." He smiled warmly and took Bothwell's hand and pressed it. "We had some good times. Remember Ainslie's?" He lifted his free hand in a mock toast. "To the old times, when everybody was either good or bad and things were that simple. I know about you and my sister," he added quickly.

"What do you know?"

"That you're . . . together. Beaton told me. I never thought it would happen. Never. I can't understand any of it. You're going to murder him, aren't you? Morton's been home a month and a half and hasn't done it for you, so you're going to do it."

"No," said Bothwell. In the distance, beyond the barren apple trees, the stone house stood enshrouded in white. He was tempted to tell John about Walker and the letters, but he was afraid John would tell it to Harry. John loved Harry. You could see it in his eyes whenever anybody at court spoke of Harry: the love in John's eyes. And there was always, whenever anyone spoke ill of the King, or made a jest at his expense, the anger in John's eyes. Bothwell had seen things like this in Denmark and Paris—men loving other men to the point of sexual embrace —but it was beyond his comprehension. As a child, when he'd crawl the rocks near his father's old castle in the north, and peer down at the Witches' Sabbat, all twisting naked bodies and colored flames leaping against the black, he'd seen men using other men like women, and women doing the same, but he'd thought them fairies from India, and fairies weren't really men and women, but air. Gossamer things. God, why am I thinking all this? He's John, Johnny. The ground's freezing, but he's one of the few friends I know.

"I said, are you going to have someone do it for you?"

"No," Bothwell said angrily.

"I don't believe you," said John, shaking his head. "Morton was here last night. With James. I watched them walking off through the snow. They looked like quill ink someone shook on a piece of paper."

"James! What was he doing here? And Morton?"

"I don't know. Maybe he was visiting with my sister."

"And Morton?"

"I don't know. After I saw them I looked over at the lodging and saw Mary's face in her bedroom window. It looked like the face of a daemon-child, a Morgan le Fay type of face. I thought to myself: Poor Harry's going to die soon. Perhaps he deserves to die. But he's so young. God gives everybody a second chance —He must!—even us. Even him. I watched James and Morton walking off until I couldn't see them any more, then—as soon as they were gone—the wind went mad. It was like penny whistles, flutes, organ sounds, trees raving up, snow throwing itself down, everything so white that it was blinding, and, off, somewhere, I heard a wolf howl, and I knew it wasn't any ordinary wolf, but that it was a man. The snow was pouring down so fast I couldn't breathe. It was as if I was drowning. I thought I heard someone behind me and looked over my shoulder at all that careening white, and suddenly, as if it were right beside me, or only a little off, I heard that howl again. But there wasn't anything there that I could see. I was frightened, more frightened than I can ever remember being before, and so I climbed up on top of the wall and stayed there until it began to lighten. At some point, I realized that it wasn't anything as simple as a wolf-man that had been howling. It seemed to me that it was the sound of God, and that there wasn't any Jesus in Him at all." He tugged at Bothwell's coat sleeve. "Am I crazy? Jimmy, am I crazy?"

Bothwell raised his head and looked toward the house. Breathing heavily, he took a kerchief from his pocket and handed it to John. "Wipe the wet off your face. It's no sleep last night. And all the cold." He was quiet a minute. "Do you come here every night?"

"Yes. I suppose I must be crazy." He stood up and wiped the snow off his cloak. "Well, Bothwell must be off to see the Queen. And Lord John must be off to his rooms at Holyrood, where he intends locking his doors, shucking his clothes, pulling his curtains, and lying down to sleep on a turkey rug in front of the fire. He hopes he does not see you tonight, Jimmy. He truthfully hopes so." He offered Bothwell his hand. "James has given permission for an Ecclesiatical Court under Hamilton. She can divorce him, Jimmy."

"Certainly," said Bothwell, getting up. "Divorce him and throw her child's legitimacy and claim to the succession into doubt forever."

John laughed. "If that were to happen, it would happen twenty years from now. God gave us all a brain. Let James Charles use his when his time comes. Let us use ours in our own time. Good-by, Bothwell, and greetings to Sister Mary. If she loves you, and you her, I've no complaint. But remember the Ecclesiastical Court."

They shook hands, then John walked through the orchard to the gate where he'd left his horse the night before, and Bothwell walked through the orchard and toward the house.

Mary was upstairs in Harry's room. He was sitting in the tin bathtub singing "Greensleeves," while Drake and another servant poured green salts down his back and scrubbed him with sea sponges. The room was filled with a peculiarly foul odor, which Bothwell recognized but could not place.

"It's not me," said Harry, dropping a ball of scented soap and rising from the tub. "Medicine. Ughh! Come in and sit."

Mary was standing by the window gazing down into the snow. Bothwell walked to her side, raised his hand, and dropped it again. She moved her fingers nervously along the windowpane. "It's not the smallpox," she whispered. "Don't you recognize the smell? A preparation of mercury. Isn't that the prescribed treatment? Before we were married, when we thought he had the measles, it was the same symptoms, less virulent. Syphilis."

Harry lifted his medicine, made a face, and swallowed.

"Well, I must go," said Mary, moving to the door.

"So soon?" said Harry.

"I have a poor-school to open, then a merchant gathering. But I'll be back tomorrow. Bothwell, your arm?"

"It will be our last night at Kirk o'Field," Harry said, smiling merrily. "Bring Bothwell to the little party we've planned. And bring us a piece of Bastian's wedding cake. Until tomorrow then."

The wedding of Sebastian Pages and Christiana Hogg took place at ten o'clock the next morning in the royal chapel of Holyrood, with the archbishop performing the ceremony, and two of his bastard sons acting as altar boys. Afterward, Mary had arranged for a pantomime and a buffet. An elaborate masque was planned for the evening. Sebastian had served her faithfully and well since coming here with her from France all those years ago, and Mary wanted to show her appreciation for his devotion.

In the middle of the performance, Maitland approached Mary's chair and told her he had a matter of some importance to discuss with her, would she please come into one of the antechambers with him?

"James is gone," he said, latching the door. "He left word he had to go to Lochleven because his wife was ailing. You know, madam, how it is between James and his wife."

"Then why did he go?" she said. "He told me nothing of this."

"Perhaps he knows something which we do not know." He

nervously fingered the frilled collar of his shirt. "But that is not all. John Knox left early this morning for Lothian, ostensibly to settle some minor dispute among the presbyterial court there. And not thirty minutes past, I received a note from Signor di Moretta announcing his immediate retirement from his post and stating that he plans to leave Edinburgh by the middle of next week."

A sudden chill ran down Mary's spine. "If there's a conspiracy, why is Di Moretta leaving? He's the King of Spain's confidant, Harry's only friend of any importance. And Knox? What have Knox and Di Moretta to do with each other?"

"For the first time in a long time," said Maitland, "I am at a loss. I think they all know something. Whatever it is, is beyond my ken. There's a saying: When the candles are out, all the cats are gray. Tonight is the King's last night at Kirk O'Field. Tonight we arrest him."

"But so soon—"

"Madam, the fat's in the fire. We're blind. Something is going to happen, perhaps it's already happening at this very moment. Tonight we arrest the King. I wish we could do it now, but we can't. But we make the arrest tonight. Tomorrow may not be here for a good number of us if we don't."

Harry sat against his pillows, strumming a London street ballad. Mary watched Maitland search through his pockets, pull out a small leather bag, and undo the strings. He noticed her looking at him, and winked. But he's a nervous man tonight, she thought; he's not Michael Wiley tonight. Bothwell, Livingstone, and Archbishop Hamilton were seated around the card table playing dice. Three or four ladies from the wedding party talked excitedly among themselves about each other's gowns, ailments, and loves, glancing every now and then in the direction of the bed. Harry seemed upset.

"Does Leicester really tint his beard?" Maitland said.

"Yes, yes, a slight purplish color," said Harry.

Maitland smiled, drew an almond from the leather bag, and thrust it into his mouth. "Bothwell," he said, turning toward the card table, "did you know the Queen of England's Leicester tinted his beard?"

"Seven," cried Bothwell.

Hamilton laughed delightedly and clapped Bothwell on the back.

"What a convivial group," Harry said to Mary, putting aside the mandolin. "Do they think I'm going to infect them? And Hamilton—why did you bring Hamilton? You know how much I dislike him. Mary, I'm speaking to you."

Mary raised her head and stared blankly at the red taffeta mask. Without thinking, she said, "Why don't you take it off?"

"What are you talking about?" he said irritably.

"The mask. I'm sorry, I didn't mean to—but why don't you take it off? The cleansing baths are done. You're well now. There's no need to—"

"I asked you a question," he interrupted. "Why did you bring Hamilton?"

"He was at the wedding. I just asked him. I don't know why. I asked him." Was he scarred? Was he ugly and ruined under the taffeta covering?

"He was a bad priest," said Harry, "corrupt and morally rotten. There'd never have been any trouble with men like Luther, Calvin, Knox, if there hadn't been men like Hamilton first. But, since he's here, we may as well make use of him. I wasn't able to attend Mass this morning. Archbishop come here." Harry snapped his fingers.

Hamilton picked up his chair, bustled across the room, and set it down next to the bed.

"Don't sit," said Harry. "I missed Mass this morning, and since you are the only 'priest' present, I thought it might be nice if you read us the psalm of the day."

Hamilton looked at Mary, then back to Harry. "I don't have my breviary, Your Majesty."

"And haven't had for some time, I think. I have one." He reached under one of the pillows and handed the book to Hamilton. "I trust you know what the psalm of the day is."

"Yes, Your Majesty. It was posted on St. Giles's door this morning when I went to marry Bastian and Christiana, but it's such a depressing text that I omitted it from the service."

"I'm sure that, somehow, we'll survive," said Harry. "And stop that infernal dicing before I go out of my mind!"

Bothwell cast the dice once more, then turned, crossed his legs, and smiled at Harry.

Mary could not keep her eyes off the taffeta mask. Was he scarred and ugly? As ugly as he sounded now? Once she'd loved him. Once she'd believed he loved her. Was he afraid, ashamed to have her look at his face?

Hamilton read:

"... the terror of death has fallen upon me.
Fear and trembling come upon me, and horror overwhelms me,
And I say, 'Had I but the wings of a dove, I would fly away ...'"

She believed the Roman Catholic Church was the Mystical Body of Christ, the one true apostolic church founded by Jesus himself for the salvation of the world. She could never be anything else but a Catholic. She knew she was not good, but she loved God. With her whole heart. Whole soul.

"Louder," said Harry.

Maitland offered Hamilton an almond.

"Engulf them, O Lord; divide their counsels, for in the city I see violence and strife; day and night they prowl upon its walls.
Evil and mischief are in its midst; treachery and fraud never depart from its streets. ..."

Walker, the letters, troops advancing to Amsterdam, all this *talk*. Disconnected. If she'd never loved him it would be easy. But she had.

"If an enemy had reviled me, I could have borne it. If he who hates me had vaunted himself against me, I might have hidden from him.

But you whose companionship I enjoyed; at whose side I walked in procession to the house of God—"

"That's true," said Harry suddenly. He looked around the room. "It's true. It's easy to accept anything—it doesn't matter how bad—but when *a friend* does it—then there's nothing to do but—that's the worst of all. A friend!" He looked briefly at Bothwell, then waved his hand for the archbishop to continue.

"We all are your friends, Your Majesty," said Maitland, dressing his face in bewildered concern. "There is no one in this room who wishes you ill."

"Go on, Hamilton," said Harry.

"But I will call on God and the LORD will save me. In the evening, and at dawn, and at noon, I will grieve and He will hear my voice. He will give me freedom and peace—"

The Pope was the Vicar of Christ on earth, the supreme ruler of all the faithful, whose definitions and pronouncements in all matters of faith and morals were infallible. If there was a plot, was it simply Harry and his father Lennox and Drake and perhaps De Gouda, and the Pope knew nothing of it at all? If there was a plot . . .

"His words are smoother than oil, but they are drawn swords. Cast your care upon the LORD and He will support you; never will he permit the just man to be disturbed—"

What she needed most was time. To think. Harry at the head of a Spanish army marching down to London! The very idea was ridiculous. She needed time to think. What if Bothwell arrested him and there wasn't any plot at all? She'd be the laughingstock of Europe. Elizabeth would laugh. Perhaps he could be brought to trial for Davy's murder, but that was almost a year ago. And she'd just signed the pardons.

". . . God will bring them down into the pit of destruction; men of blood and deceit shall not live out half their days. But I trust in you, O my Lord."

The archbishop sighed, wiped his forehead, and eased back into the chair. He laid the breviary on Harry's bed. Harry took the book in his hands, kissed it, and put it under his pillow.

Mary raised her head and looked at the taffeta mask. Why didn't he take it off?

He leaned forward and caught her hand. "Tonight," he whispered. "When you've come back. I've been cross. Forgive me."

Suddenly she felt sorry for him. His face was probably scarred. He had nobody that loved him. His father had never loved him, only used him. The eyes, over the mask, were nervous, frightened. She forced herself to smile.

Harry raised his arms and cried, "The King of Scotland shall propose a toast. Ned, pour the wine all around."

As Drake filled Mary's goblet, she studied his face. Walker had called him the dark one, the evil one, vicious, dissolute. He was an exceptionally handsome man; no one could deny that. Straight nose, smooth forehead, sculptured lips, good chin, swarthy olive skin, but not one line, one wrinkle, no hint of blood. It was a handsome, vacant, meaningless face.

Harry snatched Maitland's hat from the bottom of the bed. "Ah, a red feather; that stands for passion." He fit the hat, which was much too small, on top of his head. "A toast to the most lovesome lady," he said solemnly, "to the most constant, natural, and regal lady God ever made. Gentlemen and ladies, here is my wife, the Faery Queen." He doffed his hat, bowed his head, kissed his fingers, and emptied the glass behind the loose-fitting mask.

Everyone else did likewise, and the ladies murmured among themselves.

"Wait," cried Harry. "I'm not done." He lifted the glass high, then struck its rim with his index finger and produced a tiny *twang*.

"Thank you," said Mary, blushing. "Although I am perhaps not always the most 'lovesome' of ladies." She smiled at Harry over the top of her glass, then stood. "If I'm to dance at Bastian's masque, I must go now."

Harry's eyes glistened over the red mask. "One dance. And then you and Maitland and Bothwell can come back, and I'll take off my mask and let you look at me, and then, when the others have gone . . . then we can love one another again."

Drake helped Mary into her ermine cloak.

Harry's lips formed words and sentences. She searched his eyes, but there was nothing there. When he finished speaking, she bent down, held her breath, and raised his mask enough to kiss him on the mouth.

Harry motioned for Bothwell. "Jimmy," he said, clasping his hand, "do you remember when Elizabeth kept us in the Tower and we burst our chains and swung along all the steeples of all the churches in London with our ropes? Then Elizabeth flew overhead on Leicester, but turned into water and ran through our hands to the streets below. And we whacked the Questing Beasts. But I came up to Scotland and you went over to Denmark, instead of coming here with me. Do you remember?"

Bothwell stared at him as if he were a madman.

"I didn't think you would," Harry said sadly. "But Mary does. Don't you, dear heart?"

Mary nodded her head. The tale he'd made up for her the night of that tournament two years before, when she'd met him for the first time in her life and he was the best man she'd ever known.

When she reached the courtyard she noticed Bothwell's man, Paris, standing off a little in the ankle-deep snow and looking morosely at the window on the second floor. Bothwell called him over to help Mary up on her horse. His face was covered with black soot; he looked like a blackamoor. *"Jesu,* Paris," she laughed, "how dirty you are."

Paris cupped his gloved hands and Mary rose onto her saddle.

"It stopped snowing," she said to Bothwell. "Just this minute. It's not snowing any more."

Paris was whispering something in his ear. Bothwell rubbed his finger down the other man's cheek, then walked over to Mary and lifted the finger. "Smell it," he said. "Do you know what it is?"

She shook her head.

"Gunpowder. From the crypt beneath this house. It is a small part of approximately one hundred pounds of gunpowder. Dear heart."

She started to say something, reconsidered, and looked up at the twin rectangles of yellow light on the second floor. The back of Drake's head came into view, then his shoulders. He turned slightly, paused, and walked away from the window. Mary opened her mouth again, closed it, and looked past the misty jumble of tree limbs to a section in the sky where the outline of the full moon could be seen through the thinning clouds. Finally she said, "At midnight, you will arrest him?"

Bothwell nodded.

Torches flaring, the rest of the party was moving through the still orchard.

"He expects us back at midnight," said Mary. Her face was without expression. She gazed steadily into his eyes. "It was close to this time last year he murdered Davy. You mean only to . . . *arrest* him?" Her eyes mirrored the red cast by the spitting torches.

"What do you want me to do?" Bothwell asked hoarsely.

She dropped her head, gave the horse a fierce kick, and rode off to join the others.

Paris touched him on the shoulder. Bothwell spun around, stared into his thin face, and snapped, "Why do you look at me like that? Do you want a thrashing?"

Paris broke into tears. He fell to his knees, seized Bothwell's hands, and began furiously kissing them. "I never murdered anybody," he said in a little voice. "Not in all my life. I never killed anybody."

Bothwell pulled Paris to his feet and struck him hard across the face. "Did you hear me say murder? Did you?"

Paris threw his arms around Bothwell's neck. "She did," he moaned. "She said it with her eyes! Let us get out of this place and go back to the country and leave kings and queens alone. My knees—I'm sick, bad off. Bothwell, please, I feel like I'm hanging on top of some rock over the sea and if I let go the sea will come and get me." He fell backward into the snow. "I never did murder," he wept. "I never did it, Bothwell. Not murder."

Therobo and cithern, clavicytherium and harps and virginals. The violist flashed his bow up and down his glistening strings. Flames gnawed at the ill-smelling rush torches fastened to the walls. The bride's long black tresses were piled high on her head, circled by a silver wreath, with a tiny red galleon fastened to the top. Bastian, the groom, with his height and his long yellow love knots, fleetingly reminded Bothwell of Harry. In a flowing multicolor clown dress, John moved drunkenly among the masquers. The room stank of hot tallow.

"An amazing assemblage, Bothwell," said Maitland. "Bastian asked Lord John to design a different sort of wedding masque, and he has done exactly that. He was out early this evening along the Cowgate, the city entrance, and into sections of Edinburgh I never knew existed. These are masquers who wear their costumes all year round—ragamuffins, vagabonds, thieves, black marketeers, and whores. Though some of our Presbyterian guests have raised an eyebrow, Her Majesty does not seem to mind."

Bothwell watched the dancers dance. Maitland smiled and waved as Mary swept by on Bastian's arm. How can she dance? Bothwell thought. How can she ever be here?

Maitland took Bothwell's arm and drew him to a table of garlic-stuffed meat patties, stewed carp and pike, and little cakes and melting iced cream. "There will be no problem with Lord John," he said in a whisper. "Miss Beaton will see to him. At the last minute, she suggested that there wasn't any bedding clown for the happy couple, and he reluctantly agreed to perform the part. In his present condition, I doubt he'll be roaming about at Kirk o'Field tonight. It is now eleven-thirty, Bothwell." He waited a minute. "I think it would be the most remarkable joke if all of us simply marched over to the Kirk and lit the fuse to that gunpowder ourselves."

"God, but you can be a cold man, Maitland."

"Try some of the meats with the garlic stuffing, Bothwell. They're delicious." A grin playing about his mouth, Maitland studied the other man's face. Suddenly the grin disappeared and he said, through clenched teeth, "You are going to take ten men. You are going to take them to the King's house at Kirk o'Field. You are going to take them up the staircase to the second floor and arrest the King of Scotland for high treason. First, he will resist. Then you will kill him. Do you understand, Bothwell? The Queen understands. Do you understand?" He smiled pleasantly. "I suggest you knock before entering the royal chambers, as Drake might be in there with him." He seized Bothwell by the arm. "He meant to blow us all as high as heaven," he said, in a voice Bothwell had never heard before. "You. Me. Her. He meant to *murder* us. We must execute him for that. We must strike—now—before we are stricken. Do you understand *that?*"

In the murky glow, John jumped onto the orchestra stage and raised his tambourine. The organist ended his hymn with a final ear-shattering peal. Bastian lifted his bride in his arms and ran from the room. Mary and the others flew after them. Bothwell walked quickly after her and, in the crush outside in the hallway, roughly took hold of her arm. She turned and gave him a surprised look, then pulled him after her up the staircase with the others. John, his long gown wafting behind him, rushed the bridal couple to Mary's bedroom, where, as a mark of her favor, she had agreed that they should spend the night. John slammed the door shut. He took a jew's-harp from his pocket and played "The Daughter of the Loch" while the wedding guests clapped their hands. As soon as he was done, he threw open the bedroom door.

The bride and groom lay naked under the holland sheets of the huge bed, the lutanists and flutists on their left, violinists and mandolin players on their right. The bride flushed prettily and covered her face up to her eyes with the sheets. Bastian looked up when Mary came in, then grinned, moved under the covers, and emerged a second later with a yellow garter. He threw the garter to Mary.

John snatched up a silver cup filled with spiced wine and trimmed with rosemary, and handed it to Archbishop Hamilton. Hamilton reeled across the room, attempted to kneel by the bed, and collapsed on his side, spilling half the wine down his vestments. He attempted to raise his bulk, failed, sighed, and stretched out contentedly on his back. Holding the silver cup in the air, he announced in rich, full tones, "God bless. Long live." He burst into giggles. "A splendiferous wedding," he said, trying to control himself. *"In nomine Patris, et Filii* and so on. Johnny, Lord John, take it up. I can't go on."

John bent down and took the cup from the archbishop's hands. "Am I an ox, dog, or horse?" he said. "At whatever rate, I'm as gone as this reprobate monk at my feet." He hiccoughed, frowned, then laughed. "Bastian and Christiana," he said, in a grave voice. "May the Adversary, the Black Man, Father of Lies, Fiend or whatever he is this year, never enter your hearts."

"Not that awful *stuff,*" said Hamilton from the floor. "Get to the part about the fairies."

"The fens, pools, marshes, and hedgerows all are empty now," said John with a dramatic flourish of his arms. He put a finger to his lips. "Shhh," he cautioned the wedding guests. "The fens are empty now because all the fairies are peeping through that casement window behind me. Don't look. They'll go away if they catch us peeping back. We'll stay only one brief minute more, and then we'll go, and then they'll come, and they'll cobweb these two with their smiling, and fan them warm with Trent-fly wings, and sing them sweet idle green songs. I think I hear Will o' th' Wisp out there. Jack o'Lantern, too. But they always behave themselves on wedding nights. The Incubus is out there growling; the others won't let him in. He'll have to take his pleasure in the town tonight. As for the Succubus," he said loudly, "we know what's happened to that old fellow." He kicked Hamilton, who was still lying on the floor, lightly in the ribs.

"Splendiferous," bellowed Hamilton, propping himself up on his elbow. "Are we all still here? Amazing. Definitely amazing. Lord John waxes light when he's merry, which is when he's polluted with drink, which is to say—something or other. Don't pay heed; I always was a rotten priest. Go on. Go on."

John turned to the bride and groom. The musicians were playing a soft, lilting rendition of "Cupid Played at Cards for Kisses." "Now, Bastian and Christiana, God bless you both, and may your marriage never be as some we have seen." He handed the silver cup first to Bastian, then Christiana. After they had each taken a sip, he took their hands and placed them one on top of the other.

"Wondrous," muttered Hamilton, struggling to his feet. "Everybody present shall now cheer so loud and merrily that the dead will immediately get up out of their graves to come see what all the din's about."

Bastian took the silver cup off the bed table. "First," he said, "we'll cheer for Mary, Queen of Scots. Good cheer." He emptied the cup, motioned for her to come forward, took her hand, and gently kissed it.

John tottered against the window and slowly sank to the floor. "Wicked man," laughed Beaton, kneeling at his side and helping him to his feet. "What you need is—"

"Miss Beaton," said Christiana with a grin.

"Another drink," said Beaton.

"It's time for Farmer Pages to plow his field," said Archbishop Hamilton. He sprinkled the sheets with holy water and yanked shut the bed curtains. The wedding guests moved out of the bedroom.

Mary drew Bothwell down the hall and into a darkened alcove. She wound her arms around his neck, kissed him ferociously, and stood back. "It's late," she said. "It's time you left."

"What do you want me to do?" he said thickly.

"Don't you know, Bothwell?"

"To arrest him."

With her half-parted lips, wide eyes, and pale face, she reminded him of a baby that's just awakened and found itself alone in a dark room. She hugged him again and whispered in his ear, "He's there now. Waiting to kill you and me. Don't arrest him, Bothwell."

"You mean for me to—"

She put her hand over his mouth, kissed him gently on the forehead, pressed his hand, and walked hurriedly down the long corridor to bid the guests good night.

CHAPTER FIFTEEN

Followed by Paris, Livingstone, three of his henchmen, and five soldiers, Bothwell left the palace by way of the kitchens and led them along the back wall of the garden to the rear of the stables. A sentry cried out, "Who goes there?" They stopped dead in their tracks, then Paris cried back, "Friends."

"What friends?"

"My Lord Bothwell's friends."

Bothwell glowered at Paris.

"Friends?" said the sentry. "I make out eleven of you. Tell Lord Bothwell that, when you see him—it will make him smile, to discover he has so many friends. Pass on, God be wi' you."

Despite himself, Bothwell smiled. But as soon as they were off the grounds, he turned to Paris and said angrily, "Not to use my name, man. This is dangerous business. I'll answer if anyone questions us." As they proceeded into the town proper, Bothwell raised his hand to wipe the snow from his face. His heart was beating violently and his breath came in short gasps. I never knew her at all. Never. Or myself, either.

The little band pressed along the south side of High Street, dropped down a narrow alley to the Cowgate, and arrived finally at the Blackfriars' wall, which stood adjacent to Kirk o'Field. Bothwell told the others to wait, then climbed over the wall and leaped down onto the other side. He bent and ran quickly into the ruins of the church, climbed a rickety ladder to the nave, and looked over to the house.

A light was burning on the second floor.

Through one of the gaping holes in the church roof, Bothwell watched the restless clouds surging across the dark-water sky. He made his way down the ladder, left the church, ran back to the wall, and whistled for the others. His hands were shaking.

The door of the house was wide open. Placing his hand over the hilt of his sword, Bothwell led the men up the turnpike stair and into the antechamber. He paused, caught his breath, and threw open the door of Harry's bedroom.

Nobody was there. The brown and purple quilt lay across the floor and the card table had been overturned. A rope, attached to the wrought ironwork in the fireplace, stretched to the opened window. Bothwell leaned against the pane. Down below, six or seven men scurried across the gleaming snow and into the orchard.

"The gunpowder!" he shouted. "Out, out, get out!"

He raced after the others down the turnpike and out the door.

"God," said Livingstone, "he must have seen us coming. Now where and what?"

Bothwell pointed to the section of the orchard he'd seen the men enter, then drew his sword and ran across the slippery courtyard. Inside the orchard, someone—he couldn't tell whether it was a man or a woman—shrieked and cried, "Pity me!" It seemed to come from the direction of the town wall. With Paris and the others behind him, Bothwell dodged his way between the long rows of twisting black branches. Suddenly, one of the limbs smacked him full in the face and he fell to the icy ground. He groaned and rolled over on his back.

Above the clustering boughs, the moon passed from behind a purple cloud and colored the sky light yellow. Drake sat against one of the tree trunks, his head flung back at a peculiar angle. His eyes stared blankly at the sky.

Paris made the sign of the cross.

There was another scream. This time it was close by. Bothwell got to his feet and walked slowly to the edge of a small clearing. He stopped. Twenty feet away, the King of Scotland lay scuffling in the snow with five men.

His nightshirt was pulled over his face, but Bothwell recognized him by the long legs and fair hair. Two burly figures pinned his arms to the ground, while a third attempted to hold down the kicking legs. Another man straddled Harry's chest. The fifth man was standing with his back to Bothwell, his arms calmly folded, waiting for the others to be finished. He was a very tall man—there was something familiar about the way he stood, all the weight on one foot, the slightly stooped shoulders.

Harry shoved the man who was holding his legs back into the snow. The man cursed, threw himself forward, and pounded his fist into Harry's groin. The long white legs quivered, then lay flat.

There was a tremendous explosion. Bothwell looked over his shoulder and watched the stone house rise into the air above the branches and break into chunks and pieces of stone.

When he turned around again, the men had gone. Harry lay motionless in the snow, the nightshirt over his face.

Bothwell knelt beside the body and uncovered the head. Startled, he drew back. He'd forgotten what a handsome man Harry was. The illness hadn't marked him at all. The moonlight gave the smooth pale cheeks and forehead a pearl and ivory look. The thick red lips were drawn back in a genial half-smile and the teeth glistened in the soft light. He looked so unbelievably pure, innocent, and wronged. Then he breathed: he inhaled with a loud sucking sound, and opened his eyes.

"He's alive!" Paris cried. "Let's leave here."

"I thought they killed you," Harry moaned. The air hissed into his lungs. He tried to raise his head. His throat made a wet gurgling sound and his head fell back on the snow.

Bothwell tried to think of the words of some prayer, any prayer, but nothing came and he looked back at Paris and Livingstone and the other men, who were standing at the edge of the clearing, arms hanging at their sides, eyes wide, mouths tight; then he looked back at Harry.

"Finish it," said Livingstone.

"Lighting the lint in the crypt," said Harry, spewing air out of his mouth. "Good you heard them coming or we'd—but not." He struggled to take in more breath. "He—the Bastard—must have thought she'd come back—so he could kill her and me together, get everything for himself."

"Kill him," said Livingstone. "Before the blast brings everyone coming. Kill him now!"

Harry lifted himself up and stared into Bothwell's face. "You!"

"Say a prayer," said Livingstone, moving forward and kicking him in the side. "Say '*Giustizia, madonna, io sono morte.*' Bothwell, *do it!*" He kicked Harry again.

Harry screamed "God!" and attempted to roll away. Bothwell twisted the nightshirt across his face and pressed down with his hands. Harry was very strong, and it took what seemed like a long time for him to die.

"For Jesus' sake," said Paris, grabbing Bothwell by the shoulder, "let's leave this place."

I wish I was a baby that had just been born, thought Bothwell, just baptized, washed clean.

As they left the orchard, he looked back at the spot where the little stone house had stood. It looked as if God had struck it with His fist.

Bothwell hurriedly undressed and drew on his nightshirt. Jean sat up in bed and rubbed at her eyes. "You're shaking all over," she said. "Husband, what—"

"Nothing," he mumbled. He slid under the covers and rolled on his side.

Fifteen minutes later the door was flung open and a young watchman entered holding a lantern.

"What's the matter, man?" said Bothwell, rising against the pillows.

The watchman fought for his breath and finally managed to say, "The King's house is blown up. They think the King and Queen are killed."

Bothwell's heart stopped. "But she's here. She's not there. No."

"The Queen is alive and well," said Jean coldly. "She gave Bastian and Christiana her chambers for their wedding, and slept in Miss Beaton's room. Go now. My husband will be with you." As soon as the man was gone, she turned to Bothwell. "Are you going to kill me now? Is that it? She's free; the ring is off her finger, but you're not." She got out of bed. "Get dressed; aren't you going to help them search for the murderers?"

"I don't know—"

"Will you blow me up too? Get dressed. I must go and comfort the bereaved Queen."

The body lay naked and broken in the muddy snow. A contingent of sheriff's men kept the townsmen back.

"About one o'clock," said the captain of the watch. "House rubble, not a stone left standing. Not a mark on the body. There might be a broken rib. There's the body of a chamber servant farther off. Broken neck. Horses are saddled on the other side of the town wall—the King's livery. I don't know why they'd be there." He threw a canvas over the lifeless form. "He looks like a little lad. He couldn't have been as bad as was given about. We have some witnesses over here."

"Witnesses?"

"Two women. One May Crokat, one Barbara Mertane." He led Bothwell to a bulbous-nosed housewife of about thirty, with pretty red curly hair. "This, May Crokat, saw the most. Mr. Maitland is with the Mertane woman."

"What did you see, mistress?" Bothwell asked the woman. He avoided her eyes.

She was lying in her house, under Mr. Maxwell's lodging, with her twin babies on either side of her, when she heard a great crack. Thinking it was the house above her, she ran to the door. She walked across the street but could see nothing. Five minutes later, she saw about ten men coming out of Blackfriars' Gate and caught one by his coat sleeve—it was rich material like that worn at the court—and asked what the crack was.

Bothwell remembered.

But the man didn't answer and instead pushed her roughly

away, and four men went up the wynd, and the rest down to Cowgate.

"Did you recognize any?" asked Bothwell, looking the woman straight in the face.

"No, my lord."

"Have a deposition taken," Bothwell said to the captain. "Did you search the orchard?"

"Yes, sir. Nothing there. Except . . ."

"Except what?"

"Some slats from one of the gunpowder barrels. Mr. Maitland has them. And there were wolves when we got there. The explosion knocked out a section of the town wall behind the house. There were ten, twelve wolves. We saved His Majesty's body, not one second to spare. Weren't as lucky with the chamberman. Most I've seen of late in the hills were all bones. Not these. They were big, arrogant. Had to chase them off with hagbutt fire. I think he was strangled; throat and mouth's purple. Whatever, he wasn't in the house when it went up."

The ragged trees twisted against the night sky. Bothwell and the captain walked over to the body. The canvas cloth wasn't long enough and the feet protruded. Bothwell knelt and wrapped his wool scarf around them. They were still warm.

"Take him to Holyrood," he said, getting up.

Jean's dressing table was cleared, her clothes chest gone. The bedsheets lay across the floor, ripped in pieces. Bothwell sighed, gathered up the sheets, threw them on the mattress, and undressed. Perspiration glazed down his brow, damping the oily hair over his eyes.

Drone and moan of night. Tar. Pitch, except for a watery glimmering of moon on the joint stool beside the bed, a sliver of moonlight on the gray rug. Outside, above the steady sweep of the wind, a cat was whining like a terrified baby. What kind of love is loving when it makes a murder? Dark. Dies in a bed at night? Makes liars? *Dark*—expanding and contracting with every inhalation and exhalation. A speck crawled along the sliver of white on the floor. Bothwell pulled the quilt and torn sheets to his chin and tried to sleep.

My father was the King's good friend. He never lied, and he never broke a faith. I was the Queen's good friend, good friend. Right. That was good. The best thing, Father . . .

You put the dirk inside my chest and took it out. Then you put it in again. Your face was red when you did it. Then, they said you were mad, and locked you in the turret. When you stabbed, I thought the blood coming out would have been warm, but it was cold.

"Bothwell," Mary whispered. Then louder, "Bothwell, Bothwell." She leaned over and shook his shoulder.

"Mustn't touch," he said hoarsely. He swung his legs over the side of the bed and rested his head in his hands.

Mary said something, but he wasn't listening. Whatever it was, she said it again.

His eyes were blurring. He was remembering things: he was remembering his father. He was remembering a thin, haggard woman standing on a beach almost twenty years ago, and how she'd boxed his ears, then smoothed the hair off his forehead, and said: "You were such a nice boy once." And later how she'd said: "One more thing, please," and died. He wondered what it was she was going to say.

Mary rested her head against his neck. Her hair fell against the side of his face. He tried to picture her in hell. Then, suddenly, he wanted to take her, and kiss her, and whisper things to her, comfort her, and love with her, and tell her that he loved her, because he did. Despite everything. Instead, he said, in a dull monotone, "Best go."

Then he remembered something else. He sat up, drew on his dressing gown, and took Mary's hand.

"Impossible," said Maitland. He relatched the door, moved quickly across the antechamber, and closed the door to the adjoining room. "Speak softly, please. My wife—if she knew I had a hand in this, or that Her Majesty had, or even you, Bothwell—but did you make out the faces?"

Bothwell said no.

"But the way they stood, some mannerism, some oddity of dress—did you hear any of them speak?"

"I do not think so. Livingstone was with me, and Paris, and the others. They might have caught something."

Maitland clicked his tongue, thought a minute, then lifted a sack from under his desk. "They found this in the ruins," he said, turning his attention to Mary. He emptied a few cracked and splintered barrel slats out of the bag onto the desk top. "It's the remnants of a gunpowder case. Bothwell's crest is stamped over every inch of it. Now, nothing in the crypt could have survived the force of that explosion. Not a scrap. Therefore, this barrel had to have been placed at some distance from the King's lodging. Someone had to put it where it was, and I feel rather certain it wasn't Bothwell." He turned his attention to Bothwell. "Now, my lord, it is my advice that you try very hard to remember something about those men you saw last night. Right off, who was their leader? Don't think, answer. Quickly."

"James," said Bothwell. "I know he is supposed to be at Lochleven, but I swear, though I did not see his face, it was him. The others were shadows, but I could feel it was him, sense it. The King—the King said it too. He said it was the Bastard."

Maitland broke into a bright grin. Despite himself, he laughed.

CHAPTER SIXTEEN

Morning, Mary knelt at a prie-dieu beside the body of her late husband, reciting the prayers for the dead. She was dressed head to foot in the *deuil blanc,* the traditional white cambric mourning robes of widowed queens of France. As the priest went through the motions of the Penitential Mass, she tried to think back to the death of her first husband, little François. But her mind remained a blank. She could remember nothing. The priest completed his service. The mourners gradually left the chapel.

She smiled uncertainly at the Virgin Mary, and the votive candles, weaving madly at her feet, rose high for a second, causing her to smile back for that second with equal uncertainty. Mary dropped her eyes to the Virgin's plaster-of-paris feet and gazed at the serpent struggling beneath her heel. Both the Virgin and the serpent were the same statue, painted and lacquered with the same paint and lacquer, but the snake's eyes, in the votive lighting, glistened like rubies. Its gilded head, however, was crushed firmly under one white foot.

Mary blinked. The foot seemed to move. The candles hissed. Did God exist? She stared at the corpse lying on the bier beside her. He was still the most beautiful man she had ever known.

Our Father, Who art in heaven, hallowed . . .

She stood and gazed at the corpse. Given another set of circumstances, he could have been a genuinely good man. He had charm, spirit, beauty. He had an easy grace. But there was on thing he did not have, and never would have had: that was character.

Mary bent over the waxen face: I hope you prayed before you died. And I hope you are not in . . . that you are in purgatory, or heaven. Two nights ago you would have killed me, but I killed you instead. I wanted to kill you. I did it. Not Bothwell. But I did not want you to be . . . dead—

A shrill scream rent the heavy air. Mary jerked up. The chapel was empty.

Arms outstretched, all disheveled and witch-visaged, the women shook their fists at her, reached out, and tore at her widow's weeds. Then they moved back against the Stations of the Cross, moistened their lips, and drew their veils across their faces.

"In '59," shrieked one of them, "I got staked for fucking on Sunday. Halloo, Sister Mary."

"I had a rich old husband took too long to die," laughed another. "Welcome."

Blood smeared like rouge across his mouth, black kohl running from his eyes, Drake whirled forward, lifted his skirts, and performed an impudent curtsy. "You know my crime," he giggled. "It's so incessantly dolefully smoky and hot down here. When will you come?" He lifted her hand in his, made as if to kiss it, then sank his teeth into the palm.

"Ned, mind," said a gentle voice which Mary recognized as belonging to the old monk with the icicle on the top of his nose. "And, Your Majesty, never mind. They're jealous and vindictive because they have to spend their time haunting wynds and closes and beaches and the generally opprobrious places. But you're alive, and they no longer exist, and you don't really see them, even if they can see you. Am I obscure?"

Mary opened her eyes just as the little silver door of the Tabernacle burst open and she was suffocating in the blazing—

She was alone in the darkened chapel and standing beside the

embalmed body of her husband. The air was very heavy and
it was nighttime and she was very tired. She walked to one of the
side-doors, pushed it open, and stood for a minute breathing the
crisp night air. The moon was small and distant, soft. There
weren't any stars. There were not any ghosts.

Bothwell drummed his fingers against the Council table and
listened as the other lords debated the amount of reward moneys
to be offered for the apprehension of the King's murderers. Still
in her *deuil blanc,* Mary sat in an armchair against one of
the casements, the morning light coming into the room from
behind her. Her hands were folded calmly in her lap. Bothwell
shifted his eyes to James, who had arrived in the capital early
that morning.

Maitland had just finished saying he felt five hundred crowns
more than enough.

"A King has been murdered," said James.

"I believe we know that," Maitland said briskly. "I must say
that this burst of generosity on your part, my lord, is, shall we
say, rather—strange?"

"He was the King of Scotland," said James. "His father is the
Earl of Lennox. What will England, or France, or even Spain
think if we are niggardly in avenging our King's death?"

The other nobles nodded.

Bothwell glanced at Mary. She was still sitting in the armchair, the morning light behind her, her hands folded. "The reward will be two thousand crowns," she said in a low voice.

"Madam," said Maitland, "the treasury is depleted as it is—"

"I say it will be two thousand crowns. This country's mine;
its moneys are mine. It will be two thousand!" She fell back
into the chair, weeping.

The Council members surrounded her. Bothwell realized that
James, who also hadn't risen, was staring at him. He looked
back. The blank expression seemed to drain slowly from James's
face, and for a brief minute he looked ill, sickly white, tired.
It occurred to Bothwell that he must have exactly the same

expression on his own face. His skin was goose pricks, there was a feeling inside his stomach that felt like dysentery. But worse.

Later in the day, toward evening, Bothwell watched Paris unfold a large, crudely drawn placard and spread it across the floor of his antechamber. It showed a bare-breasted mermaid wearing the crown of Scotland. It showed her scaled tail twisting above a drawing of a ragged hare bearing Bothwell's crest and initials. The hare nibbled at Darnley's decomposed corpse.

"They were up all this morning, Bothwell. When I took this down, they recognized me as your man and called out threats. But these placards are not from the common people, but from the rich and powerful. There were other placards that had words, and all the words were the right spelling. And, unlike this one here, most of the placards were printed at a press. There is a plot against us, Bothwell, and it is from those men killing the King before we did, and if they are Lord James and Lord Morton as Mr. Maitland says, then they will be the ones who win, and not you and me."

Bothwell bit at his lip. "You go back to Dunbar," he finally said. "It will be better for you there."

"You will come too, Bothwell?"

"No. Take care, Paris." He was thinking: Within the hour, everybody in Edinburgh will know she became hysterical because Maitland suggested two thousand crowns was too much to offer for her husband's murderers. That was clever. She will put the Bastard in his box, and not he put us in ours.

That night a madman ran the length of the High Street screaming that the Earl of Bothwell had caused him to shed innocent blood.

Rumors everywhere. A different rumor every morning. At night, new placards which would be torn down by the sheriff's men at dawn, only to be replaced the following night. The snow began gradually to melt away. In the streets, they would whisper the Queen could not sleep, that she had tried to hang herself, that she was going mad. They would say Jean Bothwell had fled to Dunbar fearing for her life, that she was being held in a secret place and slowly poisoned by her husband. Lord James's life was in present danger. The King had not been killed by the explosion, but poisoned, or strangled after, or drowned in his tub, or beaten on the back of the head with a rock. The Queen was under an enchantment. Bothwell was a sorcerer, having mastered the art in Paris under the tutelage of Mary Beaton's aunt Janet; Bothwell was a sodomite; Bothwell had six wives; Bothwell had designs upon the life of the young Prince. The Queen had gone mad. Bothwell was mad.

As for Bothwell, he attended to his duties as a Council member and to the opening of Parliament. Some nights, he would go to Mary through the pitchy limanga. They seldom spoke. He would take her, mumble something, then leave. There was no love in it, only lust. He hated himself more than he hated her. During the days he would ride alone to the firth north of the city, dismount, and walk for hours along the sand and jagged black rocks. He was tortured by the thought that, without a thought, without thinking, he might suddenly throw himself into the water and drown. He didn't want to die. He never wanted to die. His father had died a suicide. The sky was blank. He tried never to think of Mary. Sometimes her face would begin to form in his mind and he would try to fill it with something else. Winter disappeared, and the days grew warm and fresh.

Peonies, double white violets, cowslips, rosemary. Insects droning above the flowering honeysuckles. Peach, wallflowers, lilacs and daisies, wrens, bluebirds, robin redbreasts, and almond trees. He was ice. His odor of soap and wine and cold sweat disgusted him. He could not bear to touch his left hand to his right.

When he slept at night, he would always sleep instantly. Then he would wake up in a nightmare. Then he would go to her again. And again, neither would speak. And again, he would leave as soon as he was done, and hate her. But still, when he was away, he would think of her eyes and hands and voice and face and lips and body. In early March, almost a month after the murder, he stopped going to her.

In April he rode down the High Street before her, carrying

the sword of state, and stood beside her throne as she convened the Lords Assembled. They did not look at each other. Her voice was weak when she spoke. The Parliament enacted a special money grant for the Presbyterian Kirk, extended certain crown fiefs to Maitland, James, and the Earl of Morton, and confirmed the appointment of Bothwell as captain of Edinburgh Castle.

The next day, Mary's physician warned the Privy Council that unless she forsook her mourning and went to a peaceful sea place her health would be seriously impaired. The Council petitioned Mary to stop mourning and holiday at Seton. She left two days later.

When she passed through the town gates, she found herself surrounded by about fifty townsmen shouting hosannas, throwing flower blossoms, and crying, "God bless that sweet face." She smiled.

James opened his antechamber door.

"Spring at long last," said Maitland. "James, you look pale; I suggest more sun. You stay here locked in your rooms and see no one. My wife is concerned." He pressed his face into a smile and sat down. "James, you look grim as a goose."

James sat down across from him. Maitland's hair, under the brimmed conical cap, was smoothed down to just above his welted shoulders with a strong-smelling rose grease. He was dressed in bell-shaped trunk hose with an ornamented codpiece, a Kendal green doublet, turned-down collar, and short loose coat with hanging sleeves. Vanity. He was wearing his I've-got-you smile.

"How is your lady?" said James.

"She is well," said Maitland. "That is, if you mean my Lady Maitland. She frizzed her hair and she's pretty as a breast of bacon. I've ordered her some gowns from Paris—orange tawny, straw yellow, white lawn. They should arrive in a month. Tawny is her best color." He drew a hanky edged with pink lace from his doublet, sniffed at it, was silent a minute, then said, "But if you mean my lady the Queen, then we have a different matter."

"I have another letter from Lennox," said James, shifting uneasily in his seat. "He makes accusations against Bothwell."

"Why does Lennox communicate with you?" said Maitland. "Why does he not address his grievances to the Queen? Or to the Council? Or the Lords Assembled? It is odd he should be writing you, who have never been his friend. It is odd that you should be defending the man who betrayed your father."

"Every man believes Bothwell to be the murderer of the King," said James. "Lennox writes to me because he knows no one else will defend his just cause." He folded his hands calmly in his lap.

Maitland's voice changed abruptly. "Now, James, I think we ought to talk. I think you ought to make a public statement sometime this week that you believe in Bothwell's innocence. I believe you might also, as a kindness to Her Majesty, request your lackeys to stop posting those infernal placards. They are very distressing to Her Majesty. Don't look surprised. Don't hang your mouth. Her Majesty and I know Bothwell did not murder the King. You did." He sniffed the hanky again, then folded it in his pocket.

"Have you become a fool?" James managed to say.

Maitland smiled pleasantly.

"You have no evidence," James said.

"I do."

"There can be no evidence."

"Then why do I know that there were two men holding down our late beloved lord's arms and legs and another sitting on his stomach smothering him to death with his nightshirt? Perhaps one of the gentlemen did not beat his fist into the late beloved lord's groin. Perhaps the King did not cry, 'Pity me, kinsmen, for the love of Him who pitied all the world.' Perhaps. But I believe that he did, and that you, James, stood a little off and supervised and watched and considered in your mind how Bothwell might be blamed. You've always been neat, James. And I've always admired your neatness. It's fresh, invigorating."

"I did not commission the placards against my sister," said James. "I never meant anything against her. Maitland, there was a plot, a Roman plot."

"I know that," said Maitland. "We all knew that three months before it happened. But there was another plot. *Your* plot. You know, James, I've never had you in a corner before. Never

until now. It humanizes you—somewhat." He waited for James
to say something. "You've always amazed me, James. At this
moment, I have you. I know you don't like that. But to look at
you, one would . . ."

James got up, walked to the cupboard, came back, sat down
again, and set a small silver casket on the table. It was inlaid with
lions, stags, and partridges.

Maitland stood up. "What is this? I recognize that box. I don't
know from where, but I've seen it."

"Sit down," James said amicably. He unlocked the casket and
drew out a handful of letters. "Lady Bothwell visited me yesterday. She had not wished to come. But my brother John persuaded her. These are letters from my sister to Bothwell. I
think you might read them. Sit down. Read them."

Maitland read several of the letters, then looked up. "It is
hardly my concern—or yours—that the Queen and Bothwell
have been somewhat more than friends."

"She now shares more than her bed with him. She shares
her kingdom, her power—in fact, if not yet in statute. That is our
concern, is it not? Bothwell is no friend of yours, or of mine.
She has given herself over to his influence, and his power grows
every day. He would be a fool not to use it against those—like
me, perhaps even like you—who might have the temerity to
oppose him."

Narrowing his eyes, Maitland stared soberly at James.

"It has not been your habit, Michael Wiley, to encourage those,
even though they may once have been aligned with you, who
have an interest in destroying you."

"No," Maitland said. "That has never been my policy. My
policy has always been somewhat more . . . practical."

"I would trust that your policy retains its . . . practicality."

"You may be assured," Maitland said after a moment, "that it
does."

The sun was a faint pink glow behind the hills. The stubbled
plain was swathed with a light green and purple mist. Sweetbriars,
gilliflowers, yellow daisies, violets, and budding lilac bushes lined

the muddy road. Bothwell liked the rush of the morning air against his face, the smell of the violets, the sound of the invisible birds. It would be a good year for crops. He let his horse slow to an easy canter, and watched the sun rise above the hills.

But I always come back to being Bothwell. *Mea culpa.* Why had she sent for him? What reason? He did not want to see her at Aberdeen, and there was no cause for her to ask for him.

At noon, he passed through a ruined monastery. The buildings had been reduced to standing stones, the façade of the chapel was stripped of its lead, clumps of coarse grass and violets grew in the dried fountain. He dismounted, sat against the fountain, and unwrapped some cheese and bread. Bluejays sqwawked loudly in the budding trees. A hand touched the back of his neck.

He jumped to his feet and turned around.

"I spoke with Livingstone," said Mary. She was dressed in a white blouse and peasant's skirt. Her face was sunburned, freckled all over. She loosened her hair. "The last time you were with him, you were rude. That was bad of you. Livingstone's your friend." She held up a flask. "Châteauneuf du Pape. I was afraid, as you got closer to Aberdeen, you would turn around and not come. So I set out early this morning thinking to meet you on the road." She took two goblets from her saddlebag and poured the wine, then sat down beside him, closed her eyes, and rested her head against the stone fountain.

"I never know what to think of you," said Bothwell. "You're all back and forth. You change."

Mary took off her sleeves. Her hair was red and gold under the sun. "You unhappy man," she said. "I love you. And you, me." She took his hand and brought it to her stomach. "You can't feel him yet, Bothwell. But he can feel you. He *loves* you."

He tilted his head and stared at her.

"Soon we must be married."

"Soon? Can't be."

"I have our child inside me, Bothwell."

He felt a tear run down his cheek. She brushed her lips across his. Her mouth was sweet.

He put his arms around her waist and rested against her breasts.

A slight flickering of the lashes, momentary confused movement of the arms and legs, and the end of the last dream Mary dreamed that night. She opened her eyes and closed them.

Everything will be well.

Rolling on her left side and pressing the satin pillow against her cheek, she tried to sleep again. Bothwell mumbled something. Mary sighed, stretched, opened her eyes again, and smiled at him.

The sky in the morning. It's the silence. The beginning of the sunlight gathering there at the window. Gauzy, green, and round earth, and a slight breeze coming from the ocean. And even the birds stop a second. One second.

A marriage means they'll do against us. They won't like a marriage. They'll march against a marriage, and James . . . my brother James riding at the head. But we'll fight. We'll fight! And if we lose, perhaps we'll win. There's a chance. God always gives us a chance. And, finally, there's us. And even if we don't, can't, or they . . . there's still, oh, still—

Us.

Short of breath, and my heart, and I— Everything, oh *you!* And I believe, I believe everything will turn out well in the end, and if it doesn't . . . it could have.

CHAPTER SEVENTEEN

A PROCLAMATION 12 MAY 1567

To all citizens of Scotland that fear God,

Whereas the Earl of Bothwell, known to be the principal author, deviser, and actor of the cruel murder of the late and much beloved King, has, finding the Queen's person utterly destitute of all good counsel, divorced his lawful wife, and seduced the Queen's Majesty to a dishonest and unlawful marriage with himself: and whereas the said Earl Bothwell is now gathering forces, and stirring himself to get the young Prince, now in Mar under our care, in his hands that he might murder the child as he did the father; the Nobles of the land resolve to withstand, and deliver the Queen out of the bondage of this wicked man, and put her in such a place as she may recover her good senses. Wherefore, we, the undersigned, charge all lieges within this kingdom to be in readiness at three hours warning to assist us in freeing the Queen from her ungodly captivity, and bringing the said Bothwell to punishment for the aforesaid murder and other crimes. All such as will not side with the Parliament of Scotland are commanded to depart from Edinburgh within four hours, under pain of being accounted enemies to the state.

Signed,
James Stewart, Earl of Moray,
  Lord Chancellor of Scotland
William Maitland of Leithington
  First Secretary
Mathew Stewart, Earl of Lennox
James, 4th Earl of Morton
David, Earl Lindsay of the Byres
John, 6th Lord Erskine, Earl of Mar
Alexander, fourth Earl of Eglington
Archibald, 5th Earl Argyll &c.

enacted in the presence of John Knox, pastor of St. Giles, John Craig, Superintendent of Edinburgh, John Spottiswoode, Superintendent of Lothian and the southern counties, this day of God, 12 May, the year of our Lord 1567.

⚓ EPILOGUE ⚓

Winter. 1570. The Lords Assembled have ratified a trade pact with Sweden-Denmark, which will more than offset the financial losses incurred as a result of the recent bloodletting in the Netherlands, where Presbyterian merchantmen are no longer welcome. In the Netherlands, the King of Spain has massacred forty thousand Protestants in the name of the Pope. But Scotland has no need for fear: the Lords Assembled has abolished papistry forever. Our ships depart weekly from the harbor at Leith bearing red and pickled herring, sea coals, and whisky products to Ireland, goatskin, linen and wool, smoked and dried and salted fish to France and ports as far as the Baltic. The new docks and warehouses at Leith are filled to overflowing with flax, hemp, iron, pitch, tar, and other imports. All is prosperity and good.

The little King is nearly four years old. Lord James has given us strong and sensible administration based upon the rule of law. He's the greatest man, and he guides us each, every step, with his goodness and his wisdom. He's like Solomon must have been. Ah, and he's a royal and godlike-looking man; his skin's copper-colored; he's muscle-armed and tall and long-legged and walks and speaks and acts in every way a king does—or, at the least, ought to.

Master Knox has not much longer left on earth. Some will say it's because he took himself a sixteen-year-old girl to wife when his first wife died. There was good laughing at that. But he was a hero once, and all his life he never was afraid of any man. And we'll give him that. But now, he'll stop sometimes in the middle of his text and lose himself in a dream. He cannot walk steady unless the young wife aids him. I heard my father say once that it was because he missed Queen Mary, that in his own way Master Knox loved to rail against her best.

In '68, when she escaped her island prison and got three thousand men to her side in the space of one day, there was great fear here in Edinburgh. But God defeated her army through a stratagem, and sent her packing into England, where the Queen of England, who is Scotland's friend, keeps her locked tight. As for Bothwell, he's in chains in a Denmark dungeon, and they say he's stark raving, just as his father was at the end.

The first years after Queen Mary's overthrow, it was madness here. Mr. Maitland went over to the Queen's men. But that is his reputation—to change sides as often as a coin thrown in the air. One day he might have been Lord James's successor as Regent—it was assured—but now the Earl of Lennox will succeed. But, thanks to God, that is a day many days away.

The tall stone houses of the gentry and municipal dignitaries cast quiet shadows onto the High Street. The sun sits softly upon the steep-pitched gables and slate and thatched roofs. Milliners, confectioners, dealers in leather, dealers in spices and oils, blacksmiths and tavern owners drum their fingers on the shiny counters of their near-empty establishments. It is nine in the morning, and business will sleep till eleven. They listen to the dull cannon bombardment in the distance. They listen as the refuse carts creak over the cobbled street. In their minds, they consider the last year's profits, go over in their minds what they will and what they wish to make this year.

South of High Street, the city palaces of dukes and barons sit serenely silent. At Holyrood Palace, young smartly outfitted guards march about their appointed rounds, and servants prepare dinner in the kitchens. Hymns arise from the dark interior of St. Giles Church and waft along the High Street, past Merkat Cross, beyond the city gates, and down toward Leith and its harbor. A small fleet of fishing skiffs move away from one of the piers.

James yanked shut the damask curtains of his bedchamber in Holyrood, then sank back into a chair and submerged his feet in a small tub of hot water. He was dressed in a patched undershirt which came to his knees. His long hair was unkempt and straggly, his eyes shot with red, and his face, beardless, recently shaved clean. He stared blankly at his thin, white legs, then brushed the hair from his forehead. "I'm certain of New England," he said out loud. "There's gold there. Has to be. Everyone's always off to the Spanish holdings, but I *know* there's gold in New England. I offered Elizabeth fifty per cent of the gathering, would have gone as high as seventy—all for the loan of six ships. We've only three in our navy. Of course, the Lords Assembled wouldn't think of building more. The Lords Assembled! They know nothing, care nothing, do nothing." He raised his eyes and looked up at the royal crest hanging above his head: a lion, imperially crowned, *gules,* in one paw a sceptre, in the other a sword, on either side a dancing unicorn.

I'm thirty-nine years old, he thought; that's old. He lifted his feet from the tub and began wiping them with a cloth. They were scabrous. They sweated continuously, itched beyond bearing. Nothing had been able to end the sweating. He looked up and saw a dark figure in the shadow of the door-close. His heart skipped a beat.

"I said you look well, brother," said John, walking toward him.

"And you," he said uneasily. At first, he'd thought John was an assassin. He finished wiping his feet, rose, and went to his clothes trunk.

John sank down on the bed. "I came to tell you I was leaving."

Leaving? John had been gone since last winter. James hadn't even known he'd come back. The last time they spoke, John had been short, abrupt. Why should he tell me he's leaving? There's a plot in this somewhere.

"I'm leaving Scotland. I won't return."

Silence.

"I don't want you to go," James managed to say. "I've . . . a need of you here." He slowly pulled on his hose, selected a white shirt, fastened his doublet.

"This isn't Scotland any more," said John. "That may be good; I've heard few complain. The land is dead; long live the body politic. There's no cause for me to stay. I don't know anyone any more. I never knew you. There was an Earl of Huntly. He had a son. There was an Italian good at singing, mandolin, and letter writing. There was even a King once—he wasn't a good King, but he might have been, given time—until you and Morton murdered him."

"That is not true," James said dully.

"James, James, I'm your brother. I know. I know you as well as you know me."

James sighed and passed his hand over his eyes.

"There was a Queen, and you betrayed her time and again, and she forgave you time and again. You accused her of your crime, and you led an army against her, and imprisoned her, and took her crown away—as if you could put it on your own head. You made her lose Bothwell's babies. It's funny, really. Everybody always gave it about that Bothwell was incapable—and there she was, as big as the world, a set of twins inside her belly. I remember the last battle. I was on your side then, not theirs. Because, like everybody else, I believed your lies. We were on one hill and they were on the other. Bothwell challenged our side to single combat. Of course, everybody on our side had given up believing in Sir Launcelot a hundred years ago, and so no one accepted his challenge. You lied and said she could have her throne back if she let him go, and because she had nothing else to do, she said yes. That was her lie. And she made it plain that it was a lie when she and Bothwell kissed each other good-by on top of that hill in full view of anyone who cared to have eyes. Later, in Edinburgh, you locked her in the Tolbooth, and all the townsmen were raving for blood, begging you to let them burn her at the stake for murder and adultery. But you, in all your august magnanimity, said, 'No; that'd be unfair.' St. James! Sometimes —all this past year—when I was up in the north and eating and sleeping with men and women who'd never even heard of a Queen Mary, who'd never heard of you, or canary wine, or the Protestant Reformation—sometimes I'd pray for your death and I'd dream I was standing at your grave, guarding it to make sure that you were dead and could never come back to kill anybody ever again!"

"I think this interview is ended," said James, avoiding John's eyes. He took some papers from his desk, then suddenly bent over and started coughing. He sat down and covered his face. The papers slid to the floor. "I must go," he said hoarsely.

"It was because I could always see," John was saying rapidly, "even in my dreams. I could always see that picture of her half naked, half mad, her hair wild as fire, screaming insults from the Tolbooth window to the crowd below, ordering them to kill her or set her free. Over and over, then over again, until you had your men pull her from the window, knock her senseless, and ride her off to her island prison. She was a great and beautiful woman, James; it was impossible to be near her without *feeling* that—"

"Had she behaved temperately," said James angrily, "there'd have been no need—"

"She was intemperate. She loved Bothwell, so she married him."

"She was carrying his bastard. She was an adulteress, a—"

"Like our mother?"

James was quiet a minute. When he spoke again, his voice came in thick sobs. "John, Johnny, understand. I've given Scotland rest. She was blood, chaos. It was necessary. Don't go."

John took James's hand. "Whom did she ever kill? How many have you killed? I love you; you're my brother. If you ever have need of me, send, and I'll come. But I don't think you'll ever send. You've gone so thin, brother. You aren't caring for yourself. You should. They say your wife is coming from Dunfermline. She'll see you eat well . . . keep warm . . . sleep. Be good to her. I remember when you married her. That was a long time ago. But if you didn't love her then, she loved you. Be kind to her, do little things; she'll love you again." He paused, then let go of James's hand. "One last thing. I don't say it to be cruel or wicked. But think . . . I mean, what do you think our father King James would say of . . . everything that's happened? Good-by, brother."

On the high-seated plain outside the city the breezes off the sea were strong. A solitary cloud stretched itself across the plain, relinquished a light flow of rain, then drifted north to the Highlands. James rode across the plain to a spot where he could look down on the sea.

For a long time he sat on his horse and watched John's ship as it sailed past the shining black rocks, then turned and moved in the direction of the horizon. He waited until it disappeared from view. James shifted and looked over his shoulder at the city of Edinburgh. He let his eyes rest on the smoke that was rising from the Great Castle, then looked past the city to the south. The green hills, dark burns, and glassy lakes stretched farther than he could see. He looked at the sea a while longer, then started riding back to Edinburgh.

It was two in the afternoon when he got back to Edinburgh. Astride a white charger, he passed along the High Street. As he came into sight, the crowds would surge forward, a blur of noise and color, squeezing their front ranks against the heaving barricades. A blizzard of roses, shreds of colored paper, and silver spangles rained down upon his head from the town's low overhanging balconies. In some places, the barricades split, and, chanting and whistling, men, women, and children would surge after him, attempting to touch his clothing and his horse.

At one point, James drew his reins before a small, hastily constructed stage in the center of which stood two imitation trees, one withered and black, the other filled with green leaves and paper daisies. An old man with a white beard announced that he was Father Time. "This is what we were," he said, pointing to the withered tree. He indicated the second one. "This is what we are become." A pretty little girl with bright yellow hair danced from behind the stage and ran to James.

"Who are you?" said James, smiling.

The child looked back to the old man, who nodded his head. She held up a leather-bound volume and handed it to James. "I am Truth," she said happily. "And this is the Scottish Bible." In a lower voice, she added, "I love you, and when I grow up I'm going to be your wife." She ran back to the stage.

"Be the King," someone shouted from the crowd. Someone else cried, "A baby can't be a King!"

James addressed the wildly cheering people. "We are a stubborn people, an independent people. No other people on earth can tell us what to do. We are—"

"Be the King! Take our crown! You! Long live! King! King!"

James had to wait several minutes before he could speak again. "A King is the equal of all his nobles. And a noble is no better than any of his servants. Because—because *all* of us are the sons and the daughters . . . and the mothers and the fathers of all the kings and queens ever lived and r-reigned here. In this country. If your crops are burned, the King's crops are burned. If your business is lost, so is the King's. And if you have a hurt, it is the King's own hurt."

The crowd surged forward. The barricades broke again and men and women poured around him, reaching up, tearing at his clothes, crying his name, sobbing.

James raised his eyes. The sky rippled light blue. On a balcony directly opposite, he saw a man in a black wool cloak lean forward over the railing.

James lifted his hand. "And this is so because *you* are the King! You, the peo—"

There was a sudden fanfare of cornets. Drums thundered and penny whistles shrilled. A cracking sound ripped through James's ear. Cracking. Bone and metal cracking. One shocked exhalation. Cracking. He lifted his hand to his throat, then jerked his hand down to his hip, then raised it to his chest, then threw it down again. And another crack. Men and women roared around him like water, then suddenly he was alone, and everybody else was running, falling into each other, scrambling away from the spot where he was slowly, ever so very slowly, sliding from his horse. He rose in the saddle again. There was one last crack, he looked up at the sun, he heard one woman scream, and he hurtled from his saddle.

A rough arm pulled him into a sitting position, and James opened his eyes. Lennox was kneeling beside him. "They're clearing a path through the crowd," he said. "They'll take you to St. Thomas Hospital."

James felt something wet and sticky trickling from his mouth, but he had little difficulty in speaking. "Let go of me," he said to Lennox. "You don't touch me, touch your hands on me, you. Let go." Somebody stumbled over his leg and his teeth gritted down into his tongue.

Lennox cursed.

James stared at the light blue of the sky, above the rushing heads. "I can feel it happening," he said.

An elderly woman cautiously reached out and wiped James's mouth and chin with a thin piece of fish paper. James looked at her and said, "Why, I know you, mother. I've passed your stall many times. And bought good salmon off you." He closed his eyes and whispered, "Was anyone—else—hurt?" He opened his eyes.

She shook her head no, and wiped the wet hair off his forehead.

"I feel it coming, mother; I can feel it stretching itself out inside me." He caught blindly at her hand. "I'm afraid," he mumbled. "Afraid. My father the King . . . you see I . . . wanted . . ."

The old woman closed his eyes.

PRINCIPAL CHARACTERS

Mary Stewart is the Catholic Queen of Scotland, the daughter of King James V. As a child she was sent to France to marry the Dauphin François. She was Queen of France for a year, but on her young husband's death was forced to return to Scotland, which she found under the control of the Presbyterian revolutionaries.

James Stewart is Mary's half brother, the illegitimate son of James V and his mistress Lady Margaret Douglas. He is the leader of the Presbyterian revolutionaries who seized power during Mary's absence in France.

James Hepburn, Earl of Bothwell, is the Lord High Admiral of Scotland, a Protestant but a faithful supporter of the Crown.

Henry Stewart, Earl of Darnley, is the son of the Earl of Lennox, who betrayed James V at the Battle of Solway and has been living in exile in England. Henry Stewart is Mary's cousin.

John Stewart is another bastard of James V and Lady Douglas.

John Knox is a former Catholic priest who studied under Calvin at Geneva and returned to Scotland to become the spiritual leader of the Presbyterians.

The Earl of Huntly, Lady Huntly, and their son Sian and daughter Jean represent the last powerful Catholic family after the Presbyterian overthrow. They control all rents, fiefs, and rights in the Highlands.

William Maitland of Leithington is a brilliant Scots diplomat, known for his ability to find a place in whichever side has the upper hand at any given moment.

David Riccio is a Piedmontese musician and singer who comes to Scotland in the train of the Duke of Savoy and is later made Mary's personal secretary. He is suspected by the Presbyterians of being a papal agent.

Elizabeth Tudor, Queen of England, daughter of Henry VIII and Ann Boleyn. Considered by Catholic Europe to be a bastard usurper of a throne which is by right of hereditary succession Mary Stewart's.